D0014087

DELIVER US FROM EVIL

DELIVER US FROM EVIL
CLINT KELLY

T 15796

BETHANY HOUSE PUBLISHERS
MINNEAPOLIS, MINNESOTA 55438

Deliver Us From Evil
Copyright © 1998
Clint Kelly

Cover illustration by Fran Gregory
Cover design by Dan Thornberg,
Bethany House Publishers staff artist.

Published by Bethany House Publishers
A Ministry of Bethany Fellowship International
11300 Hampshire Avenue South
Minneapolis, Minnesota 55438

Printed in the United States of America by
Bethany Press International, Minneapolis, Minnesota 55438

Library of Congress Cataloging-in-Publication Data

Kelly, Clint.
    Deliver us from evil / by Clint Kelly.
       p. cm. — (In the shadow of the mountain ; 1)
    ISBN 1-55661-955-3 (pbk.)
    I. Title. I. Series: Kelly, Clint. In the shadow of the mountain ; 1.
PS3561.E3929D45   1998
813'.54—dc21   97-45420
                                                          CIP

To my mother, the storyteller,
as brave and dear a woman as ever lived.

ABOUT THE AUTHOR

Clint Kelly is the author of *The Landing Place* and *The Aryan*, as well as a publications specialist for Seattle Pacific University. An ex-forest ranger, Clint's inspiration for his novels comes from his wife and four children and from the landscape of the Pacific Northwest where they make their home.

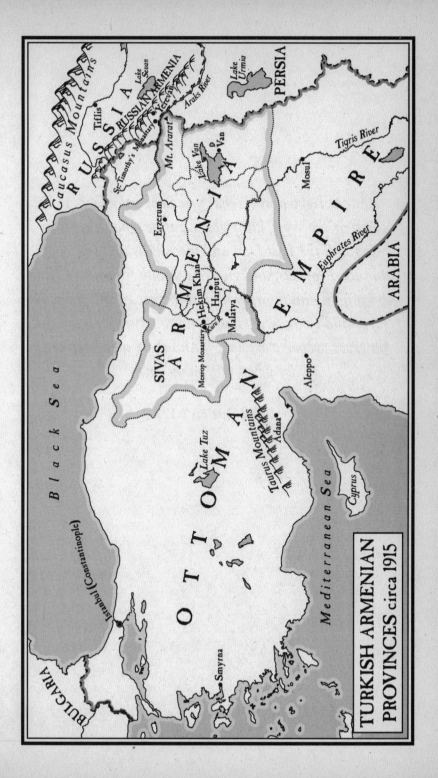

TURKISH ARMENIAN
PROVINCES circa 1915

BULGARIA

Istanbul (Constantinople)

Black Sea

Smyrna

OTTOMAN

Lake Tuz

Taurus Mountains

Adana

Cyprus

Mediterranean Sea

Aleppo

SIVAS

ARMENIA

Msrop Monastery

Kuru

Malatya

Harput

Hekim Khan

Erzurum

Msrop Monastery

Mt. Ararat

St. Timothy's Monastery

Caucasus Mountains

RUSSIA

Tiflis

RUSSIAN ARMENIA

Lake Sevan

Yerevan

Araks River

Lake Van

Van

Lake Urmia

PERSIA

EMPIRE

Mosul

Tigris River

Euphrates River

ARABIA

"It is not righteousness that you turn your faces to the East or the West, but righteous is he who believes in God and the Last Day and the Angels and the Book and the Prophets; and gives his wealth for love of Him to kinsfolk and to orphans and the needy and the wayfarer and to those who ask, and to set slaves free, and observes proper worship . . . And those who keep their treaty when they make one. . . ."

The Qur'an 2:177

Chapter 1
Early Harvest, 1915

Adrine Tevian took a deep breath. It was all she could do to keep from shouting the stunning news that traveled through the towns of Anatolia like water from a burst dam. If the news was true, then maybe the salvation of Armenia was at hand.

Despite being young in years—just seventeen harvests to her account—Adrine carried herself more maturely than some women twice her age. Her features revealed upon close examination a dark desert beauty. The long slender neck, high cheekbones, and proud tilt of her head revealed an ancient Armenian heritage, descending from Hayk, great-great-grandson of Noah the Patriarch. Beneath concealing streaks of river mud and charcoal, a smooth determined chin and bold brown eyes flecked with gold spoke of generations of industrious, devout followers of God the Father. Even the lustrous black hair, now dulled and chopped short, hinted of tortoiseshell hairbrushes and garlands of bright orange poppies.

The plain straight covering she wore said little about the bloom of womanhood underneath it and hid the eroding effects of meager rations on a slender body yearning to be free.

Adrine held to the same skepticism about the future as her remnant people, but she tucked it tightly inside the hope of a steadfast Christian faith. It was her belief in an omnipotent God that gave her the will to carry on.

Her beloved town of Hekim Khan was occupied by the Turkish army, the town square converted into a sprawling commissary. She cooked for the enemy and did his laundry. For that he let her live, if scrabbling for scraps from the military soup pot and bedding down in a rodent-infested straw hut could be called living.

Adrine squeezed nut brown eyes shut and chewed lips chafed raw by the relentless sun. "Forgive me, Jesus," she breathed. "Of course this is living. I thank you. Air is free. Sunlight is free. Sleep is free." If sleep would come. She shuddered against the dark thoughts that tried to nest in her mind. The enemy had ways of taking air, sun, and sleep. *Extermination*.

A cat, her belly fat with kittens, poked a pink nose and wiry whiskers from the hole beneath a stump near the cooking fires. The Turk soldiers fed her scraps and allowed her the pampered life of camp feline. Adrine kept a watchful eye to make certain Giaour didn't end up a hungry Armenian's main dish. "Giaour" meant "infidel." In a fit of indiscretion, the dusky puss had taken up with a Muslim cat the next street over and was soon pregnant. *What useful purpose do Muslims serve?* Adrine thought. Shame followed, but it was slow in coming.

She wouldn't permit herself to daydream about punishing the Turks, for in doing so she knew she would become the god of her fantasies, finding pleasure in paying back Turkish wickedness with ever more innovative forms of torture. But vengeance was the Lord's, and Christ Jesus never struck back at His tormentors. If He had, even once, Adrine Tevian would have made an effective and willing Angel of Death.

It was the guilty knowledge of her own vengeful spirit that made the news now particularly welcome. She was not without sin and had cast more stones—in her mind and heart— than ever fired from David's slingshot.

What an incredible report! A half hour earlier a rider from north of Erzurum had entered the heavily fortified Hekim Khan. His travel papers identified him as Eugin Karpat, a Turkish rug dealer traveling south to visit his dying father before joining the Turk forces at the Russian front. The fact his eyes were never still suggested otherwise.

The commissary where Adrine worked was separated from the parade grounds by a hundred feet of brick commons. Between gulping mouthfuls of Adrine's savory artichoke hearts and potatoes simmered in olive oil and lemon, Karpat spoke quietly of wonders in the sky. He kept his voice low so as not to attract enemy ears. Here at the commercial and political crossroad of race and language—Armenians to the east, Turks to the west—each could easily comprehend the other.

Adrine, conscripted to satisfy the ravenous hunger of the Turks and attend to their washing, pretended to busy herself with cooking and serving, but her hearing was sharply tuned to the merchant's every word.

With wild eyes darting from his steaming bowl to the dried blood on the scimitars of restless Turk soldiers milling about the square, Karpat spun his fantastic tale for Armenian ears, sitting close but never looking directly at them, careful to speak with head bent. He told of Russian airmen from the 3-D Caucasian Aviation Detachment who had recently returned from flying a reconnaissance mission. Two of them, 1st Lt. Alexander Zabolotsky and 2d Lt. Vladimir Roskovitsky, had flown toward the mountain, parachutes on their backs, oxygen canisters strapped to their faces in the open cockpit.

They looked down upon the great stone battlements surrounding the base of the mountain and were reminded of childhood stories of pilgrims ascending Ararat to scrape pitch from the Ark of Noah. The devout travelers then crafted the pitch into necklaces, which they wore about their necks like amulets to protect the crops from battering rains and searing heat. Mother Ararat, protector.

Twice the aviators circled the snowy white dome, then glided downward toward a sparkling blue lake, still frozen at one end but melting at the other. Suddenly, in the forward cockpit, Zabolotsky whirled and yelled at Roskovitsky in the rear. Roskovitsky looked where his companion pointed and nearly fell out of the aircraft.

There, grounded on the shore with a fourth of its bulk projecting out into the water, was a massive wooden structure enclosed like a chest. The lower they flew, the more extended it became until the amazing object stretched impossibly long, longer than any ship ever built. A catwalk ran the length of it, and one side of the craft near the exposed end was partly dismantled. On the opposite side was a great doorway. Scattered along the shore lay piles of stones, some of them quite elaborate.

"Altars!" Karpat said, louder than intended. The Turk captain of the guard strode near, then stopped to examine shirts on a rack that Adrine and her enterprising neighbors had sewn for the occupying Turks. Karpat attacked his artichokes with gusto and held his bowl at arm's length for more, eyes ever darting. Adrine obliged, dredging up some extra large chunks from the bottom of the steaming pot.

"Much activity along the road?" inquired the Turk captain. He was a tall, hairy fellow with boots to the knees and a riding crop he enjoyed using to lift the chins of his weary men. Though the men smiled into the fierce face of their captain, an almost imperceptible flicker in their eyes said the touch of the crop was unwelcome.

Karpat looked at Adrine, but she kept eyes downcast, shoulders suitably subject. She must not meet the gaze of a male of a superior race, even if he was a Turk impostor spying for Armenia.

Karpat wiped his slick mouth with the back of a sleeve. "Not a great deal, my Captain," he answered the officer. "A few female refugees, quite abandoned, I assure you, and a dead boy or two. Shot, I think. I didn't encounter any companies of forced marchers, but I suspect that will change with the weather."

The captain grunted. The hot days and cold nights of late summer were giving way to a frigid fall. The plains in August broiled the displaced Armenian refugees by day and froze them by night. The relentless exposure quickly claimed their famished bodies. Milder daytime temperatures would ensure more of them reached Hekim Khan, as would the fact they inhabited the northern and eastern edges of Armenia. But for the deportees north of Lake Van, it was just the beginning of a three-hundred-mile death march south to the deserts of Syria.

"Any spoils?" The way the captain hissed the latter word made Adrine stiffen. The Turk leaned toward the carpet man and gave a wink as if they were coconspirators.

"No, nothing," Karpat said, an odd strained quality to his voice. Rather than look at the Turk, he stared at the ground and marked in the ashes of past fires with a soiled finger. "The bodies were naked, of course, and split open by the sun. I did not search long in that stench, but it was certain they had been previously examined. It is difficult to hide gold when thieves rob you first of your dignity, then your jewelry."

The Turk glanced sharply at the recent arrival. Adrine's heart raced. Karpat had displayed too much emotion for the ravaged Armenians. If the captain detected the tiniest shred of sympathy for the Christians, Karpat would be cut down where he sat.

The hairy Turk commander advanced on the newcomer slowly, deliberately. "Armenian Christians are sacks of dirt who plot against their hosts and court the enemy. For too long they have lived off the kindness of their Turk benefactors. They do not deserve a drop of caring concern."

The captain lifted Karpat's chin with the crop.

Adrine held her breath and watched as the rug dealer smiled disarmingly and arched his eyebrows. The captain's stern face relaxed. A joke! Chuckles turned to guffaws and soon they were laughing riotously. The captain returned to the nearby group of officers to retell the joke of "dignified refugees." Indeed!

He had missed the sign of the cross etched in the ashes. But Adrine saw it, looked about anxiously, and quickly obliterated it with the toe of a ragged shoe. She bent with another ladle of vegetables and placed a slip of paper between the carpet man's fingers and the upraised bowl. The paper vanished into his sleeve.

A burst of laughter erupted from a knot of soldiers as the captain retold the tale.

"Go on," she whispered and turned to stir the pot.

As if by secret signal, other Armenian camp slaves sidled closer under the pretext of sweeping the packed earth of the square, straightening the shirts on display, tending to Karpat's horse.

"Altars of worship to almighty God!" he rushed on in an urgent whisper between bites of vegetable. "Those Russian airmen saw the altars of the forefathers! My uncle Karnig's altar!"

"What *else*?" pleaded Adrine, lips barely moving, her body turned from him. They must not appear to converse beyond the bare necessities. She tingled all over and was so afraid he wouldn't be able to complete his story before the captain returned for a new joke.

"The rumors say the pilots immediately flew back to their commanders, and the news raced to the ears of the czar," Karpat mumbled, bowl raised to hide his mouth. "Nicholas ordered two companies of one hundred fifty men to be dispatched from the headquarters of the Fourteenth Railroad Battalion at Bayazit, and under the leadership of a Sergeant Rujansky, the Zamorsky Brigade ascended the mountain early last month. After nearly four weeks of difficult climbing and trail construction, they claim . . ." He paused, barely able to contain his emotion. "They claim they encountered the Ark!"

The officers' laughter subsided. The Turk commander's group would soon break up. Karpat must hurry.

"According to their eyes—let us hope it is not the view from inside a vodka bottle—the Ark contains hundreds of small rooms like animal stalls and others very large with tall ceilings. Fences in the biggest rooms are constructed of immense timbers so thick"—he paused with agonizing effect—"that they would contain creatures nine, ten times larger than elephants!"

The Armenians gasped despite themselves, but the preoccupied Turks took no notice.

"All was covered over with a dark, waxy seal, hard as a helmet—a substance the Russians could not identify. Farther up the mountain were the blackened remains of timbers severed from the Ark. Some had been formed into a small shrine that contained a rough assembly of stones such as those upon which the Israelites might have burned their animal sacrifices. It looked to have been charred by lightning, the roof disintegrated.

"Think of it! The Ark of Father Noah! We are saved!"

As if by signal, Karpat's enthusiasm carried his audience's gaze to Ararat, a five-day's journey away by swift horse. Each strained to see through the shimmering air to the amazing object that the Bible, and now the Russians, said kept Noah, his wife, their three sons and three daughters-in-law, and remnants of every animal safe from a flood that covered the earth. Surely the Russian discovery was a sign of Armenia's salvation.

But Adrine was leery of jumping to conclusions based on

hearsay. She'd seen unfounded rumors kill faster and more surely than ignorance ever did. Not knowing was its own form of hope.

"Turkish butchers care little for the things of God," she said. "They desire heaven only long enough to steal the streets of gold."

"Really?"

Adrine jumped, her blood turning cold. The captain of the guard suddenly towered over her as if by magic.

"Fascinating," he said, breath sour from drinking *raki*, "but not very amusing. Let me tell you a joke of mine. Why do all Turks have bad backs? From all that stooping when extracting gold from dead Armenians. Or this. How do you spot a good Armenian? Listen for a heartbeat, and if there is none, that is good!"

He grabbed Adrine by her once long black hair, now short and ragged and thick with dirt. She deliberately did not bathe, smeared her face with charcoal, and slept and worked in the same thin, shapeless garment the color of wasted earth. Ugly women were less likely to be raped.

Karpat tensed and slid a hand inside his cloak.

The captain pulled Adrine by the hair to the center of the square and bellowed for attention. The Turks smelled sport. Some of them were violent criminals only recently released from prison and assigned to special "butcher battalions" by the Teskilati Mahsusa, or Special Organization. The town of Hekim Khan was a staging center for assaults on villages and cities within a hundred-mile radius. Its Armenian population had been decimated and the men, including Adrine's two brothers, taken away. Her father was already dead at the hand of brigands, and her mother and grandmother inexplicably vanished the day after her brothers disappeared. Perhaps they were killed, perhaps they threw themselves and their grief into the Euphrates River. She might never know. The remaining Armenian women and children in Hekim Khan were allowed to live as slaves. Their food rations were larger and more frequent because their conquerors wished to keep the women healthy enough to service and refresh the Turkish troops.

"Insolent Armenians who harbor secrets from their benevolent Turkish masters may be more useful as fertilizer," the captain shouted. With a contemptuous shove, he released Adrine.

"Observe," he sneered, then turned to a tall thin woman, a yellow scarf tied tightly about her head, who stirred an enormous iron cauldron that boiled the sweat and trail grime from a load of military uniforms. She was Sosi Emre, a Turk, but a decent one who did not take unfair advantage of the Armenian situation. A three-year-old boy played about his mother's feet.

"Has this woman treated my men well?" he asked of his troops crowded about, emphasizing the question with outstretched riding crop.

A loud enthusiastic murmur ensued among them before one smooth-faced youngster replied, "Yes, Captain, the ten of us who stayed in her home last night were well taken care of!"

The companions of the ten jabbed one another in the ribs and commented obscenely on the implications of that statement.

"Aha. That would mean, of course," the captain continued, obviously enjoying the opportunity, "that this loyal subject of the grand vizier met your every need and dutifully slept with each of you?"

The young man faltered, uncomfortable with the question and the jibes of his companions. "No, sir, we did not ask for such a thing of her."

"Really?"

Adrine's blood went cold at the contempt in the commander's voice.

"A truly loyal subject would not wait to be asked but would assume her duty. You two men, place more wood on that fire."

The two men indicated by the riding crop hesitated, wary of the turn events were taking.

"NOW!" the commander roared.

The men hurriedly stacked several large chunks of wood around the base of the cauldron. Flames shot upward. The water erupted in a furious boil and billows of scorching steam.

"Please, Captain, she was most generous with her home and her possessions," pled the smooth-faced soldier. "We do not wish any harm to come to this woman." A hush had fallen on the others, many of whom nodded their agreement.

"I see," the commander said. "Then bring me her child."

The mother fell at his feet and clasped her hands to her breast. "Oh no, good Captain," she begged, tears streaming down a weary face. "We are Turkish, good sir. Turks like you. You must not mistake us for infidels. Please, do not hurt my baby."

The captain, his face a mask of determined hatred, nodded at the little boy.

The mother screamed, "Run, Kenan, run little one!" He ran as fast as his chubby legs could move, but the captain was on him in an instant.

Hoisting the boy by the back of the shirt, the commander strode to the cauldron and held the crying, choking child above the hot, wet steam. The boy squirmed and tried desperately to avert his face from the scalding billows. Buttons popped, the chubby legs dropped with a jerk, and the boy shrieked. The mother beat against the officer's tunic with her fists. The child wailed in terror, dangling by a shred of cloth.

The captain snatched the boy away from the cauldron and threw him against his mother. "Lie to me again, woman, and your precious son will boil with the trousers!" He turned and gave Adrine a look that froze her blood, then marched off in the direction of the barracks.

"Stop, butcher!" The mother rose to her knees in the square and turned her son to face the captain. "Face us, monster, face us now!"

Adrine stared at her in horror. Why didn't the stupid woman hold her tongue?

The captain stopped, balled his hands into fists, and whirled to face his accuser.

The mother tore open her child's trousers, yanked them down, and thrust him forward. "Circumcised," she sobbed. "He is circumcised like every good Turkish boy. Take a good look. You would boil your own!"

The captain covered the space between them in six strides. He raised the riding crop above her head. The venom in his eyes said he would whip her to ribbons.

As one, the regiment of Hekim Khan stepped forward and stopped within arm's reach of the weeping woman. Faces grim, they locked eyes with their commander, and a clear message passed between them. Slowly, the riding crop descended harmlessly to the captain's side. He spat against the side of the cauldron, and the spittle evaporated with a sizzle.

Then he turned and quick-marched away.

Adrine gathered the sobbing, hiccuping little boy and led him back to his mother. She put her arms around her neighbor and held her for a very long time.

Cold despair settled on Adrine's shoulders like a soaking blanket. Why had the beast Ozal turned his anger from her to Sosi? Was he saving Adrine for an appropriate moment when he would drag her into his headquarters and take his spoils of war?

And how long before the next pathetic procession shuffled and whimpered through the streets of Hekim Khan? The refugee caravans were on the increase, and some weeks saw three or four arrivals of displaced Armenians. Evacuated from their homes by official decree, they clutched what they could grab before the bayonets lowered and turned them south toward the internment camps of Deir-el-Zor in the Syrian desert. Those who survived the weather, starvation, rape, suicide, and execution arrived at the camps more dead than alive.

Adrine shivered and wrapped thin arms more tightly about her friend. She missed her family with the most intense pain she had ever known. She endured dark daydreams and night terrors of what they must have suffered. One of her few pleasures was the thought of God's judgment raining fire from heaven and broiling the Turks alive. But revenge was the guiltiest of gratifications, and she wrestled against it. They could strip her of her dignity, but by Christ's grace they would not take her decency.

So she remembered her entire family as alive—gathered in a circle about the *tonir*, the covered fire set recessed in the floor in the center of her home. With their feet and legs tucked beneath the communal blanket, they would spend the winter nights cozily eating raisins, singing hymns, and telling stories. Memories of those happy times sustained her.

The two women and the little boy remained huddled together for a while before the soft mewing from under the withered old stump finally caught their attention. Adrine took a grubby little fist in her hand and led Kenan to the stump while his mother watched in numbed silence. Giaour's whiskers greeted Adrine's hand. Adrine fished about beneath the stump, then withdrew three downy gray balls of new fur and watched the smile of wonder dawn on the innocent, forgiving face of the child. A little more exploration revealed two still-born kits, which Adrine quickly but carefully placed back beneath the stump.

Eugin Karpat joined them at the stump and stroked a fuzzy newborn with the back of a heavily callused hand. "Thank you, sister," he said, barely above a whisper, "for the message. The Fedayeen value your risk and will consider your plight."

The Fedayeen! Adrine's heart leapt despite the thick sadness coating her spirit. The Armenian sisters had little to feed on besides scraps of food and Scripture, but the heroic tales of the mountain guerrillas who struck like vipers and vanished like apparitions fed their hopes of eventual rescue. All muscle and cunning, the Fedayeen bedeviled the Turkish supply lines and assassinated infidel generals in their beds. The Black Wolf and his men were masters of invasion who derailed trains, intercepted top-level military strategy, and confused the enemy by lightning raids and daring impersonations.

Adrine looked about and her heart faltered. Who could afford the luxury of legend surrounded by the realities of war? She, least of all. "And what shall we name these three kittens, brother? How about Famine, Pestilence, and Sin?" Her voice shook now that the tension was gone, but there was no mistaking the bitterness.

"Courage, sister," Karpat responded, lips barely moving. "God is a just God. This will not last forever. There may even be enough of us left to begin again."

Adrine lifted her eyes to Ararat. "Then repeat the news for me, brother. And tell of the Flood. And the eight who began again."

He started to speak, but she interrupted him. There was such sorrow in the words. "One thing more, brother. Tell me if I shall ever love and be loved by someone kind and good. Tell me!"

CHAPTER 2
Late Harvest, 1915

Tatul Sarafian buttoned the neck of the roughly woven coat and blew into his hands for warmth. The nights were frigid. A shiver of apprehension made the fine hairs at the back of his neck stand at attention. He should be home watching and listening, muscles spring-loaded for attack, but he preferred the cow shed and the company of cows. He loved the mornings when the bawling bovines spilled into the street from neighboring courtyards to lumber out onto the prairie to graze. By evening, back they came, fat udders swaying, to dash in at their own open doors for milking and a rest.

Tatul loved to sleep with them, snuggled against their gently heaving sides, the mixed smells of manure, warm cowhide, and moist, grassy breath sweet in his nostrils. Undisturbed by the escalating terror peeling the sanity from the cowherds and the milkmaids who attended them, the cows were content to eat and sleep and make milk.

It was the only constant left in the Sarafian household.

The boy, now nineteen and strong from the planting and harvesting and lifting that he did for the people of Erzurum, wondered for the hundredth time in three days if he would ever marry and father children. Would he own a fine vineyard like Mustafa Sukan? Tatul snorted. Sukan was a Turk, an infidel, the husband of four wives, and the father of twenty-three children at last count.

He lifted his head, drawn by the magnet of Mount Ararat. How beautiful her shoulders, lit silver by the moon! From his father Tatul had learned, as had every Armenian boy, the way to the Landing Place and the Holy Thing high on her shoulders. It meant climbing her icy sides and entering the sacred sanctuary of her glaciers. It meant preparing oneself before God, living sinless for a season, asking permission of heaven.

Tatul sighed. He knew of no one younger than his father, Serop, to have climbed to the Place and worshiped at the stone altars erected by his Armenian ancestors at the base of Noah's Ark. Serop had been preparing to take Tatul and his brother Haji on the journey when the horrors had begun. Now their father spoke little and shook his head much. Most frightening of all, the fire in his eyes, usually so intense, burned more feebly each day. What would his family do if it went out altogether?

Suddenly the young man's heart beat faster. Brown eyes the color of leather flashed fire in the darkness. He bolted from the cow shed and ran, arms outstretched, toward the mountain. He dropped to his knees and drank in the sight of it shimmering silver in moonglow. An endless blanket of stars floated above her crown.

"*Agri Dagi!*" he cried. "Mountain of our agony, possessor of the Holy Ark of Noah. Ararat, mother of the world, why do you watch us die and do nothing?"

Tears spilled onto the peasant coat of the farmer's son. The question was meant for God, but God did not answer. As far as Tatul could tell, God came and went, but the mountain remained, and it was to the mountain that he now appealed. She was the eternal backdrop for an entire Christian race, the oldest on earth. She was Ararat. She was Armenia.

Would she watch and do nothing while her people fell beneath the sword? Or would she stir, erupting in a river of molten anger to halt the slaughter, consume the Turks, and reclaim a stolen land?

Tatul gave a half shout, a half sob of challenge. "Burn the flesh from their bones! Save us, Mother Ararat. Save us or we will perish!"

He dropped and hugged the ground, berating himself for his carelessness. *You fool! They'll hear you!* He waited, heart pounding, but no torches parted the darkness, no cursing voices raised in pursuit.

He jumped to his feet and raced farther onto the plain. Tatul Sarafian ran until the muscles in his legs threatened to collapse. Then he stood still and waited while his lungs quit heaving. He was hungry, always hungry now. Without warning, the Turks took their food, ate their cattle, stole the milk meant for families with babies. But Tatul felt the hard, ropy muscles beneath the cloth that covered him and knew the satisfying leanness of young manhood. He felt the power of a righteous loathing and swore that the Turks would live to regret their actions.

The terror had been building for some time now. It began with soldiers in the streets. Dark, mistrusting glances and appraising stares. Turk neighbors, once friends, averted their eyes or begrudgingly served Armenian customers in their shops. Turk children no longer roamed the fields with their Armenian playmates. Donkey carts and bicycles were appropriated for vehicles of war. The thunder of combat dominated every guarded conversation, though the battlefront with Russia was still two days' journey north.

Russia. "Uncle Christian" was the code name of Russia to the increasingly jittery Christian Armenians. The Way of Escape. Those for whom the handwriting on the wall was all too plain fled to the mother of all mountains, skirted her frozen flanks, and slipped across the Aras River to freedom inside Russia. One evening they would eat a loaf of Aunt Seri's nut bread hot from the oven, the next morning their home was empty.

Tatul frowned. How could true Armenians just walk away from their homeland without so much as a backward glance? There could be no freedom for him were he to slink away in the night. He was prepared to resist the Muslims and their Germanic allies even unto death. It was unwelcome talk in his family, but Tatul Sarafian was prepared to die for Mother Ararat, for Armenia, for the sake of God's people.

His dark, expressive face had lengthened in gathering maturity, and the thick eyebrows and shadow of a budding mustache promised the same high-spirited handsomeness that so marked his father and grandfather. He had a lopsided way of smiling that made him appear shy even when he wasn't. And to his chagrin, whenever he frowned, as he did now, women thought him endearing.

Veron would have him for a husband, of that he was certain. She was splendid-looking, if lofty-minded. A man could overlook a little vinegar when the sweet main dish was so carefully arranged.

He laughed at his own conceit but felt the delicious thrill of possibilities. Surely this nastiness with the Turks would soon end. He and Veron would wed, have many babies, and become wealthy landowners and artisans with hired workers and a villa on the Mediterranean Sea.

"Arrogant fool!" chided Tatul the Practical.

"A *small* villa, then," replied Tatul the Dreamer.

Hands clasped at his back, he began to dance the *bar*, a traditional folk dance. He was alone in the moonlight. On and on he frolicked beneath the heavens to music only he could hear. The stars were his audience—and the immense, brooding Ararat.

He stopped abruptly and stared hard at the mountain. *If you won't spew forth your venom, then show us the Ark of Father Noah. Give it up for all the world to see, and the Turks will drop their weapons and fall to their knees.*

He cursed his fanciful thoughts. The only reason a Turk fell to his knees was to pray for another throat to slit.

A familiar rising panic eroded Tatul's confidence. In the late summer of 1915, people had begun disappearing from his town. Now, just a few months later, thefts were reported almost daily from the four churches and two monasteries just beyond the village. Beatings for no provocation were frequent; Armenian goods were confiscated and protesting storekeepers silenced. Christians were accused of collaboration with the Russians. Some Armenians looked for salvation in the arrival of the Russian army. Others refused to wait and took their chances fleeing across the border. In this atmosphere of growing fear, scattered retaliations were initiated by Armenian freedom fighters, giving the Turkish government confirmation of a massive Armenian conspiracy and justification for their own routine acts of numbing humiliation and increasing numbers of executions.

Tatul hefted a fist-sized rock and hurled it as far as his frustration could throw. Didn't anyone in the world see what the Turks were doing? Why did no one stop them? Never had he felt so alone.

"Touch me!" he screamed at the dark. "Touch me and I

will make you regret the day you were born!"

A wave of revulsion swept over him. Revulsion for himself. He had been baptized in water melted from ice carried by his father from the summit of Mount Ararat. As an infant he had traveled on his father's back by donkey to the monastery at Echmiadzen where the Armenian Patriarch, the spiritual head of all Armenians, had pressed a holy cross of gopher wood from the Ark against Tatul's bare chest and pronounced him hereditary Child of Noah.

And now this "holy child" spat common profanities at the enemy and questioned God's very existence. Tatul Sarafian couldn't remain sinless for one evening, let alone an entire season. When could he dare ask permission of heaven to visit the Ark? The water from high on Ararat had been wasted on him.

What it was, he didn't know, but suddenly his scalp prickled with a strange foreboding. He turned toward Erzurum, and it was as if the vastness of the plain narrowed suddenly into a thin arrow pointing home. He needed to be there. Now.

He ran, but it was through a thick mud of doubt and fear. Sharp pain stabbed at thighs and calves, and the more he ran, the farther away he seemed to be. A third of him said go home. Two thirds of him said flee to Ararat.

And the one darkest thought of all: *I am too late. A great danger is already there.*

At the end of his street, Tatul collided with a runaway horse snorting and foaming its alarm. People wandered the streets dazed and confused. A woman screamed, "My child! Where is my child?" Shouted demands for silence followed. More screams.

A stone flew out of the night and caught Tatul over the left temple. Blood trickled into his eye. He staggered backward, the flicker of fire and sounds of struggle failing to register their meaning. He stopped and leaned against a wall until his vision cleared, then barged on toward the home where lived the twelve family members. Tatul had been given by God.

The loudest confrontation was coming from the cow shed. Tatul made straight for it and entered the open doorway just as a bearded man in police garb fired two bullets through the forehead of the matriarch of their cowherd.

The military gendarme turned the gun on the matriarch's

latest offspring, a sunset red and snowy white calf with large, trusting eyes. Tatul's mother wailed and flung herself in front of the cow's dumbly innocent face. The soldier matter-of-factly took aim at the woman.

"No!" shouted Serop Sarafian, Tatul's father, throwing up a hand and coming between his wife and the gun.

Time stood still. It seemed that everyone was there in the crowded shed, including a contingent of five more gendarmes. The youngest children were crying, and Grandfather looked stricken. One gnarled hand clutched at his heart. His mouth opened and closed, but no sound came out. His son Serop had been attending him until the current threat to his wife. Haji hurried to his older brother's side, and Tatul wrapped his arms around the boy's head and held him close. Tatul kissed the sweaty brow and felt his brother's body tremble. His brothers and sisters attached themselves to Tatul's legs and feet, each wailing in misery. Tatul watched his father.

In one corner of the stable, Uncle Vartan and Aunt Seri worked on, seemingly oblivious to the commotion, their faces grim, their backs bent to their carvings. They were very old. Far into each night for the past week, they could be found in the shed hard at some task. Tatul had paid them no attention, but the events unfolding around them on this night appeared to have given them renewed vigor.

"The cows are needed to feed my men," the gendarme announced, his voice measured and cold. "One should be sufficient for now. I will post a guard at the door, and I want every able-bodied man to immediately butcher this animal and stack the meat for our use."

Suddenly, a booming voice from the street declared, "All men, women, and children of Armenian descent must vacate their homes and places of business three days from now. You will be taken to deportation camps for removal to another district where you will be detained until war's end. There are no exceptions to this order from Talaat Pasha, the Turkish minister of the interior, who is acting upon the direct orders of the grand vizier."

The chief gendarme surveyed the room with a lordly smirk. "You see," he said, "everything is under control." He lowered his gun, nodded curtly, and left, the other gendarmes close behind. They took up their positions just outside the shed.

Serop Sarafian left his wife, who continued to weep softly and clutch the orphaned calf. He returned to his father, whose breathing was more even now. Serop's eyes locked with Tatul's. One word the town crier had said hung between them like Damocles' sword. *Removal.*

"*La illaha illa'llah,*" Serop prayed into the air of the stable poisoned by the police visitation. "There is no god but God." Outside, the commotion began to die down, order restored.

The sun would rise tomorrow on a town emptier of men.

Gently Serop lowered his aged father to a pad of straw and covered him with a blanket. It was best to let him rest where he was.

"I will sleep here tonight," Tatul said. "I will watch over Grandfather and the cow shed."

Serop nodded. "Take the children to bed first. I will stay with your grandfather until you return."

Tatul hugged Haji and the girls tightly, kissed them all, and took them to bed in the house. Cousin Sarkis, almost thirty but still without a wife, was left in charge.

Tatul returned to the shed. His father had already begun the task of butchering the family cow to feed the occupying troops. Tatul took a skinning knife from a drawer in the side bench, but before joining his father, walked over to inspect Uncle Vartan's and Aunt Seri's handiwork. They sat back and let him see. Two slabs of stone lay on the table, each two feet high, a foot thick and eight feet long. Each family member's name and date of birth were followed by a blank spot for their dates of death.

The gravestones were a neatly etched labor of love. But Tatul quickly turned away lest Aunt and Uncle see his troubled face. They were resolute against the unfolding conflict. Older by twenty years than their nephew Serop, they had spent their years in a rich swirl of family and farming. Now they were ready to end their lives as they had lived—on their own terms.

Tatul felt the edge of the blade and wondered how many gendarmes he could reach before a bullet found him. *Mother Ararat, send forth your molten river of anger. . . .*

The cry of a wounded animal rent the night, shrill and unearthly. But as it died in volume, it took on a new quality, human and familiar. Tatul whirled and fell over a small milking stool. He met his father's stricken eyes. Then a moan of grief and despair escaped his lips.

He bolted from the shed, slashing the air like a dervish, but the gendarmes made no attempt to stop the young man with a knife. Another scream erupted from two houses down, and Tatul knew. It was his beloved Veron, and he would not find her alive.

And God would have to find himself another Child of Noah. Tatul would not ask the permission of heaven to kill every Turk on earth.

CHAPTER 3

The American looked eastward along the shore of Lake Goljuk and adjusted the binoculars for a sharper image. Stomach churning, he took in the ghastly view and fought the urge to retch. He ate little these days because little stayed down, and little was to be had anyway. The red roan nickered softly and shifted its weight.

The man shifted, too, and wiped the sweat from his neck with a faded blue bandanna. Broad shouldered and deep chested, he looked big for the land, as if horse and rider had been chiseled from the same block of granite.

At first what he saw resembled a field of round stones dotting the sands of the lake. But the glasses confirmed the worst. They were heads of Armenian refugees poking through the sand of shallow, hasty graves. Many more bodies, some bloated and swollen, most shriveled from the relentless sun, lay unburied. A few bobbed at the water's edge, more than likely killed while bending to drink. All were naked, forced to disrobe before they were killed, for the opportunistic Muslims believed that clothes taken from a dead body were defiled.

There were not enough scavengers. Vultures by the hundreds hopped among the dead and wheeled overhead. Wild dogs and rodents picked at the edges. But the fallen numbered in the thousands throughout the valleys and plains of the Harput District. In his journal, he had written that it was the Slaughterhouse Province.

A hot, stifling breeze from the lake blew over horse and rider. The man's gorge rose. Hell couldn't smell worse, he was certain. He would have to wait another month before he could bear to ride to the end of the valley opposite and inspect the killing field thoroughly.

A shadow fell across the saddle horn, and Frank Davidson, American Consul at Harput, looked up, the great plane of his forehead and the closely cropped scalp of salt-and-pepper hair glistened damply. Close-set dove gray eyes squinted tightly and scanned the sky. A giant of a vulture swung in a descending spiral, its eight-foot wingspan ending in long individual feathers like stiff fingers. It glided low to inspect him, its great long neck outstretched, fierce eyes blinking as if in disbelief that he was still breathing.

Davidson wanted to take his rifle and blast the bony sack of filth out of the sky. But that was anger talking. He knew their value. Vultures were specially designed for cleanup of the worst that man could do to his own species.

"We were forced to kill them," a wizened old Kurd had told him two days before at the last valley of death he'd inspected. "The military gendarmes herded maybe two thousand or more between the hills and told them to make camp. An armed company of Turks then rode to my village at the head of the valley and ordered us to fall on the Armenians or we would die. To sweeten the offer, they told us that for a modest fee, we would be allowed whatever plunder we found on the bodies in excess of that sum. We did not have to give it much thought."

The Kurd hung his head in brief shame. After all, his own people fought the Turks for an independent Kurdish homeland. But quickly his features hardened and the pragmatic survivor of desert and mountain emerged. "So little space and so many bodies piled one upon another! For two and three weeks they rotted in the sun and our poor village reeked from the stench," he had complained. "Many of us died from handling the decomposed bodies."

The vultures were a grim necessity.

Davidson, head aching, squeezed his eyes tightly shut against the glaring vision of hell and fought not to retreat. Someone had to record the atrocities, or one day the Turks would deny the whole thing. That's how they operated.

They had sealed off the high, narrow end of the valley with a couple of armed gendarmes. Two dozen more gendarmes at the water prevented anyone from attempting to swim to freedom or flee along the narrow paths that skirted the lake. Then they stood by while the weakened refugees were attacked by "invading" Kurds. He'd seen it time and again, the Turks always claiming their hands were clean of innocent blood. After all, they were outnumbered by the sword-wielding bandits. What could they do?

Davidson hadn't smiled in months and wondered if he ever would do so again. He urged the roan forward down a dry, dusty draw. The animal's nostrils flared and it shied sideways as they neared a cluster of bodies. It appeared to have been a small family of three children and their mother. The father had most likely been destroyed earlier when the first wave of killing decimated the male Armenian population.

Davidson wanted to cry for the defenseless family, so pitiful and beyond recognition as they lay against the scorched earth. But he hadn't cried in months either, squeezed dry by day after day of unceasing horror. All four of the dead bore bayonet wounds. He expected to find very few gunshot victims. Bullets were too precious with a war on.

"They are the People of the Book," Davidson mumbled, shaking his head. "For sixteen centuries, through conquerors and conquests, the Bible has been their sacred text, and now"—he faltered, wanting the analogy to be an apt one—"now they face annihilation, as helpless as kittens in a rain barrel."

Three hook-beaked raptors hopped into Davidson's peripheral vision. He turned to stare at their ugly naked necks and bare heads. Quietly they waited for Davidson to move. When he did not, they hopped forward another ten feet, then waited again in silence.

Davidson reached for the rifle strapped to the saddle and fired over the birds. They flapped a safer distance away, unhurried, eerily patient.

Slamming the rifle back into the saddle straps, he turned the horse more roughly than intended, the heels of his cracked leather boots digging into the gentle horse's sides. As horse and rider wheeled about, Davidson shook a baked fist at the sky. "Why?" he demanded. "These little ones were made in your image and now they are vulture scraps. Why, dear God, why?"

The sky did not answer. The vultures waited.

He wanted away from the murder and mutilation. He wanted someone to pay for this enormous crime. He wanted to feel rain against his face, to smell rose petals in the air.

Instead of this.

"Catharine, my love," he said, as if she rode behind him and was not a world away in New York trying to regain her fragile health, "I cannot say when I'll be home again." He squeezed eyes tight against the slaughter and thought of his beautiful, strong-willed Catharine. "I long for you, darling, but I know what you would think of this madness." He fought a rising nausea and tried to remember how lovely she smelled in his arms, the soft, radiant warmth of her—except for her feet, which were always cold. "I must do what I can to help these people before they are all dead. These poor, undefended people . . ."

He opened his eyes again and was glad she was not here. Not for this unholy scene of death. She was a strong woman and saved her tears for the living. He was glad his Catharine was not here because she would have stormed straight to the nearest Turk magistrate's office and said things that would have placed the entire American consulate in great danger. She would, without a moment's pause and in the name of all humanity, have jeopardized the whole of her husband's efforts to smuggle Armenians into Russia.

But Frank Davidson would be hanged before he would let these outrageous criminal acts go unpublished. He would send a detailed account of the Lake Goljuk massacre to Ambassador Morgenthau in Constantinople. To President Wilson in Washington, if necessary. And woe to any Turk who put himself between Davidson and the telling of this awful truth. He would personally ensure that the silenced voices in this forgotten hole of a place would be heard.

Davidson straightened in the saddle and set his jaw determinedly. It was such senseless bloodletting, yet strangely appealing to those in the heat of war. For a barrel of beans and a chunk of cured meat, the man on the horse might have swooped down on the nearest Turk village and exacted his own retribution.

Instead, Consul Davidson swallowed hard and urged his horse back to the dead mother and her children. He bowed his head and, with vultures for witnesses, hoped he could find it in his heart to pray.

And then the tears came.

Chapter 4

Twenty-eight ragged youths crept on silent feet to the edge of the playground, mock rifles primed and at the ready. Eyes blazed with resolve, faces tight beneath tall sheep's-wool hats.

Tatul Sarafian blew on his fingers in the gathering dusk and watched. And did nothing.

Neither did Kevork Basmajian, the provincial governor, at his side.

Unaware, unguarded, the barefoot children of Van chased one another around small blackened pails in which they were to collect the watery soup dispensed by the Armenian governor. Into the pitifully thin base would go bits of coarse black bread. The meager mess was the broth of life to the haggard residents of the historic Armenian capital.

The children danced on in the village square, oblivious to the menace bearing down upon them or of the young man of Erzurum who raised no alarm. Van's youth strutted like the conquering kings whose names were carved in Castle Rock. Raiment of ragged royalty flapped about their thinning bodies, threadbare and held together by mothers' prayers and ingenuity. Dirty toes punched the dust, and playful taunts reached the neglected gardens of the once choice city of Oriental luxury.

"Rumor and hunger keep us alive, keep us in motion," Van's villagers said. Reports of food would galvanize them as few other things could. But most often when the forced marchers reached the rumored site of the miraculous manna, they found that famine had arrived first.

Thin was the governor's soup, but reliable.

Upon the captain's signal, the twenty-eight spread out

along the low piled-stone wall, dropped to one knee, and leveled their weapons at the laughing, breathless dancers.

Tatul smiled a tight, grim smile, one matched by the provincial officer in drooping black mustache.

The soldiers sighted, tensed, and waited for the command to fire.

"Rise to attention!"

The order was barked in a high, pre-pubescent voice. As one, the twenty-eight boys rose and stood unflinchingly straight, eyes forward and unblinkingly fixed, nonplussed by the steady, critical gaze of their twelve-year-old captain.

"Right face!" The unit of eight- to thirteen-year-olds turned smartly and shouldered their mock rifles. "Heroes forward!" All but two of the youngest started off on the same foot, and the two quickly compensated. The boys assembled in the street in front of the governor, smartly alert, rifles ready.

Sarafian watched their smudged faces for signs of defeat. He found only courage and fire. Despite the cold pit in his stomach, he admired the firm determination in each child's jaw. Sadly, few if any would live to love a woman, or cradle a son, or fall facedown before the Holy Ark. But for this moment, before this magistrate, they were men of valor.

"What can the governor do for these loyal citizens?" The respect in Kevork Basmajian's voice was genuine. Tatul's throat tightened. Though Turk butchers were bearing down on the mostly defenseless Van, the governor took time to honor a rough collection of humble warriors whose patchwork shirts, coats, and pants were the clever transformation of a pile of scavenged scraps.

"We are from Artemid and have come to trade these wooden guns for real guns. We want to protect our country."

The governor thoughtfully stroked his mustache, his countenance as serious as the words just uttered. "We can only issue armament to those who can drill."

The boy captain filled his chest with air and came to stand firmly before the magistrate. "We can drill, sir!"

"Let us see."

Without hesitation, the young captain turned to face the troops. A guttural "Huh!" flew from his throat, and the butts of twenty-eight wooden rifles came to the street with a thud.

Up they came again to "Present arms!" Back they snapped to "Right shoulder arms!" and forward ready at "Charge bayonets!" Not a smile or averted glance altered the sober fresh faces of Armenia's littlest defenders.

"Company front!" Untanned skin moccasins shuffled in place, feet in perfect rhythm, the miniature soldiers reassembling in a straight line, shoulder to shoulder.

Governor Basmajian, impressed, nodded to the captain. "Permission to review the troops," the governor said.

"Permission granted, sir!" replied the captain smartly.

Into each young ear, the governor whispered, "God sustain you, my son." At the end of the line, one young man's stoicism threatened to crumple. Quickly, the governor called him out.

The boy stepped forward, trembling, his tears frightened back into hiding.

"Name?" demanded the governor loudly but not unkindly.

The boy's voice cracked. "Aram Garo, sir!"

"Well, Aram Garo, why have *you* come?"

The line of snowy mountains that separated the Armenian homeland from the Tigris Valley glowed a gentle rose color beneath the sun's last rays. The little boy did not speak at first but breathed hard, eyes wet with tears. His dirty face twitched with panic, then Aram turned and caught the steady gaze of his captain. The leader was looking away past Lake Van's lovely waters to hazy Nimrud's cratered peak, then north to Sipan's graceful cone. It was there, tradition said, the Ark first sought harbor, only to give it up and come to a final rest on Mother Ararat still farther north. Father Noah. Father God. Christ His Son.

Aram Garo's breathing slowed. He sniffled loudly and found again an expression of military restraint. "I came, sir, because my father disappeared and was last week found murdered by the road to the Turkish lines. His teeth had been cut out of his head, their gold removed...." The boy's reserve broke and he wept. The others did not move, but the struggle showed in their faces.

His captain put an arm around him and wiped the tears with his fingers. "Most of my troop have had their fathers murdered or their mothers commit suicide rather than be raped," he said, voice flat.

He looked deep into the governor's eyes. "Please, sir, let us fight for the homeland. Though we could not keep our parents alive, perhaps we can avenge their deaths." The boy soldiers lost their precision and fell out. Their eyes grew guilty and distant for the lack of brawn and cunning each was convinced could have saved their mothers and fathers. Several began to cry.

To fight with their last breath was their reasonable penance.

"It is too late to travel tonight," Governor Basmajian said brusquely. "And too dangerous. You will be my guests." He motioned to two aides standing in the shadows. "Feed these brave soldiers a ration of black bread, tea, and sugar, and put them in a room at the city troop quarters. Find them some hot water and ensure a good scrubbing is had by all. Air their clothing. Find each a pair of heavy wool socks."

The boys brightened at the litany of luxuries and managed to regain some of the military bearing they'd brought with them.

"Sir?" The boy captain removed his wool hat and attempted to smooth the tangle of hair beneath. The governor turned and waited. The captain cleared his throat, his bravery beginning to slip. "Sir, with all respect, we will not leave without real guns."

The governor nodded. "I understand, Captain, and if I had guns to give, you would have them. But there are not even enough for the defense of my own people. When this war is over, people will again collect guns and shoot game. You must join me then for a hunt, but for now we are the hunted, and the game flees to the empty places. You understand."

He did. Tatul watched the dignity with which the young commandant silently saluted the governor. The salute was returned.

"But I wish you to keep up your discipline and training, for the time may come when we shall need your assistance. Hold your command in readiness, Captain, for your country may call upon you yet."

"We shall be ready, sir!" The captain turned to his ragtag company. "Right shoulder arms!" The pretend rifles flew into position. "Column right, march!" And the volunteer army of

Artemid stepped proudly on their way to bath and bed.

Sarafian fought a lump in his throat and again felt hatred for the Turks, a now familiar and loyal emotion. *"Veron died protecting her virginity. She was saving herself for you. It was her wedding gift."* The words of Veron's grief-crazed mother seared his flesh. *"They broke her neck because she resisted so fiercely."*

Sweet Veron. Dearly beloved. They will regret the day they took you from me.

"Sarafian!" Apparently the governor had been calling his name repeatedly.

"Yes?"

Governor Basmajian sighed and his shoulders sagged. He stared into the distance as if he could separate Turkish invaders from the gathering gloom. "This used to be such a beautiful place, my Van," he said, seeming to forget what he'd meant to say. "Gardens so green, homes so well kept, choice carpets and silk hangings at every turn. There were tons of matted wool to be cleaned, carded, spun, and woven for clothing of the finest cut. Everyone wanted clothing from Van."

He looked down at the coarse fabric of his own ill-fitting suit the color of dark earth. In wartime, homespun was the only available cloth in the Caucasus region. "And now the seat of government is a modest mud house. And your dear father taken, and . . . God knows what."

"My father is alive!" exclaimed Tatul. He seized the old family friend by the biceps and tried to yank the slump of defeat from the man's weary frame. The strong young hands urgently clamped the aging arms as if renewed vitality and hope could be transfused through a grip.

The governor looked at Tatul, and the young man released him in frustration and embarrassment. To transmit hope, he first needed to himself be blessed with an abundance of optimism. What Tatul Sarafian had in abundance was pure loathing. Any residual hope left in him was a bitter determination to see Turkey burn and writhe for its sins against Armenia.

Serop, my father, do not let them defeat you. Wherever they've taken you, hold fast to the homeland. I love you, Father, and will do my best to honor all that you have given me. He squeezed his eyes tightly shut until golden comets streaked behind the eyelids.

He tried not to think of his dear mother or little Haji, coy sister Shapur and gentle cousin Sarkis. He remembered instead the feel of his father's powerful hands lifting him beneath the arms until he was astride his thick neck, high above the ground, little hands reaching for Ararat. He had pretended to scoop the creamy snow from her sides and fed it to his father, who smacked his lips and declared it the most wonderful food on earth. Angel food.

And when he was too old to drape his father's shoulders anymore, the two had slept by a fire in the wilderness, and Tatul listened again and again to the stories of bravery from Scripture. They had dreamed together of the day when the eldest son would follow in his father's footsteps to the holy ground at the foot of Noah's Ark. They had prayed for sinlessness so that Tatul might be worthy of the journey. Tatul would pretend to sleep until he heard his father's breathing deepen. Then he would wriggle forward on his elbows until their heads touched. Only then could Tatul relax, the tingle of excitement subside, and sleep overtake him. For he believed that even as father and son slept head to head, the wonderful things that his father had seen would jump from his brain into Tatul's.

Then came that terrible night when Veron was killed and Erzurum sacked, and the family was forced into exile. But Tatul knew that he could not wait to be herded off to the desert. The sight of Veron lying stripped and broken on the floor of her home was as much a part of him now as his heart—and as vital. It was the spur that would enable him to help Armenia survive the terrible sentence she was now under.

He had announced to his father that he would slip away that very night and join the Fedayeen, the legendary freedom fighters who were hard as steel, alert as ferrets, brave as lions, and, it was told, possessors of several lives.

The two Sarafians argued bitterly at first.

"What of your mother and sisters?" his father had demanded. "It will take all of us men to defend them on the road to Syria. Their hearts will break without you."

"Come with me, Father!" Tatul shouted back. "Let all Sarafian men take the battle to the bloody infidels and feed them their own brains! They won't allow you to live. You know this.

You will be murdered or forced to rebuild their smoldering ruins. I would rather die defending the homeland than die while being herded down the trail like a mindless goat or while placing a single brick for a home to be inhabited by a Turkish devil!"

The words stung. His father's shoulders dropped, and he shook his head. "So hot, so hate filled!" the elder said. "You must spill some of that venom or you will be poisoned by your own bite. Not everyone can abandon the women and the little ones, or Armenia will never begin again."

The two generations glared at each other. Then quite unexpectedly, Serop Sarafian threw his arms around his son and kissed him. "Go with God," he whispered huskily. "I cannot leave your mother or the little ones. Uncle Vartan is too old, and cousin Sarkis too sensitive. But you are strong and swift. You can do much good on your own. All I ask first is that you go to my old friend and yours, Kevork Basmajian. If anyone can tell you how to find the men of the dark, he can. I do not even know if the Fedayeen exist, my son. I hope to God they do. The Turks and the Kurds are afraid of something out there, something they call the *Koords*—human wolves. But Kevork knows. Just . . . just remember one thing." His father had hesitated, searching Tatul's face before going on.

"What is it, Father? Tell me."

"If you become a Fedayee, you will never see the Ark. To be a true Fedayee, you will never know sinlessness. Never." The last word was a sob. The father bowed his head.

Tatul reached out and tenderly took his father's head in his hands and drew him close. Their heads touched, and the nights in the wilderness again passed between them. "The way of heaven may for me lie along another route," Tatul said. "You have ever taught me the way of grace, and for nineteen years I have embraced it. But the Turks do not understand grace. The sword is their grace, and for them to ever change, they will have to feel the bite of their own blade. Let us pray that it is but for a short season."

And then he had wept great tears of sorrow and mourning while his father held him tightly, their mingled tears washing off some of the madness that threatened to swallow them. Tatul's father, the farmer, had loved Veron, too. Her radiance was like having the heart of the sun inside the house.

"Kiss Mother for me," Tatul said as they parted, "and Auntie and the children. Tell them this is for them, that I didn't kiss them myself because I will return before good-byes are necessary. Do you have enough to begin again, Father? How will you live?" Though it was not said, they both hoped to heaven that would indeed *be* one of the challenges in Serop Sarafian's beclouded future.

"Yes, yes," his father had replied, brushing aside the concerns as if they were just contemplating a day trip to see relatives. When Tatul did not take his eyes off his father's, Serop mustered up a smile and patted his son's cheek. "We have your mother's and your grandmother's jewelry for money and plenty of places to hide it."

Tatul, the son, had gone to Governor Basmajian and received his blessing and an entry into the armed camp of the Fedayeen. The Black Wolf, great barrel-chested commander of the mountain guerrillas, had boisterously embraced him and taken him under his private tutelage.

Now Tatul Sarafian swallowed hard and thought of the boy soldier's father whose teeth were torn from his head for gold.

"You were good to bring supplies," said the governor. "We needed supplies. The defenders of Van cannot feed forever off anger and pride."

Tatul nodded but did not trust himself to speak.

He looked to the mountains instead and felt a stirring deep in his heart.

CHAPTER 5

Adrine Tevian trailed her feet in the cool, rushing water, then lay down among the bright yellow blossoms of the *loriki* shrubs that grew in profusion along the riverbank. She dare not be gone long, but the well had run dry. A water jug was her passport to a few stolen moments alone with the steadfast River Kuru and away from the hungry eyes of the young Turk soldiers and the murderous glances of their leader.

Adrine turned onto her stomach and plunged her head beneath the cold, clear water. She remembered how she used to come here as a child and completely submerge her body in the shallows for long periods until her mother gave up calling for her. She'd learned to swim in that river. She was baptized in its frigid winter waters, and in the river's mud had first seen the print of a human foot with six toes. A monster, she'd screamed to her mother, a two-headed beast that ate children.

She was no less shocked to learn that the monster was her mother's brother, Uncle Saras. But he had one head only and a taste not for children but for *achot*, a mixture of cheese, walnuts, and yogurt. To her horror, he'd demonstrated the sixth toe that very night by the fire, wiggling it as vigorously as the other five. She didn't know why, but whenever her brothers and sisters clamored for Uncle Saras to remove his shoes so they could count his toes, Adrine hung back and said nothing. For years, the surplus digit made her anxious. She dreamed of cutting it off, yet was so ashamed of the dreams that, each morning following a bout of nocturnal mayhem, she would insist on polishing her uncle's shoes to a mirror shine. He chuckled and assumed it was just her shy way of expressing affection.

Adrine turned on her side in the shaded shallows and looked across the river to the Monastery of Mesrop, known as the Fortress of the Golden Casket to the Armenian faithful. There, behind the ancient walls of one of the oldest monasteries in the world, resided hoary and ageless monks in black robes and head coverings, keepers of a treasure most rare.

Deep within the monastic library of priceless manuscripts never translated or published was an ornate gold chest. Behind its lavishly adorned little doors rested a piece of reddish-colored petrified wood, carved in the shape of a cross. It measured thirty-nine by twenty-four centimeters and was about three centimeters thick. It was fashioned from the Holy Ark itself.

So the rumors said.

Like most children of Hekim Khan, indeed of all Armenia, she dreamed of the day when she would cross the Kuru on the rickety old cable ferry that brought the supply monk to the town market and see that marvelous cross. And like all Armenian children, she fled in terror from the stately, high-hatted holy man that deigned to tread the dusty, profane streets with his sacred sandals. The monks looked so dark, almost sinister in their somber black trappings, and parents added to the fear by telling their children not to venture into the path of a Mesrop monk or their eyes would remain forever crossed. Even Armenian adults shrank back into doorways and averted their eyes at the passing of a consecrated man of Mesrop. Old superstitions died hard, and no one knew anyone from the town who had ever set foot inside the monastery walls.

Soon after the new year, the Turks slaughtered the monastery's mules that for years had pulled the ferry from shore to shore and back again. The two wooden rafts that carried priest and freight across the racing waters were secured to the Turk-controlled shore in a deliberate attempt to starve the monks, whom the Turks said performed human sacrifice and drank one another's blood for communion. The Turks hated the monks, for they were the keepers of Christianity and centuries-old manuscripts that spoke of God having a Son born of an earthly mother. It was blasphemy to think that Allah, the Highest and Mightiest, would soil his divinity in the womb of a commoner.

So speculation about the monks flew among Armenians and Turks alike. Did manna from heaven sustain them? No cloud of vultures soared above their sacred compound. Though Adrine strained to see them at their holy rounds, it appeared still at Mesrop. Either the holy men were at prayer for deliverance, or they had been caught up into heaven by God.

Adrine shuddered, prayed for their protection, and dreamed of the cool mountain caverns and icy snowpacks far to the north in the mysterious Caucasus Mountains, the disputed borderland between Russian Christians and Turkish Muslims. Did these sweet, cool waters originate there along with the wild, exotic stories of giants and gold that so amazed the people of the plains? Her missionary teachers said no, but it was fun to dream. The rugged ramparts of the Caucasus flexed their granite muscles from the Black Sea in the west to the Caspian Sea in the east and were home to one hundred twenty colorful peoples and tribes. These mountains hid the stronghold of the legendary Fedayeen.

They had to be legendary. Her plea for help had gone unheeded. Or had Eugin Karpat the "rug merchant" met some terrible fate along the way and not delivered her message? She bit back bitter tears. Wishful thoughts of the Fox came unbidden. He was reported to be among the bravest and most cunning of all the Fedayeen.

Legend had sprung up quickly around this one. It was said that he was part animal, part man. That if caught in a steel trap in the form of a forest fox, he would gnaw through his own leg to escape. The joke that followed was that one righteous fox on three good legs still held the advantage over a Turk with none to stand on.

She imagined him tall as a tree, swift as a hawk, silent as the snow. And as fanciful as a young girl's daydreams, she chided herself. Armenians were born storytellers. If the Fedayeen were as good by half as the tales told, Armenia would run the country, and the Turks would shovel the barnyard waste.

The last two days in Hekim Khan had brought a flood of Armenian deportees staggering south. To what? They had no flour, no seed, no farm implements. They had been picked clean by vultures in uniform. A lucky few of the condemned had wagons, but most wore burlap and bound their bloody feet in sacking or torn carpet. To wear shoes, if one had them, was a dangerous risk. One could be killed for shoes that then would be sold to a once wealthy merchant for the equivalent value of two horses.

Faces waxen, emaciated bodies streaming rags, the displaced Armenians carried little wrapped bits of maggoty dog meat; others, their faces pitifully swollen, were herb-eaters who hadn't seen meat in weeks and were reduced to swallowing leaves and blades of grass.

A low moan, like the mindless chant of the insane, rose and fell from their open mouths. Occasionally one would approach and plead, "Mercy, have mercy!" and be beaten back by the military gendarmes.

The children were the most pitiful. Like ancient dwarfs, foreheads wrinkled and cheeks deeply creased, they shuffled past, eyes down, searching the packed earth for anything eatable. A near stampede had occurred when one of them spotted a spill of candle wax by the steps of the troop barracks.

Adrine often hid little handfuls of nuts and pieces of withered apples inside dough balls. She watched the deportees for mothers with children, then joined the inevitable knot of Turks who threw insults at the passing parade and pelted the infidels with stones and rotten food. Adrine tossed the small balls of nutrition as gently as possible, willing them to be fished from the dirt and confusion. They nearly always were, the mothers alert as ferrets and lightning fast for anything with which to feed their babies. Last night a tall, bone-thin mother, hair dull and stringy but with a still proud bearing and two starving little girls at her side, bent and retrieved three dough balls at once and slid them inside the folds of the shabby burlap barely covering her body.

Then she straightened and searched the faces of the angry mob. Her tortured eyes at first scanned past Adrine, then returned. Unsmiling, she halted with her children amid a hail of sticks and curses and bowed ever so slightly. Adrine furtively made the sign of the cross against her breast, and the woman bowed again, then hurried off, sheltering her girls by the thin protection of her body.

Later that night, Adrine slipped down to the refugee encampment in the hope of seeing the proud mother again. The stench of unwashed bodies and death made her forget her own hunger. At least she had a portion to eat twice a day. If she was watchful, she could even count on an occasional extra scrap falling from the soldiers' table. It galled her, but she had to eat to be of use to the brotherhood, to God, to any hope of a future.

She watched a bent Armenian couple walk their granddaughter to the home of a Turk at the river's edge. The girl was fifteen or sixteen with vestiges of beauty still evident in her thinning frame. Obviously her grandfather had been more resourceful and had planned more carefully than most. Their clothes were worn but whole, and less of their bodies had wasted away. The fact that the grandparents were still among the living was remarkable in itself. The old were the most expendable, and if not killed early in the march, sometimes they committed suicide to allow younger family members access to the rapidly dwindling food supply.

They were greeted at the tumbledown river home by a dark man yelling threats. While she could not hear exactly what was said, it soon became evident to Adrine that some kind of negotiations were underway. First, the high-pitched cajoling of the old man. Next, the Turk farmer waved his arms and circled the young girl as if inspecting a new plow horse. He squeezed and measured and considered. The old woman said nothing.

The Turk disappeared inside the mud brick dwelling, then reemerged with a sack, which he passed to the elderly Armenian. The burden slung across his shoulders and steadied by the old woman at his side, the grandfather kissed the girl—who showed no emotion—and made his way back to the refugee encampment. His wife was carved from rock and moved only when he did. The Turk farmer took the girl's hand and led her through the door to his home.

Cold inside, Adrine watched the old couple and the sack of flour trudge past. Could she judge them for a transaction made by mutual consent? They'd ended their granddaughter's nightmare and in the bargain given her to a master able to care for her. In return, they'd been spared starvation. Love had nothing to do with it.

That is what she told herself. But that morning when she heard of the riot at the refugee camp over a sack of flour, she felt such a flood of vindication for the granddaughter that she had to sit down and pray for balance. The flour was stolen, the old people's wagon ransacked, and now the shrewd bargainers had neither food nor granddaughter.

Oh, God, are we reduced to this?

The glad rush of water over gravel coaxed her from the dreary memories. Adrine was tempted to swim, to drift downstream to the mighty Euphrates, free from the insanity of Hekim Khan. But where would she go? How would she live?

If she went anywhere, it should be upstream to the mountains, to the stronghold of the *Koords*—the Fedayeen wolves. No one knew exactly how they lived, but it was certain from whom they drew their strength—*Kara Koord*—the Black Wolf, and the Fox, his adopted son. It was said the Wolf had ten hands and six eyes and the strength of three men. Would his son possess any less? So why didn't they answer a sister's cry for help?

Adrine laughed aloud at the exaggerations and thanked heaven for the sound. It had been so long since . . . joy.

She returned to her stomach and stared into the wide, panicked eyes of a small boy.

He was so entangled in a little floating bed of dried rushes that at first she mistook him for a frightened animal caught in the weeds. But the thin face and dark hair were unmistakably that of a desperate human being escaping downriver.

He couldn't be more than nine or ten. His boat had no rudder and must have taken the wide bend in the river and been swept into the thicket of birches that grew along the edge. It stuck fast, held there by the force of the racing water. He lay facedown on some bits of wooden planking lashed together with cords of hemp, his back disguised by a thick layer of rushes, just his head and feet exposed at either end.

"Hello," she called in a loud whisper. "Don't be afraid."

He looked warily up the bank to the town, and she could tell he was anxious to get away.

"Are you Christian?" he asked.

"Yes." Adrine felt a sudden flush of hope for this boy, out of all proportion to his sad predicament. Most of what turned

46

up in the river these days were the corpses of dead Armenians. Two days before, the bayoneted bodies of a man, woman, and child swept downstream from some ill-fated caravan and were found at the ferry landing. Adrine wanted to help this boy, to send him sailing down the Kuru to live to be somebody's father.

She scrambled to her feet and waded out to the little reed boat. It was a rude craft but rather ingeniously woven of whatever was at hand and sturdy to the touch. She glanced anxiously at the top of the bank. Seeing no one, Adrine grabbed the sides of the boat firmly in both hands and pulled it free of the birches.

Clumsily, the water pulling at her legs, she struggled and maneuvered the boy in the boat until they were both pointed at the middle of the river. Then stumblingly she guided the craft as far from shore as she safely could. With a prayer, a shriveled bit of apple, and a quick kiss to the top of the boy's head, she shoved the rough vessel out into the current. It wobbled for a moment, unsure of which way to go, then swung into the strong pull deeper out. The child's bare feet hung over the end of the contraption and paddled with renewed vigor. A small hand emerged above the floating tangle and gave a jaunty wave.

"God go with you!" she cried, loud as she dared, hoping he could hear her above the gurgle and rush of the water.

The boat and its crew of one entered the chop and swirl and picked up speed on its voyage downstream to join the River Euphrates.

Adrine wanted more than anything to run along the riverbank and cheer on the brave little boy, to make certain he kept kicking up a plucky silver wake all the way to the sea and freedom. But she couldn't, not without attracting unwanted attention. She watched until he bobbed from sight, then waded back to shore and picked her way up the bank to town.

Weak with hunger, it took her longer than usual. At the steepest part of the bank, she reached for a handhold and felt a strong, unyielding arm envelop her, pull her up, and press her tightly against military hardness. Her eyes squeezed tight against the horror, she breathed in the dank body odor and felt the stroke of a hairy hand against her cheek. Above the roaring in her ears, she heard the methodical slap of leather.

Adrine stiffened at the touch of the riding crop beneath her chin. Her head rose against her will, and she looked into the veined, feverish eyes of Neelam Ozal, the Turk commander. She saw the undisguised hunger, the utter contempt, and felt herself falling into sweet unconsciousness.

———

The skin on Frank Davidson's arms crawled. He had never before seen an entire people hounded to death.

The silence was deathly. Hundreds of innocent Armenians incapable of talk. Mostly women, children, and the elderly, they stood dazed and terror-stricken in the open expanse before the police station of Harput, Turkey. It was hauntingly dark, the surrounding streets deserted. A few policemen stood guard but no one said a word. Even the children, frozen in fear, did not cry.

Davidson, the neutral American consul, moved among the remaining Armenian residents of Harput, desperately wanting to meet their frightened gaze, doing everything within his power not to. More than once he went to speak, only to stop and cover his embarrassment with a cough. He had nothing to say to them. He was powerless to help, so anything he said would be false, glib, meaningless. How the neutral consul hated the word "neutral." It was obscene that he just stood there, arms at his side when women and children went marching past to their deaths.

His nerves were so frayed that he began to lose composure. If only Catharine were here, she would know what to do. Without saying a word, his wife would minister to the sick, bring a moment's compassion, comfort the children. She had that quality about her to breathe new life into sad old places. They'd never had children—could not—but it was just as well with Davidson's constant foreign postings. Still, without the freshness that children bring, she had put a shine on his life that made each day new. Those early mornings when he would wake beside her in the dark, he would relish her warmth and excitement as she planned the day's activities.

Davidson shook his head, tried to dislodge the demons there. Catharine's absence took its toll, especially whenever the Turks rounded up a new caravan and marched them out of town. But she was not well, and Harput was not safe.

The extermination was methodically planned, that was certain. Davidson heard reports that all Armenian soldiers had been disarmed and later shot. Then followed mass arrests and the execution of Armenia's political, financial, and intellectual leaders, which they had kept him from viewing. Thus beheaded, the communities were finally fully emasculated by the murdering of the remaining male laborers. Officially, the men were sent to work on the roads. In fact, they were taken a few hours from town and killed, their mass graves or unburied remains grisly reminders to their families that they too would soon meet a similar fate. Davidson had watched the wagons roll out full of men, their hands tied behind their backs, only later that day to observe their return. Empty.

Soon after, news arrived that Armenian saboteurs had retaliated by ambushing the Turkish army at Van, burning the Muslim quarter to the ground and killing thousands of Turks, Kurds, and other Muslims in the process. It was supposedly then, and only then, that the Ottoman government decided to "relocate" Turkey's Armenian communities—for reasons of national security—to the Ottoman provinces of Syria, Lebanon, and Iraq.

Davidson stopped in front of a young boy seated on the ground, a sleeping infant cradled inside his thin coat. The boy's eyes were incredibly empty of hope. Davidson knelt, removed his jacket, and placed it around both boy and baby. He touched the boy's face and forced a smile. The boy, shivering from cold and fear, pressed against Davidson's rough, chapped hand, but his expression did not change.

Suddenly overcome, Davidson gathered the children to his chest with a groan. A guard—as if women and babies needed to be guarded—moved to intervene but stopped when the people around the American closed ranks. Better to look the other way than to start a bloody uprising in the middle of the night.

The baby was soiled, but Davidson didn't care. He prayed to God to lift them straight up to heaven, and when God didn't, he prayed for the earth to open. He was a second away from ripping at the ground with his bare hands, to chewing out a hole with his teeth if need be, anything to hide these children and spare them a death they did not deserve.

A skinny arm slid around the back of the American's neck, and Davidson hugged the boy and baby, the only sweet embrace he had known for so very long.

"Attention!" Turk guards shouted in fractured Armenian. "Collect only the belongings you were permitted to remove from your homes and prepare to begin the march. Do not be alarmed. You will be taken safely to resettlement camps in the desert between Jerablus and Deir-el-Zor to await the end of the war. At that time, you will be returned to your homes." Guards on horseback at the rear of the crowd pressed forward and herded the deportees in the direction of the march.

Someone reached down and tore the children from Davidson's grasp. Before he got to his feet, they were gone in the press of anxious humanity.

"Wait!" Davidson shouted, but there was no waiting. The crowd surged forward, activity and noise a needed distraction from the dread of waiting.

"Don't go." He felt foolish saying it and barely uttered the words. The Armenians abandoned their city with something like enthusiasm now that they were moving, motivated by false hope, by a belief that no man, not even a Turk, could be as monstrous as the stories claimed.

"Maybe what we've heard is lies," called one man over the melee. He was almost giddy at doing something—anything. "They said we'd get our homes back. The war won't last too long, and then we will return to Harput and begin again!"

The American consul wanted to grab the stupid man by the throat and force him to read the communiqué received just that afternoon from the neutral observers in Trebizond on the Black Sea coast. Turkish authorities there loaded Armenians onto barges with the assurance they would be safely put ashore in Romania or Bulgaria, where they could seek asylum and a new life.

Instead, the barges were towed far out to sea and their cargoes of screaming humanity deliberately sunk.

Davidson groaned. The cold rush of despair rapidly replaced the warmth of the children. He laughed a harsh, mirthless sound. Even if by some miracle anyone lived to return to

Harput, they would find their homes and stores and shops and goods in the hands of others. Hundreds of thousands of ethnically diverse Muslims, themselves displaced by the conflict at the Russian front, were heading south toward Harput and filling in the towns and occupying the lands left vacant by the forced expulsion of the Armenians.

His despair turned to anger. White-hot fury. Davidson charged a little shakily toward the consular office. He would send a scathing wire to Washington and tell them precisely what he thought of neutrality. Neutrality was for cowards. Neutrality was just another form of favor. Ask Pontius Pilate. Neutrality was killing Armenians by the droves.

His president would listen, surely. He began to mentally compose a telegram. *"My dear Mr. President, I believe that you should reconsider the United States' involvement in the war. Turkey does not understand the inhumanity of its systematic destruction of the Armenian way of life. The Germans do not understand the gravity of lying down with Turks. It will take the resolve of American policy, and I am sad to say, the muscle of U.S. military might, to get them to see the error of their ways."*

While he was at it, Davidson would add a lighter postscript. *"And, Mr. President, as I really do not see how morality can be federally mandated, I believe that you should bring the considerable weight of your office to bear in the prohibition of legislated Prohibition. Otherwise, you and I shall have to take our brandy in the cellar of the White House with guards at the door!"*

Davidson paused at the gate to the U.S. consulate and listened. In the night stillness, the sound of tramping feet could be heard fading ever so gradually to the south. The consular official looked up at the starry heavens and sighed. Even if one day those feet should come tramping back again, would there be anyone left in Harput to greet them?

Frank Davidson nodded to the watchman at the gate, and the wrought-iron barrier parted to allow him entrance. He made determinedly for the office door. While he had breath left in him, Davidson would make so much diplomatic noise that he couldn't be forever ignored—or he would take matters into his own hands, whatever the consequences.

God help him, someone in a high place was going to have to pay attention.

CHAPTER 6

Crablike, Turk soldiers scrabbled for the top of the craggy ridge. Nerves taut, eyes straining, attention riveted on the lead man ten yards in front. If his hand came up, they froze. When it dropped, they advanced. Knee-high black boots scraped softly against unyielding rock, but the defenders of Prime Minister Talaat Pasha climbed the steeps as silent as falling snow.

Teeth clamped on hard steel knives. Steamy breath entered and exited flaring nostrils. Muscles protested. Hearts raced. The frightened Turks felt the mountain cold penetrate to bone. Detached from the earth by an enveloping mist, they forced their thoughts away from the hidden places beyond the trees.

Their unseen enemy did not eat. Nor sleep. Each was seven feet tall, the color of bronze with a stride twice that of a normal man. They were not men at all, but furry, feral mountain beasts, harder, stronger, more cunning than any animal.

They were the legendary Fedayeen.

They rose with the moon and picked off their victims one by one. Thus the special Turk army unit had not moved in the night when they could too easily be cut off from one another. Two were posted guard but none could sleep. At every howl of a distant wolf, every chatter of a night owl, stomachs churned. The lieutenant berated them for their cowardice, spoke darkly of their fate should they fail. But they listened only halfheartedly, for the lieutenant's own qualms were betrayed by an uncontrollable twitching just beneath his left eye.

The hand was raised. They halted. Lungs bellowed in and out against the steep ascent and thinning air. Steam poured in streams from red noses. None dared drop a knife. The taste of metal was a constant reminder of what they'd come to do.

Kill the Fox.

The rumors said he was the shadow of *Kara Koord*, the Black Wolf. The Fox and the Wolf turned as one, fought as one, thought as one. By night only one slept, but both awoke refreshed. Each morning they told the same dreams—in unison. Should one conceive a son, the legends said, the child would call both "Father."

Together, they and their deadly pack swept out of the Caucasus Mountains, which straddled the border with Russia east of the Black Sea, and pounced upon the Ottoman troops and supply lines struggling to the Russian front. Sometimes with the coming of dawn, Turk soldiers awoke to find every other man slain. At other times, all survived the night only to discover that the ammunition cartridges they'd worn to bed were missing. The sly, random attacks did more to unnerve the Turks than did a full declaration of war.

Kill the Fox and cripple the Wolf, the orders said. Kurd mercenaries, posing as goatherders, served as paid lookouts. For weeks, sightings of the Wolf's band had been carefully tracked and plotted on a map, the Kurds and their herds acting as decoys. By patient, strategic positioning of the herds higher on the slopes in an ever tightening circle, the Black Wolf was himself gradually and imperceptibly herded onto the upper reaches of a narrow ridge with limited access and, more importantly, limited escape.

If Turk intelligence was correct—and Allah see to that, blessed be his name—in another hundred feet they should crest the ridge and take Black Wolf's pack by surprise.

No one wanted to think of the consequences should the Wolf and the Fox somehow slip the net. Each man felt often for the reassuring hardness of the pistol at his side.

But there was ample reason for optimism. The Wolf was apparently unaware of the ruse, or he would have long ago eliminated the Kurd herdsmen, fed the goats to his men, and filled the steep canyons with derisive laughter. No, the Wolf apparently was aging, his mind losing its edge. The legend was flawed after all, and now the Turk lieutenant and his men would have the privilege of ending the Wolf's reign of terror.

The strategists who planned the attack thought it unlikely that the Wolf could be taken in the secret raid. They believed in his heightened animal instinct for self-preservation, if not his immortality. The orders were to target the Fox. The younger Armenian anarchist, by virtue of his brash youth and relative inexperience, was more prone to mistake. He was unseasoned, and the Turks counted on a cocky defiance to be his downfall.

Here, now, belly flat against damp stone, each Turk soldier felt coldly distant from home and happiness. And where were the military strategists, the men who sent others to stop the unstoppable? Likely arranging their chairs at the victory party.

The last of winter was in the drifting fog. The lieutenant, twitching with unease, crept to the top of the ridge while his men waited below. He fought the urge to flee down the mountain. Capture the Fox and be Turkey's hero. Turn tail and run, be Turkey's goat.

Dead goat.

He took three deep breaths, then rose to a crouch. He quickly scanned the forest vegetation ahead for movement, prepared to drop at the first sign of detection. Nothing moved. He started forward, stopped, peered through the wet gloom. A small forest clearing formed a level widening in the spine of the ridge—free of trees, dotted with many low bushes, here and there a few patches of ice and shaded drifts of snow, covered in a thick carpet of needles. It would in happier and drier times provide soothing relief for the weary climber.

Something odd and decidedly out of place caught his eye at the far end of the clearing. He straightened to gain a better view, then quickly resumed the crouch and ran forward, knife in hand.

The men below watched their leader disappear over the top of the ridge and for two long minutes heard not a sound, the worm of doubt gnawing at their bellies. At last, unexpectedly loud in the stillness, they heard the lieutenant's voice. "Advance men. All is well. Come and be refreshed."

For a split second they looked about to see if anyone thought the words strange. Everyone thought it, but none betrayed it. Neither did anyone move.

Ten seconds more of indecision passed before the second

lieutenant raised his eyebrows and urged them forward. The soldiers stood and followed their commander over the top and onto level ground.

The second lieutenant's hand went up. They halted. The mist lifted and at the far end of the clearing a lone man lounged at tea.

This was no ordinary man, nor was it their lieutenant. Long and lanky, he appeared even taller with his high hat of black wool. His bright costume consisted of a short, multi-colored woolen jacket across broad shoulders, baggy trousers embroidered in red and yellow, and a long winding sash of solid red bound at the waist and reaching almost to the tops of the soft leather moccasins.

Bandoliers of ammunition crisscrossed his chest and fastened at his waist. The long barrel of a Russian Mosin rifle protruded above his back and a ten-repeater Mauser pistol from his waistband. A knife belt strapped above this contained an ugly curved blade stained red with blood—the Dagger of Damascus worn by every devoted Armenian rebel. A wooden staff lay alongside the man, standard issue, a third leg for treading steep mountain paths.

There was no mistaking the stranger. From top to bottom, he was *Fedayee*.

He eyed them coolly, silently, and sipped thick, sweet Turkish tea from an ornate crystal glass. He reclined at a black lacquered tea table, richly inlaid with mother-of-pearl and set low to the ground in Asian custom. It was a peculiarly jarring scene set against the wild, looming mountains now rapidly materializing from the vanishing fog.

The man was alone. *Where was their lieutenant?*

The second lieutenant slowly removed the knife from between his teeth. The other men uneasily followed suit and looked to the senior officer for orders. His mind raced to interpret the odd tableau. Skin clammy, he fought to ignore the sour acid at the back of his throat.

Wiry, wound tight as coiled wire, the lone Fedayee held the twenty at bay with no more than an air of controlled contempt, sipping placidly at his tea.

It was then that all became plain to the second lieutenant. They had earned an audience with the Fox, protégé to the

DELIVER US FROM EVIL

Black Wolf himself. Young, brash, full of himself, the Fox believed his own legend and thought himself so invincible as to take tea in the company of the enemy. He'd forced the lieutenant to call them forward, then slashed his throat. He'd guessed they would be so unnerved by the sight of him and the strange circumstances that they would turn and flee. A bizarre initiation rite for the Fox, to be sure, but one which would enliven many a traitor's fire in the years to come, each time told a bit more fancifully than the time before. Well worth the gamble.

Well, the reckless young Fox has gambled and lost, thought the second lieutenant. Obviously no hairy-faced veteran this. Young, smooth-skinned, handsome, he'd recklessly pressed the fates once too often. Now he would experience the very flesh-and-blood consequences of his actions.

The Turk officer hesitated two seconds more. He hated to make another Armenian martyr, but these days Armenians expired in such huge numbers, what matter one more?

His amusement quickly turned to rage. The forest clearing was carefully chosen for the ridicule of the Turk forces. The very sovereignty of Turkey was questioned by feckless, unemployed infidels. This one did not even shave. Outrageous!

The lieutenant clenched his jaw, drew his pistol, and raised the knife in his hand toward heaven. The Fedayeen were fools.

The greatest of battles sometimes occurred on the smallest of stages. The arm and the knife dropped.

With a defiant roar, the Turks, pistols drawn and knives in hand, surged forward. Their weapons aimed but for one mark—the black heart of the Fox.

They were halfway across the clearing when the ground beneath them erupted.

Bare-chested men in baggy trousers sprang from beneath the carpet of needles and threw a stranglehold around the necks of the attacking soldiers. Two pistols fired harmlessly at the treetops as a curved dagger for a necklace held each Turk a prisoner, abruptly ending the battle charge.

No attacker dared swallow at the risk of a razor's death. Nor dared they meet the fierce gaze of the bearded Fedayeen who embraced them. Excruciating seconds passed, broken

56

only by the loud blowing and sipping of hot tea, and the heavy breathing of men under strain.

They watched the Fox calmly survey the bloodless battle-field. A slight smile played at the corners of his mouth. He pursed his lips and warbled a perfect imitation of a songbird. From the trees behind him emerged the second Turk lieutenant, a Fedayeen dagger pressed against his back by a tall Armenian in a wild, stringy mustache. Though the lieutenant found it difficult to look at his captured men, he remained rigid with defiance.

Without rising, the Fox motioned for the lieutenant to be placed with his men, facing the Fedayee legend.

"I am disappointed," the Fox said. "You have wasted many days and failed to do your people proud. We have watched your approach with great interest in the hope you would put our cunning to the test. But a small band of squirrels heavily armed with nuts could have taken you captive. Most disappointing." The Fedayeen shook with laughter, each Turk in their grip trying frantically to shrink back from the jostling blades that threatened to slice throat and windpipe.

"I would do well to execute each of you here and now. After all, your graves are already dug." The Fedayeen laughter turned to shouts and hoots of derision. The Fox had cleverly commanded them to clear the forest floor and hollow out depressions for their bodies. Once in place, it was an easy matter for other brothers to cover them over with dirt, debris, and a final, convincing layer of needles. They were experts at it. Fedayeen campsites were notoriously undetectable, the smallest of animal bones and tiniest of food crumbs removed. Every displaced rock along a stream bed was carefully replaced. A rear guard was responsible for covering all telltale tracks by straightening broken foliage and dragging behind a tree branch or sheaf of leaves.

To betray the company by overlooking a single footprint or snapped twig incurred the terrible wrath of the Black Wolf.

A cloud obscured the spring sun, and with it the Fox's pleasant demeanor vanished. "Show them to their graves!" he shouted.

The Fedayeen bellowed their approval, quickly disarmed the captives, and yanked them about by the hair. The ground rushed at the Turks, each shoved facedown into a shallow hole, arms at their sides. A Fedayee straddled each hole, dagger poised.

Again, agonizing seconds passed—nothing said, nothing done. Nothing but the sipping of tea.

"Kill us, you animal!" screamed one of the soldiers. His face was roughly rammed into the earth, pressed down by a boot, held, then released. He choked and coughed, nose and mouth clotted with dirt.

"Leave him alone. He's absolutely right. I am an animal. I am the Fox!" He laughed at his own joke, and the Fedayeen joined in. "You know," the Fox chuckled loudly, "I believe that is the first time in recorded history a Turk has told the truth!"

The Fedayeen rocked with laughter, some of them doubling over, others holding their bellies to contain the mirth.

To the men in the ground, it was the laughter of devils. They prepared to die.

"Allah be merciful! Allah be merciful!" cried one.

"What did he say?" mocked a Fedayee.

"I think he said, 'All of us Turks are pitiful!' " rejoined another.

"It's nothing but camel gas!" hooted a third.

The Fox got to his feet, and the Fedayeen fell silent. The men in the ground held their breath in the sudden quiet. Death walked among them . . . and stopped by the head of the Turk lieutenant. The Fox crouched down, grabbed the man's hair, and jerked back. Dirt and sweat mingled in rivulets of grime. The Turk spat and tried to clear his mouth of strings of matted drool. He fought to meet the gaze of the one he'd come to capture, but the fires of bravery in his eyes flickered low. Through the pain and humiliation, he was startled to see something entirely unexpected cross the face of his conqueror. As they peered deep into each other's souls, a fleeting look of uncertainty and something like compassion crossed the Fox's face. For a brief instant, the Fox looked away. Then came a mask of hard, brash contempt. The Fedayeen legend threw a glass of tea into the enemy commander's eyes.

"Stand them up!" The Turks were jerked to their feet in front of the Fox, backs to the clearing. Several hands shook. Some had their eyes closed, lips moving in silent prayer.

"I now pronounce sentence on this band of pathetic insects. You are to be set free to return down the mountain in disgrace and dishonor, your ultimate fate to be decided by your own kind. From what I know of the Turk, even Allah will be hard-pressed to save your miserable skin."

Wild relief showed in the disbelieving faces of the Turk soldiers. They looked at one another, wanting to smile and sing, but not daring. A couple looked to the sky, tears streaming. Most shared to some degree the expression of the lieutenant, one of incredulity and, for a few, outright suspicion.

"Just one thing more before you leave. Remove your clothing and pile it here by me."

The faces of the captives drained of all color, their elation short-lived. "I do not understand, sir," the lieutenant said. Something in his eyes suggested he understood only too well.

"I will repeat the instructions once for the Turk scum who have difficulty hearing. You will remove your clothing—all your clothing—and leave it here." The Fox motioned to the ground beside him. "Because the Turkish military insists that all Armenians disrobe before they are butchered, we wish for you to do the same. Of course, like you, we only do it out of respect for the tenant of Islam that says dead bodies defile any clothing they touch."

The lieutenant strained to hear exactly where the treachery lay in the Fedayee's instructions. "But, sir, respectfully, you did say that we were not to die by your hand."

"No, not by my hand. But I sincerely doubt you will find your way out of these mountains before the wild beasts have torn you apart or you have eaten one another. Should you by some miracle make it back, unless I am sorely mistaken, your people will not be happy to see you coming naked and empty-handed.

"I would retain at least a shred of optimism, however. Once you're naked, we have no immediate plans to disembowel you and explore your body cavities for hidden jewelry."

The full import of the Fox's words sank in. No map, no fire, no food, no weapons with which to hunt, no protection from the chill high mountain nights. No shoes.

They *had* been sentenced to die.

"Lieutenant, instruct your men to disrobe. Now." No mistaking the menace with which the quiet command was given.

The lieutenant considered resistance, but he knew the Fedayeen would simply strip them and leave them to die regardless. Without looking at his men, he gave the order. "Disrobe!"

Quickly the pile of uniforms grew. Soon twenty-one frightened Turks stood naked and harshly pale against the dark browns and greens of the forest. Most had abandoned any attempt to hold their heads defiantly erect but did try to cover their shame with their hands. They were quickly chilled to the bone, the fog returning in heavy wet billows.

"Nightfall comes rapidly in the Caucasus," said the Fox, "and it feels like snow. I would waste no time descending to lower ground. But first, we will take tea together." With a wave of his arm, tea glasses were brought, enough for every captured soldier. The hot tea was ladled from a tin bucket. Another camp with a fire must lie beyond the trees.

Awkward as they felt, naked and drinking tea in front of the smirking Fedayeen, each Turk knew it might be his last warm beverage. They drank for survival.

"Enough!" The tea glasses, empty or not, were removed. "Leave us now, and if you live to report anything of this incident, it should be of your humane treatment. Of drinking tea from glasses when you should be watching the earth turn red with your blood. Say that all Armenian People of the Book are like this, not exacting an eye for an eye, though absolutely within our rights to do so. Turkey's undoing will be at the hands of the Turks. Go now."

The lieutenant straightened, and when he did, many of his men straightened too. With every measure of dignity and pride they could muster, they turned to face their retreat, only to be met with a grisly scene of horror.

Scores of severed goat heads littered the open space between them and the tree line. Stomachs roiling, the naked men were forced to pick their way between the bloody remains, half expecting to stumble over the heads of the Kurdish goatherders who had joined the plot against the Fox. Laughter filled the deep canyons. Taunts and curses burned bare backs, and unshod feet grew numb from the biting cold.

When the last of the enemy's stark backsides disappeared in the trees, the Fedayeen lit two small campfires for a victory meal of premium Turkish wine, roast bush hen, and millet dipped in buttermilk, broth, cream, and butter. The Kurd spies had been well supplied and had put up little resistance.

With brow furrowed, the Fox reclined on a soft bed of tree boughs. His personal squires, men specially assigned to the first and second in command, sat vigilantly by. The squires carried the commanders' knapsacks and acted as bodyguards. The leaders carried only binoculars and a compass.

The Fox watched the Fedayeen recount the shame of the Turks, sides splitting whenever one of them gave a particularly skilled accounting. But he did not join in.

He had been a Fedayee for a season, and his rise in the ranks was itself the stuff of legends. With all the brains of a centipede, he had met with the contacts he'd been given and demanded without preamble to see the Wolf. To his amazement, he was taken three days' travel into the mountains to the lair of Kevork Chavoush, the Black Wolf. Immediately upon facing the fierce countenance of the famed commander, the young man was slapped to the ground.

He got up and was slapped down twenty-five times more before losing consciousness. When he awoke, he was lying on the floor of the Wolf's house dressed like a Fedayee. The great man taught him the ways of the Armenian revolutionary and took to calling him "my shadow." When he allowed six men to hurl daggers at him simultaneously to practice their controlled aim, taking one knife in the thigh without comment, the Wolf christened him "Fearless Fox."

He was far from fearless, but no one suspected it. The old Wolf loved the youth for his daring disregard for life and limb. Others hated him for so quickly gaining the famed leader's favor. There were three attempts on his life before the Wolf declared anyone a dead man who would harm a single hair of the Fox.

He loved living among the tall, fearless freedom fighters. Handsome, erect, impressive in bearing and determination, they were vastly different from the common Armenian, who was fast losing strength, nerve, and self-respect in the face of the Turkish juggernaut. The Fedayeen believed in the homeland and devoted every waking moment to its restoration.

They were the fighting knights, the hope of Armenia's future. Their bellies never bloated, nor did their faces turn yellow with jaundice, like those of the common peasants. They fed off the land and did not sit about waiting to be beaten. Their steely features implied neither a life of sorrow nor one of pleasure. Instead, they seemed chiseled from the rock, never relaxed, eyes ever on the alert.

They were lions, and they had taught him the ways of lions.

A small knapsack comprised the Fox's few earthly possessions beyond weapons. There were repair tools, a polishing cloth, single spares of shirt and underwear, and moccasins for camp. A Sarkisov watch and chain, a small purse with a meager five to ten piasters, a small pouch of rations (a pound of ground millet, a little salt, some rock-hard biscuits). That was all he permitted himself of creature comforts. But there were three more things without which the others would matter little.

One was a bit of Scripture torn from a Bible. It was from Genesis and spoke of the mountains of Ararat where Noah's Ark had come to rest thousands of years before. Brave Noah had battled ridicule and wickedness and flood to start again, to establish a new homeland. The Fox believed he was no longer worthy to carry the promises of God, but he kept the worn pages all the same.

The second prized possession was a chip of the Holy Communion wafer given him by the archbishop. Should he lie fatally wounded in battle, his dying act would be to place the portion of the wafer upon his tongue and to depart the world with the knowledge of Christ's supreme sacrifice his last mortal thought.

The third most valuable thing among his meager belongings was also most personal. Each Fedayee, men of fiery resolve that they were, carried a small snippet of hair from a dear friend, a mother, a wife, or the woman they loved. The Fox's treasure was a lock of his beloved Veron's hair. In the privacy of the night, he held the silken treasure between his fingers and breathed deeply of the scent of her. It made him sad, but it gave him the strength to fight for Armenia. The homeland was his wife now. He was too cold inside to ever love another.

He did wish he'd thought of getting a lock of his mother's hair. Was she alive?

He was always on the move, never more than seven days in any one place. It kept the Turks in turmoil, foiled many a government trap, and allowed the grateful peasants to provision their national heroes. But to stay in a village beyond seven days strained security and taxed the generosity of the beleaguered peasants.

The Fedayeen marched at five to six kilometers an hour. In the dead of night they easily covered twenty-five to forty kilometers. Roadside villages were avoided to prevent discovery, and rivers were forded with extreme caution. On those occasions the baggy trousers were removed for ease of crossing, but never the bandolier. To be separated from their weapons was in violation of the Fedayee code.

They were required to reach a possible safe village by daybreak in order to be carefully hidden inside before the sun rose. First, a lone Fedayee scout scoured the village for the enemy. Next, two Fedayeen entered the village and roused a known sympathizer (from which there were many to choose). They explained their need, then returned to the Fedayee camp with the villager. He then proceeded to lead them by the safest route to four or five homes he knew to be best suited against surprise attack.

Once the visitors were safely quartered, the host families feasted their guests with the best of what was at hand, then sent them to bed in the corner of a stable or barn. They slept with their rifles, one Fedayee posting guard. Before they retired the first night in a village, a public meeting was held at which the Fedayeen told their tales of daring and the villagers offered up the latest news about government troop movements and the best places to stay in the villages farther on.

The Fox had learned to stand guard as motionless as a statue. Sometimes birds alighted on his head, mistaking him for a stump. Once, in the highest, coldest place he had ever been, he dug an ice cave and spent three nights huddled against his brothers for warmth. In the morning he had taken a snow bath, bandolier still in place, rubbing his bare skin with the freshly fallen fluff while the veteran Fedayeen, who rarely ever removed their clothing, snickered and called him a woman.

The next morning he discovered a guard fast asleep at his post. The Fox crept forward without a sound, cut off the leather strap of the man's rifle, and released the weapon without waking him. The rest of the band beat the miscreant and voted to expel him from their ranks. The Fox rose to the man's defense, humorously and half-seriously describing what would happen should there be a second offense. The brotherhood relented and let the grateful man stay. From that day forward until the redeemed guard was killed in a Turkish raid, the shadow had a shadow of his own.

Once a king, now a gypsy. Today a feast, tomorrow berries and wild roots. Extra food meant fewer cartridges. Pack animals meant certain discovery. He fast learned to prize bullets over bread. Travel light, travel swift. Stay agile, stay alive. In times of battle, slip a pinch of millet into the mouth and feel renewed energy.

On the move, there was an occasional heifer from a farm, dripping red blood, a dusting of ashes coating its seared flesh. Or a sheep from a shepherd, broiled shish-kebab style on skewers of green branches. Three or four voracious Fedayeen would devour a whole sheep, then, like horses, plunge their faces into water holes. It might be a week or more before they saw meat again. To kill wild game took precious ammunition needed for war.

When the Fedayeen got on each other's nerves, the Wolf had a simple but effective solution. He ordered the offended parties to take thick sticks and, in turn, beat each other twenty severe blows without resistance. Should either man not show enough muscle in the punishment, the Wolf waded in with his own stick to the cheers of the spectators. The penalty ended with laughter on all sides.

The Wolf could not be contradicted even if the order given was a foolish one. His rule was sacred, and the Fedayeen were bound to carry out all orders at the cost of their lives. Any disobedience meant swift execution. Should the offender flee, his ex-brothers would hunt him down and exact the ultimate punishment themselves.

It was a harsh existence, but a proud one. The bond between the Fedayeen was unbreakable.

"It went well?" asked a gruff but kindly voice. The Wolf separated from the darkening trees, his squire at his side. He came and stood over his protégé.

"Yes, I think so, my brother," the Fox replied. He started to rise. Before he reached full height, however, the Wolf backhanded him a staggering blow.

The Fox landed on his back and shook his head, trying to focus. He made it to his knees before catching the second blow on the ear, hot and ringing. "Do you intend to knock me unconscious, brother?" the Fox asked groggily. He turned on his side and felt to see if the ear was still intact.

"I intend to give you exactly what you deserve," the Wolf said, flashing the assembled Fedayeen a giant wink. "Only one flaw in how you handled the Turks, my son."

"Too kind?"

"No, just adequate."

"Too harsh?"

"Hardly."

"What then?"

"Too *polite!*" With a roar of laughter joined by a Fedayeen chorus, the Wolf went to all fours and cuffed the Fox affectionately about the shoulders and face.

The Fox grinned hugely. "My mother trained me well." Another roar of laughter. Soon several took up goat heads and began butting one another spiritedly about the clearing.

The Fox had passed the initiation. He could negotiate with daring and creativity. Should even one of those naked cutthroats make it out alive—and there was probably a Kurd or two left to see to that—the fame of the Wolf and the Fox would take another mighty leap. There weren't too many ways to explain losing your clothes in the high country. Besides, as a guarantee, the Fedayeen knew a few Kurds who, for a price, could tell the story as convincingly as if they'd been there.

The Wolf extricated himself from play and pulled his young friend aside. The old veteran looked glum. "I have a dangerous assignment that you are free to refuse. But you have proven your wisdom and discernment, unusual in one so young. To give this charge to anyone else is to doom it to failure. Though it places you squarely in the jaws of death, I hope you will accept out of love for me."

The Fox knew of no man on earth besides his father that he loved more. "I accept."

"You do not know what I'm asking, reckless boy."

"I need know only that you ask it."

The Wolf looked at the boy, his eyes filling with tears. "If you do not succeed, I will die at the news."

"*When* I succeed, your shouts will trigger an avalanche on Ararat!" They both stared off to the south in the direction of the mother of all mountains. They loved her. They would die for her. She was Armenia. If the Turks killed every living Armenian, she would give birth to more, just as she had cradled Noah, and he had been fruitful and multiplied.

"A message, then, a cry for help from an Armenian sister. The plains city of Hekim Khan is in the iron grip of a Turk tyrant by the name of Neelam Ozal. He is tired of feeding the largely female remnant population because supplies become increasingly more difficult to procure. The city is a major staging area for the Turk army, and much damage is inflicted under the sanction of Ozal. They prey unmercifully on the refugees passing through.

"The cry for help came long before Advent, but we could spare no one. Many sons of Noah talk of freedom, but few will sacrifice what is required to secure it. The Fedayeen are spread thinner than the membrane of a newborn kid. Just ask any she-goat." He smiled, yet looked anything but lighthearted.

"If Ozal is mad, I fear that soon there will be an unprecedented massacre. I want you to go to Hekim Khan. You know the language well and can easily pass for a Turk—no offense meant. Take what brothers you need with you. Seize the situation from the inside, create havoc, and rescue those women. If you can find a permanent solution to Ozal in the process, so much the better."

The Fox felt a mix of dread and excitement. "Yes, my brother, I will do as you have asked. Do not look so worried. I can be most charming and convincing when I want to. Just tell me where you want Ozal's clothing sent."

The Wolf laughed, but halfheartedly.

Tatul Sarafian, alias the Fox, grinned a shy, lopsided grin. *Serop, my father, I do this for you, for the sake of Armenia. Pray for me, Father, as I pray for you. God help me.* He fervently hoped that God heard the prayers of spies and assassins.

And then he thought of his beloved Veron, so beautiful and soft and capable. Ruined. Dead. Oh, he would make a convincing Turk, to be sure. They would rue the day they preyed on old women and virgins.

Quickly the grin faded. He was glad when Kevork Chavoush, the Black Wolf, gathered him into a bone-crushing bear hug and would not let go.

CHAPTER 7

The screams startled Adrine awake at daybreak.

Bewildered, wrenched from sleep, neither she nor the other camp slaves could tell where the terrible night dreams ended and the real horrors of the day began.

But the snarling, gun-waving attack was all too real. Turk soldiers and released convicts kicked in the doors to the abandoned hotel where the Armenian women slept and hauled them from slumber by their hair. Panting, swearing, and shouting at the "whores of Jesus," the Turks tore at the women's clothes and groped them even as they kicked and shoved them to their feet.

"Stop! Stop this! Have you no regard for anyone? Have you no mothers or sisters of your own?" But the men did not listen to Adrine.

She watched as a suckling was torn from its mother's breast and tossed to a man bristling with daggers. The mother wailed for her child, begging that it not be harmed. The man laughed, held the baby by its feet and shook it up and down and side to side. The baby screeched, and the mother fought like a wild animal against the soldier restraining her. He threw her to the floor and jammed his knee into the small of her back.

She groaned. "Be merciful to my little one. Do not harm him, I beg you."

Adrine ran to help but was shoved back by a beefy hand. The man with the daggers gave the child another hard shake. The thin swaddling cloth fell to the ground and was trampled in the chaos. The naked male infant held his breath, turned beet red, and squirmed to free his tiny feet from the huge paw that trapped them.

"Nothing of any value hidden in this one's covering!" he bellowed, and the other soldiers laughed. They were looking for secreted jewelry, unable to accept that although a dozen previous surprise raids had turned up nothing, there wasn't something still to be found.

"Please don't hurt the boy." Adrine Tevian had to yell to be heard above the wails and shrieks that filled the old hotel the Turks had commandeered to house the captives. She held out her arms to take the child. The man looked from Adrine's pleading eyes to the gasping, wriggling infant as if amused that anyone would want it. He tossed the baby to her, and she caught the little bundle in midair, wet with tears, gasping in terror. She quickly retrieved the cloth from the floor, carefully swaddled the boy, and knelt beside the mother's head. She showed her that her little boy was spared, then appealed to the soldier who held the woman to the floor.

The soldier was as young or younger than Adrine and saw the plea for mercy in her eyes. Nor did the look of reproach on the older soldier's face escape his attention. He released the mother and jumped to his feet, embarrassed at having to choose. To save face, he grabbed the other arm of a woman savagely resisting the search and helped haul her from the room, facedown and beseeching God to condemn them all to death.

Adelina Yanikian hungrily gathered her baby into her arms and lay over it, rocking the little one and protecting its head from the mayhem.

"Why have you come? Why do you treat decent people this way?" another woman shrieked in anger.

"In punishment for crimes against the government! For traitorous conduct! For attempting to lure with lust and for eyes that wander!" the Turks roared. The woman turned in amazement and gave a bitter, cold laugh. She and her sisters were weary, pallid, ill-clad, thin, and unwashed. All they could attract were fleas and gnats. They were about as alluring—and capable of allurement—as sacks of seed.

Adrine rushed among the chaos, trying to calm the hysterical and prevent injury. Despite how thin and threadbare she was, she was not easily dismissed by friend or foe. There was purpose in the way she moved, an inextinguishable light in the passionate brown eyes. Adrine Tevian possessed a self-confidence and purity of soul that belied her menacing circumstances.

"Sweet angel of light," she sang loud as she could, "spread thy golden wings above us. Lift us to His realms of glory. . . ." Adrine turned to quiet a bawling child and received a thick-handed blow hard in the ear. Pain shot through her neck and head, the room exploding in yellow stars, nearly dropping Adrine to her knees. She staggered back and tried to ignore the roaring all around and inside her. Her vision cleared, and she saw that she was on her knees beside a girl of thirteen or fourteen, glaze-eyed with fear.

Adrine gathered the girl to her breast and gripped her about the neck to keep from falling. "Swift sweet angel, angel so bright . . ." She continued singing as the women and children were being herded outside. The room reeked of sweat and unwashed bodies, but Adrine smelled an excitement in the Turk soldiers that could only mean an interrogation.

Adrine helped the weakened girl to her feet and, arm around her quaking shoulders, moved toward the door. They joined the rest of the one hundred Armenian women and thirty children remaining in Hekim Khan, many of whom turned to look at the Armenian peasant who had not yet had all determination and compassion stripped away. Something more powerful than guns or intimidation leapt in the air between them, drawn from Adrine Tevian as from the sun. Imperceptibly, a number of them stopped cowering as the girl who once herded geese drew near.

Adrine nodded at them despite the nausea she felt from the blow to her ear. She could cry if she weren't so dry. Three thousand Armenian women, including her own dear mother and grandmother, had been deported from Hekim Khan over the winter, sent south, never to return. Those who remained were military property. As long as they possessed the health and strength to cook and clean and meet carnal desire, they had worth. Those who became sick or resisted or did not have a benefactor to protect them disappeared.

Adrine understood that the Ottoman rulers demanded

much of Captain Neelam Ozal's command. Daily he grew more irritable, and she had heard him curse the pressure he was under to make the Armenians pay for Turkey's ills. Almost weekly she saw Turk troops from the battlefields beyond flow through Hekim Khan, yet supplies grew ever more scarce. The last to be fed were the Armenians. Nearly a score had committed suicide, and Adrine mourned every one. But tragically, a quick death was preferred over slow, agonizing mistreatment.

It was one of those desperate ones found dead in the river who, the night before taking her own life, had confided in Adrine that she had sold herself to Ozal for a dish of food. It was a cruel mockery of intimacy that left scars in her flesh and a soul all but dead from the awful words he poured into her ears. He told her how his own father, made an invalid in a previous war, had been abandoned by his Armenian wife when Neelam was just eight years old. Neelam's mother had refused to convert to Islam, had beaten his father whenever he was too paralyzed to use the toilet, and some days would not come near her "infidel" son. When she became angry at little Neelam, she would shriek that his misbehavior was no mystery since he was the devil's offspring. "You are so large and have so much hair. Your eyes are strange lumps of coal," she mocked. "You smell like you've been singed in the fires of hell. Get away from me, Satan's child!"

Neelam Ozal had ever since attempted to flush the blood of Armenia from his veins.

Adrine smiled at Adelina Yanikian, clutching her infant son, and leaned close to murmur assurances. From a fold in her head wrap, Adrine took a small lump of dried fig. "Here," she whispered. "Chew it fine, then pass it to your baby in a kiss."

The frightened mother, aged before her time, looked deep into Adrine's strong, warm eyes. She drank of the love and courage found there and palmed the precious fig as if it were a nugget of gold. "You are God's own sister," Adelina said, tears welling over. "Christ be with you!"

Adrine looked quickly away and willed the gnawing in her own stomach to be stilled. How much more she would do if only she had the means! It was good work and healing. The more time spent considering the needs of the Armenian sisters, the less spent pitying her own lack.

The Armenian women of Hekim Khan were herded into the square, facing the little stage Captain Ozal had erected for his frequent addresses. They were little more than harangues against the schemes of the "foreign visitors in our land," but they never failed to draw a good number of the city's Turks. Today was no exception. Many of them disagreed with their government's harsh treatment of the Armenians. Many counted Armenians among their closest friends and business acquaintances. A few of their neighbors had even provided asylum in the early days of the deportation, but now their bones littered the plains alongside those they'd harbored. It was those bleached bones and a dwindling food supply that bought the silence of most sympathetic Turks.

Adrine watched as Ozal took the stand beneath a faded yellow sun, as drained of color as the hopes of a dying Turkey. Dark, unblinking eyes swept the smaller crowd of huddled women with unmistakable menace. And then he did something rarely seen—he laid his riding crop down on the platform.

He rose with two long white objects, one in each hand. "In my left hand, I hold the thigh bone of an Armenian. In my right, I hold the thigh bone of a Turk caught aiding an Armenian. As you can readily see"—he thrust both grisly artifacts forward at arm's length—"you cannot tell them apart. Dead bones have no nationality."

He clapped the bones together, and they shattered in a dusty burst. "The Holy Qur'an tells us that God, the Most Gracious Master of the Day of Judgment, gives rule and deprives rule to whomsoever He chooses." The captain's voice rose steadily. "God exalts and God debases. He makes the night penetrate into the day and the day pass into the night. God brings the living from the dead and the dead from the living and bestows sustenance upon some without stint.

"Today, God, the Infinite Boundless One who is, sorts the weak and the fraud from the genuine and the obedient. All of your troubles originated with your fabled descendancy from Noah the Great Messenger. That lie has separated you from Muhammed the Last Messenger!"

Ozal paced restlessly from one side of the stage to the other. His angry gaze raked each woman upon whom it fell, and few could meet it.

"Your mythmakers say that you are the children of Hayk, great-great-grandson of Noah. They say that the Ark came to rest on Mount Ararat and that eastern Anatolia became the original Armenian homeland. Fable! In fact, it came to rest on el-Judi, a great distance from Ararat. Anyone's historians can be convinced to say anything." He looked slyly down his nose. "Perhaps you descended from the lizard pair aboard the Ark. Now that would make sense!" He laughed, but save for a few of his men and a handful of Turk civilians, he largely laughed alone.

"The truth is that two thousand years ago your people enjoyed one brief forty-year empire under Tigran II the Great. The Romans invaded, and ever since then you have been a dispersed people, an inferior race living off the kindnesses of those you exploit. You cry and complain to the Russians, and those dullards become the next in a long line of gullibility.

"The time has come again to stop the Armenian complaint!" He swooped up the riding crop and pointed at the women accusingly. "Your people hated Byzantine rule. They welcomed the Turk conquest of Anatolia with open arms. Well"—he spread wide his arms and his voice changed to syrupy mockery—"now we offer you *our* arms. Accept them and live. Reject them and be the first to die!"

With a victory yell, Ozal's men ran among the Armenians and grabbed them in sloppy embrace. The women recoiled. Some were slapped into submission, others thrown over shoulders and carted around the square, the spoils of war. Someone in the watching crowd began to play a lively tune on a stringed *saz*, and the Turks towed their sobbing, begging victims across the clearing in a macabre dance of humiliation.

Ozal's eyes fell on Adrine, and one eyebrow lifted in invitation. She stood still, arms rigid, willing him not to touch her. He strode to her side and put his arms around her. She was hard and unyielding as rock. He stepped back.

"*Silence!*" The music stopped. The dancers stopped. The command reverberated through the square. Ozal was livid.

"This woman is guilty of treason," he wheezed, barely able

to control the fury. "She is withholding an item of jewelry, even while knowing that all Armenian valuables are to be confiscated by the state and held in trust until the temporary exile of their owners is declared at an end. Execute her!"

Adrine felt the world spin out of control. *My God, remember me this day. . . .* Rough hands grabbed her, but from somewhere behind came the voice of another.

"Stop! Don't harm her. She gave me the gold pin in the event we were freed. It was for my wedding day."

A babble of voices arose, and a young girl of no more than sixteen came forward, Isabel Petrosian by name. She reached out and, with a tremble, placed a sparkling gold pin of shimmering leaves into the captain's hand. It was wet. He appeared captivated by her clear eyes and amazed at her daring.

"Forgive me, Commander, the thought of marriage clouds the mind and poisons sound judgment."

Adrine felt a reassuring hand beneath her elbow. What was this sweet, brainless girl doing? Ozal's claim of withheld jewelry was totally fabricated. Anything of value Adrine owned had long ago been surrendered or stolen, including her grandmother's ruby necklace. This girl owed her nothing, yet came forward at great personal risk and created a defense.

Ozal fingered the moist pin, admiring the craftsmanship. Armenian artistry brought a handsome price. "You are a fool, daughter," he said, the fury gone. He stroked her hair with the crop. "A fool for love, a fool for friendship. Who danced with you?"

Confused by the question, she hesitated. "I danced with her, my Captain." One of Ozal's men came forward. "How may I serve you?"

The captain snorted. "You may serve me by following orders, mule! Why did you not find that pin before the young woman brought it to me?"

The soldier took a faltering breath, clearly sensing grave danger. A scapegoat was required, and he had drawn the short straw.

"It was hidden in my mouth, Captain," the promised bride spoke up. "See, it is still damp." She permitted herself the faintest smile, and he returned it.

"I see."

Adrine heard something deadly in the captain's reply. He stared at the girl until she could no longer meet his gaze. He was reading her, sucking her secrets. The viper was about to strike.

Before the horrors began, Adrine had often watched Isabel in the market and vicariously shared in her growing joy as the wedding neared. The husband-in-waiting might have gained a most devoted and attentive helpmate in a different place and time. By some miracle after the Turks descended, Ahbet had been one of the few Armenian men allowed to remain and work himself thin loading military supply wagons. By publicly ignoring each other, their relationship managed to escape the detection of the Turks. The bride's Armenian sisters had forged a kind of underground telegraph that ferried messages between the two lovers. Adrine had delivered a few herself and been forced to eat one when a soldier demanded her business in that end of town.

But certainly the bride owed her nothing to warrant this reckless act of kindness. And now the girl was defending a Turk soldier as well! Without parents to protect her, to safe-guard her words and grant her permission to wed, the girl had promised herself to another and was flush with love. How could she rationally measure the jeopardy she had placed her-self in?

The air above the square thickened with a palpable tension.

"Do you know what I see in your eyes?" Ozal asked the bride.

Her eyes dropped. "No, my Captain."

"Come now, I'm certain you could make a good guess. One clue. I see far too much hope of future happiness when you speak of a marriage that should have no expectation of hap-pening. Do you know what that tells me?"

The girl's show of bravery evaporated. She wept. "No . . . no, my Captain." Her voice was nearly inaudible.

"It tells me, little one, that your betrothed lives, and more, that he lives here in Hekim Khan. And that where you are, he will not be far off." Ozal raised his head and shouted, "Will this woman's intended husband come forward *now*?"

No one moved. No one spoke. All were statues in the stifling silence.

Ozal unhooked the pin from its clasp and held the golden point to the sky as if sighting along its tip. Slowly the riding crop rose beneath the girl's chin. Slowly her head rose with it.

"*Look at me!*" he shouted, and her eyes flew open. Inch by inch his arm descended, and with it the piercing needle of gold.

Adrine could not watch. She prayed with every fiber of her being. Would that she could peel back the sky and pour her request straight into God's ear.

"Here am I, Captain." The deep baritone was startlingly close at hand. A shirtless youth in soiled apron, with muscles hard and bunched against a lean frame, stepped to the side of the weeping girl. She fell against him. With a fatal tenderness, Ahbet held her and shushed her with comforting reassurances that he could not keep.

In a lightning stroke, the riding crop sliced across the young man's ear and left an ugly red slash that spilled blood onto his beloved's neck and shoulder.

"Mercy, Captain!" cried Adrine, reaching a hand toward the couple.

The crop slashed across her wrist. Searing pain shot the length of her arm, and she cried out.

"*Allah* is merciful," Ozal said, cold as the grave. "I personally incline more toward business. This is bad business and must be corrected." With a flip of the crop, four soldiers swarmed over the young man. After a brief but valiant struggle in which he was able to blacken an eye and nearly tear an ear from a man's head, they knocked him unconscious and tossed him into a freight wagon. His bride dropped to her knees, inconsolable in anguish.

With sinking heart, Adrine watched the wagon pull into the road south out of town. Four armed men jumped on. They would not disappoint the captain.

"Idleness is a waste of good daylight," Ozal told the crowd. But she heard how smugly he said it. The morning had been quite profitable. The People of the Book had been shown a valuable lesson.

Then he turned and looked quizzically at Adrine, the serving girl. "Why do you think me so unfeeling?" he asked. "Did I not spare the bride?"

Chapter 8

The morning gave way to afternoon at the outdoor commissary for the occupying Turks at Hekim Khan, and Adrine Tevian was allowed a brief break from washing and cooking for an army. Tea, a small portion of stringy mutton, a cup of hot, watery broth—gone all too soon. She could snatch an extra bit from the pot under cover of darkness, but it was never enough.

Sometimes with a surge of will she could step outside herself and not feel the gnaw of famine. But never yet had she been able to quiet the whine of hunger. Unspeakable, inaudible, it nevertheless droned inside her consciousness like a fat winged beetle. Never did it give her a moment's peace. Even when fed the meager day's ration, it merely changed to a low ominous thrum.

She longed to go south, but not to the dusty desert death camps of Syria. The destination of her dreams was the region of Adana on the Mediterranean. Caravaners told of lovely groves of oranges and bananas stretching beyond view from the balmy shores of a crystal sea. She hoped that heaven would be dripping with fruit. But for now—for the terrible, soul-crushing *now*—heaven was Adana.

Adrine heard that a hard day's walk west of Adana was Tarsus, where the good Saint Paul was born and first preached Christ crucified, Christ resurrected. Whenever her father read from the Scriptures of the great apostle's journeys, she had thrilled to think that they themselves lived only a few days' travel from Tarsus.

She sighed wistfully. Tarsus was also the place Anthony fell in love with Cleopatra.

Love. It seemed so long since she had indulged in girlish fantasies of tall dark men with slender waists and fabulous wealth who would admire her for her fine mind and musical laugh. A sigh, hollow and habitual, seeped from Adrine Tevian's thinning frame.

Today she would readily settle for a squat, nearsighted bricklayer with six toes on each foot, as long as he had breath to call her his *yavroos,* his dear one. Considering her shabby condition, more than that she could not ask.

But all the Armenian bricklayers, she was quite certain, were either dead or stumbling toward death. Yesterday, in a haze of self-pity, she had actually resigned herself to maybe marrying a Turk bricklayer who would call her his cow and feed her as often as he fed his dogs. What Turk would starve his dog?

After the incident in the square, love seemed a crushing impossibility. She sensed the danger was escalating. After today, there could not be many more tomorrows. Five thousand Armenian citizens of Hekim Khan were already gone. Only the poor remnant of camp slaves remained. But Turk civilians could easily take over the tasks performed by the Armenian women. The only purpose for using Armenian slaves was to humiliate them.

Adrine favored the stable adjacent to the hotel for sleeping. She had endured the harsh winter nights by lying beneath layers of filthy stable hay, wrapped in discarded military rags. As soon in spring as she could survive in the open, she took to sleeping on the stable roof, where the vermin were fewer and the stench much diluted. And where she was not within easy reach of the soldiers.

Some nights she watched shooting stars and chewed her fingers to stave off hunger. Other nights she fantasized life as a princess or countess in some far-off castle where her parents were still alive and her grandmother tended geese in a secure little cottage just inside the castle walls. Her little brothers, Nartou and Keghi, would play the hiding game with her again, and she would kiss away their hurts and yell at them for being pests. She longed for the pageantry of the church she and her family had attended. They had not been allowed near St. John's since the occupation. Her eyes had grown wide when the choir entered in their snow-white robes, big red crosses on their backs. Her heart had soared at the sight of the good archbishop in his high-backed velvet chair. How he loved the children. She could still feel the warmth of his big hand upon her head. Every Eucharist, he not only administered the sacraments but slipped each child supplicant a grape sweet. When she was very little, she thought the seated figure in regal vestments sitting on his velvet throne must be an angel.

Had the angel survived? She doubted it.

Incredibly, Captain Neelam Ozal, the riding crop a leather extension of a left hand in perpetual motion, found her appealing—dirt, rags, and all. Equally incredible, he had not yet taken her to his bed. Was he incapable of fulfilling his desire? Still, she felt violated by his every look. The dark, moist eyes roamed freely, taking in every imagined detail of her body. His touch, which came with increasing frequency, at times fell light and yearning about her face, but more often landed rough and heavy about her arms and shoulders. Once, he'd wrapped his arms about her waist in a hungry, wine-soaked embrace. Still, he'd never taken her. She winced at the pain in her wrist. The slashing riding crop had left an ugly welt. She was afraid his patience with Adrine Tevian was fast dwindling.

Had he not yet taken her because he was so closely watched by his own troops? Their curious code of conduct certainly permitted rapacious treatment of female refugees. They roamed among each new batch of arrivals and selected the youngest and prettiest of the captives for drunken revels in the desert or in the soldiers' barracks. Yet, that same code of conduct was undoubtedly the one thing that had stood between the women who served the military camp and similar full-scale abuse. For the time being, they enjoyed an uneasy protection with only occasional demands to service the troops. But let no one mistake this most fragile truce for actual safety.

Perhaps the captain suffered a physical or mental debility that mercifully kept his passions in check—except when they flared and he became dangerously mean. The probable reason for that was more horrifying than if he had made every woman in the region his concubine. The fulfillment of his desire was written large across his face every time he administered "justice" on a deportee or sent a new batch south to die. He took his real pleasure in making the Armenians pay for collusion with "Uncle Christian."

Adrine shuddered and clasped her hands prayerfully at the sky. Even her prayers had died. The awesome, wonder-working God of Saint Paul was as far removed from Hekim Khan as the moon. Or was the fact she still drew breath a sign that God heard? Grandmother said that God the All-Knowing was in no way defective. *"If there is a hearing problem, my little goose, it is with you."* And magically the old woman would withdraw a fat purple grape from Adrine's ear and feed it to her.

She fought her mind away from Hekim Khan and the magical grandmother she missed so much. The books at the missionary school told of the region southeast of Adana, around the head of the Gulf of Iskenderun and ancient Antioch, called Antakya by the infidels. Her father had told her that was where the first Christian church was formed and the followers of Christ first called themselves Christians. Antioch, jewel of commerce, once one of the world's most dazzling cities. Adrine could almost taste its exotic richness.

Luke, the physician, had come from Antioch, and it was from among the Gentile believers at Antioch that missionaries were sent to other parts of the Greek and Roman world.

What Adrine wouldn't give for an anointed man of God like those early Christ followers. Instantly she felt guilt for Ahbet, the young groom struck down that morning. Poor Isabel, his betrothed. How could Adrine yearn for someone for herself to grow old with when the promised bride now carried a broken heart, a heart broken courageously defending another? The expensive gold pin had been no gift from Adrine. It was Isabel's from the beginning, carefully hoarded for the wedding day, yet so quickly sacrificed to save a life. The generosity of her love, expressed in a lie, had cost her the chief object of her love. One life saved, one lost.

A tear made a dirty track down Adrine's cheek. The Lord forgive her desperation, but she could see her dream man. He was tall, made taller by a fire in his soul and an unquenchable thirst for the things of heaven. A strong man, not overly muscular but mighty in character, resolve, and action. A man with little time for pretense and pettiness but all the time in the world for a woman of passion, a woman of principle, a daughter of God. Adrine looked into the creases of hands made old by baking sun and hard work and felt the burning rash beneath rough clothing. She sighed in frustration and regret. What man of character would give a second look at the plain, shapeless peasant slave that was Adrine Tevian?

Angrily, she chastised herself. *This* was a disguise. *This* was forced upon her by circumstances beyond her control. *This* was an evil hatched in the minds of power-mad Ottomans without conscience. The real Adrine Tevian was a proud, optimistic woman who would support a family and a husband with every fiber of her being. The real Adrine Tevian would tend orchards of pomegranates, figs, and nectarines while her husband took an important seat in provincial government. He would design a better tomorrow for the populace while she created a better tomorrow for their children and their children's children. He would fight courageously for a homeland for his people. Confident and accomplished, she would have a private compartment on the Berlin-to-Baghdad Railway and conduct their export business by appointment only.

If the message got through. *If* the Fedayeen had men to spare. *If* they could read her mind from the distant mountains and would ride the wind to her rescue. Then off she and her fearless hero would gallop to the upper heights where the eagles nested, and she would become the first female Fedayee. She would cook for them and clean their weapons and stoke their courage.

She shook her head, dizzy with fancy. What a pathetic, impractical creature she had become. Perhaps her dream man was the legendary Fox, who neither ate nor slept. If so, his valor was in no need of a foolish servant girl such as she.

The missionaries at Urfa were to blame for her fanciful thoughts. She'd spent two years in their school, and they had taught her to dream, to look beyond the narrow confines of Hekim Khan, to believe that all things were possible through Jesus the Christ. Her father actually began saving money aside to send her to college. And then on that one most awful day of her life—until now—her father was taken from her by robbers and with him, her dream.

She smiled despite the madness.

What she wouldn't give for a plate of Grandmother's sweet *khourabia* right now. She had taken those sugar cookies for granted. . . .

"Ah, a little amusement to share with your captain?" She did not start at Ozal's presence. She'd grown accustomed to his sudden appearances, the perpetual jeer in his voice. When he had not taken advantage of her the day she'd fainted in his arms by the river, Adrine had exploited the man's weakness. He seemed to like a strong woman—within reason. Her struggle for dignity fascinated, perhaps amused him. But if she went too far, he would probably dash her brains against a rock. Until then, it was one of her only defenses.

"I was thinking of my grandmother, my Captain," she replied evenly, hunched over, arms crossed inside the voluminous sleeves of her cloak. "She was the lady of the house, along with my mother, who shared the household duties but was frail from pneumonia. They were both taken south, and I've received no word of their fate."

"Pity." Ozal eyed her moistly, the riding crop beginning its familiar journey about the contours of her desert wrap. "Your father?" The crop stopped at the cowl and slipped it from her head.

Adrine jerked the cowl back in place and, turtlelike, withdrew as much of herself inside the folds of clothing as humanly possible. "Brigands robbed him and shot him to death on the road to Vil. Years ago," the flat voice reported from deep inside the cowl.

"Ah," answered Ozal. "Not unlike the conditions we find today. Kurdish thieves at every hand. No respectable citizen is safe. Kurds!" The last word was a curse. All the nation's present ills could be summed up in it—or worse, *Armenians*.

Adrine emerged from the cloak, eyes ablaze. "The Kurds are puppets. It is the Turks who pull the strings!" It first alarmed then exhilarated her to discover that at that moment she did not care if she lived or died.

She thought he might lash her face with the crop. Instead, he used it to draw serpents in the sand.

His voice was ice. "At least their fees are reasonable."

She shouted, "You'd come cheap, too, if your entire village was threatened with annihilation!"

A south wind whipped about them, on it the unmistakable scent of rot and death. The Turk commander looked past the edge of town to the rocks and hills beyond. He wore the sneer of the conqueror. "Smells like something died," he said slowly and turned to walk away.

Adrine leapt up. Every fiber of her being screamed to attack this human vulture who took so much pleasure in the ruin of others. "God in heaven peel the flesh from your bones and feed it to you in front of your children!" It was the worst thing she'd ever said aloud. Her knees threatened to cave under her, but she refused to go down. If this was the end, she would go standing.

Without turning, he gave a little wave of dismissal. "That would, I assume, be the great Christian God of heaven who takes note of every fallen sparrow? Perhaps now they fall too fast for Him to count? Face the truth, woman. Allah is repaying the Armenian for years of lies and opportunism and blackmail. You have bitten the hand that fed you, and now that hand slaps back. I'd watch your tongue, woman. You have already been responsible for one man's death this day."

"I hate you!" screamed Adrine, tears streaming. "I hate Turkey. I want to die!"

"By all means," the captain replied, "you are free to go." Without another word, he disappeared inside the barracks.

For a minute she did not move. The Ararat of her soul, that great mountain kingdom of faith once as fresh and clean as the snows, had crumbled. Nothing remained but a wretched bare frame like a drawing she'd seen of an Indian wigwam from the American west, its animal-hide covering burned away and the thin ribs of tree saplings exposed beneath. One mighty kick and the whole thing would collapse.

She knew to go north, but her body was pulled south by an irrefutable force. Thinking was not her first priority. She wept as she ran, arms wrapped tight about her, feet striking the earth by the side of the road in little explosions of silt.

Past the home of the Turk who had paid a sack of flour for a wife. Past the camp where the old couple had lost a sack of flour in trade for one granddaughter. It was probably the ruts of the death wagon she now followed south to the desert. She stooped to retrieve a tiny torn sandal from the grime and thought of the young mother who stopped before the mob and acknowledged a Christian sister's meager offering with a bow of gratitude. The round, vacant eyes of the woman's two little girls loomed sadly in Adrine's memory.

Many more had come and gone. All as stunned and gray as those who preceded them. Baggage on their backs, babes in their arms, bent beneath the load of shattered lives. Periodically rifle shots echoed back from the hills beyond town, as they had that morning soon after the wagon left with the beaten Armenian boy. Riderless mules and empty wagons occasionally made their way back to town and were immediately appropriated by the eager Turks of Hekim Khan. It seemed as if the animals guiltily averted their eyes, not wanting to be questioned on the whereabouts of their human burdens.

Confused, she stopped. The wagon ruts veered from the main road and followed a rocky draw around a wall of rock. So did many hundreds of overlapping footprints—old men, women, teenage girls, and little ones of both sexes marching away from the customary route taken by droves of Armenian villagers under the guard of Turk irregulars and Kurd militiamen.

It was a place Adrine as a little girl had been warned never to go. *"Do not wander there, little geese,"* Grandmother had cautioned her and her sisters. *"There are cliffs and canyons and wild beasts to eat you up."* Then Grandmother had smacked her palms together sharply, and four little girls jumped. *"The only geese down there are dead geese!"*

Adrine felt sick, smelled death on the wind, but still she did not turn back. Almost none of the footprints came *out* of the draw. Six sets of boot tracks, the hooves of a horse or two, but no civilian footprint. *Dead geese.*

Long before the end of the wall of rock, the stench intensified. Vultures soared overhead on their way down the draw, riding the updraft from the boulder-strewn ravines below.

At the turn around the end of the rock outcrop, her heart beat wildly, and she was forced to cover her nose and mouth with a tattered sleeve.

Nothing could have prepared her for the horror beyond the wall.

The first sight was that of bits of clothing strewn about

the top of the ravine, undergarments and a few shoes too worn or damaged to fetch much in the marketplace.

She forced herself to the edge of the cliff and looked down upon hell itself.

Hundreds of naked corpses lay four and five deep. They had no doubt been forced to disrobe at the top of the cliff, then were herded over the edge by armed soldiers.

She was so afraid she would recognize someone . . . and then she saw him. Ahbet, the brave young groom, Isabel's love, lay hunched over as if in prayer. He must have struggled mightily, for the body was still clad in the work apron, feet still shod in the thick-soled shoes he'd worn that morning. She felt a flood of love and pride for him that he refused to be robbed—and stripped to naked shame—even in death.

Paralysis quickly followed. Every emotion and thought fled her. It was enough that her body remembered to breathe and pump blood. By the time she saw the lone figure approaching her, she was panting for air in sobbing gasps. A giant hand squeezed her heart, and she teetered on the ledge, not wanting her people to die without her. Why should she be privileged to live while they lay rotting in the sun? How many more ravines across the land held the multiplied dead?

She did not want to go on, nor could she. She began to remove her own clothing.

"My boy would like one of Giaour's offspring. I have money. Can you help him choose a cat?" It was the Turkish washerwoman whose son Captain Ozal had nearly boiled alive. She came from up the road. Why had she followed? Adrine shook her head to clear it of the headache that battered her temples. The woman was not alone. Pressed tightly against her chest was little Kenan, no longer as chubby as the day he'd tried to outrun the captain.

"I . . . I saw that you were distraught," Sosi Emre said. "This is no place for the living, so I came to see if I could help. . . ." Her voice trailed off. No explanation seemed needed in the presence of such evil.

"You may have these clothes," said Adrine dully, folding her cloak. She placed it carefully on a flat boulder. Flies scattered. She fumbled with the buttons on the patchwork dress she'd fashioned from the bits of discarded army uniforms.

The other woman spoke low to her child in Turkish and set him down on the ground. He shrank back toward the shade of the rock wall, his child's mind uncomprehending. "Take my hand." She extended it toward Adrine. "I'm frightened. Please, I need your hand."

Adrine hesitated, not certain what she should do. A world of flies and stench and dead bodies swirled about her, gained speed, pulled at her with a frightening, magnetic power.

Eyes never leaving Adrine's, the other woman walked slowly forward. Their hands joined, and Adrine was grateful for the strong, cool grip that enveloped hers. She clung to it desperately.

They held each other on the stony lip of death, stood a long time in the company of hundreds forever silenced. Adrine's sobs echoed back an elegy from the rocky crags.

The older woman helped the younger back into her cloak, then called the little boy. Hesitantly, Kenan came, and hand in hand the three headed slowly back up the draw. Halfway to the road, Adrine raised the woman's hand to her lips and kissed it.

"I am sorry for what my people have done to your people," Sosi said.

It was all Adrine could do to turn back north, to set foot once more on the road into Hekim Khan. From somewhere in her memory a voice said, *The road that leads away also leads back.*

Kenan's mother stopped to wipe his nose with the hem of her dress. "Isn't it almost your Easter?" she asked.

Numb still, Adrine looked questioningly at her Muslim friend and nodded. "Sunday."

The woman set off toward town at a brisk pace. Kenan pumped his little legs to keep up. "Let's tend to our business, then," his mother said. "We have a cat to choose and an Easter to observe."

Adrine felt her friend's grip tighten.

Then the dam of her emotions burst. Adrine Tevian fell to her knees and wept inconsolably. Tears spilled from the Turkish woman's eyes, too, and even little Kenan sniffled sorrowfully. They clung together and rocked one another on the road of death.

Sometime before the sun slid out of sight, the mother clucked soothing words, and it was as if Grandmother were suddenly there. *"One hand cannot clap,"* she had often said, *"but two hands make a sound."* Adrine smiled for the second time that wretched day and hoped she lived to be old and wise.

They were yet a stone's throw from the edge of the city when they saw the sign. Erected on a post of the sheep gate, the new order was a model of brevity:

ATTENTION ARMENIAN MILITARY ATTENDANTS:

The services of all Armenians previously employed by the Turkish military command post at Hekim Khan are hereby terminated. For the preservation of the order and security of the region, and for their own safety and welfare, at dawn tomorrow former employees of Armenian descent will be escorted under government guard to the Syrian resettlement zone. This notice is subject to all conditions outlined previously in the official Proclamation of Deportation. Anyone attempting to circumvent this order will be executed.

A mule brayed in the distance. A water cart clunked past, one wheel out of round. Wind gusted dust in their faces and made the neglected gate creak in protest.

The two women said nothing. They were from two different worlds. One could stay; one must go. Kenan's mother reached to comfort her friend, but the young woman raised worn hands and shook her head. Ozal would have his revenge. With a long shuddering sigh, Adrine Tevian turned and walked alone toward the stable where she slept.

CHAPTER 9

The night was unseasonably hot and sticky, still as the grave. A silver moon, full and shimmering, hung above the flat housetops of Harput. In the time of sanity, many residents slept in the open on the roofs to escape the swelter. This night, in the time of madness, armed Turks stood atop the dwellings like sentinels. Ears strained and eyes scanned the deserted streets for unauthorized movement.

Frank Davidson knew the back routes and sidetracks, the shadows that concealed. He slipped from doorway to garden to wall, ready with an answer should he be challenged. "Official U.S. consulate business." He would evoke the name of the chief of police, who he well knew was away in Mezreh chasing a troublesome knot of Armenian males barricaded inside a French Catholic mission station.

The Capucin monks who manned the station could sell sand to a Bedouin. The chief of police would not be back anytime soon.

Davidson shifted the tin document box to the other hand. A soft sloshing penetrated the metal confines of the box. Food and drink would be welcome. The pharmacist and his family had several loaves of bread with them, but they could not be eaten. Thousands of dollars in gold—their life savings—were baked inside. It was all the family had to start again in Europe or America.

He thought of Catharine, how he had reassured his wife that he would invite no unnecessary dangers. Neutral meant neutral. But what choice did he have now? If President Wilson continued to drag his feet, there wouldn't be an Armenian left alive. They were Davidson's friends, his employees. He'd worshiped with them, danced at their parties, was the godfather of two Armenian babies. Because of his name, they called him "Frank, the son of King David" and baked him special treats because his wife and home were so far away.

He'd taken the remote post at Harput to immerse himself in the people, the language, the culture of Armenia, and they had won his heart.

And now this people who loved to laugh, to sing, to gather fresh flowers and raise large families was in terrible trouble.

The danger was escalating. From the official dispatches received by the U.S. Consulate at Harput, Turkey, it was obvious that the more despondent the Ottomans became over the misfortunes of war, the more those "foreigners" living within their borders would feel the lash. Turkey suffered repeated defeat. Now word came to Davidson that the Russians had crossed the Caucasus Mountains and invaded Turkey, and the mighty British navy had successfully blockaded the Mediterranean and engineered an "Arab revolt" of the eastern provinces.

Reports poured out of the most remote hovels and important administrative and commercial centers of Turkey. U.S. State Department officials, Protestant missionaries, and Red Cross workers filed ever mounting evidence that a wholesale extermination of unprecedented viciousness was underway. Davidson did everything in his power to keep Washington appraised of the increasing atrocities.

Posts in Aleppo, Baghdad, Beirut, and Damascus took in the haggard surviving remnants of desert death marches from the interior of Anatolia and received the Armenian refugees shipped in cattle cars from the Aegean coast.

The Turks' hatred for the People of the Book was fueled by the interception of letters between Armenian anarchists dreaming of salvation from the Russians and the discovery in Harput's Armenian quarter of enough explosives to level the entire province. Much of it was uncovered in and about the home of the bishop of the Armenian Georgian Church.

The churches began to fall then—bells, stained glass, and organs, all ground to fragments beneath the boots of the betrayed.

Reaching his destination, Davidson felt for the northwest

corner of the supply shed and froze. The wet, gusty sound of a large animal disturbed the night. Then there were two, maybe three. The muffled snorts were too deep for horses. He flattened against the cool stone wall, heart hammering, and waited.

Three massive dogs lunged from the shadows, their heavily armed Kurdish masters in tow. Mercenaries. Hired to patrol the empty markets and hastily abandoned homes of the Armenian quarter, they were ever alert for hidden assets and illegal escapees. The bounty for goods: a portion thereof. The bounty for human life: use of the criminals for sport. The fields beyond town were riddled with the decaying carcasses of those so foolish as to defy the Young Turks and their Kurd hirelings.

The great heads of the straining monsters jerked up from the street. Jaws snapped in agitation. Nostrils flared and strained the air to identify the odor. Moonlit strings of spittle dripped silver from blackened jowls. They were on limited rations, the animals' huge bones clearly visible beneath their thin coats. The Kurds pointed at Davidson's hiding place and with an excited roar, the dogs sprang forward.

Davidson braced himself, but to his greater horror, the creatures and their keepers made straight for the door of the supply barn. The pharmacist, his wife, and their six children watching through the cracks lay fear-soaked just beyond that door.

"Hello! Nice night." Davidson stepped from the shadows, arms raised high overhead. The tin file box glimmered from one hand in ghostly reflection.

Without stopping, one of the Kurds handed his leash to another, leveled his rifle at the American, and came close to running him through with the bayonet affixed to the barrel of the weapon. "State your business," he growled in thickly accented English.

The dogs, all teeth and dark muzzles, growled and choked at the leash, ribs heaving, ravenous for diplomatic flesh.

"Frank W. Davidson, official United States Consul posted to Harput and Mezreh, at the behest of Wilbur J. Carr, director of the Consular Bureau of the U.S. Department of State. I am a neutral observer with attending diplomatic immunity and an enormous appreciation for superior canine flesh. Yours are quite handsome beasts. Mastiffs, I believe, used by Assyrian kings to hunt lions. Bread? Cheese?"

The Kurd with the bayonet backed Davidson up against the supply barn door. They held each other's gaze for a moment, then the Kurd's distrustful eyes darted past Davidson as if trying to penetrate the door.

"Government property. United States government," Davidson said, nodding his head at the building behind him. The Kurd's gaze returned to Davidson. Neither man blinked. The frenzied dogs pulled mightily against their restraints. They wanted what was beyond the door. There was no time.

Davidson prayed and lifted the lid on the tin box.

The dogs snarled and lunged at Davidson, barely held back by their keepers. The Kurd swung the razor-honed tip of the bayonet within an inch of the American's throat. Davidson smiled reassuringly and pulled forth a ring of flat bread and tossed it to one of the mastiffs. Caught in midflight, the bread was wolfed from sight in three frightening gulps. More bread followed in quick succession, the animals yipping like pups one minute, fighting like crazed bears the next.

The American and his three Kurd companions made a strange tableau in the silver night of Harput, picnicking cross-legged at the edge of the street, making wary peace with goat cheese and *raki*. The liqueur, distilled from aniseed, was forty-five proof. It could be consumed in quantity before the drinker fully appreciated its effects. Davidson sat with his back against the supply barn door and was an affable host, though neither food nor drink passed his lips. The visitors finished off a bottle of *raki* apiece, and when Davidson fished up a chunk of jerked mutton and an even rarer handful of apricots, the mellowing Kurds thought him a magician.

All the while, the consul's mind raced from the family on the other side of the shed door to the forty Armenians camped in his courtyard to the three males hidden in his attic to the young father who slept in his broom closet. *"God keep them all,"* he silently prayed.

The dogs grew restless. The skin stretched tight over their broad skulls spasmed impatiently. They rose and paced until they were shouted back to their bellies in the dust. Their muzzles strained toward the barn. They whined and woofed, but the sated Kurds seemed not to notice.

"Medicine?" The head Kurd belched and repeated the word. "Our detachment is falling to the tearing head. You have medicine to fix?"

Davidson had him describe the malady. Severe, tearing headaches. Coughing, achy limbs, high fever, mental confusion, rash, weakened heartbeat, delirium.

Typhus.

The dread epidemic raged among captives and captors alike, wherever unwashed and lice-infested people crowded together. Refugees and soldiers both, fifty to a hundred a day in any given locale, died from heart failure, kidney failure, pneumonia, or septicemia. The Turks weren't just killing Armenians. They were killing their sympathizers—and themselves.

"I don't have any drugs for you," Davidson said, voice raised, one eye nervously watching the agitated dogs. What limited pharmacy he had was needed by those to whom he gave refuge. "You must burn all affected clothing and bedding, shave heads, wash scalps and bodies with strong soap. And then you wait."

The dogs were on their feet, straining at the leash, front feet dancing off the ground. Eyes fixed on the barn door, they barked and fought to be released. The drowsy Kurds cursed and yanked at the leashes and yelled at each other in their own language.

"The barn," said the head Kurd, speech slurred. "Inspect . . . we have to inspect . . . make certain no escapees . . ." He got to his knees and moaned. He held his head with one hand. The other arm flopped and jerked with each pull of the dog.

"I think, my friends, that your dogs are likely typhus carriers." Davidson helped the dizzy Kurds to their feet. "There's probably droves of fleas imbedded in their fur." Flashes of apprehension flickered in the Kurds' eyes. "Those headaches you're experiencing right now? Could be first-stage typhus." Panic pierced the raki-induced fog. The mercenaries sobered quickly, collected their weapons, and punched their dogs into submission, the barn now forgotten.

"I shall pray for your protection," Davidson called after them. "People do survive typhus. Whatever you do, don't scratch." He watched them involuntarily scratch themselves at the mere suggestion. "And you might want to have your dogs destroyed as a precaution." He listened a moment to men and beasts shout and yelp back into the shadows, then mumbled, "May the fleas of a thousand mastiffs nest in your beards."

He suddenly felt weak from nervous tension. He slowly sank to the earth and again rested his back against the crack in the supply barn door. Watching him from a distant rooftop down the street was a heavily armed Turk soldier. Davidson lifted an empty wine bottle and tipped it toward the guard, who remained immovable. The lone sentinel must have witnessed the visitation and hasty leave-taking of the Kurds and assumed Davidson was authorized to be on the streets.

Empty. Everything was empty. The file box. The city. But not hope. As long as God gave breath, there was hope.

He jumped. There was a slight pressure in the small of his back. Careful to keep face forward, he clutched the *raki* bottle like an old friend and sang "Camptown Races." With his other hand, he felt behind him and encountered several little fingers poking him gently. "Hello, little one," he murmured between stanzas of "Camptown." He squeezed the child fingers, and they squeezed back.

"Thank you." The two words were whispered from just behind his left ear. "We all thank you."

Davidson felt a flood of such remorse, he almost burst into tears. "I . . . I have no more food left," he whispered back. "Do Dah! Do Dah!" he belted into the night.

The guard down the way returned to his patrol and left the obviously drunken American to sober up before dawn.

"Your kindness is our food," the pharmacist said. "There are crumbs in the cloth wrappings? We will content ourselves with those. If you please."

Slowly, sadly, Frank Davidson gathered together the corners of the cloth towel. A starving family had been forced to watch the enemy devour the food meant for old women and children. Davidson checked about for prying eyes, then half turned and carefully stuffed the cloth through the gap in the door. More fingers squeezed his in gratitude.

He coughed and said gruffly, "It is dangerous to remain longer. It would arouse too much suspicion to return again for some days. And once those Kurds come to their senses and think about this night, they will be back to search the barn. Before noon tomorrow, a wagon will come and the doors will open. Do what you are told and do not ask questions. Understood?"

Without hesitation came the reply, "Yes, quite clear. Go with God."

Something rough and sticky was hastily forced between his fingers. He removed his hand and with it a tiny, misshapen lump of worn candy, long hoarded.

He stood abruptly, threw a couple of additional off-key "Do Dahs" into the night and melted into the shadows.

The gritty candy tasted bittersweet.

———————

The four horsemen thundered through the night, two days distance from Hekim Khan. From Igdir to Somkaya, Caldiran to Timar, hooves flying, their senses were gloriously filled with the startling presence of Ararat—to the Armenians, the Mother of Earth; to the Kurds, the Mountain of Evil.

Down from the volcanic highlands they had flown, down from the land of cones and craters, down from the snowy vaults so near heaven. The horsemen rode hard and swift, taking fresh half-wild steeds from eager sympathizers at villages and encampments along the way. It was an honor to lose one's mount to the cause of the Fedayeen.

Rough and weathered, on they came. Gone were the telltale sashes and colorful cords. Gone the tassels and bandoliers. Knives they carried and pistols, but the Russian rifles and Sarkisov watches were left far behind.

Just four things of the past did each carry astride his flying steed: the wafer for emergency communion, a portion of Scripture, one lock of a good woman's hair, and the burning desire to see Armenia free forever.

At their head rode Tatul Sarafian, alias the Fox.

Fatigue seduced him to make camp. The dry wind of the plain stung his eyes, and dust storms raked his throat and lungs with grit, but the great heart in his chest thudded a constant refrain: "Save the women ... save the sisters of Armenia...." He rode for Veron, the one woman he had believed with all his mind and strength was divinely fashioned by God to bring Tatul the passion of the young and the solace of the old. God had slept while evil men tore her from him and murdered her where she stood. He would avenge her death by restoring life to a hundred more.

"For you, Black Wolf, and for the brave sisters of Hekim Khan!"

Like blazing wildflowers after warm spring rains, colorful rumors sprang to life at the passing of the horsemen. Some said they were going to throw holy water in the face of the grand vizier, and it would burn his eyes from their sockets. Others said the riders carried vials of disease and were on their way to infect the entire Turkish army. One blind old man who heard their passing and felt the wind was pelted with the clods of earth tossed by flying feet and legs. "I shall receive my sight before those four are done," he crowed. "All that we have lost shall be restored!"

"*Oughour!*" the people cried. "God be with you!"

"*Shen mnak!*" the horsemen shouted from the backs of their lunging steeds. "May you be prosperous!"

At towns thought to be heavily saturated with Turkish military, the Fedayeen entered separately, one or two coming from the north, the remainder circling around and entering from the south as if separate parties. They listened for news of the latest troop movements and planned their continued route and detours accordingly. At Tepedam, a small military supply depot emptied of all Armenians, one of the horsemen slipped undetected into town and tossed a stick of dynamite through the door of a munitions warehouse. Once they were shot at but swiftly outraced the feeble pursuit.

Always they kept moving. The stench of death greeted them with increasing frequency the farther south they rode. They wept and seethed at the killing grounds of Nazik and Uramus. They buried five sisters, horribly mutilated, and vowed to one another they would avenge the murdered ones. Hekim Khan was their goal. They must not turn away now. Old though the cry for help now was, God willing, there were still living Armenian sisters counting on them for rescue.

The four horsemen pushed their horses faster and

changed them more often. Each thought of loved ones and homes that were no more.

On the eve of the final deportation of all Armenians at Hekim Khan, the riders reined to a stop outside the northern boundary of the city. The moon lit the town's emptiness with a sinister glow. The only sound was thin, distant music and the blowing of the winded horses.

The Fox looked at his dirty, desperate men and knew he could not reclaim the years they had aged on the road to Hekim Khan, nor retell all they witnessed on the murderous passage they had just made. Their dead must number in the tens, if not hundreds, of thousands, and unless God intervened, Armenia was about to be erased from earth's memory.

They could do no more than try to save one small pocket of the living.

Tatul Sarafian jerked his head in the direction of the music. "They drink the blood of fallen Armenia to the sultan's health," he said, barely able to contain his emotions. "We must save our sisters and at the same time not lose our ancestry. We are a proud and noble people. We do not dash the brains of others about for sport but rather use our brains to confound and humble the enemy. We enter Hekim Khan now, sent by the Wolf, empowered by God, inspired by Mother Ararat, and filled with the righteousness of our cause. If we do not survive, we will die as we have lived—Fedayeen first, Fedayeen last, Fedayeen for all eternity!"

They formed their horses into a solemn circle and leaned to the center, right arms extended, palms down. Horses moving, they linked thumbs and little fingers, prayed the Lord's Prayer, and broke with a soft shout of solidarity.

The four horsemen turned toward Hekim Khan and rode abreast into the unknown.

CHAPTER 10

The combatants eyed each other coldly. Heads bobbed and weaved in hypnotic unison; feet dug in for a more secure foothold on the bare dirt floor, lit from above by a single hissing lantern. Blood streamed down the left leg of one fighter, from the right ear of the other. The spectators cursed and screamed their preferences, the air rancid with the smell of blood, sweat, and dust. Drunk with gambler's lust, bettors thrust wads of Turkish lira at the betting clerks. Bare knuckles sealed a few private deals, and the betting clerks carried small clubs with which to settle the more heated disputes.

They loved their blood sports, this all-male mix of Hekim Khan townsmen and occupying Turkish troops. And though the Turks of Hekim Khan loathed the enforced occupation by the Turkish military, especially the strutting lordship of Captain Neelam Ozal, the men fell to their knees and bowed low when he announced that the Armenian Church of St. John the Apostle would be converted to a cockpit. The raised spectators' gallery was made of church pews, and the altar was stripped of its sacramental furnishings and converted to accommodate Ozal's hand-carved cockfighting chair.

Beautiful Armenian frescos adorned the two side walls: Adam and Eve in the Garden, and David in combat with Goliath, on the east wall; Noah and the Ark and the mountains of Ararat on the west. Reliefs beneath the roof ledge depicted angels, Abraham and Isaac, Jonah and the Whale, Jesus the Christ Child, Jesus Crucified, and the Risen Christ, as yet undesecrated.

The cockfights had waged all through the night. Dawn approached, and with it would come the deportation of the last of the traitorous Armenians of Hekim Khan. The crowd was in a testy, drunken mood.

In the cockpit, My Sultan puffed up like a swollen cobra, black feathers and crimson comb flashing royally in the lantern light. Sturdier and stockier than its rival, Ucman Sungur's prize fighting cock had a smoky black head, bare as a buzzard's, and an elongated beak that clacked menacingly.

Captain Neelam Ozal's gamecock, though it weighed approximately the same, was dirty white with blood stains and devoid of the showy feathering that so glorified its rival. It was scrappy, but fought tentatively at first, hanging back, never allowing the proud show bird of Ucman Sungur to come close inside with its deadly pecks and kicks. The glory was all in Tekke's interior, a coiled spring package of explosive strength and vicious intent patiently waiting to deliver the telling blow.

Both birds wore three-inch razor-sharp bone spurs slipped over the natural spurs that grew midway between claw and hock.

Most of the men foolishly rooted for My Sultan. They simply could not believe that Ozal's tattered, bloodstained warrior, making its fighting debut, was any serious match. They made sly comments behind their hands and cast mocking glances at Ozal in his private cockfighting chair.

What they did not know was that the captain had purposely trained his fowl for just this night. Reward and punishment. Command and response. The fighting cock of Ozal's own making reflected the captain's own thinking. The good men of the town with their great smirking faces and wet, flabby lips were about to be taken for a fortune. Ozal looked at his soldiers and drank in their mocking glances and felt a stirring in his loins. He took pleasure in the demise of fools such as these. This was about the last amusement left in the grimy little hole of Hekim Khan. He could taste their defeat, and he liked the flavor.

A bell sounded, ending the round with neither bird sustaining much damage. A musician began to play a lively tune on a stringed *saz*. The crowd erupted in a babble of expectation and further bidding. No matter how slow this match went, the crowd had been promised a battle royal at the end—several birds set in the pit at once to fight until all were dead but one. They could tolerate one dull match in anticipation of the finale.

Ozal made his way down to the outer ring of the pit where each cock was cleaned and talked to by its handler in preparation for the third and final round. He saw that Tekke was in excellent shape for the finish. The ear wound was superficial. Ozal motioned for the musician to cease, then he turned and addressed the gallery.

"Friends!" He waited for the crowd to quiet. "I know that these have not been the easiest of times for any of us. You have welcomed us among you in difficult circumstances." As if they'd had a choice.

Ozal strode to the center of the pit and swept an arm over the murmuring spectators, stopping at the cockfighting chair of Uncman Sungur. "To my worthy and esteemed rival, let me say that your bird has fought valiantly. May it be as fearless in death!"

Sungur jumped to his feet and leaned over the pit, grinning in contempt. "The wind blows exceedingly hot from the bag within you!" he shouted, standing straighter with the cautious laughter of the crowd. "Once we have relieved you of your wealth, how will you take to the role of street beggar, O Illustrious Captain of the Guard?" Though everyone knew it was the *raki* talking, a few moved away so as not to be associated with the reckless Sungur.

But Captain Ozal appeared to be in an expansive mood. "Ucman, Ucman, such careless talk from a school administrator! As much as I would like to, I must decline your kind invitation to dine with you this evening. Pity. I understand that you are serving a new dish called My Sultan Had a Bad Day!"

The laughter was riotous and deafening and drowned out anything further the sputtering Sungur wished to say. He received a few friendly slaps on the back as the spectators resumed their seats for the concluding round.

The crowd sensed something about to happen. Ozal returned to his chair. His and Sungur's verbal sparring match had ignited new interest. The noise swelled to a fever pitch. Jokes, insults, jeers, and cheers filled the old church to the rafters. The bell rang. The cocks were released. The fight was on.

My Sultan made its first and last attack of round three,

ten seconds after the bell. A miss. Then, before the church full of horrified onlookers, Tekke countered in a blur of wings and feet and raking beak that eviscerated its opponent in under one minute. My Sultan fell to the ground, sliding its mangled head across the floor. The former feathered majesty was no more.

With lightning swiftness, Tekke seized the advantage, dug its claws into My Sultan's soft underbelly, and sliced a death-dealing blow. End match.

The crowd sat silent in disbelief, counting their losses. Tekke's handler announced the official results. "Tekke, owned by Captain Neelam Ozal, defeats My Sultan, owned by Ucman Sungur the educator! Judgment is final, all debts to be paid on demand."

Two hands clapped loudly in measured rhythm. The sound reverberated through the stunned atmosphere, and the crowd turned to the doors of the church where stood four strangers, the youngest and handsomest applauding the scene. All were rough, blackened with grime, and horsemen, to tell from their smell and their stance. Who could they be?

Armed soldiers materialized at the strangers' backs. Ozal rose from his altar seat and looked the visitors over. "These are dangerous days to be on the road and so late at night to be traveling. State your names, your origin, and your business. Be brief, be truthful, or be gone."

The youngest flashed a crooked, shy smile, teeth strikingly white in the blackened face. "I am Bolu Bergema and these the brothers Mentese. We are recent residents of the prison at Murat. Justly held, to be sure, but eager now to repair our foolish ways, to become contributing citizens, and to pledge our patriotism to the Turkish Republic by enlisting as your humble servants. Turkey needs soldiers; we need work. And as for the lateness of the hour, it is actually early morning. We camped a couple of hours to the north, then rose at first light so as not to raise suspicion by arriving in the night watch." The pronunciation and inflection were flawless Turkish, the sincerity unimpeachable, the facts probably impossible to verify.

"Check with the authorities at Murat," Ozal ordered one of his lieutenants.

Bolu Bergema laughed bitterly. "With all due respect, my Captain, the prison at Murat is a pile of rubble and the authorities dead or scattered. It is the work of Armenian anarchists intent on freeing other scum like themselves. Our proof is much more common. We have breath like camels and a desperate yearning to be sentenced to a year in a harem!" The crowd laughed, and all four of the dark horsemen grinned disarmingly.

"Check with the authorities at Murat," Ozal repeated, matching their grins. "And ride north two hours and locate their campsite. The fire should still be warm."

"We built no fire, my Captain," Bergema replied evenly. "Again, we did not wish to cause alarm. We only wished to verify the fame of Neelam Ozal by our own witness. And to find gainful employment in the army of the grand vizier."

"Fame?" Ozal sniffed the air for the scent of deceit and fear. None presented itself. "Who speaks of me outside this town?"

"Ah, many know the exploits of Ozal the Swift. You are known for just and rapid retribution at the expense of Armenian dogs. It gives the true Turk patriot courage and hope to go on in these trying days when hearts fail and spirits flag."

With the barest flick of an eyelid, Ozal signaled his men. Four of the burliest grabbed Bergema, slammed him down on a low-lying table, pinned his arms and legs, and carted the entire affair to the pit beneath Ozal's private box. A half-dozen soldiers restrained the brothers Mentese with rifles in hand.

The crowd, sensing an unscheduled contest of wills, bent eagerly forward and craned their necks to see around the beefy guards restraining the brash young stranger.

Ozal summoned Tekke's handler and whispered long in his ear. The man reentered the pit, lifted the scrappy hero, and set the conquering gamecock on the table next to Bergema's head.

The stranger and the gamecock eyed each other without moving. The handler stood behind Bergema's head. Tekke straightened, strutted over to the young man's face, craned its sinewy neck, and peered close. Bergema pulled back from the wicked beak and squeezed shut his eyes. In one swift stroke, the handler fastened meaty hands on either side of Bergema's jaw, pushed his face toward the gamecock, and held him fast. He spread the stranger's eye wide open with dirty fingers. Tekke peered closely at the bright, moist object, neck jerking, head turning side to side.

Bergema fought to lie still. The head of the gamecock loomed in his vision like a hideous monster, pink wattles flapping each time the neck jerked, the vicious needle point of the beak poised to peck the white orb of the eye. It took a supreme focus of the will to keep from crying out. Despite himself, he gave a half moan, half gasp, muscles rigid.

"A small wager, Bolu Bergema," Ozal called down. "If for three minutes, you stare down my handsome Tekke, you win. If, however, within three minutes he attacks your eye and renders you half blind, I win. At any time you decide to tell me the truth, then it's a draw and we go settle this according to Turkish law."

The gamecock's head darted downward, beak striking the table. Bergema jerked but chewed his tongue rather than make a sound. Up came the naked head, a beetle squirming in the savage beak. With a sharp gulp, the beetle disappeared, and Tekke twisted lower for a closer look at the white eye with the dark, terrified center.

"My Captain, I accept your wager and raise the stakes!" Bergema cried, amazing the crowd with his pluck.

"Speak," Ozal commanded.

"I have heard it said that you keep women—Armenian whores. My men and I are ravenous after so long a time without female companionship. If I outstare your fine bird, allow my men and me nightly access to your collection of slaves. What say you, Captain?"

"I say you are desperate indeed!" Ozal laughed and the audience with him. "You have not seen these creatures you desire. They are one hundred of the most disgusting females you have ever laid eyes on. In fact, to blind you first would be a mercy!" The room dissolved into husky, ribald laughter. "One for each of you, then, but the rest leave tomorrow for the deserts of Syria. I can no longer keep them on government requisition. They drink too much boiled water!" More laughter, pouring of raki, and poking of ribs. Too much boiled water! The captain was in fine form tonight.

The slashing beak was so close to Bergema's drying eye, he could feel the push of air with each jerk of the gamecock's head. Suddenly, the optic nerve began to twitch and his eye jumped, attracting more attention from the curious bird. Bergema's mind screamed. At any moment the beak would plunge deep into the soft tissue of the eye. At any moment the world would go black, and the pain would pierce the center of his brain. He prayed, he fought panic, he called upon Abraham, Black Wolf, and the Son of God to work a miracle.

"My Captain, I am shocked." Bergema sounded calm. "You are a just man. Surely a man's sight is worth *at least* the hides of all your infidel prostitutes. Give them to me, and I will be your personal pair of eyes, sighted or blinded, it matters not. Think of the legend *that* will spawn!"

Captain Ozal contemplated the outrageous bid. At six o'clock in the morning after a full night of raki, wagering, and bloodletting, it held a strange appeal.

"Done!" the captain cried. There was little chance the bird would not strike and turn this young upstart into just another maimed pauper. "Three minutes!"

Tatul Sarafian's heart sank. He'd hoped the three minutes had already started. *God help me.*

Wagering took on a renewed urgency with everyone racing to place their bets before a bloodcurdling shriek would signal the end of the challenge.

Time stood still. Tatul's brain went numb, and his ears filled with a roaring like that of the sea. He sensed rather than saw the leering, smelly spectators who largely bet his eye would go any second. To the credit of a few, it seemed a waste of the future to deliberately blind a promising servant of a new Turkey.

"Two minutes remaining!"

Ozal looked nervously about. This was taking too long. Tekke agreed and struck with surprising force. Blood oozed from the bridge of Tatul's nose, sliding down into his nostril. Seeing the crimson stream, the cock's fighting instincts were aroused, and it struck again, a sharp tearing blow to the lower lip. The bird tugged at the lip and widened the wound, spilling blood in a crooked rivulet.

Ozal smiled and tensed for the telling blow.

With each strike the crowd drew a sharp, collective breath. The sight was appalling, yet ghoulishly entertaining to the denizens of drab, shriveling Hekim Khan.

Now Tekke puffed up, ruffling its ragged feathers in indignation that this opponent provided even less fight than the last. With a serpentine glare, it turned its head sideways and lashed at the young man's eye.

It caught him a glancing blow off the eyebrow, and the beak imbedded in the wrinkled skin of the eyelid at the corner of the eye.

Tatul bit his lip to keep from screaming, the fighting cock monstrously huge at close range.

"One minute remaining!"

Ozal liked a close match, but not this close. He began to look about for some way to goad Tekke into a fighting frenzy like the one that had finished off My Sultan. He rose to leave his private box but encountered the sweaty, heaving bulk of the baker and the opium trader practically wedged in place by their drunken excitement.

"Out of my way, you stupid beasts!" They did not budge and somehow absorbed Ozal into their perspiring embrace. He looked wildly about for his soldiers, but they were intent on the drama below, and he was trapped, smothered in bearded, odorous enthusiasm.

The angry fowl tugged at Tatul's eyelid as at a fat worm, dug its claws into the table, and pulled back with a snap of its head. The beak sliced through the eyelid; the bird lost its hold and tumbled backward off the table. The crowd roared in derision. The bird fled in search of its dignity across the twenty-foot circle to the far side of the pit. By the time it was cornered and returned to the table, the timer struck the final bell a smart clanging ring, and the match was over.

Tatul Sarafian had two good eyes and one hundred women.

"Your gamecock, Captain," he shouted gladly, "it must know the truth when truth presents itself!"

The spectators, though cheated of a blinding, cheered the stranger's mettle. They may have been earlier tricked and bilked of their wagers by the captain's cunning and now by the young man's improbable win, but they felt good about

Bolu Bergema escaping an even crueler fate.

After slapping and congratulating the stranger for his lucky escape from the razor beak, the crowd did not stay for the promised battle royal. What could beat the rare display of courage by Bolu Bergema from Murat Prison? They were exhausted. The cocks were caged and removed from the pit.

Tatul fell back on the table in the emptying hall, eyes shut, his own body like jelly from tension and fatigue. Gingerly, he dabbed at torn flesh with the back of a sleeve. Though they hurt and would undoubtedly fester, compared to the alternative, the minor wounds were blessed assurance that he had found favor. *Thank you, God, for hearing my prayer. Could it be that we are still speaking?*

A cold shiver passed through him, and he opened his eyes to stare straight into Ozal's.

The piercing look was an icy knowing. It appeared the captain didn't believe the story of Murat Prison. Bolu Bergema and the brothers Mentese had interrupted Ozal's big triumph. They had halted his planned exodus of the useless Armenians and stolen the glory of Tekke's impressive win. And Bergema had refused to lose an eye. All in all, a very dangerous start as Hekim Khan's newest residents.

"Welcome to my province," Ozal said with a sneer. "As my new pair of eyes, I think it best we begin by showing you something worth seeing. First, take a little sleep, for you are tired. Then come, let us take a short trip into the hills just beyond town. It is a sight that should gladden your loyal Turkish heart!"

Tatul shivered at the malice in the words and stood to follow the captain. From the young Armenian's sleeve slid an exquisite dagger, all gold and silver inlay. He studied the base of Ozal's neck. With one quick thrust, he could end the tyrant's reign and ask questions later. The hand that held the dagger trembled even as it rose.

Ozal turned and Bolu Bergema dropped to one knee, head bowed, the costly hand-tooled stiletto extended haft-first on open palms. "My Captain, a gift from your humble servant. If I had but more to give. . . ."

The captain's eyes narrowed. He grasped the beautiful weapon and held it to the light of dawn that was just now breaking rose and azure through the stained-glass windows of roughshod evangelists and passionate fishermen. "On your feet, Bolu Bergema," he ordered. The former prisoner stood.

Ozal ran a finger over the shiny flat of the finely honed blade and studied the young man's Adam's apple. "Where did a member of Murat Prison obtain so fine a blade as this?"

Despite his sore and bloodied face, Bergema smiled a sly smile. "I appropriated it upon my release by the strategic application of piano wire to the person of the prison administrator who mistook me for an Armenian. Under pressure, he was only too pleased to part with the knife."

The captain laughed, a dry and unpleasant sound. "This way, Bergema the Garrote. Now I am certain that after you have rested you will like what I have to show you."

Tatul Sarafian of Erzurum swallowed hard. As they passed beneath the painting of Jesus the Christ Child, he reached a shaky hand inside his shirt, felt the comforting locket of Veron's hair, and crossed himself.

The lies were breeding like rats.

CHAPTER 11

At dawn, Frank Davidson awoke to pandemonium and groaned. The Muslim devout filled the street in front of the U.S. Consulate at Harput—as they had for days—praying at the top of their lungs for the righteous destruction of all Armenians and for the success of all Turk "surgeons" who "skillfully remove the festering canker from the back of the nation." There would be no more rest this day.

He knew the worshipers had risen from their beds and immediately begun the ritual washing. Hands, mouths, nostrils, faces, arms, and feet, three times each.

These were the ablutions required to enter prayer worthily, even prayers for holy destruction. Great care was required not to nullify ablutions by the passage of gas or urine, scratching a scab, or falling asleep. Should any one of those occur immediately after washing, ablutions had to be repeated before prayer could commence.

"*Allahu Akbar!* God is the greatest!" The preamble to worship began, repeated four times. "*Ashhaddu An La Illa-L—Lah!* I bear witness that there is no god but the One God!" Repeatedly, the prayers bore witness to Muhammed and exhorted the faithful everywhere to join in. Davidson certainly could have. He knew them all by heart and had had more than one sound sleep destroyed by them.

"*La Ilaha Illa-l-lah!* There is no god but the One and True God!"

Davidson sighed, punched his pillow, and sat up. He knew they had commenced ritual bowing, prostration, and kneeling, each position accompanied by prayerful utterances carefully prescribed for their symbolic significance. The rote prayers completed, the air filled with impromptu declarations of hatred.

"They do blaspheme who say, 'Jesus is coequal with God.' Death to blasphemers!" On and on they droned, beseeching God to kill all Armenian "liars" who believe in the Bible and salvation through Jesus Christ.

The Muslim worshipers surged forward and beat on the gates of the consulate with sticks and fists, then fell back to petition the sky with renewed fervency and volume.

It was harassment against the Armenian employees of the consulate, pure and simple. It was an act of aggression against a sovereign neutral power that went unpunished.

Consul Frank Davidson tossed and turned and tried cramming his head between pillows to block the savage prayers. He could not. It was as if the peoples' faith was validated by the slaughter of innocents. But they saw little of the atrocities and were ignorant of much. Travel on the roads was greatly curtailed. Few ventured beyond the city limits. News was filtered and colored by national self-interest. If he could take them to the valleys of death and rub their noses in the rotting carcasses of their neighbors, their hands and faces would never come clean for such prayer again.

Davidson thanked God for the thousandth time for the large three-story consulate and the high-walled garden with its thick canopy of mulberry trees. Back home in Port Jefferson, New York, a quiet seaport on Long Island's North Shore, such an arrangement would be quaintly known as a "privacy hedge." It was a term that here held enormous meaning.

The American was not surprised to hear women among the noisemakers this morning, at times even outpraying the men in volume and menace. Though many were draped in the Islamic veil, they knew no masculine equal, and while publicly subservient, in truth they ruled their devout husbands behind closed doors.

How he missed Catharine and the family home in Port Jefferson, but he was meant to roam. Thankfully, he had friends in Harput and regularly entertained them; or rather, he used to have friends—workers from the American hospital, teachers from the German and Danish orphanages. Particularly stimulating had been the five teaching colleagues from Euphrates College. He had attended the college graduation ceremonies soon after first arriving at the consulate. So had the Turkish officials of the region. At that time goodwill had flowed between Christian and Muslim.

What a difference a year had made! Recently, five college missionaries of Armenian descent had been arrested. Yesterday came the crushing news they had been tortured to death. "Seditious intent" rang the ridiculous charge. Davidson lodged a formal protest, but it would be filed and forgotten.

Euphrates College was a work of the Congregational American Board of Commissioners for Foreign Missions, a Christian missionary presence in the area for sixty years. Since conversion from Islam was legally punishable by death, they labored among the Greek, Armenian, and other Christian minorities. All of them were friends, all good people. Many of them, more than fifty in number, labored at outlying mission stations, some with children.

They were a regular feature of Davidson's circuit, the nearest ones three days away, the most distant two weeks on horseback. It used to be a pleasant change in routine. Now he dreaded the time away from the consulate and feared what he might find when he arrived at their homes. One fine lady had died of typhus while treating the Armenian sick. Others simply disappeared under suspicious circumstances.

A soft knock came at his door. Davidson sat up with a jerk. It was only Fetty, the sweet Muslim serving girl who brought him hot Turkish tea each morning. Still, his heartbeat increased and his eyes flew to the painting of the rock dwellings at Cappadocia. Behind it was the safe. In the safe were tens of thousands of dollars entrusted to him by sad-eyed deportees. It was weird, this island of wealth in a sea of death.

How long would the nest eggs last? How many would actually ever be claimed? It had become one of his unspoken duties to preserve these savings for those Armenians who, by whatever miracle, survived. He swore to track down as many of the few addresses and contacts with relatives in other countries as he'd been given and send their valuables on. It was the least that he could do.

There was more hope for those who attempted the dash over the border mountain country west of Ararat to Russia. Some were shot fleeing, others caught in the cross fire at the war front, but those who made it eked out a living among Russian peasants or found a home with relatives in Russian Armenia. Some had made their way as far as Moscow or the United States and sent small amounts of rubles or dollars to support loved ones still caught in Turkey's web.

Dangerous though it was, the American consulate was a stop in a loosely organized underground escape route through the remote hill regions where, for as little as a thumb's worth of fresh cheese, a man dressed as a woman could book passage on a mule's back or cling to the underside of a wagonload of chickens. The underground railroad's next stop was Hamit Batu's farm. From there, it was four days, maybe five—and as many peasant hideouts—into Russia. Sometimes refugees were met short of the border by a Fedayeen escort, but most swam the Aras River or floated downstream on whatever they could find until they bumped against Uncle Christian's shore. Others floated into rifle range of Turkish troops and eventually came ashore as bullet-ridden corpses. Some of mixed blood had been killed with Russian bullets for failing to convince Uncle Christian they were not Turks.

He wished he could learn the fate of those he harbored and handed off to Bantu. Only twice had he heard of safe arrivals. Word had come through for their savings to be sent with the next batch of "railroad passengers." It was too dangerous to make inquiries, and nothing could be mailed from Russia without being confiscated by Turkish postal authorities.

Thebes, a twenty-pound tabby, thumped from the bed to the floor and stood by the door purring in sonorous encouragement. Davidson opened the door and sent the cat out to his roamings.

He drank his tea and dressed. The shouted prayers from the street below intensified. He sighed. It was going to be a difficult day.

A thud hit the ceiling above the bed. Davidson looked up in concern. He hoped the Naskarian family didn't harbor a hothead about to lob a bomb out the window. The little daughter was a lamb and only cried with a soft mewing, but the teenage son hated the confinement and wanted nothing more than to make a few Turks pay with their lives.

The Naskarian boy endangered everyone in the compound.

Order and separation of sovereign states had thus far been maintained, but it was a fragile peace. Should an unauthorized Armenian be discovered inside the American compound, it would be all the excuse the mob needed to storm the palace. For that reason, the consulate's Turkish staff was carefully screened, and they served with a loyalty that was the envy of other offices in the region. As a condition of employment, few outsiders knew about the bonus pay and extra food consular employees received, thanks to Davidson's overtaxed contingency fund. He did not slight in this area but worried that betrayal was never more than a couple of bread loaves away.

Davidson smiled thinly and lingered in the steam from the cup. He had enjoyed this posting, for all its risks. Compared to some of the diplomatic hovels offered in Turkish backwaters, the United States government offices at Harput *were* a palace. It was, as rated by a superior in the State Department, "the best house in town." It boasted three stories of spacious rooms, and the previous occupant's taste in Oriental rugs and paintings had left a refined mark. It was handsome and dignified and altogether fitting for an official of the United States government.

And compared to his last posting in the port city of Batum, on the Russian Black Sea, Harput was a resort. But for the adventurous Davidson, the hiking and horseback riding near the more temperate shores of Batum were the two things superior to the sun-baked bleakness of Harput. His one regret was that the Batum climate did not agree with his wife. She had fallen ill and returned to America. So far, they'd been married almost three years but together barely one. Sometimes the ache for her was scarcely bearable.

Catharine took upon herself much of the blame for their separation. If only she were stronger, more resilient, like Abraham's wife, Sarah. If only she could have gotten pregnant in Batum and right now been raising their child to present to proud Father Frank upon his eventual return. Instead, no child and only a sickly, barren wife to look forward to. She couldn't imagine any man would be eager to return home to that.

He wrote love letters exalting her courage, her talent for watercolors, and her quiet, steadfast work on behalf of women's suffrage. She was an officer in the General Federation of Women's Clubs and gave stirring speeches against socialist-feminist trends and for democratic self-determination. He'd never forget her response to a politician who told her that given the vote, women would lose their femininity. Rising to her full five feet one inch, head erect, eyes ablaze, she smiled sweetly and said, "Women in the garment laundries stand on their feet for fourteen hours a day in scorching steam and searing heat with their hands immersed in scalding hot starch. Do you honestly think these daughters and wives and mothers would lose one ounce more of their feminine charm by putting a ballot in a ballot box once a year than they are likely to lose standing in foundries and laundries year-round?"

No, the fault for their separation was entirely his. Frank Davidson was born to the diplomatic corps and a fascination with the plight of refugees. That he, a foreign officer of low rank, should be placed by God into an explosive confrontation on the other side of the globe and given a protective shield of U.S. sovereignty behind which to rescue the defenseless was both humbling and exciting. Not that his superiors would always approve of his extracurricular activities. But in a nation where life was cheap and the rules of the frontier as capricious as a pirate's heart, he was paid to use his wits, whether or not it always jibed with official protocol.

He was hired to make decisions where little direction or precedent existed. No one should be required to stand by while women and children suffered for being born into a subject race. Let the strategists in Washington tell him what they would have done differently had they been in his place.

Davidson's personal requirements were few. Half his wages went home to Catharine, and since his room and board were provided by the U.S. government, the remainder of his earnings was spent on entertaining Turk officials and "maintaining" a few miles of track in the underground railroad that saved Armenians.

The Muslim prayers still filled the air outside the consulate. "God the All-Seeing Eye, kill the Armenian infidel ... cleanse our land of their festering filth! Kill them ... kill them...."

His cup clattered against the saucer. Davidson flushed and felt like hurling the whole business down on the mob outside, maybe even boiling up some oil to rain down upon their ill-begotten heads. Because of their hatred, he could not go home. Nor could he turn his back on so much as a single little one threatened by the butchery.

He rubbed his eyes and ran a hand through what little prematurely gray hair was left. He'd had a full head when Catharine literally waltzed her way into his soul that Christmas ball at the Waldorf in honor of William Lewis's appointment to assistant attorney general of the U.S. She could have had her pick of the room, but she said it was the six-foot Frank Davidson in brown tweed who stopped the music for her that night. And she him.

"Kill the Christ-lovers! Kill the Jesus-worshipers! Favor us with their spilled blood. . . ." On and on the prayers droned.

Diplomacy was dangerous work, but Davidson's audacious style took its toll in other ways. His rugged wanderings had earned him an uncouth reputation in diplomatic circles. In 1913, he had taken a leave of absence to hike the heights of Uzbekistan and climb Mount Ararat. The consular superior, Gottshalk, was not amused and thought the hiking episode open to ridicule by the local peasantry. "Most Russians think a consul might ride," he had sniffed. It was Gottshalk who recommended Davidson for "a remote, uncivilized, and unexacting place." A place like Harput.

Davidson shook his head. He must stop these ruminations. He was a no-nonsense man with an incautious streak. One did not last long in the diplomatic corps unless willing to take risks. Time was running out for the pharmacist and his family. There was only one more train out of Batu Station until a month of no activity passed to quiet suspicions. Besides, the Kurd mercenaries and their mastiffs would come to their senses in the bright glare of day and return to the site of the supply shed, suspicions aroused. Davidson must hurry and take the fugitives in the wagon to Hamit Batu, the sympathetic Turk with the heart of an Armenian. Some said there were missing military officers buried on his land, but he was prominent in local government and shouted his detractors down.

Davidson dressed hastily, suddenly anxious to be away, each button a prayer for divine protection. The mirror told him that the dusty, worn riding attire would earn a sound reproof from Supervisor Gottshalk. "Perfect!" Davidson pronounced, giving his image a smart nod of approval.

Outside, the American consul took the wagon reins from

the groom and nodded politely. Nudging the horse to the back gate, he gripped the reins tightly, took a deep breath, and nodded sharply to the groom. The gate swung wide.

Two or three snoopers were knocked aside and a quartet of worshipers dove away from the racing wagon in a barrage of very un-Muslimlike curses. With a quick glance back to ensure the gate closed before the offended pedestrians recovered, Davidson cut the corner onto the main road, scattering a bevy of chickens and dogs right into the path of Feroz Akarli, the Harput chief of police. Davidson instinctively hauled back on the reins barely in time to bring the careening wagon to a clattering halt. A cloud of grit and chalky dust enveloped Akarli, who frowned and wiped his mustache clean with thumb and forefinger.

"Reckless endangerment, for a beginning," Akarli said, informing the American of his crimes. "Cruelty to animals, failure to yield the right of way to a pedestrian, religious disregard tantamount to persecution, and disturbance of the peace. How plead you, consul?"

Davidson breathed easier. Akarli was in a good mood. "The only peace disturbed here was my sleep by those prayer machines. I thought neither road construction nor devout shouts were allowed to commence before ten o'clock in this fine municipality." He and Akarli had mutual respect for each other, despite the impossible times. It was often difficult for the commander of the rural gendarmes to justify the orders he was sent from the seat of government in Stamboul. He followed them nonetheless, yet always with professionalism and at least a slim measure of humanity.

Akarli looked as if caught on the horns of a great moral dilemma, then brightened. "Ah well, you've committed no breach of the public trust that couldn't be repaired with another jar of those New York raspberry preserves. Tell me again, what is this secret ingredient? Peck-tan?"

Davidson chewed his lip. Akarli's favorite form of capital punishment was talking people to death. It was still the shortest route to getting back underway.

While sitting atop the wagon and carefully explaining pectin and the whole canning process to the fascinated policeman, Davidson caught movement out of the corner of his eye.

To his shock, a window in the upper story of the consulate slid open and out crawled the Naskarian boy. The mulberries grew thick and dense there, a small forest of forty trees, but as the youth grabbed for a handhold, the leaves and branches shook. Suddenly, the boy gave a mighty kick backward as if to dislodge someone attempting to grab his leg.

"The principle being, of course, to seal or preserve vegetables, meat, fruit, drinks, whatever, in a jar or can for future use." Davidson was glad the policeman's back was to the compound. He scanned the street carefully from side to side, but Akarli's presence had magically caused the good citizens of Harput to disappear.

He'd begun to calm down when, to his shock, Mr. Naskarian came through the window and grabbed for the branch in pursuit of his son. Fortunately, whoever had hold of the father on the other end maintained a grip and hauled him back inside. Unluckily, the Nakarian boy lost his hold and fell.

It was the worst possible time for a lull in the noisy prayers, but there it was. No disguising the sound of boy and ground meeting behind the garden wall. Akarli whirled around. "What was that? Someone attempting to escape the compound? If you are hiding Armenians, Consul Davidson, you are an accessory to unlawful flight, and that is punishable by death! Open that gate!"

Davidson jumped down from the wagon and shouted over the wall to the stable. The gate swung wide again and a yowling Thebes the cat shot through the opening like an orange comet, the groom in hot pursuit. The yard beneath the spreading mulberry trees appeared otherwise empty.

The policeman bent and picked up a fresh fallen branch and examined its broken stump. He looked into the latticework of foliage above, a scowl on his face. Davidson laughed. "My cat. After the songbirds again. I swear if he doesn't lose weight, I'll need to reinforce the floor joists!"

Akarli studied the consul's face, the corners of his mustache twitching. "This is a quite isolated outpost, Mr. Davidson. Things could happen here that the outside world might never hear of. Should the people decide to investigate the Armenians alleged to reside inside the consulate, I'm not altogether certain that my men, as thinly spread as they are, could stop them. Perhaps you should stop feeding your cat, and this will result in an appropriate reduction in excess weight. It is particularly objectionable at this time when so many are in want."

There was no mistaking the underlying intent of Akarli's last words. He believed there were illegal deportees sheltering inside the U.S. Consulate. This usually congenial man had his limits.

"Your point is as well taken as it is well made, sir. From this point forward, Thebes will do with less. Now if you will excuse me . . ."

The policeman walked deliberately to the horse and stroked its head. "Permit me a last question. Be assured that my concern extends to all those who look to Harput for safety and protection in these harrowing days. Where exactly are you going this morning?" The brows of his eyes arched into dark exclamation marks.

"I don't know that I need to inform you of official consular business, but it is no secret that I go to the farm of Hamit Batu for foodstuffs—vegetables, some grapes, a little milk." Davidson's frustration at the delay and the nosing about was beginning to show.

Feroz Akarli ruffled the horse's forelock. "Does the chief consul do the work of servants?" He watched the American's reaction carefully.

Davidson dropped all genial demeanor. "That is your *second* last question, sir. Suffice it to say that my man is a bit under the weather today, and despite how complimentary these fine quarters are to the host country which so graciously provides them, I should like from time to time to get away from the confines of this little corner myself. *Now* will you excuse me?"

Akarli stepped away from the horse. "By all means," he said with exaggerated politeness. "But I wouldn't be away long. Not as long as you were away last night. In these perilous times, it takes little to ignite much."

Davidson glanced sharply at the police chief. Last night? How much did Akarli know of last night? The consul was beside himself but tried not to betray agitation. If he left now, would he be followed? While the master was away, would the mansion burn? The element of a surprise getaway had been thoroughly dashed.

The police chief stepped aside with an exaggerated flourish. "Go with Allah! And remember the definition of neutrality."

A frigid chill seized Davidson's spine despite the day's growing heat. He felt the lingering memory of little fingers poking him in the back. Jaw set, he nodded curtly to the officer, clucked at the horse, and set off down the street at a moderate trot past the determined pray-ers.

Despite the clenched fists and dark, resentful looks that greeted his passage, Davidson willed himself a brighter outlook the farther Chief Akarli faded from sight. Gone were the sinister shadows and demons of the night. Primed with the taste of their raki, the Kurd mercenaries of last evening would have returned to their camp in search of further libations to quell the fear of typhus. And if their reputation for sodden revels was half true, they'd have had their dogs drunk by three o'clock in the morning, and they themselves would have been unconscious by four.

"There is luck that brings ill and ill that brings luck." Davidson muttered the old Armenian bromide. "Let us wait and see which of God's doors will be opened to us."

He permitted himself a faint whistle and allowed the wagon to wend its way casually through the streets. The aging harness nag appreciated the stroll, and what few townspeople were about took little notice.

His rescue strategy was simple. Back the wagon into the barn away from prying eyes. Place the false wooden frame assembled to mimic stacked crates into the back of the wagon. Arrange the pharmacist and his family of seven inside the hollow assembly. Cover the whole with canvas and cinch the cover secure with rope. Continue on to the farm of Hamit Batu. Once there, transfer the "cargo" to the vegetable wagon, cover over with a layer of cabbages, and wish Hamit a profitable day at the market.

Others were smuggled by sympathetic Kurds across the Euphrates River on primitive little ferryboats to Dersin, Turkey. Beyond was Kurdish-controlled territory and again the safety and freedom of the Russian mountains. Increasingly, Turk river patrols shot and killed anything that moved along the banks of the Euphrates. Questions, if asked at all, could be asked later.

Hamit's underground did not come cheaply. But life savings in exchange for spared Armenian lives seemed a bargain price for escape from Turkey's charnel house. Sadly, only the wealthy could afford survival. The prosperous pharmacist had struck an arrangement that placed a portion of his gold in a trust account. For taking a risk and for his kindness, Frank Davidson could draw upon that gold reserve to buy another poorer family their freedom.

Davidson leaned back and let the rising sun bathe his face. A ring of low-lying mountains circled the Armenian Plateau that contained the twin cities of Harput and Mamuret-ul-Aziz and many agricultural villages. The region was part of the ancient Armenian homeland trampled by Byzantine, Arab, and Turk. The last census put the Armenian population of the Plateau at slightly more than 110,000. Davidson figured it closer to 150,000—before the deportations. Each day now the number dropped, but even in the best of times the government had typically underestimated the true strength in numbers of the Christian minority.

He banished the gloomy picture of a shrinking people from his mind. It was the only way to function. All in all, it felt good to be about to smuggle eight souls to a new life. Just like the eight spared in Noah's Ark to start a new world. It didn't take many to begin again.

He slapped the wood at his side and actually felt a slender thread of cheer, not at all a familiar feeling for the past year. The sudden *thunk* earned him a soft whinny and a curious look from the pair of patient, watery eyes up front. Sure the wagon was a rickety old ark with creaky wheels and gaps in the floorboards—not nearly the awesome vessel that rode out the Flood—but the good Lord had done more with less.

Very early on the first day of the week, just after sunrise, they were on their way to the tomb. . . . He jerked straight in the seat and earned a second quizzical look from the horse.

"Easter!" he announced to an impossibly bent old man aimlessly sweeping the stoop in front of his equally crooked house. The Christian holy day had dawned in an increasingly Christless land.

He averted his eyes from the burned-out Church of the Saintly Martyrs. Two months before, two hundred had huddled inside her sanctuary, slowly starving to death, until the day the doors were beaten in and the refugees clubbed to the floor. All were killed. The grand pageantry of Easter would not spill out its shattered windows and splintered doors this day. Today, the infidel was king.

The wagon creaked past shuttered shops and a dreary procession of dusty brown homes with flat roofs, as inviting as piled skeletons. Despite the times, Davidson savored the remembrance of the day, as if he alone in all this wretched land knew of the world-changing Resurrection. Easter in New York was pretty hats and frilly dresses. Succulent hams, fervent prayers, an empty grave. Holy, holy, holy.

Davidson chuckled. Drop a ham in the middle of these Muslim purists, and they would scatter like a bomb had gone off. Pork, the Christian's secret weapon!

He hoped the Armenians, what was left of them, did not forget Easter. Their faith above all else was their distinguishing mark. People of the Book.

Their only hope.

Ahead was the little shed *cum* stable the U.S. consul had purchased for repository of stores and desperate people. Davidson yanked back on the reins. The wind exhaled in misery. A dust devil spattered his face with dirt. A window slammed closed. An infant whimpered, gagged, and wailed from somewhere behind Harput's shackled walls.

There was fresh blood on the shed, at the sides and over the door. Dread curled about Davidson's stomach and squeezed.

"Heeyah!" He snapped the reins, and the wagon careened the last hundred feet in one frantic plunge. It was still rolling when Davidson hit the ground and yanked on the barn doors.

Empty. A smell of old sweat and straw. Dark droplets of blood trailing over the dirt floor to the haymow.

Davidson dashed inside the barn, past a wall of bridles and tools, running from crate to haystack in search of something—anything—alive. Mad, breathless, he hurled packing crates, knocked aside a pile of rotting onions, dug at the straw, and imagined tiny fingers squeezing his. A child's sticky candy. *"Your kindness is our food."*

He had led murderers to his little family of eight. The monsters had killed them and hauled them away like so much venison. He did not even know their names. Anonymous, in case of official inquiry. But in death, they should have names, bodies to bury, next of kin to notify. . . .

"Here."

Davidson straightened, heart pounding, straining to hear.

"In here." A patch of straw rustled, and again came the hoarse whisper. "Be still, good consul. We are all safe beneath the straw." A solitary eye glittered from a space in the hay.

Davidson almost wept. "You are injured, pharmacist?"

"No, friend. After you left, I cut my wrist for blood to smear the doorposts, that the Angel of Death might pass over. If it worked for our Jewish friends, my family deserved no less."

Davidson flashed with anger. "Fool! The smell of your blood might have led the dogs right back here. Why did you not just stay hidden? I said I would be back for you."

From somewhere deep behind the glittering eye, a child whimpered in muffled fear. "Do not be annoyed with me, kind friend. I did what any father with little to protect his family would do—I thought of something. Would not God honor this symbol of his ancient protection?"

"Oh, God has, pharmacist, God has." Davidson shook his head and expelled a shaky breath. "Be still, now. Eat the bread and fruit I have brought for you while I back the wagon up to the mow."

On the second attempt, Davidson coaxed the nag to maneuver the wagon right where he wanted it, tight against the haystack. Quickly, Davidson installed the false floor of wooden crates into the bed and motioned the refugees forward. "Youngest first, oldest last," he directed, giving each member of the family a drink of water and a hasty hug and kiss before passing them inside the narrow confines of the cramped compartment. With stoic reserve, they crawled into place, each child with a fresh piece of candy clutched in a grubby fist.

"Lie facedown and breathe through the gaps in the floorboards, using your hands to cushion the bumps." The American demonstrated with his own hands and arms. He gave them each a handkerchief. "Place these over your eyes and mouths to keep the dust out." *And Lord*, he prayed, *protect them from the sun*. The heat inside the closed compartment of packed humanity would be unbearable—but for the hope of freedom.

The mother folded herself inside the wagon alongside the oldest son, head and feet jammed painfully against the wooden sides. The pharmacist was last, only inches of space remaining. Eyes wet with apprehension and gratitude, he embraced the American and, without complaint, climbed in on his side. Davidson covered him with sacking, completed the preparations, and forced the gate closed.

He looked up and down the dusty street. Seeing no one, he climbed back into the wagon seat. All was deserted, everyone hid behind closed doors and shuttered windows.

Then he saw atop a distant rooftop an armed Turk soldier shifting his weapon and watching his wagon come down the street to the outskirts of Harput. Davidson hoped he'd let the wagon pass without inspection. It was a common enough sight, the U.S. consulate wagon headed to the small farms for provisions.

But apparently it wasn't to be. The soldier signaled a rural gendarme, who stepped into the road in front of the wagon and put up a hand to halt the American.

"*Gun aydin*. Good morning," the gendarme said with an officious clip. Another gendarme, hands on hips, circled the wagon cautiously as if it were in imminent danger of exploding.

Davidson reined in the horse and inquired evenly, "*Ingilizce biliyor musununz?* Do you speak English?"

"*Evet*. Yes," the gendarme replied. "What business brings you out so early this day?"

"I go for vegetables," Davidson responded. "My kitchen staff became ill on the last load from Bilug the Onion Monger, and I go to settle with him."

Both gendarmes snorted in amusement. "Have you supped his wine made from fermented onions?" asked the first. "It will take your head in its hands and crush your skull as easily as a house of sugar."

For one terrifying moment, Davidson thought the gendarme circling to the rear of the wagon was going to crouch down and look up under the bed, but he swatted an insect from his leg instead. "No, I've not had the pleasure," said Davidson with a companionable laugh. "You good men have a splendid day. I will convey your kind thoughts to Bilug and ask him for a flask of onion poison to warm your appointed rounds." He made to snap the reins and leave.

"Let down the wagon gate," the chief gendarme loudly ordered. He betrayed no alarm, but neither did the tone in his voice countenance further delay.

"Certainly, if you feel that detaining a member of the United States diplomatic corps on his way to market is within Turkey's national interests." The sarcasm seemed not to register in the least.

Davidson stepped down, walked to the back of the wagon, and met the plainly distrustful stare of the second gendarme. With a prayer and a snap of the stays that held the gate closed, Davidson opened the back of the wagon.

A wormy pile of moldering onions released its dark stench in an eye-watering cloud of decay. Both policemen jumped back as if bitten.

"Eeeyi!" exclaimed the chief, face wrinkled in disgust. "That is fouler than beggar's waste! You tell Bilug that if he does not compensate you for this swill, he will personally have me to deal with. On your way, Mr. Davidson, and may you be upwind of this the whole trip!"

Davidson grinned helplessly and resumed his journey with a turn onto the road to Hamit Batu's safe house. He willed his nerves to calm themselves and only hoped the passengers behind the fetid onions did not gag to death before he got them to safety.

CHAPTER 12

Adrine knew something was amiss the moment she opened her eyes to a sun midway up the morning sky. The leaden weariness, the steady whine of hunger, the thick gauze of impending doom—all the same.

But when was the last time she had awakened emptied of sleep?

She leaned back on thin elbows and blinked first at the cloudless sky, then threw off the sacking that served as covering and peered over the edge of the stable roof. The street was empty of soldiers, guards, men. Some children played tag and swatted stones with sticks. Two Turkish women in veils were discussing the lack of fresh melons in wartime.

No men. No military. No deportation.

It was Easter, a day for miracles.

Adrine picked straw bits from the shapeless gray cloth, torn and thin, that formed her pitiful dress. She did not know why she took sudden care with her appearance.

She went to the knobs of her knees, careful not to sit improperly, even though there was no one to see her. *"When a girl dies, the ground must approve; while she lives, the public must approve!"* Grandmother again, ever ready with colorful basketfuls of social etiquette.

Grandmother. Sweet old woman. Gone.

Adrine smoothed and patted the dull muddle of her hair, eyes closed. "Almighty Father, as I have survived the dawn unmolested and rested, might I ask for another miracle or two? Will you help me bring Easter to my sisters?"

It was the most ridiculous of requests, and she glanced about anxiously to ensure no one else had heard the foolish words. The streets were as empty as before.

She grew angry with herself. "Faith is expecting the unexpected." As if God didn't know. "God can do anything." Was this a prayer or a lecture?

Agitated, she got to her feet, swayed a moment, then paced the small patch of rooftop. She almost stepped into a small plate of *manti*.

Adrine blinked as if to clear away the mirage. The meat dumplings remained. She stooped and brought the little plate to her nose. Two lumps of heaven stayed put and gave off a sweet aroma. She touched them with her tongue. They touched back. She gulped them down and missed them immediately. She should have been kinder to her taste buds. Rolled the miracle meat around on her tongue. Now they, too, were gone.

But if Easter manna, then Easter anything was possible!

She examined the pretty plate, its blue border, its roundness and glazed finish. It had been a very long time since admiration had been part of her morning. Adrine permitted herself a small smile, murmured a quick amen, and hurried down the ladder, missing the last rung and falling into the arms of Kenan's mother.

"I am Sosi Emre and this is your Easter," greeted the washerwoman, grinning son in tow. "Happy Easter, Adrine Tevian!"

Adrine's eyes welled with tears.

She hugged Kenan and touched Sosi's lined cheek with a trembling hand. The woman wore a bright yellow and peach wrap that was the prettiest sight Adrine had seen in months. "You are God's own miracle," she whispered. "The dumplings?"

Sosi nodded. "The dress is a good color for today?"

Adrine took a deep breath. "Oh yes. Good color. Will you help me spread Easter joy?"

"I told you yesterday we have an Easter to observe," Sosi replied. "What do we do?"

"We are like the two Marys of the Bible. Come, let us run and tell His disciples that He is alive!"

The puzzled look on the older woman's face delighted Adrine. "You can start"—she laughed, a strong new desire to live bubbling up from deep within—"by telling me why I'm still alive!"

But Sosi kept her in suspense while they made the rounds of the Turkish woman's friends and shopkeepers who proved surprisingly generous while Ozal and his legion were sleeping off a long night. They even looked upon the Armenian woman with some pity and clucked sympathetically at her servitude to the arrogant Ozal.

Along the way, the two "Marys" accumulated three circles of flat bread, two tomatoes, two cucumbers, a bottle of olives, a small pot of honey, a chunk of badly molded goat cheese, some cooked rice, a handful of fried eggplant, a cup of pistachios, three fistfuls of dried fruit, six zucchinis, a fresh onion, a quarter pail of milk, and a half pail of lamb broth. The rice came dear at the knotted hands of Zarene, the imposing carpet weaver who, with fiery eyes and high drama, argued and shouted and counted every kernel. Hands waving as fast as they flew with needle and thread, the immense Zarene swayed and cast her eyes at the ceiling in astonishment at these two women and their unholy request. Though Adrine could not fathom all the rapid Turkish with which Sosi negotiated, there was no mistaking the titanic struggle of wills. As they were leaving, Zarene, draped in a mountain of black cloth, stopped them and shot a last question at Sosi.

Sosi weighed the request with lips tightly pressed. Finally, her shoulders dropped and she nodded resignedly. A self-satisfied smile crossed the merchant woman's lips, and from her great sleeves she produced two slim leaves of mint and laid them atop the rice. A fragrant hint of mint wafted among the three women, and Adrine nearly fainted. How long since she'd tasted the pungent plant?

With the folds of their garments full, they hurried along the street toward the shabby, abandoned hotel where the Armenian women were housed, afraid they would be stopped and their treasure confiscated. They only spoke once.

"What was Zarene so upset about?" Adrine asked.

Sosi almost didn't answer. When the reply came at last, it was clear from the tone that protest would be futile. "I agreed to clean her shop once a week for a month in exchange for the mint. I will do it at night after Kenan falls asleep. The rice would be bland without mint. It is only four nights."

Adrine knew it was four eternities. The military camp workers slaved fourteen to sixteen hours a day and were drained when their heads lay down. And if the Armenian women were deported, extra work would fall to the Turkish workers.

But she said nothing. When Sosi's hand reached to lift the catch on the hotel entry, Adrine placed hers on top of the dry red fingers and pressed.

Stagnant air, redolent of unwashed bodies and sweat-soaked clothes, greeted them. A few coughed sickly, but so far no epidemic had invaded their fragile group.

The ragged women inside the dim expanse of lobby and adjacent deserted tea shop came quickly alive at news of an Easter feast. They excitedly questioned one another about why they had not been taken away that morning on the journey to the desert camps. Wild were their speculations.

"Wolves came in the night and ate our captors!" said one.

Another offered her theory: "The earth opened up, hell was exposed, and the devil took the demon soldiers home."

"That means we do not have long," said Adelina Yanikian with a laugh. "As soon as the devil smells Ozal's breath and feels the riding crop beneath his chin, the old deceiver will realize his folly and return them at once!" Her little boy pulled himself up by the hem of her dress and stood wide-eyed and wobbling before the colorful eatables that had just whisked through the door.

Sosi and Adrine organized a food brigade to cut and prepare the scanty rations for the Armenian women and children.

"It's not the first time God has stretched a few loaves and fish," said Adrine by way of blessing. She read the wariness and defeat permanently etched in her sisters' once beautiful, loving, laughing countenances. *Dear God, give them a few moments' peace.*

The women removed their sleeping bundles to the sides of the big room, long ago looted of its furnishings, where they slept on the hard dirty floor. They seated themselves in orderly rows in the now empty space. The brigade passed out slices of cucumber until they were gone, then resumed the distribution with slim wedges of tomato. Each precious item was thus apportioned with every effort made to see that each woman received two or three small but equal portions of something, especially if weak or with a child, and milk, water, or a source of juice to quench their thirst.

Adelina poured tiny portions of the available liquid while young Isabel Petrosian, eyes closed, face etched in the deep sadness of a lost love, rocked Adelina's son. "What thoughts have you this Easter sunrise?" asked Adrine gently. "Does your fine strong man live on here, inside?" Softly, she stroked Isabel's head, feeling guilt and sorrow for the brave young couple, one gone, one clinging to a dark and uncertain life.

The answer surprised her. "I think of the children," Isabel replied, kissing the cheek of the boy in her arms. "I've the heart of a parent but can have no children. When the war ends, there will be Armenian children who have no parents. I will be mother to as many as I can so that they may know love and grow up to marry and have babies in freedom."

Adrine kissed the top of the selfless girl's head. *Father, grant her wish*, she prayed.

Worn faces and haggard eyes searched Adrine's countenance for permission to eat. Those few who did not wait were soon halted by the quiet in the room.

Adrine felt the overpowering sense of a holy presence. It was so strong, she looked for it in the corners and out among the famished women who would not eat. But there was something else. Something she remembered from her childhood with the giggling cousins and Grandma Goose. She pictured the dear old hands giving out raisins and nuts and little balls of fragrant cheese. Slim young hands eagerly reached, but before anything was devoured, the spoiled children first traded for the most prized items.

"I'll air out your bed each day for a week if you give me your raisins."

"Here's six nuts for a ball of your cheese."

But no one in the hotel traded. Every item was a wonder.

The childish memory so amused her that Adrine laughed aloud. "Christ is risen from the dead!" She cried the Easter greeting of her youth.

"Blessed be the resurrection of Christ!" came the fervent response.

"Christ is risen from the dead!"

"Blessed be the resurrection of Christ!"

"Christ is risen from the dead!"

"Blessed be the resurrection of Christ!"

Each declaration and affirmation was stronger than the last, until at the third, the room reverberated with the healing words. And, as if there were no pain, no hunger, no extermination, the young women turned by ancient habit and kissed the hands of the few elders among them. The old women wept, and the young women joined them.

After a few minutes, Adrine stood and raised the bit of bread and the small ladle of milk she'd been given. She looked up and closed her eyes in thanks. "The body and blood of the Lord Jesus Christ! Take, eat and drink, in remembrance of the greatest sacrifice ever made!"

We need a priest. We need wine, she thought. *Don't we?*

Christ is our priest, and milk comes from grass, which comes from the ground as surely as grapes.

They ate in reverence, and all too quickly it was gone. Some gulped greedily, others savored each bite and rolled it over decayed teeth and gums to prolong the moment. One woman choked on her rice and was soundly thumped between the shoulder blades. A child cried for more.

Adrine whispered to four of the sturdier sisters who got up from their places and soon returned with crockery basins and cloths. Water was brought and poured.

Without saying a word, Adrine took a basin of water and set it at Sosi Emre's feet. The Turk woman started to protest, but Adrine waved it off. Tenderly, she removed her friend's shoes and those of little Kenan.

Adrine smiled at the pinched and swollen feet that had walked so many steps to fill a condemned woman's last hours with a little joy and dignity. Carefully, she lifted each foot in turn and bathed it gently in the water. "Let this be the water of health."

"Health be yours," rejoined the assembly in the old bathhouse custom of washing the feet of one's neighbor.

Sosi nodded and reached to do the same with the feet of Adrine Tevian. Adrine responded by washing the feet of the grinning Kenan.

Next, the feet of Isabel, the almost-bride. They smiled into each other's eyes, tears of awful pain streaming down their faces. Adrine hugged the girl's knees and lay her face in the lap of one so generous.

"No! Not mine!"

Suddenly, the gentle murmurs of concern and cries of goodwill ceased. All eyes turned to the woman who refused to be washed. Two elder women knelt on either side of Hannah Mereshian, reassuring her with their presence that it was all right, that they were bound by faith, and by faith they would find a way out of the horror—together.

Hannah, her face drawn in hard bitter lines, looked at the ceiling and let out a long, wretched moan. "Let the roof fall on me! I am not worthy that you should touch me. . . ." Her sobs trailed off like the last whimpers of a mortally wounded animal. She shrank back from the kind hands that held her and beat weakly against her face with balled fists.

"Shh, mother, shh," Adrine comforted. "What is this that you aren't worthy? Jesus the Christ washed the feet of—"

"I hated you all!" Hannah shrieked. "Each night in the dark I lay awake wishing there would be fewer of you in the morning. I opened my eyes each day and cursed the sight of you. W-why wouldn't you die? Each of you was a chipped and broken mirror in which I saw the depth of my own ruin. To look at you day after day becoming less and less was a reflection of what was happening to me, to my plans, to my future. You with children have someone to live for and to busy yourselves with! I have none. They vanished in the night. I awoke one cold morning and they were gone. I had to ask if I had ever given birth!" A wail of abject sorrow tore from the broken woman, and she went limp. The elders gathered her in their arms and laid her carefully on an empty sleeping mat, unfurled by another. The old women lay down beside Hannah Mereshian and held her. The rest knew instinctively that the elder mothers would not leave her side until God saw fit to restore her.

Adrine scanned the drawn and somber faces in the room. She clasped worn hands prayerfully to her chest. "There is healing in these basins, sisters. Your hands become Christ's hands, and whether we live or die, we can walk on holy feet above the hatred and the evil. If we don't complete what we have begun, the Muslims will have their victory."

For the next hour, the women bathed one another's feet, the two basins passed from hand to hand. Some feet were bone thin and infected; most were sore and bug-bitten. Often, someone would empty the basins, draw fresh water, and the ritual would resume.

When Hannah revived, she felt their acceptance and tearfully consented to the foot washing.

It was worship. Symbolic and little that it was, it cheered them and reminded them of their worth in God's sight.

"Father God," Adrine prayed in a loud and grateful voice, "you are Jehovah Jireh, the Great Provider. You are the Father of Noah and his bride, his sons and their brides. This sad and bloody land was your choice for a new beginning, and not far from here is Mother Ararat where the ship of salvation landed. . . ."

"Father God, Father Noah, Mother Ararat . . ." softly chanted the women.

"Father God, we bless you and thank you for this communion meal and ask you to reward the kindness of all who added to our Easter rejoicing. We have no priests—they are all dead—but we have a High Priest who knows our pain, and by His stripes we are healed. We have hungered, but He has hungered more; we have been tortured, but He was tortured more; we are lonely and abandoned, but He was lonelier than we all. We ask you, Father, to protect us and give us strength no matter how dark it becomes. We are but weak daughters of the High and Mighty, People of the Book!"

One of the women stood and read from a portion of Scripture she kept carefully hidden beneath her clothing. " 'Blessed are you when people insult you, persecute you, and falsely say all kinds of evil against you because of me. Rejoice and be glad, because great is your reward in heaven.' "

"Rejoice! Rejoice!" The cries of the women filled the room.

"And, Father God, one thing more we ask of you," Adrine prayed, quieting the room. "Please convince Sosi Emre to explain to us the miracle that finds us in worship and not in the stinking company of Ozal's bullies!"

The women laughed at the unorthodox benediction and

clamored for an explanation from the washerwoman.

Sosi held up her hands to calm them before excitedly explaining the events of the previous night, breathlessly told her by the wife of the opium trader. They laughed when she strutted about like Tekke the gamecock and gasped when she described the dramatic facts surrounding the four horsemen. Adrine felt her heart race.

"What did they look like? What did they sound like? How did they state their business? Their exact words now, leave nothing out!" Could these men be the answer to her long-ago cry for help?

But when Sosi, eyes averted, told how Adrine and her sisters were the wager in the incredible challenge between man and fowl, the assembly disintegrated into an outburst of shock and outrage.

"Now we are traded like wheat or currency?"

"Worse than that. Grain and money at least have value!"

"Are we to become the common whores of conniving road bandits?"

"I say we attack them before they come lusting after us! And if Ozal is sleeping off a drunken carouse, let's stone him as well!"

Adrine, eyes ablaze, shattered a crockery basin against the wall. Every eye met her look. "The captain thinks we are disgusting, and Bolu Bergema, the escaped prisoner, *gambles* for us all with his sight and wins one hundred infidel prostitutes for his personal use and that of the brothers Mentese. Well, the *sisters* Armenian are no longer the property of brutal men.

"Prepare for travel, each of you. Let the cowards come for us on the road, in the open, before God and Allah-fearing Muslims. Not here behind sealed walls to be extinguished like vermin. Rise up, sisters, and walk with noble bearing into the arms of Jesus!"

With shouts of "Father God, bless us!" the women rushed for the doors.

"Do not do this, Adrine," Sosi pled. "They will hunt you down and slaughter you on the way. I beg of you, stay here, give them what they want and live a little longer. More than one miracle has occurred this day. Is it impossible to expect another?"

Adrine looked determinedly at her friend and stroked Kenan's soft cheek. "Then the miracle will follow us onto the road. I cannot bear to think of some thief or murderer putting his filthy hands all over me, thinking little more of me than the spit in his mouth. No, Sosi, pray for me but do not hinder me. Good-bye." She kissed the washerwoman on the forehead and ran from the barracks.

The Armenian women of Hekim Khan went to the road and instinctively turned south toward the Syrian detention camps. It was where their parents and husbands and children had gone.

They carried all they possessed in small bundles tucked beneath their arms.

"No, no! You are going the wrong way!"

They turned. Adrine Tevian stood alone in the road that pointed north and east. "There," she gestured. "To Mother Ararat and the mountain strongholds of the Fedayeen. To Uncle Christian. The rivers come from there. The snows come from there. The Ark is there. It is the source of new life and new beginnings. All that lies south is sand and death." She turned forward and strode through the streets of Hekim Khan.

Some of the women looked uncertainly at one another. Gradually, in twos and threes, all followed the lone figure northward.

CHAPTER 13

Tatul's heart raged within him. The unspeakable stench of two thousand decaying bodies was so thick upon the air, it was difficult to draw breath. He stood at the brink of a carnage so vile, it was all he could do to keep from flying at the captain of the Twelfth Army Corps of the Turkish army and hurl them both off the ledge. He would want to survive the fall long enough to ram Ozal's head deep into the rotting flesh of his victims. With hands strengthened by hatred, he would squeeze all but a flicker of life from the man, then pin his arms and legs while a vulture black as sin scissored Ozal's eyes from their sockets.

He wanted Neelam Ozal to know that living could be worse than dying.

"Gruesome, isn't it?" Ozal held a soiled yellow scarf over his nose and mouth. "This should teach Ottoman citizens not to turn on their benefactors." His eyes never left Bolu's face. They seemed to be sifting his every reaction for the truth behind it.

"Indeed," Tatul forced himself to say. He was Bolu Bergema, ex-prisoner and Turkish patriot. Forget that for a second, and he would be rendered powerless as goat droppings to save his people.

The lives of the Armenian women of Hekim Khan were in his hands.

A wave of putrefying gases wafted up from the pit. Tatul swayed dizzily on the rim of hell and gripped his sides. He shot a sideways glance at the captain, who crouched farther back from the edge as if from there the smell would float above and away and miss him altogether. *Or does he suspect me? Is he afraid to come too near the edge for fear I'll push him over? Oh, God, take my mind captive. Save me from my own venom.*

Tatul couldn't return to the city without Ozal. The Turks would never believe an accident of Ozal stumbling to his death or choking on the foul, air-sucking cloud radiating from the dead. The Turks would slaughter all the women because the Fox couldn't stomach the Valley of Death.

He felt again the last bone-crushing hug of the Black Wolf, and it gave him strength.

"They should never have massacred Allah's own," Tatul said, repeating the official Turkish claim that Russian-armed Armenians killed thousands of Turks, Kurds, and other Muslims in a purge of Eastern Anatolia.

"Agreed," said a muffled Ozal. "Their poison is lethal. To leave any alive is to risk the breeding of more assassins. Men, women, children—all must go. If the Arabs want them, the Arabs can have them!"

"You are so right, my Captain," Tatul said vehemently. "An Arab would sleep with a scorpion on the chance his sons might have tails that sting!"

Ozal laughed and idly flipped over a fig-sized rock with a finger. "You are right, Bolu Bergema. An Arab is not so particular when mating. I have known several that did not know until years later they had married their cattle."

On the outside, Tatul laughed. Inside, he loathed the perverse creature Ozal had become. He sat down on a boulder facing the captain and gripped the rough granite with hands that sought the madman's throat. His fingers could not be trusted. He forced them instead to dig into the hard, unyielding grit.

Ozal rose and surveyed the ravine of death. "Relocation was not meant to be punitive," he said. "They were to be paid rent for their vacated properties. They really brought this all down upon themselves." He spoke as if the Turk citizens rotting by the tens of thousands across Armenia were merely victims of a gross civil misunderstanding.

"Bravo, Captain. Outstanding! Only a learned Turk like yourself could, with a few carefully chosen words, turn a misdemeanor into a capital offense!" Tatul forced a mighty laugh and gave the captain an exaggerated wink.

Again Ozal's eyes searched his face, then apparently satisfied with what he saw, he laughed in return. "I think perhaps I should now fine them for polluting this garden land!"

Tatul laughed again but turned and bit his tongue. *Father! Mother! Little Haji, my brother! Think not ill of me. . . .*

Tatul the Fox fought the urge to slide a dagger from his boot, lean forward, and thrust the blade home between Ozal's ribs and into his black heart.

A hot wind stirred and with it came another wave of foul stink. Sand rained down their necks and stuck to the corners of their mouths. The vultures quarreled below and cast an occasional malevolent eye at the two living humans on the cliff.

Quite unexpectedly, Ozal's shoulders sagged. The soiled cloth slipped from his face, and he said, "It's a civil war of their own making. Though they are a distinct minority, they are murderous in their intent to have an Armenian state. We have a war to fight with Russia, and the opportunistic Armenians take advantage of our distraction and internally bleed us dry. Is that not treason?"

Tatul felt his nails crack and tear against the boulder. *Careful.* "It might seem that way, my Captain. Many Armenians of Byzantium welcomed the Seljuk conquest with thanks to God for rescue from Byzantine oppression. Did not the Seljuk Turks protect the Christian church and abolish the religious taxes? Sultan Melikshah treated the sons of Jesus very well. Some Armenian noble families were so impressed by the sultan's high character and charity that they voluntarily converted to Islam and joined the fight against Byzantium."

Tatul shifted uncomfortably. If the tales of conversions to paganism were half true—and the Turk telling was highly suspect—then those Armenians were not nobles but spiritual traitors. "And it is true that later the Ottoman rulers permitted the establishment of an Armenian patriarchate, which resulted in the immigration of thousands of Armenians from outlying regions. The Armenians prospered, to be sure, but used that prosperity to greatly strengthen the Ottoman Empire. They became the most able of bankers, merchants, industrialists, and government officials."

Tatul became dangerously caught up in the telling of his own proud history. How far the Turkey of today had fallen from the loftier ideals of the past! He felt too passionate and was not careful to see Ozal's countenance change from curiosity to resentment.

"In the last century, twenty-nine Armenians rose to the highest rank of pasha," he said. "Twenty-two others became ministers, including the ministers of foreign affairs—"

"Enough!" shouted Ozal, jumping to his feet. He stuck an accusatory riding crop in the younger man's face. "Do not defend betrayers to me! They used their positions of influence to undermine the sovereign state in a diabolical attempt to make the faithful of Allah pay with their lives!"

Tatul leaped up. "Do not misunderstand me, wise and honorable Captain. I merely admire that which is admirable, no matter the source. Surely you cannot deny the many rich and lofty contributions to Turkish heritage of Armenian art, culture, and music. Where is the political intrigue in that?"

Ozal raised the crop and slapped it hard against the palm of his hand. "Yes, so lofty were their poets that we've executed two hundred of them this year for seditious writings. Perhaps you know Varoujan and Siamanto?"

Tatul had not heard. To hear the names of such talented lyricists among the dead was a hard blow. He gulped but did not betray his pain. "Second-rate buffoons, both! I speak of Hovakim and Daniel Danielian who wrote of the creation and the wonders of this great land, of courage and honor, the good-hearted and the faithful." He bit the inside of his cheek, fought his emotions, and held back the tears that threatened to fall. He spit on the ground and flung a rock into the pit. "How will we ever recover from this slaughter?"

"If you mean the Ottoman spirit, the pride of Turkey, the human will to regenerate and move ahead, those are not dead, Bolu Bergema," Ozal replied flatly. "The Germans will not forsake us in our fight for justice and inviolate borders. Frankly, my dear former prisoner, you sound a great deal softer than the man whose eyeball was a peck away from landing in a gamecock's belly."

"You do me an injustice yourself, good Captain," Tatul demurred. He grinned at the Turk. "I wish to present more facets of my character than merely those shaped by prison swill. 'My world is stamped in colors new, my soul in silver stars of thought; O grant me shine of day and glow of night in which to paint a new world for all to hold.' "

"Danielian," Ozal said. "Second ballad."

"You see? You know it!" Tatul cried. "Art speaks not just to Armenian or Turk, but to human hearts. And it is my heart you're trying to read. I know you brought me here to test my thinking, did you not? To see, in fact, if I might actually be an Armenian rebel, perhaps even a reckless Fedayee who decided one bright afternoon to leave his mountain ramparts and stroll down to the plains to see—what?—how goes the war? How fares the price of rice? How many dead Armenians can pack a rail car?" The grin did not fade, but the dark eyes threw sparks.

Ozal smirked and visibly relaxed. "Of course I took you for a man of culture the moment I smelled your clothes soaked in horse sweat," he said sardonically, "and when I laid eyes on the muscle brothers who accompanied you to my gaming arena. Every pasha should travel in such elegant style and educated company."

Tatul chuckled and fought the sickening rumbles in his stomach. "If this little excursion to your private killing ground was meant to unmask me, it has, good Captain, it has. You wouldn't expect it of one who has had to live by his wits as I have had to do. The law has seldom understood the brigand's life. But hardened rogue that I am, I'm nevertheless appalled that you've been forced to this by a stubborn people who do not know how to live as guests. But that is my secret. I am too sensitive and easily upset by civil villainy."

The Turk officer sighed heavily. "Yes . . . yes. I sometimes wish I'd followed my father into the opium fields. Soldiering, like highway robbery, is little understood by either civilian or magistrate."

Tatul nodded understandingly and gestured at the dead. "You were able to recover sufficient valuables from among them to repay at least a portion of your trouble?"

Ozal sighed again. "By the time they've come this far, belongings of value are considerably less in number. They've already met with so great a collection of thieves, fugitives, police guards, dogs, and Kurds that they either have nothing or have become so expert in hiding jewelry that we have little choice but to bayonet them in two and dig it out of them."

He said it as routinely as if he were speaking of the dressing-out of a lamb for the evening meal.

Tatul clenched and unclenched his fists. If he sat there a moment longer, he would tear Ozal's tongue from his throat. "Well, my Captain, what have you next?" He arched his eyebrows and forced an eagerness into his handsome face.

"Hmmm," Ozal mused, giving a look that almost said he was beginning to like him. "I think now it is time to test both your stomach *and* your stamina!"

Tatul looked at him warily.

"Your *harem*, good man, your own private love slaves. Though I would never pollute myself with the body of an Armenian woman, I can appreciate the needs of a man who has been so long under lock and key. Come, let me take you to them. It is time they got to know you. While I cannot vouch for their scurvy condition, between them there must be a dozen or two that can still generate enough heat to warm the night chill."

Tatul forged ahead of Ozal to the road leading up out of the vale of carnage.

"Conserve your energy," Ozal called after him. "Your one hundred females are worn thin and good for nothing, but they might mount a concerted attack on your manhood. Best be ready for anything!"

Tatul moved farther ahead, not with any thought of violating his Armenian sisters, but to swiftly distance himself from murdered people and the slaughter of one man he might be powerless to prevent.

————

Ozal watched him go and smiled enviously. "Ah, youth," he muttered. The courageous Bolu Bergema really deserved a harem of vigorous Turkish concubines. But in war, one took what one could get. He thought of his scheming mother whose Armenian blood had left his invalid father and eight-year-old son to fend for themselves.

"Where did you say you were born?" he called after his companion.

"I didn't," came the reply. "But since you have asked, I was a boy in Mardin. My family were craftspeople, ornate wine jugs and weavings mostly."

That shouldn't be too difficult to verify, thought Ozal. *Bolu Bergema—clay shaper, wagon robber, prison inmate, poet—a truly complex figure. You had better not be lying to me.*

———

The Armenian remnant of Hekim Khan heard the thunder of horses' hooves long before the Turk regiment caught up to them.

"Be strong, sisters!" Adrine sang out.

"Be strong! Be brave!" the others admonished one another.

At the head of the straggling procession of patched and bedraggled humanity, Adrine squared her shoulders and sang in her grandmother's resonant voice: " 'Christ, my Christ, my heavenly shield, thy Word, thy Word, thy Truth I shall wield!' "

Back rang the cracked but sincere declaration: " 'Behold, believe, our crucified King; revived, alive, His hosannas ring!' "

The thunder bore down on the Easter parade and vibrated up from the ground into the bruised and wasted legs of the processioners like tuning forks of flesh and bone. One frail matron started sobbing.

"Courage, good women of Christ. Let not your hearts be troubled." Adrine was again like the tiny girl in the yard of Grandmother's house, teaching the geese to be faithful followers. "He has gone to prepare a place for us. He will come back and take us to be with Him that where He is, we may be also."

"Halt! Stop or you will be shot!" Twenty-five horsemen charged the women, knocking some to the ground, whipping at them with short leather thongs. Others took aim with their rifles.

" 'Christ, my Christ, my heavenly shield . . .' " Adrine was kicked from behind—a glancing blow off one shoulder—and fell forward to her knees. The rider was on her and pushed her face flat against the ground.

"Is this the way of the good Muslim soldier?" Adrine mocked. A heavy boot mashed the back of her head. Brave attempts to keep the hymn from dying were punctuated with screams and cries. Adrine strained to see what was happening and was wrenched to her feet by a dark young man she had never seen before. He looked at her—no, he looked *into* her— and she met his striking gaze and did not look away. He seemed spellbound by what he saw in return.

The sharp slap of flesh upon flesh broke the spell. Captain Ozal was administering Ottoman justice on a young girl whimpering and cringing against two hairy brutes who immobilized her arms.

"Mercy, Captain," the girl cried. "I renounce Jesus as Christ and do bow before you, servant of Muhammed, the Messenger of God. Muhammed came with the same authority as Moses and Jesus. Muhammed is the Seal of the Prophets, the last and final messenger from Allah." Ozal looked at the confessor with contempt and raised his hand above the woman's bloodied cheeks. His swing was arrested by Bolu Bergema's firm grip on his wrist. The rifles of Ozal's men turned on the man.

"Easy, my Captain," Bergema said with forced joviality. "I cannot do my lover's best with damaged goods!"

Ozal wrenched his hand free. "Do not touch me, thief!" he snarled, then saw that a crowd from town had gathered to watch the retrieval of the Armenian women. Ozal's manner experienced an immediate—and some later said *supernatural*— refinement.

"Lower your weapons, good warriors. Allah is One, the Eternal God. He begot none, nor was he begotten. None is equal to him." Ozal intoned the foundational belief of Islam as a blessing upon the convert. The woman fell to her knees and wept inconsolably, unable to look at the ashen faces of the other Armenian women.

"Behold her joy," Ozal beamed to the little crowd. "By this confession, she has saved herself for all eternity." He smiled benevolently down upon the woman sunk small in the sand by the side of the road. He reached down and took her hand. "Come, daughter, you must no longer live as the Christian livestock do, but rather take your place with the undefiled. Here, I give you to Zarene the carpet weaver, who will care for you until you find a good Turkish husband with whom to have children and thin that infidel blood that flows in your veins." The imposing woman in black, procurer of mint leaves, stepped forward.

"No!" Adrine Tevian eluded the soldiers and planted herself between Ozal, Zarene, and the weeping woman. "Her confession was falsely obtained under the threat of death. She is Christian born, Christian raised, and will a Christian die. You cannot have her!"

Adrine braced for the searing slice of a riding crop, but none came. Instead, a small hollow voice spoke up behind her. "I have made my confession before a company of witnesses and do not wish to recant. I have violated the law of God and am forgiven by Allah, who is more loving and kind than a mother to her dear ones." Never once did her eyes rise from the ground before her.

Ozal looked at Adrine Tevian with a mixture of pity and disgust. When he spoke, the volume was for all gathered, the flying spittle for her face alone. "Because of this one good woman's conversion, I choose not to punish you remaining whores of Jesus, despite your pathetic and unlawful attempt to desert.

"I must, as the pasha's representative in this unwashed hole, honor the terms of my wager to this bold lad who so foolishly entered my cockpit and nearly lost an eye. My philosophy is that a man may disown a woman, put her away for any manner of offense, but he is bound by duty to a gambling stake. Turn around now, you scabrous she-dogs, and I will for today continue to afford you the protection of the Turkish government. And in the future"—he paused and looked at Adrine in scorn—"in the future, you would be wise to be much more selective about where and in whom you place your trust and confidence. Now back to the camp. There is work to be done!"

"One moment, Captain." The young horseman with the dark eyes spoke loudly. "As you have noted, I won these women in a fair wager last night—actually, quite early this morning. . . ." He cast a knowing glance at the troops, who responded with ribald laughter.

Tatul stretched an eye open wide with the fingers of one hand and pointed to it with the index finger of the other. "No less than this fine eyepiece was at stake," he boasted, "and I, in a demonstration of unrivaled daring, did stare down the scrappiest gamecock in all Turkey. Many of the eyewitnesses present then are present now. I do believe that it is only a just clause in my winnings that I be allowed to illustrate for my newly gained harem what happens when they are disobedient to their master, as our good captain has so eloquently outlined."

Ozal looked angry at the interruption of his command but apparently saw the number of eyes staring back at him and thought better of it. He settled on amusement. "Well then, Bolu Bergema, what have you in mind?"

The name elicited a gasp from the sisters of Armenia. Bolu Bergema, gambler, criminal, who thought no more of them than to use them for a rash bet and soon for his own personal pleasure.

Tatul bowed expansively to the Turk officer. "I believe this punishment is worthy of you, good Captain. I want my harem to return to Hekim Khan . . . on their hands and knees!"

There was a surprised pause before Ozal roared his delight and the crowd burst into amazed chatter. And another brief pause before his men leveled their rifles, muzzles pointed at the breasts of the reluctant women. Adrine was the first to go down, her flashing eyes never leaving the satisfied smirk on Bolu Bergema's lips. Quickly the others followed her example. The Christians who had so determinedly paraded out of Hekim Khan in Easter triumph now returned creeping like insects.

Adrine burned with hatred toward Bolu Bergema.

A single tear spilled onto the bright Easter wrap of Sosi Emre, who held Kenan tightly in her arms and watched the humiliation.

Sosi set her child gently down and told him to follow. Slowly, she sank to her knees, then to all fours, and, gaze riveted ahead, began to crawl after the others.

Chapter 14

A door opened and slammed shut. A lone female in drab gray flattened against the door, wanting out. Packed earth felt cold against her dirt-encrusted bare feet. Her knees were bloody and scabbed.

The noon sun held no heat. It lanced the dimly lit room with six dusty shafts through six dirty narrow windows. In the far corner, body knifed into sections by shadow and light, he sat. Stool tipped back, shoulders against the wall, booted feet crossed and propped on top of a small chipped table on which resided an oil lamp turned down. Face, thighs, hands curtained in shadow. His bare chest rose and fell in slow, steady rhythm.

The only sound in the room was their breathing—his easy, hers ragged—and occasionally the distant sound of reduced city life.

And then another sound. Leather slapping flesh.

The sound of death.

The hands came into view and with them the riding crop. She was to be punished for her insurrection. He would use her, then cut her to ribbons with the crop. Many would hear her dying shrieks, but none would dare help.

She prayed to God to stop her heart.

The slapping ceased, and the riding crop thudded onto the tabletop. The booted feet dropped to the floor and the stool came level. A face suddenly loomed in light.

Bolu Bergema.

Her sharp intake of breath came from the shadows. The pale light against the door revealed the folds of a threadbare gown and a pair of abused feet. Her arms crossed. Thin hands gripped shoulders and steadied both.

"Step forward where I can see you," he commanded firmly but without threat. Slowly, she took two steps and was blinded by a shaft of light. Her frightened face looked ghostly pale.

"I asked for you," he said, as if paying her a compliment. "I asked for the one with backbone."

She said nothing. She could not.

He smiled warmly, but the set of his jaw and the flex of his muscles hinted at cockiness. "From what I've heard, this would be the first time in history you've had nothing to say."

Silence.

"I see. Then listen. You are to be my *bash kadin*, the head woman of my harem—"

"This country outlawed the harem in 1909 at the fall of Sultan Abdulhamid. Perhaps you were in prison and not informed." She half expected him to fling the riding crop at her head. But again he smiled, and the mustache, the thick curly black hair, the dark flashing eyes ... She shuddered at the thought of one of those expressive lights forever shut by a filthy barnyard bird.

And then she remembered that he was willing to risk an eye to feed his perverse sexual appetites, and she vowed he would lose another precious part of his anatomy before she would ever submit to his slavering.

"Ah, you do have a tongue after all," he said. "Perhaps you would do well to go back to holding it. In case the lesson has been lost on you, Armenians seem suddenly unprotected by Turkish law. Let me assure you that I am well aware of the reformers' attempts to abolish the age-old practice of couching. But no one asked if I thought it wise to abandon the kept women who have for so long been such a rich feature of our national heritage.

"Therefore, you will continue to look after the others as you do now, but you are to be ready at my beck and call night or day. I have not yet decided just how to divide you all between my men, the good brothers Mentese, but you, Adrine Tevian, shall be mine alone. I suspect a woman of your fire knows something of the finer arts of lovemaking, despite your inferior ancestry."

She took a menacing step forward, ruined nails digging little trenches in the palms of her hands, then remembered the precariousness of the moment. Her lip curled in disgust and rendered the rest of her dirt-smeared and matted visage all the more grotesque. "Yes, I have seen the sum total of what you know about art. Herding us back on our hands and knees was a magnificent display of your artistry. What have you planned for tonight's sport? Licking clean the hooves of your horses with our tongues?"

He laughed at her, throwing back his head and crowing at the ceiling. Fingers laced behind his head, he shamelessly exposed hairy underarms and a naked torso, letting her know the great gulf fixed between their stations in life and the utter contempt in which she was held. She was property of a common thief, slept on top of a smelly stable, and stole scraps from a Turkish stewpot. A far cry from the elegant merchant woman of her dreams, riding a private car to Berlin. Far from the wife of a good and honorable man who would not make a spectacle of his underarms when a lady was present.

Despite her fear and disdain, she could not stop herself. The goose, as Grandmother never tired of saying, was out of the pen. "You, Bolu Bergema, are nothing but a sexual forager, a beast without a brain that is forever in the grip of its appetites. If you were a man, you would find a way to mercifully end our pain."

Bergema folded his arms across his chest and snorted. "Yes, by Allah, I was thinking of weighting your necks with stones and drowning you in the river." He leaned forward and thumped the table with both fists. "That was not mercy you received from Ozal on the road today, you stupid, impulsive woman; that was Ozal ingratiating himself with the crowd. *I* demonstrated mercy by showing the captain that I could be as innovative as he when humiliating those too weak to hurt me. Until he's convinced I'm as cruel and arbitrary as anything the Young Turks can produce, you're about as safe as those rotting away in the hills all around you!" Angrily, he grabbed the riding crop in both hands as if to pull it in two.

Adrine ignored the voice of caution and laughed in scorn. "And for that we should thank you? We should trust in a common criminal with a demolished prison for a home? Oh, thank you for allowing me to crawl the road, perhaps the very road upon which the Great Bolu robbed and raped the innocent!"

The veins in his arms bulged and snaked from wrist to biceps. "You are a very foolish woman." The ice in the voice froze her bravado. He stood and stepped around the table, riding crop slapping against palm. She shrank back, afraid.

"Very foolish—and very brave," the icy voice continued. "That may afford us a chance, albeit a slim one."

She could make no sense of his words. Her own came tremulously. "You speak in riddles. Do what you came to do, mighty Bolu, but know this. Though you begin with a live woman, you shall finish with a dead one. I will not be your *bash kadin*. In the name of Christ, I have been set free."

She shut her eyes and waited for his hands.

"So, Fark, what do you think of this red-hot Armenian ember?"

"Ah, friend, she is too much garlic and onion, too little cloves and cinnamon." Adrine's eyes flew open at the soft, high-pitched response. A third person in the room stepped from total shadow against the wall. He was short and compact, his small head topped by a green felt hat like an inverted pail. His clothes were worn thin by war, but his pants and jacket with high collar and long waist billowed in the style of the royal courts of old. He peered at her from an old patrician face that was smooth and closed from knowing too much.

"This is not some slave market where I am to be handled and ogled like meat for the evening meal. Please, sir, take your revolting eyes from me!"

The little man called Fark sucked air noisily, and his eyes winked shut. "She is certain to get us all killed. She is correct about one thing, however. She is not fit for the slave emporiums. The hair needs a coating of butter to restore its sheen; the breasts want training to overcome a decisive downward tilt; and the mouth warrants an ocean of discipline and a general good scrubbing. Even then, I doubt she would render a feather's worth of pleasure. I say kill her and save the rest. This one is trouble." One eye popped open, thought better of it, and popped closed again.

Adrine moaned in shock and dropped to her knees, the

still-raw wounds shooting with pain. She was no more human than Giaour the cat. Half dead already, she was judged unfit even to satisfy a convict's lust.

"Stand, Adrine Tevian, and allow me to introduce one of your own. Fark is an Armenian eunuch who served ably during the last of Abdulhamid's reign. He championed the constitution and the abolition of polygamy, even though he himself had been permanently maimed for love of God. We owe him a debt."

"I owe him nothing!" said Adrine in a voice as dead as she felt. "Where are the women this toad of the sultan liberated, whom not even their relatives came to claim? Those harem girls were a part of a past everyone wanted to bury, and so they were discarded to end their days as outcasts."

Fark's eyes winked open. "I, too, am an outcast, young woman. I have lived here in Hekim Khan in obscurity ever since leaving the harem, my high voice a brand of condemnation. No one will hire me for fear of appearing sympathetic to the old ways. You forget that it was I who prevented merchants and fortune-tellers from entering the harem at will. It was I who insisted on Christian teachers for the women when the sultan wanted to prohibit their employment to save his precious social order. I am old, and with any good fortune I will be dead before this interminable conversation ends."

Adrine stood and looked from the old eunuch to the convict and back again. She gave a short burst of laughter, almost a bark of derision. "I have not met a man of real influence since my father was killed by road robbers. Perhaps your friends slit his throat, Bolu. Perhaps even *you* river!"

He came at her, the riding crop raised as if to strike. She cringed and waited for the blow.

Instead, he pinned her against the wall, the heat of his anger radiant against her skin. Then he pushed back, grabbed her hand, and forced the riding crop into it. "For you," he said. "You'll only get one chance to use it. Choose well." Then he gripped her arm, yanked open the door, and muscled her into the blinding daylight.

She cried and stumbled, shoved ahead of Bergema, the harsh grip on her thin elbow a painful fire. *Where is he taking me? My God, no, not the river . . . yes, the river!*

Down the bank they plunged. Thickets of brambles scratched trails of red across his chest and back. Her feet bled freely, new wounds joining old.

Adrine half fell into the water and he waded in after her, water filling his boots and staining his dusty pants dark.

He's going to drown me! she thought.

Wildly she fought his grip and tore at his arms, but with a strength borne of milking cows and climbing mountains, he easily grabbed her hair and flung her head and shoulders beneath the noisy flow.

But instead of holding her there until her breath gave way and her lungs filled with water, he knelt, yanked her face out of the water, and held her gasping across his thigh. With a slender shaving of lye soap he'd fished from a pocket, he vigorously massaged her scalp until sufficient lather formed. She cried and choked and ranted, but to no avail. All ten strong fingers worked the burrs and dirt and snarls from the disheveled nest, then plunged the head under for a good rinse.

Up she spluttered for a second head soaping and a sorely needed face washing. By now spectators had gathered along the top of the bank, laughing and pointing at the sight below. Fark stood apart, a short, dark anomaly. The little eunuch did not invite their curiosity.

"Hold still!" Bolu shouted. The cleaner Adrine Tevian became, the more slippery she was to hang on to. But the emaciated camp slave was swiftly tiring.

Soon she lay still across his lap, feet soaking in the healing waters. She hadn't touched the river since . . . since the day the little boy came floating by, except to quickly fetch water for the camp. It surprised and saddened her that she didn't feel much revulsion, much of any feeling at the memory of the murdered family bobbing in the shallows. She was gradually embracing death.

Gentle fingers worked through the tangles. Whenever they encountered an especially matted portion, they stopped and carefully separated hair from foreign matter, then proceeded again to comb and stroke away months of neglect. Despite her confusion and fear, Adrine lay still and, God help her, enjoyed the attention.

"Listen to me," he said low, for her ears only. "Show no

149

reaction, for all eyes are upon us. Make it appear as if you have been tamed"—he felt her stiffen—"although I hasten to add that we both know that could not be further from the truth."

She cocked one eye open and saw that he was smiling. He had a very nice smile, not at all lecherous. He was, in fact, quite pleasant in his features.

Her eyes strayed to the angry scarlet welts on his bare skin and wondered if they hurt, then wondered why she wondered.

"They're nothing," he said, and she quickly looked away. "The sky is my roof, the earth my bed. I am quite used to minor injuries such as these."

Again she stiffened. *What does he mean, the sky is his roof? A prisoner rarely sees the sky.*

"I am not who I pretend to be. For now I think it's best that is all you know. But whatever transpires in the next hours, I ask you to trust in me. The pretense cannot long survive, and every passing hour the peril grows. Now I want to give you a sign that your prayers have, in part, been answered. Do as I say, or we shall all be dead. Eyes closed." Despite a thousand warring questions, she closed her eyes.

He rummaged a moment in a small leather pouch at his waist. "Now kiss me," he half mumbled, "and look like you welcome it."

Hand behind her back, he raised her face to his. "Now open your eyes." She did, and just before their lips met, she spied the pale white wafer protruding from his lips.

Her mind exploded with the implications. The communion wafer now disintegrating in her mouth meant God had heard her prayers, and this was her brother in Christ! It was a shock, a joy beyond measure.

Dare she hope? Was she held now in the arms of a legend?

But what did the warm, yielding lips mean? The strong arms holding her with so tender a compassion? The electrical charge that wrapped every cell of her being in its voltage? Suddenly her body surged with more life than it had at birth. Here, by the river of death in a city of death . . .

He stroked her hair back, hesitant, and as if suddenly in command, jumped to his feet and roughly pulled her to hers.

"Now, my moist little hag," he said loud enough to be heard aboard a freighter in the distant Mediterranean, "now

I can see that you once, in fact, were a woman and, with a diet of honey and caviar, you could be again. That, and Allah's divine intervention!"

The crowd laughed and watched the brash young horseman from the north drag Adrine Tevian back up the bank. It was obvious to all but the youngest that he intended to take her off to a private place and begin to sample the fruit of his bone-weary harem.

A bellowing was heard afar off. The cursed Captain Ozal was venting another complaint and fast making his way to the river. "Before the dignitaries arrive," Bolu Bergema announced, and again the crowd laughed, glad to have so effusive and interesting a newcomer in their midst, "I declare your experiment a huge success. Armenians when not fed become as irritable as the rest of us!" The crowd snickered and smirked, and Adrine fought the rising resentment in her heart, the sick, helpless feeling of the taunted and the weak. *"Whatever transpires in the next hours, I ask you to trust in me."* She did not know if she could.

"I wish to propose a perplexity to my little camel to see if her brain is as far gone as the flesh from her body. It is an old harem riddle and quite appropriate to her present situation. Here it is, my little beast of burden: What is yellow like saffron and reads like the Qur'an? Either you'll solve this riddle, or tonight your death will take you."

Adrine trembled. The awful crowd, openly grinning at her plight, leaned in to hear the answer. Some of them were the same women who had supplied bits of food for the Easter sunrise service. Now they were back in step with the times, heavily veiled against any evil challenge to their sanctimony. Those males who knew the answer, or thought they did, made wise eyes at those who scratched ignorantly for the solution.

Bolu Bergema circled Adrine like a cobra, head bobbing and weaving, leaning forward for the kill.

He struck without warning, and several in the crowd stumbled back in shock. He kissed his way from her shoulder to her ear and whispered a clipped, quiet, *"Gold!* The answer is gold!"

Bergema jumped back. Ozal's fury drew nigh. "Time enough! What is your answer, my skinny little poppy seed?"

"G-Gold," she stammered.

"What was that?" Bergema mocked, cupping a hand behind one ear. "The river made you *cold*? Perhaps all that dirt was what really kept you warm!"

More laughter. "*Gold!*" she screamed. "The answer is *gold!*"

Bergema looked amazed. "That's it, my brilliant little egg yolk! With one word you have cheated Azrael, the angel of death, and now Eros, the god of love, awaits. . . ."

Another roar of accusation and Ozal was upon them, uniform askew, lips rimed with spittle. "My crop! Which of you miserable dogs has my crop?!"

Adrine thought she might faint. The hard bulge of the riding crop was lost in the folds of her dress, but she thought it must shout its very whereabouts. She felt Bergema's hard arms envelop her and practically drag her away from the confrontation. She had but one chance to use the crop, he'd said, and she'd better make it count. Adrine shuddered.

"Come, my queen, to our seaside villa, and let me show you how this miserable dog treats his harem." He turned to the fuming Ozal. "I assure you, Captain, I will closely inspect my property for any signs of a tool for whipping horses. Should I find anything, may I use it before its return?"

Despite his anger, Ozal had to smile at the lusty youngster. "By all means, Bolu, whip away."

"But what if she converts before I'm through?"

"Then your harem will again be reduced by one."

"At this rate, I shall be out of a harem in three days at most."

"A blessed sacrifice."

"My loss, Allah's gain?"

"Exactly."

Bolu Bergema gave a little wave and left the captain to his stormy interrogation. The captain called after him, "Do not forget in your eagerness to bed that unfortunate creature that in the Ottoman Empire, a wife's place, even in paradise, is beneath the soles of her husband's feet."

"Oh no, good Captain," Bergema shouted without turning around, "it is the very first lesson we shall cover together!"

Fark kept pace with the horseman and harem girl from a distance, gliding from pillar to post with practiced ease. He was near seventy and quite used to remaining invisible.

He thought it ironic that it was possible to be a Christian eunuch, but not a Muslim eunuch. Islam prohibited castration. As a consequence, most Turkish harem keepers had been black eunuchs from Africa or white eunuchs from Armenia. He was a self-inflicted eunuch and remembered how at thirteen he had crushed himself between two rocks as a means of achieving chastity. That single selfless act had been in keeping with the Book. "For there are eunuchs which were so born from their mothers' wombs," wrote Matthew the tax collector, "and there are eunuchs which were made eunuchs by men, *and there are eunuchs which made themselves eunuchs for the kingdom of heaven's sake.*" He was the latter, and that made him feel closer to God.

But he knew many eunuchs who were that way because other men had chosen to mutilate them to serve other ends. Young boys ripped from their mothers and brutally altered forever, sentenced to a life of caged servitude in a surreal world of forbidden sex and unnatural relations. It was that deranged realm of self-indulgent sultans, polygamy, and murderous intrigue that he had worked so hard to end—and to escape.

Now he was called back into service for one last grand rescue of a miserable harem indeed.

Fark snorted. The chances of the reckless scheme succeeding—Fedayeen, or no Fedayeen—were thinner than turtles' hair.

CHAPTER 15

The thumb screws tightened, and with each crushing twist, the shrieks of agony intensified.

With every scream, Consul Frank Davidson flinched and wished to be anywhere else. On stage, the tortured Cavaradossi writhed and panted and begged heaven for mercy. Each prayer earned another twist of the screws.

And this is only the first act, thought Davidson. *Chronologically, we shall yet be treated to attempted rape, suicide, murder, execution, and more suicide.* He shifted uncomfortably in his seat at the Harput Opera and glowered. There wasn't enough money in all the U.S. Treasury to keep him in this godforsaken hovel of a city.

His companion noticed the American's agitation. "Puccini is popular precisely *because* he's vulgar," the sweating Neman Beyit said in a loud nasal rasp. "Wagner is too mystical, Strauss too pretentious. To be any good, and here I speak symbolically, opera must have blood all over the stage."

If it is Turkish opera, thought Davidson darkly. Art imitating life. The real-life bodies of the tortured and slaughtered littered the landscape while government officials studied the finer points of physical abuse through their opera glasses.

Steady, Davidson old boy. You are of far more use to the Armenians present than absent. Upon his request, word had come from Hamit Batu that the pharmacist and his family had safely fallen into the arms of Uncle Christian. *That sweet little girl made it.* By God's grace, it was a higher calling than any other he'd received in Uncle Sam's employ. Now, if he could only get the Neskarian family out, that would make room for the Anjikians. They were an old couple with two nieces who badly needed medical care for asthma. The times grew riskier by the day. He would have to bribe more Turks to look the other way—some of the consulate furnishings would make appropriate "gifts." Two silver candlesticks could ransom a family of six. Besides, Ambassador Morgenthau's plate was too full to take inventory until the war ended.

He looked beside him at the *vali*, the provincial governor of the district, and marveled that the portly official didn't leap from the seat. Beyit was a mass of unease—unease with his position, his clothes, his skin—and continually in motion. He pulled at his cuffs, strained at his collar, tugged at his lips, sucked his teeth, cleared his throat with maddening regularity, and worried his considerable nose with either thumb or, if in an especially high state of excitement, both.

And judging by the buttons popping from his frayed uniform, he tapped a secret source of rich foods unknown to most of Harput's inhabitants, including much of the region's armed forces.

The agonized cries of *Tosca*'s brave hero rattled the mostly empty seats of the theater. Both of Beyit's thumbs were busy. The singers were third rate at best, but the governor turned to Davidson with eyes streaming tears.

"What are you looking at, good consul?" he asked with a sad, all-embracing smile. "Be glad it is not Russian opera. Then you would see vulgar!"

Davidson nodded curtly and closed his eyes. Here was a man of such tender emotion he cried at a fictional performance by an amateur theatrical company. Yet on any given day this very same man would, without a twinge of regret, order the cruel eviction of a thousand human beings, most of whom would perish from violence or hardship. Was Beyit really just a pawn of the central government at Constantinople? Was he the least of all evils, and far better than most?

Then Davidson remembered that increasingly his diplomatic communiqués and official U.S. State Department pouches were intercepted, tampered with, delayed, and in some cases discarded in blatant violation of international law. The twitching, weeping man beside him was responsible. Increasingly, too, Davidson sent strongly worded mail to the embassy in Constantinople urging the U.S. contingent to keep the pressure on the Turks to allow free and unmolested communication flow. Unimpeded mail between Harput and the capital now took three weeks each way, more than twice the time it took a letter to travel between Constantinople and New York before the war. Telegrams, at three times the cost, rarely arrived the same week they were sent. Bribery did nothing but line the pockets of thieves. It was an outrage.

And, he thought, *exactly what I deserve for accepting a post so remote as to require a solid month's travel by horseback, rail, and wagon to reach the seaport at Constantinople. How easily arranged my "disappearance" could be!*

The singers tripped on through *Tosca,* but Davidson was not with them.

"Bravissimo! Bravissimo!" Beyit leapt to his feet and applauded as the curtain rang down on the first act. "Such courage in the face of so much adversity. Splendid! Splendid! Frank, are you listening? If I had not gone into public service, I would have managed an opera house—the Teatro Lirico in Milan or the Teatro Costanzi in Roma. Do you know that eighty years ago there was one opera seat for every ten people living in Genoa?"

Davidson did not know. Nor care. He missed his wife, the captivating Catharine Carman of Wading River, New York. He could feel her in his arms, the soft way she brushed her hand against his whenever he read the paper and she thought he should be paying attention to her. He missed the way she made kissing sounds at the robins at the window feeder. He even missed the way she brewed tea, and cupped his chin and pecked his nose each time she poured. She would make lovely sense of his life again, and with her he could speak the French, German, Russian, and Spanish he'd learned as a student guiding tours in Europe, before teaching her. A cosmopolitan education was all but useless in rural Turkey.

He also missed his father, who'd died of cancer the previous year. The pewter Civil War chess set belonging to Henry Davidson was now the son's, but the reason for playing chess at all no longer lived. *I should have been there, war or no war.* The consul had been on his way home to see the elder Davidson via the southern overland route to Beirut. However, by the time he reached Egypt to set sail, the war had begun. The cable from his chief in Washington was terse and unyielding: "War declared. Stop. Leave canceled. Stop. Return Harput. Stop." His mother had gone to live with her sister in Rochester. They'd not been as close as he and his father. Nor did she play chess.

"I want the American schools reopened," Davidson said aloud.

Neman Beyit, an animated mix of tugs and adjustments, added a quick chew to the back of his hand. "Out of the question. The closings are necessary to prevent the spread of typhus among the people."

There was little typhus in the city, but the American school buildings made excellent military depots. "Two days," Davidson said. "I want them open in two days."

"For someone who has no official standing in Turkey since the abrogation of the capitulations, your wants are of no concern to me," Beyit replied with a stretch of his neck and a yank on his cuffs. "Did I tell you of the old Armenian gentleman I met on the road last evening?"

"Three days or I contact the embassy," Davidson answered, eyes shut. "No, you did not tell me of the old Armenian gentleman."

"Ambassador Morgenthau has a new puppy," Beyit mused. "The man uses your frequent dispatches about our behavior to train the puppy where to make water.

"But I digress. The old Armenian gentleman was driving a wagon with a long wooden box in the back. I asked him to state his business. He replied that he was taking his coffin to the deportation camps in the south. While he did not fault us for making the trip necessary, he was concerned that a shortage of wood in the desert would prevent his burial. Whatever happened, he did not wish to be cremated. I naturally relieved him of his wagon but allowed him to keep the box."

Davidson glanced at the perpetually moving administrator and marveled at the man's ignorance. He had made a monstrous joke of misfortune rather than change it, as was within his power to do. Did he even know what he was doing?

"If Ambassador Morgenthau waits upon the Turkish mail for my dispatches to paper his puppy, his floors must be wet all the time. Tell me, Neman, what use have you for all those dispatches?"

Beyit gave a mighty suck on his teeth that, had the roots been any shorter, would have pulled them from his head. "You must have me confused with the mayor, Consul Davidson. Official United States correspondence is inviolate."

"Then how do you explain the breaking of the American seals placed on the doors of the American schools you commandeered?"

The throat clearing went on for a ten full seconds. "As Molière said, 'It is an odd calling to make decent people laugh.' Yours is an odd calling, my friend."

"And it was your Puccini who said, 'I have more heart than mind.' It is to your heart that I appeal, good vali, as my friend. Open the schools."

With one giant calming, all Beyit's tics called a brief halt. He looked in astonishment at the American consul who had quoted the vali's beloved Puccini. He sighed melodramatically. "I do hate to see American citizens and their dependents suffer. If you invite me home with you now for a drink and some of that American chocolate, I will reopen the schools in two days."

Davidson tried not to reveal his panic. "Now, Neman? Surely you mean after the final curtain? Yes, yes, by all means come along to the consulate once this whole miserable mess concludes." He grinned weakly.

Governor Beyit stood up and made for the exit. "This is the fourth time this week I have seen *Tosca*, but I have not been to the consulate in a fortnight. Suddenly, I thirst like a herd of steamy camels. Fill the pool with cognac, my friend, I wish to go for an evening's swim."

It was Beyit's way of harassing Davidson, of trying to catch him in the act of smuggling Armenians. Though he himself for some unexplained reason had allowed several hundred Christians to flee across the river and make their way to Russia unpursued, he persisted in making little surprise raids on the consulate under the pretext of urgent business or casual visits. And Davidson was under no illusions that if the vali discovered undocumented Armenians on the premises, he would have them removed and shot without a second thought in order to save face and prove his importance.

"How is Fetty the maid?" A look of desire washed over the governor's features. "Is it true what I hear, that she desires to go to America to study law?" He was highly enamored of the liberated Muslim girl who would have nothing to do with him and hid whenever he entered the consulate. Davidson did not force her to serve the governor against her will.

"She is well and eager as ever to study judicial process. She wants nothing more than to help the new Turkey come into the twentieth century." *And to abolish female slavery once and for all.* He dared not state Fetty's real reason for seeking the American's help in getting to the West. She was a bright girl with no more than a third-grade education, thanks to Old World repression. Her father was killed at the Russian front, and Davidson just about had her mother, a secret suffragette herself, talked into permitting her daughter to emigrate.

But if for any reason Davidson was unable to sound the warning, Fetty might well lose her benefactor before the night was over.

The only reason Davidson agreed to join Beyit at his interminable operas was because that was the one certain time when the governor was thoroughly occupied. Beyit hated having his operas disturbed, even by the most urgent matters of state, and always stayed riveted to every note to the very end. Some went on for three hours or more and provided an ideal block of time to free a group of refugees living in the attic, feed them, and transport them to the "railroad" that whisked them over the river and well along the highway to Uncle Christian's.

Tonight was no exception. There were thirty Armenian adults and six or eight children preparing to leave the consulate. To return this early would be certain disaster. These precious ones to whom he had pledged his personal protection would be sitting ducks. He might even be ordered to leave the country for illegal conduct, and that would be the end of so many hopes.

He felt again the pressure of a little hand in the small of his back. It haunted his every waking moment and prevented him from falling asleep. It awoke him in the predawn watch, and he would lie awake praying for the little children.

A crowd of urchins squatting about the governor's carriage scattered at their approach, then swarmed about the two men as they attempted to board. "Back, you little devils!" shouted Beyit, swinging at their heads and slapping away their outstretched hands. "Back, or I'll tear your eyes out!"

Davidson, stuck behind the governor's attempts to cram his bulk through the carriage doors, urgently searched the milling mob until his eyes alighted on one boy. The lad looked questioningly at the American, who reached out a hand and quickly whispered something in the youth's left ear. The boy bolted down the street toward the consulate, naked heels flying.

Go, Garabed, go. Davidson jammed himself in after the governor. *Go warn the others.* "Well, Neman, I must say you are full of surprises tonight. Usually you have at least one of the children beaten as an example."

"Halt!" the governor shouted to the carriage driver.

The carriage jolted to a stop and with it the excited clamoring of the children. This had never happened before. Davidson blanched. "I . . . I was merely making conversation."

Beyit gave him a curiously studied look, and Davidson felt a chill in the man's eyes that made his skin crawl. He tried looking pleasant, but Beyit wasn't twitching. It was not a good sign.

Beyit bellied from the carriage and bellowed to a half-dozen rural gendarmes to round up the children. When they had most of the youngsters corralled, they dragged them over to the carriage. "These devils are in violation of the street ordinance that prohibits the loitering of people with no business in the vicinity. I hereby sentence them to—" He paused for dramatic effect, a large smile spreading from one thick ear to the other—"to attend the remainder of the opera!" With that he slammed the carriage door and, narrowly missing Davidson's toes, collapsed back into his seat.

"That," he said, showing enormous pleasure, "will teach them!"

As they pulled away, Beyit was humming the Scarpia motif that accompanied the secret police baron in Puccini's *Tosca*.

Feet flying, Garabed raced for the soft yellow lights that blazed from every window in the U.S. Consulate. He did not want the Armenians to die. He had played with some of them and thought they were nice. He liked to be a lookout for the kind American who gave him money and candy and asked if his mother was well.

A blurred movement to his left. A streak from the shadows.

The hard wooden stick smashed against the back of his legs, and Garabed fell facedown in the rough street. He tried to rise, but the stick caught him in the back of the head, and he lay still, barely conscious, hoping his assailants wouldn't notice. He strained to hear them walk away, but all he heard was a thin young voice crying for its mother. He thought he recognized the voice. It was the last thought he had.

The jangling carriage of Vali Neman Beyit rolled unseeing past the still body of the Turkish street urchin who was a friend of Armenians. The horses and their consignment made for the main gate of the U.S. Consulate. Inside the carriage, one man thirsted for cognac; the other prayed for a miracle.

CHAPTER 16

Beyit smacked his lips and set the carriage to jiggling with his twitchings. "Ah, cognac, the only thing the Russians ever got right!"

"The French, the *French*," Davidson muttered under his breath, thinking now would be the ideal time for the end of the world.

The alarmed face of the stable keeper greeted them at the consulate gate. Davidson rudely shoved his way out the door first. Anxious glances raced between him and Gomidas Kerkorian, the stable keeper. Gomidas, an amateur boxer born in the Old City sector of Ankara, had learned piano and pugilism during a two-year stay with relatives in upstate New York. The burly Armenian had two things in his favor: an American passport and biceps the size of cannonballs. One of them bore the tattoo of a well-knuckled fist coming straight for the viewer's nose. Sleeves kept rolled to his shoulders, Gomidas made certain no one missed the fist. No one but the blind and the foolish did.

While the governor's broad posterior maneuvered slowly backward out of the carriage like an ocean liner feeling for the dock, the stable keeper gestured wildly at his employer. Though unspoken, the meaning of the frantic waving was clear: *You are not due now. There is contraband in the open. We are doomed!*

"Is anything amiss?" asked Beyit, even before he turned around to face them. The question, far from conveying genuine concern, brimmed with amusement.

How the governor enjoyed these impromptu visits.

"Ah, no, no, my friend, of course not. When are you going

162

to defend Turkey's honor with a suitable opponent for Gomidas here?" Davidson smiled expansively and gave the bicep with the fist an admiring squeeze.

Curtains in a lighted upper window fell back in place. The movement did not escape Neman Beyit's notice. He studied the upper floor carefully, eyes darting from window to window, room to room. "Goliath, you mean. As soon as my David returns from herding the sheep, we shall gather at the Valley of Elah and bring the giant down." In his expansiveness, Beyit's twitchings were reduced to an occasional cuff straightening and the odd neck stretch.

"Marquis of Queensbury rules specifically state no slingshots," babbled Davidson, looking wildly about for something, anything, with which to distract and detain the governor long enough for those inside to conceal the contraband.

"Yes, yes . . ." Beyit mumbled distractedly, moving off toward the living quarters without invitation. And then he was gone.

The governor made straight for the culinary door and burst in upon a scene of frantic preparations lit by hissing gas lamps. Two flour-covered cooks and three sweating kitchen maids were kneading great mounds of dough and wrapping fresh loaves and packing them into baskets. Windows were coated in steam; iron ovens radiated heat into the too hot space; the rich aroma of flaky new bread demanded, and got, the appreciation of every nose in the room.

A breathless Davidson and Kerkorian tried in vain to find their way to the center of the room, but Beyit plugged their passage. "An occasion?" he growled at the startled kitchen staff.

"Your visits are always an excuse to bake," Davidson called from behind the governor. "What we don't need for your repast is kept for the following week."

Beyit patted his ample girth. "Now that you make mention, I am famished. Puccini increases the appetite. Some of that fig spread, if you please, and the peach compote would work in harmony with the bread." He smacked his lips and tugged them for good measure. "I do not suppose you would have a small basin of the *tarhana* soup in storage?" The thick chowder of yogurt, tomatoes, peppers, and onions was a Beyit passion. His little eyes twinkled hungrily.

"For you, my unrepentant opera buff, it is a pleasure to comply." Davidson made a sharp face at the nearest maid and scowled. *Quit standing there with your mouth open, woman, and set the governor a place!* He arched his eyebrows and jerked his head toward the table. As if she'd been slapped, the maid jumped to and knocked over a crock of milk in the process.

Davidson fired the others another stern look, and they, too, leapt into action. "Sit here, Neman my friend, here at the kitchen table. The dining room has not yet been properly laid."

"Thank you, no, Frank, my brother," the governor replied with exaggerated warmth. He made for the door connecting the kitchen with the main hall where most parties of state were held before the war, and where now there was more likely to be a gathering of illegal Armenians preparing for travel. "Bring it to me in the dining hall. Has a fire been lit?" His hand reached for the doorknob.

"Cognac!" Davidson called out. Beyit stopped and looked thirstily at the American.

"You must take a glass with you. Nothing better for soup than first a firm foundation of brandy and conviviality! Besides, the *tarhana* will take time to warm."

Beyit saw the sense in that and reentered the kitchen. The others visibly relaxed, abandoned the baking, and set about fulfilling the governor's every wish.

"That will be all, Gomidas. Thank you for seeing us to the house." As much as Davidson hated to see those biceps vanish into the night, it would be inappropriate for the stable hand to remain. The boxer hesitated, but Davidson waved him out.

Despite one glass of cognac quickly gone and another instantly before him, Beyit's scratching and adjusting returned. He stood without touching the second glass and walked toward the door to the dining room. "Too hot in here," he grumbled. "Too hot."

Before Davidson could think of what to say to stop him, Beyit grabbed the door handle and gave it a nasty twist.

The dining room was uninhabited.

A fire crackled in the hearth and cast its golden flame over the room. The only other light was from three kerosene lamps turned low, one on the mantel, one on a small, highly polished Steinway piano to the far right of the fireplace, and one in the center of the elegant table for eighteen that graced the space beneath a hand-cut crystal chandelier from Bavaria. Electric lighting had not yet reached remote Harput, but the fixtures had.

"Charming, charming, always so charming," Beyit huffed, nostrils testing the air for foreign aromas, eyes darting to the corners of the room in search of movement. His search ended at the open door on the opposite side of the room through which was clearly seen the foot of the back stairs leading to the upper quarters. "Once this bad business is concluded, you shall have to invite the powers at Constantinople to dine. Maybe then they will deign to leave their opium pipes long enough to visit me and assess the real needs of poor Harput."

"Governor Beyit, by the power vested in me under the flag of the sovereign nation of the United States of America, I decree that you are forbidden from railing against the Young Turks for the remainder of the evening," said Davidson with a joviality he did not feel. *Why does the blasted man examine every inch of the room as if feeling for explosives?*

"The Ottoman Parliament pays far too much attention to the Armenian problem, and far too little to Turkish woe. Talaat Pasha, our minister of the interior, swears the Armenians won't recover for fifty years. How nice. Turkey won't recover for a hundred!" He headed for the stairs.

Davidson urgently signaled to the servant girls to go around to the front stairs and run up to warn the others. They fled as if pursued by demons.

He trotted after the surprisingly quick governor and waved an empty glass at him. "Now, Neman, if you persist, I shall be forced to get on the subject of Woodrow Wilson. Neman, wait! Where are you going, man?"

The sound of footfalls, someone running, someone falling, were distinctly heard on the ceiling above. Beyit paused on the lowest step and cocked an ear at the noise. "Rats?" A smile, wicked and triumphant, spread over the broad landscape of his face. He squared his shoulders, grabbed the banister, and started up.

Out of the dark beyond the stairs came a hand with a butterfly's touch. It settled on Beyit's big beefy one and was followed by the lithe form of Fetty, the serving girl and bedroom maid. She kept her eyes down and averted in the Muslim way, and the governor was thoroughly smitten.

Davidson was amazed and relieved. Though she loathed the fat official, instinctively she knew the extreme danger he posed.

"See how quickly she takes to your American customs, so forward, so unrepressed. Good riddance to the veil, I say. Yes, my child, what is it?" He placed his other hand over the top of hers and held it tightly, moist eyes seeming to memorize the tilt of her head, the curve of her throat, the play of firelight in her hair. Though one of his eyelids twitched uncontrollably, all else was still.

"I wonder would you be so kind as to allow me to accompany you on the piano?"

Beyit caught his breath. He looked as though she had promised him her hand in marriage and the national treasury in dowry. He seemed awash in her light, transported by modest, brief glimpses of her face, and stunned that she could play the piano—or any instrument, for that matter. Muslim girls traditionally took a very limited role in anything except cooking, cleaning, and bearing children. Turkish girls, like their nation, were rapidly changing.

Davidson recovered from his surprise. Fetty had worked hard at the keyboard under the tutelage of Gomidas the boxer, whose mother had wanted him to be a concert pianist. Though his strongly muscled hands were no longer ideal for the finer points of a Beethoven sonata, he worked hard to pass his talent on. Fetty had proved an apt student.

"Oh yes, Neman, please do us the honor of singing some of your favorite arias!" Davidson exclaimed, leading the big man back into the dining room. The last thing in the world he wanted was to hear Beyit's foghorn voice mangle the language of love. No, the *last* thing he wanted was for those hunted Armenians upstairs to be caught and executed. Davidson could put up with an assault on his eardrums for one evening. It served him right for getting into this mess. With a last anxious glance up the stairs, he reached for the cognac bottle and freshened Beyit's glass.

His eye fastened on a four-inch gold cross with a broken chain lying at the edge of the blue and gold carpet. It was the cross of St. Andrew, the first-called disciple of Jesus, the patron saint of the Armenians. It was in the form of an X because tradition claimed Andrew was crucified on an X-shaped cross. One of the refugees must have dropped it.

"What are you doing, Davidson? Don't be so aloof," Beyit called across the room. "Little Fetty and I don't mind if you join us, do we?"

Fetty set her lips in a tight line and sat at the piano, playing a quiet little scale exercise that was a Gomidas favorite. The governor flipped through the collection of operatic pieces and settled on *La Traviata*.

Davidson kicked the cross under the carpet and glanced sharply at Beyit. He needn't have worried. The beefy official, enraptured with his proximity to Fetty, was barely in the room.

"I so *love* Metastasio. Now *there* was a poet! Few captured human emotion such as he. *Amore! Amore!* Some of his dramas were set to music by more than forty composers. Ah, the beauty of sentiment, the elegance of the language of which he was capable! Some find him tiresome, but not I. Love ruled by reason. *That* was Metastasio. Don't you agree?"

Davidson sighed. "No lectures, Neman. Just *sing*!"

Beyit, dripping with infatuation for the gentle Fetty, acted wounded. "Americans! Always in a hurry!" He cleared his throat once because he had to, twice for emphasis, and three times because he was Neman Beyit. "Violetta, act 1, *La Traviata*," he announced. He took a giant breath that sucked in half the oxygen in the room, then let go in his best Turkish Italian:

Godiam, fugace e rapido
e il gaudio dell'amore;
e un fior che nasce e muore,
ne piu si puo goder!

Davidson's eyes watered, not from Fetty's delicate playing but from Beyit's nasal attempts to punch the high notes, breaking instead into a falsetto that was laughable. Only the thought of those many upstairs who faced certain death escaping Turkish tyranny kept Davidson sober-faced. Fetty, bless her heart, played on with a magical intensity.

Beyit tapped her shoulder. "Repeat," he said. She did and the governor sang the English translation:

> Let us enjoy;
> love's bliss flies swiftly by;
> it is a flower that blossoms and dies,
> then can no longer be enjoyed!

Davidson nearly lost his composure when Beyit slurred "flower" and pronounced "blossoms" *bloo-sums*, but he busied himself with cognac and glasses, and the governor seemed not to notice.

From there, Fetty shocked them both and requested act 1 of *La Bohème*. They listened to her sweetly sing of a cynical love:

> *L'amore e un caminetto che sciupa troppo,*
> *dove l'uomo e fascina*
> *e la donna l'alare;*
> *l'uno brucia in un soffio*
> *e l'altro sta a guardare.*

> Love is a little stove that consumes too much fuel,
> where the man does the burning
> and the woman the lighting;
> the one burns in an instant
> and the other stands and watches.

At the end, her traditional upbringing prevailed. In the stunned silence of the two males, she blushed and ran from the room. They called and coaxed her back, and Davidson studied her closely for any sign that this was simply a part of a very cleverly orchestrated ruse deliberately meant to flummox the governor. Either way, it worked.

"Fetty, child," the large man demurred, again holding her hand like a love-struck troll in an ancient fairy tale. "Fetty, I believe Rodolfo and Marcello sang of love in such a way only because they never knew one as fair as you. There is far more hope and romance in *Tosca*. Though it is not scheduled to perform tomorrow evening, if I say it performs, it will perform. Might you—"

He was interrupted by the sudden appearance of a kitchen maid who looked astonished to see Fetty at the keyboard, even more so to see her hand in the governor's.

"Yes?" Davidson said.

"Mr. Davidson, sir," the girl spoke softly, "the soup is heated to serve. May we bring it in?"

Davidson practically slammed the keyboard cover and, with a mannerly sweep of his arm, bade the governor be seated.

Fetty knew her place and slipped quietly from the room.

The servants entered with a steaming tureen of soup, two cutting boards burdened with soft loaves of newly baked bread, a dish of goat's butter, and little ceramic pots of peaches and fig. Neman Beyit stared forlornly at the place where he last saw Fetty. He waited until the other servants left for the kitchen and closed the door behind them. When the men were alone, he asked, "This once, Frank, couldn't you make an exception?"

"I think not, Neman. She has her studies and is quite strong-willed enough without letting her eat with the guests. She plays and sings beautifully, though, don't you agree?"

Neman nodded sadly, bones brittle with *amore*. "I could insist. You know that."

Davidson looked at his pale visitor and smiled ever so slightly. "Yes, and you know as well as I that a woman like Fetty would hate you from that day forward. Let us give thanks," he said and stood. Beyit hesitated a moment and reluctantly rose. The prayer was an especially loud and fervent one, of sufficient length to allow time for the guests of the consulate to descend the back stairs and slip quickly out the back entrance into the four waiting wagons.

When Davidson had said the amens, three of them, and resumed his seat, Beyit gave him a peevish glare. "You addressed the divine being as God the Father," barked the governor. "It is against the laws of heaven to be so familiar with the Supreme One. How arrogant to suppose that a man who relieves himself in the morning and belches throughout the day is related in any way to the Holy God."

"Ah, my dear Neman, you forget that in the Holy Scriptures God himself calls us His children, and Jesus himself was a man like as we. If God in His infinite wisdom made us, and into creation we came belching, then it only follows that God made the belch!"

It was by no means an elegant apologetic but adequate under the circumstances. Beyit, however, rolled his eyes and stared with increased suspicion as a third, and then a fourth wagon rolled past the dining room window.

"Where do so many empty wagons travel at so late an hour?" Beyit said warily. He started to rise.

"Good Governor!" Davidson exclaimed. "What think you of the sinking of the *Lusitania*?" He attempted to change the subject but was fully prepared to upend the tureen of soup into Beyit's ample lap if need be.

Governor Beyit sniffed and fell back into his chair. "You have the brain of a camel, Frank. That sinking came nearly a year ago."

"Yes, I know, but one hundred twenty-eight American lives were lost, and I fear it will bring us into the war. Germany seems to ignore Wilson's protests, and German saboteurs have been found in New York City. Really, Neman, your country needs to get out of bed with the Germans or suffer terrible retribution. I mean, several German consulate officials and German-Americans have already been implicated—"

"Frank."

Davidson stopped the prattle and looked at the stern mountain of Turk rule for the Harput District.

Beyit tapped the tips of his fingers together, then tugged at his nose. "The wagons?"

Davidson took a deep breath. "They travel to Malatya. Sasun Heyd, the stationmaster for the railroad, wired that he has procured some difficult items for us. More cognac, my friend, some liqueur for baking and candy making, clothes from Europe, and more bandages and antiseptic for your hospitals! Good news?" Placating the Turks was a tiresome business. Davidson hoped he hadn't overdone it.

"*Four* wagons, good consul?" Beyit swept outstretched arms toward the ceiling in amazement. "I can't get a package of Egyptian cigarettes, but you, a foreign guest in my district, can provision four wagonloads of fancy goods when most Americans have had the good sense to leave the country? What business is there left for you to conduct but to ride your circuit and bury what dead you find? *Four* wagons?"

"One I must leave in payment for Heyd's resourcefulness," Davidson patiently explained, hearing the sound of the retreating wagons no more. "Another provides added protection on the highway against brigands and Kurds. You know the dangers. And my business, as if you need reminding, includes entertaining half the Turk officiate from here to Stamboul!"

"But venture out at night? Why not wait until morning?"

"Neman! You sour the soup with your incessant questioning. I have the police chief and a full contingent of his gendarmery here tomorrow evening and need those supplies by midday at the very latest. Now, will you give your attention to the meal and stop interrogating the grocery list?" Frank smiled to put an end to it, but Beyit was loaded with one more question.

"Then you won't mind if I send an inspector to ensure the wagons meet compliance and are safe to travel?"

The American dropped his spoon with a watery plop and fell back against the chair with a sigh. This answer was the trickiest. He must betray nothing. "Suit yourself, Neman. Call out the troops and send them charging after the deadly bandage wagons. But just think about how much cognac and chocolates will disappear once your inspectors learn of the cargo they go to retrieve. The fewer ears—"

"—the more cheers," Beyit finished with a defeated look. "Perhaps Fetty could serve the dessert?"

"I think not, Governor. Fetty has gone to bed by now. Eat up!"

The rest of the meal was uneventful. The lovelorn governor would not touch the cognac, his soup grew cold, and he twitched not at all.

Davidson, however, ate with renewed gusto, and when the soup ran out, called for more. That finished, he pushed back his chair and stood to his feet. "Bring your drink, Governor, and let's retire to the upstairs parlor. A fine fire has been laid and the backgammon board awaits, freshly polished just this afternoon. Best two out of three matches. If you win, you may end the evening with an Italian lullaby. If I win, I am excused from a week's worth of bad opera. Agreed?"

Neman Beyit looked up at his friend and smiled ruefully. "In your country, Negroes are lynched, striking mine workers are shot, and children lose their thumbs in industrial accidents every day. Why in the face of your own miseries have you come to save Turkey from hers?"

For the first time in his life, Frank Davidson was at a genuine loss for words.

CHAPTER 17

We are not human.

The ugly thought stabbed Tatul Sarafian's brain like a stiff straw through the ear. He tossed and sweated in the sour hay, the pungent scent of manure and cowhide in his hair, his clothes, his soul.

For a few blissful minutes he was home again in Erzurum, coaxing the cows in a soothing whisper to fill his pail with the creamy contents of their bulging udders. He felt again the warm comfort of their musky hides soft against his face where he rested and dreamed. The sound of roughage pulverized between bovine teeth, the tug of the teats in his strong fingers, the rhythmic spurts of fresh milk striking into the rising contents of the pail with explosions of foamy white—these told him that he was alive and human after all.

You are not human.

That is what the Turks wanted the Armenians to believe. That is what the Turks wanted to believe. Humiliation, emasculation, loss of property, loss of ownership, loss of humanity. Cut the cord of family unity. Desecrate the national house of worship. Destroy the cultural fabric. Eliminate the ethnic distinctions. Bury the Armenian national character in order to preserve the "purity" of the Turkish one.

Armenia was a boil to be lanced. It was a Turk's patriotic duty, a religious imperative, an economic necessity to drive the Armenian snakes out of the land. The means to that end—the rapings, burnings, knifings, and torturings—were simply being done on *animals*, after all.

Tatul flopped on his back and stared at the dark cob-webbed ceiling above, past the wooden garden stakes bundled in the rafters, past the hanging scythes and forgotten planting tools, right through the ceiling itself—to her. Had all trust been starved out of her? Did she fully understand who he was?

And what difference did it make if she did? Just how were he and the three brothers Mentese supposed to steal a hundred and thirty women and children from beneath the noses of the mad Captain Neelam Ozal and the garrison at Hekim Khan? He had discarded several half-formed ideas and was no closer to a solution. So thoughtlessly had he assured Kevork Chavoush, the Black Wolf, that the mission was safe in his tender, inexperienced hands. All swagger then, all danger now.

Trust in me.

That day at the river he'd taken Adrine Tevian's last slender thread of hope and had woven it into the colorful garment of the Fedayeen. *Trust in me.* He had slipped the communion host into her mouth because it was a burning ember in his own. And with lips blistered by doubt and wavering faith, he had kissed her with a promise of more.

Trust in me.

What the Fedayeen took for courage and invincibility was in him arrogance. He had maybe fooled the Black Wolf, the mountain brothers, the Turks of Hekim Khan, but no man can fool himself for long. It was one thing to stare down a chicken, quite another to pit four poorly armed Armenians against the murderers and thieves of Ozal's army.

He felt again her river-slippery hair, her warm lips chafed but respondent, the thudding of her heart against his. For all the grime and wear, the lack of food and comfort, she was a comely woman and good to hold. He smiled for the hundredth time at her bravery, yet wondered if her fire, like his, was many parts desperate bravado.

He had seen the flicker of despair in her beautiful almond eyes. He would do anything to take it away. Anything.

Tatul ached for his family and their ways. Little Haji. Grandfather. Old Aunt Serpouhi. Mother. Father Serop. The singing of the special hymn on the Feast of the Holy Translators of the Bible, called *Vork Zartaretzin* by his people. "O you who masterfully bedecked the wisdom of the living letters to lead the flock of the New Israel . . ."

Angrily, Tatul flipped onto his stomach and punched the

hay. His fist struck something hard, and he fished it out. Ozal's riding crop. It must have held too many bad memories for her, and she hid it there.

Tatul sighed in frustration and stuck the crop in his waistband. The Armenian flock had placed its hope in the New Jerusalem, and now untold numbers of them lay rotting. He had to stop trusting in legends and reach down deep inside himself for some new cunning. The day of hymn singing was long past. Every minute was survival. The People of the Book, what was left of them, had better become People of the Sword, or they would soon be little more than a footnote in history.

He lay awake wondering if Adrine lay awake thinking of him. And then her face became the face of his beloved Veron. He groaned at the terrible loss of one so dear and fair. The bile of vengeance rose within, and he thought to peel Ozal alive and feed the strips to the hungry dogs.

The Lord gives and the Lord takes away again. Blessed . . . no, not blessed. BRUTAL be the name of the Lord! Well, Tatul could be brutal too.

Sarafian tossed onto his back again and lay still. "You must not let them turn you into one of them," he whispered into the dark. He thought of how earlier that evening he and two of the brothers had retired to their own quarters with six of the Armenian women, two for each of the horsemen. The third brother kept guard with one of Ozal's men over the remaining women. If it was suggested that they sample the wares while the master of the harem was away, Tatul knew Ashkhen Mentese would pull an enormous blade from a leg sheath, spit on it, and rub it with great care. Ozal's man would take the hint or regret it. The men about to sample the harem had laughed lecherously and assured everyone within earshot that that night they would plant the seeds of righteous Islam into filthy infidel receptacles.

"If a child grows, what shall we call it?" Ozal hurled back, and his men roared.

"Anything if a boy. Nothing if a girl!" Tatul the Fox shouted back, and Ozal's men roared louder still.

To the trembling women's astonishment, once the door was securely closed and barred, they were led instead to beds of clean straw matting and told to rest. The strangers from the north wrapped themselves in blankets and lay back against the door.

Late into the night, long after prying ears had abandoned listening at the door for sounds of revelry from within the harem, Tatul had slipped outside for air and had come here to the stable to be near Adrine.

He had let slide the steely reserve, the careful discipline drilled into him by the furry Wolf. A cry for help, a call to duty, and yet he became so easily disabled in his mission not by the enemy, but by a poor, half-starved victim he had sworn to do all within his power to save. And there was a huge roomful of them and their children counting on him not to be distracted, not to betray the many for the love of one.

Love?

Whatever it was, he'd admitted to it. Now he could whip himself raw for ten minutes, then return to a focused mission and begin to plan how they were to escape the talons of death into which he'd so brashly ridden.

But thoughts of her would not let him focus, would not allow him to think of anyone—or anything—but her. How still she had lain across his lap. How relaxed she had appeared. Content, that was it. *Content* to let him massage her scalp and loosen her worries. . . .

Ah, she was so good to hold. He heard a stirring above on the roof and slowly raised his arms toward the ceiling and smiled.

———

The incessant drum of insect wings awoke her.

It had been long hours before sleep came. Bolu Bergema had stayed inside with her until dark, ending speculation in anyone's mind that the reckless stranger had at long last tamed the brazen serving girl. So much for the appearance of evil, she thought ruefully. *What reputation I have left wouldn't fill a thimble.*

They said nothing, but something unspoken filled the air between them. She caught him looking at her, and each time she did, he quickly looked away or shifted his position. But not before she read an intense interest in his eyes and a masculine kindness that caused a weakness in her sore knees.

Two hours after dark, he'd ordered one of the brothers to escort her to the stable. En route they had passed but two whispered discussions, accompanied by knowing glances in her direction. Despite herself, she had tossed her newly washed hair defiantly and straightened her spine.

Now she lay beneath the shimmering stars long after midnight and felt again the river wash over her, the strong hands and soap bring new life to the itching, tortured scalp.

But more than that, much more than that, she tasted again the warm yielding lips, saw again the dance of life in the dark smiling eyes. She wrapped her arms around herself and pretended they were muscled like his, the hands sure and gentle like his, the embrace as full of as much promise and hope and love as she could squeeze into it.

She released herself with a jerk. There, she'd acknowledged what it all boiled down to in her senseless, ridiculous brain. "I am such a soft-headed schoolgirl," she scolded the night. But the more she thought about that, the more it pleased her. Here in the midst of a living hell, she had been stirred by a mysterious rider who had resurrected her emotions, however silly.

Then she saw just how absurd that thought was. She was charmed by what? A swindler? Forger? Slayer? She knew nothing of the man except he pretended to be all manner of things. What could she believe? If Bolu Bergema was the answer to her prayers, then God was a friend of thieves and scoundrels.

Adrine gasped at her insolence toward heaven. Here she lay on a filthy stable roof, weak, used, the property of one madman, on loan to another, less than two miles from at least one mass grave, clinging to her own life, however slender, by some unseen grace, and she dared to spit invective at God Almighty, her one and only true hope. Perhaps her mind had snapped. Perhaps she should throw herself from the roof and break her neck. Perhaps she should pray to die.

She wished he were near. He could sleep at the other end of the roof and . . . watch. Grandmother Goose would say that right now she needed a lot of watching.

Numb with self-loathing, Adrine dozed at last.

She awoke to the drumming of insect wings, filled with a darkening dread.

There, in a corner of the stable roof upon which she slept, a moth was caught, tangled in the straw she'd piled up behind her as windbreak. She tried ignoring the beating of wings, but the sound and the dread grew until they filled her head with fear.

Adrine crawled closer, and there in the stark light of the moon, she saw a magnificent pale pink moth locked in the bite of a hardy brown barn spider.

Wings frantically beat a pink blur, but the hoary spider's grip was sure. The struggle intensified, the larger moth nearly able to lift off with the spider attached.

To Adrine's horror, the moth rapidly collapsed from the inside, its juices sucked into the mouth of the spider so securely fastened to the victim's soft abdomen.

As the magnificent pink moth deflated, the barn spider swelled. The wing beats slowed, the now empty husk of what was beautiful still impaled in the jaws of its bloated predator.

Adrine burst into tears and pushed back from the horror. The Turks would stop at nothing until they'd sucked her people dry. She was going to die, and the world would pay no more attention than it did at the passing of a moth.

A voice like fine silk called softly from the dark. "Mistress Tevian, are you all right?"

It was he! But where? Thrill and despair fought over her remains, and for the life of her, she could not answer the man's question.

————

Neelam Ozal awoke just before dawn and called in his night watchmen.

"Did anything transpire between the visitors and the Armenian whores after I retired?" he barked.

"No, Captain, not that we could determine. All was still as the grave."

Ozal didn't doubt the guardian buffoons drank half the night away and would have missed the cosmic mating of Zeus and Hera. But it didn't feel right. That nothing had apparently gone on meant that something truly odd was going on.

He needed to take his foul temper for a ride. It was clear from all reports that either Bolu Bergema and his companions were the quietest lovers ever born, or, for whatever reasons, they had entered the chambers of Eros with a rooster's intentions but were immediately put to sleep by some unnatural spell.

On the grave of Muhammed, he would know the reason why! Bergema's whole approach to the winning of a harem was most curious, and Ozal's suspicious streak ran a mile deep. Any other lecherous convict just released from prison would have instantly embarked on a three-day orgy and emerged on his belly without an ounce of amorous intentions left.

Top it off with the fact the riding whip was still missing. It was like losing a constant companion and aide. Nothing commanded respect faster than a flick of its wicked tip.

The captain rode north, flanked by two of his largest and best-armed escorts. The times were perilous, and one had to err on the side of caution.

Reports had come through that another wave of refugees from Sivas was streaming southeast and due to pass through Hekim Khan before midafternoon. He wanted to convince the Turk drovers to bypass Hekim Khan. They could encamp on the riverbank at the wide flat above the ferry landing, then when they decamped, loop east of the city, then south to rejoin the main road. As long as those stinking priests across the river stayed in their monastery and the deportees were gone by noon the next day, there should be little incident. The last thing the city needed was imported vermin or a typhus-cholera epidemic. The saddlebags he carried contained wine, opium, and foodstuffs with which to seal agreements. For the refugees, he carried nothing but good advice: Keep moving and do not cause trouble.

For good measure, he had sent a speed rider on ahead to the Kurd camps in the Bingol Mountains to learn more of the legendary Bolu Bergema, thus far a legend only by the testimony of the man's own lips.

The chill was barely off the morning when dust, kicked up by hundreds of shuffling feet, was seen rolling toward Ozal and his men. The next sign was audible. An eerie kind of lowing as of sickly cattle. Then a sight most startling. At the front of the procession were easily more than three hundred naked women and girls—mostly old, lame, and ravaged after six days in the relentless sun. Hair flowing in the air like wild beasts, they stumbled forward reaching out their hands, arms thin as sticks, and emitted that awful inhuman lowing.

Ozal and his men reeled back from the terrifying sight and kicked their horses farther on to three mounted guards.

"Why are those women in that condition?" Ozal demanded.

The guards looked uneasily at one another. They'd seen a few officers unhinged by the mass killings. There was a cold edge to this one. Cooperation seemed best for the moment. "We were set upon by a band of renegade Kurds near Malatya," replied a tall, rail-thin guard with a wandering eye. "We were carrying more than a thousand women then and thought it best to make peace by offering the females. They would have taken them anyway. The Kurds selected the best-looking ones. The women fought back, but it was no use. About two hundred died. The old, the ugly, and the immature they stripped and took their clothes. That is what's left of them."

Ahead, commotion brought the procession to a halt. The only wagon in the caravan sat buried in a rut up to its axle, one of the two mules that pulled it coming up lame. Another bone-thin man, threadbare and tattered but having retained a shred of his former dignity, stepped down from the driver's seat upon which a wide-eyed boy and girl sat. He ran an affectionate hand over the animal in distress. "Now, Poghos," he clucked, "this is no way to do. We need to get to our new home. We must hurry so the paintings do not become dirty and cracked."

"Paintings?" Ozal snapped, fury making his chin and lower lip twitch. "What paintings?"

"My life's work," the man said. "I am Alexander Stepanian, painter of oils. Would you like to see them?"

"Yes, yes," Ozal sneered. "Do let us have a showing." The moaning, teetering Armenian remnant of Sivas were drawn to the wagon like winter-starved birds to seed.

The man ignored the captain's tone. With large pride made enormous by the pathetic surroundings, he untied the canvas protecting his precious output and extracted a thick gilt frame. His short, slight build visibly swelled inches when with a flourish he turned the painting around for all to see.

It was a highly accomplished rendering of the magnificent fortress and pleasure palace near Mount Ararat, built in the fourteenth century to guard the Silk Route. In a stunning view from high on an adjacent hillside, it showed in beautiful detail the outer and inner courtyards, flamboyant doorways, the harem and men's quarters, all done in a satisfying blend of Seljuk, Ottoman, Armenian, Georgian, and Persian architectural styles. Stepanian had captured the rich brick reds, umbers, and creams with skilled eye and hand. He was quite obviously a master craftsman.

All eyes that could still see were riveted on the painting. The lowing ceased. The famished refugees swayed wearily on their feet, tatters waving in the breeze, but now they had something to feast upon. They devoured the colors, the play of light, the angles and curves of the palace. For one very brief moment, they were transported there in a reprieve of gracious hues and subtle strokes. As long as they looked, the stay of execution held.

Alexander Stepanian, creator in oils, beamed with the pleasure his art brought the audience. His applause was in their silence.

"Have you permission to transport these paintings?"

Ozal's question brought a look of stark fear to Stepanian's face. "I . . . I thought I was free under official deportation orders to take what movable property I desired."

"A matter of interpretation," Ozal countered. "You seem better off than the others, less wasted. How do we know you do not surreptitiously sell a painting here, a painting there along the route, something strictly forbidden in the articles of capitulation?"

"Oh no!" the little artist protested. "I would never sell one of my paintings under . . . um . . . these conditions. Please, if I seem less depressed than the others, to suffer less from deterioration, perhaps it is my outlook. An artist knows hardship, rejection, misunderstanding, financial times of feast and famine. His is a heart and a hope not easily broken." He looked earnestly at Ozal and, as if sensing a great, coiled danger in the man, made an offer. "Please, Captain, I would be honored if you took one of my paintings for your personal collection.

That is not selling, that is giving. Here, take this one. It is one of my favorites, but I can tell that you admire it as well."

Ozal took the painting of the palace, studied it, and smiled an enormous smile. The painter, obviously relieved, added a grand smile of his own.

Without looking up, Ozal issued a command. "Unload the wagon."

The other men on horseback dismounted. Shocked and confused, the artist rushed to Ozal's side. "Good Captain, I do not understand. Please do not move my paintings. They require expert handling. . . ."

"Remove the children and give them into a female's care. Pile the paintings over against that rock," Ozal ordered, brushing the distraught Armenian aside like a hovering fly. "This wagon is hereby commandeered under wartime rules for the use and transport of the young and the infirm. We need to speed this train up in order that this company may be safely encamped by nightfall. Unharness the injured mule."

One soldier released the hobbled animal. Four soldiers peeled the canvas covering from the wagon. Rough hands yanked at priceless paintings of detailed ancient stone sculptures, a teeming marketplace, women harvesting tea, the ruins of a Seljuk castle, and the Dervish monastery at Meviana. Without regard, the labor of a lifetime was unceremoniously dumped at the base of the rock.

Stepanian wandered after them, lost and in shock. "No, no, good Captain. Please, no. I confess! Yes, I confess. I sold a painting here and there along the route for money with which to encourage the guards to let me keep my wagon and its belongings. It was difficult to part with my work, but soldiers need to make a living as well, and these are hard times. Such beautiful paintings aren't easy to sell unless you know their proper worth and can describe in detail their technical execution. I did that, and it kept us moving along."

He stood by the growing pile and pulled at his ears. Each time an armload of paintings crashed down on those beneath, a little yelp of recognition and loss burst from his throat. His shaking hands fluttered in front of disbelieving eyes. He called for his grandchildren, but they were crying too hard to hear.

When the wagon was bare, Captain Ozal stepped beside

the lame mule, placed a pistol to its head and pulled the trigger. The creature swayed once, crumpled to the ground, and was still.

"Poghos!" A high-pitched shriek tore from the old painter as he staggered back against the rock. The mouth worked to express his anguish, but no sound came. Huge tears streaked the sun-baked cheeks and stained the dusty front of a frayed and faded coat.

"Frankly, Mr. Stepanian, I would have thought that the soul of an artist would see a certain poetry in all this," Ozal said, shoving the pistol back in its waistband. "A mule lame is of no use. A mule dead is food for the masses. I can, on the other hand, see no earthly use for a cargo of paintings. You can't eat a painting." He turned and flung the rendering of the palace at Mount Ararat on top of the pile.

"Burn them."

The tattered painter gasped and clutched at his chest. "No . . . no—" he choked. "Please . . . I beg . . . leave them, leave me . . . don't destroy my life . . . my joy. . . ."

Tongues of flame licked along the base of the pile, then raced upward. Gold and copper frames, most heirlooms of the nineteenth century, turned brown, black, twisting misshapenly in the searing heat. Scenes, sumptuous and serene, bubbled and buckled. Slowly at first the oils melted and ran in a molten soup, then in one great whooshing column of flame, they were devoured in an angry pyre of colored memories.

CHAPTER 18

The hand slid over his mouth and clamped down. "You are in deadly danger," said a high-pitched whisper, "and so are the mothers of Ararat!"

Tatul Sarafian arched his back and nearly hurled himself and his attacker from the roof of the stable. He jammed back with his elbow and felt the crunch of bone and heard a familiar cry.

"Fark?"

"It is I," moaned the little eunuch, kneeling at the edge of the roof and patting an injured eye. "Are you always this pleasant in the morning?"

Tatul examined the swelling. "Only if I've had a truly good night's rest. You might want to soak that down at the river. It should turn a nice shade of black and give you a pleasingly sinister air."

"An invaluable addition to my efforts at being invisible," snorted Fark. He looked to the opposite side of the roof where the still form of Adrine Tevian rested peacefully in the early light. She was covered with Sarafian's coat and saddle blanket. Fark gave his friend a watery-eyed look of curiosity.

Tatul looked over at Adrine with concern. "I kept watch through the night. She won't say it, but she trusts us. The thought ages me."

"Good. For what I have to say will make you old in a heartbeat. Ozal rode off in a rage this morning to intercept a refugee caravan north of here. He knows you have not slept with your harem and thinks you are a few parts skin and hair and a great sum of lies. So the wager is off. When he returns, he swears to make you tell the truth and to execute the women.

Quickly now, you and the brothers must attempt your escape before the captain returns!"

To the eunuch's troubled amazement, Tatul slowly shook his head. "No. The only way to stop a rampaging camel is to stand your ground and call its bluff. Saddle my horse, Fark, I have a camel to meet."

"Take Adrine, the other headstrong one, with you, but do not think it possible to save anyone else. I shall offer to accompany the women south and do what I can to get them to Aleppo. As the good Lord made clear on the cross, we do what we can, but He alone holds the keys to life and death."

Tatul hugged the flustered old man. "You are a brave old husk, but I cannot pick and choose who goes and who stays. I came on behalf of them all, and for all of them I must strive." He herded the protesting elder to the ladder and over the side. "And, Fark," Tatul called down. The green felt hat tipped back, and the old patrician face lined with frustrated concern, one eye rapidly blackening, peered up at him. "Let nothing happen to her while I am away."

He watched Fark descend the ladder and fought against the doubt that threatened to overwhelm him. It was humanly impossible to expect to safely move so many people out from under the armed Turk soldiers and convicts of Hekim Khan. The odds might favor the escape of twenty to twenty-five at most, and then only by the sheer number of people to begin with.

He could not bear to think which mothers and babies would die, which few would live. Nor could he bear the certain knowledge that he would fight hardest for Adrine Tevian and leave the rest to God and the angels.

Sarafian shook off the deviling thoughts and recalled the words the sisters had sung on their aborted attempt to escape Hekim Khan on their own. *"Christ, my heavenly shield."* How much thought had Adrine Tevian given to that ill-conceived act of defiance? Little, most likely. But her shield had been up, and every one of those unarmed women and children still lived.

Perhaps the Fox should raise the shield of heaven and let caution drift in the wind.

Tatul knelt beside the sleeping woman on the roof and put

a hand out to awaken her. He hesitated, hand hovering above her shoulder, eyes unashamedly focused on the rise and fall of her breast. He barely understood the emotion that welled up in him with an intensity never before felt for anyone, not even Veron. It must be the terrible times, the brevity of life, the awful things he had seen. Here was life, the promise of life, persisting with a fierce and unlikely fervency of its own. In the face of such awful famine of food and love, Adrine Tevian held on.

And in that faint tremor of life lay a new Armenia, a new world of hope and laughter and faith. No more toppled saints and slain priests. No more shoot or be shot. No more child soldiers. No more run and hide and lie.

No more.

The hand remained suspended in midair, the back of it wet with tears. This had to be the end and the beginning. It had to be.

"Adrine," he said, lightly pressing her shoulder, startled to feel hard bone.

Her eyelids fluttered open. She studied him wearily but confidently and gave a faint smile.

"Come," he said, "we must go to the others and prepare them for flight. We haven't much time, but they must be told what is required of them."

He swallowed hard and smiled as bravely as he could. He tried to look confident, but the fox inside the cowherd from Erzurum trembled and hid its face. For as certain as the rising of the sun, between the End and the Beginning must come the Flood.

———————

The unshod hooves of the swift range ponies rained chips of dried earth behind the two flying Fedayeen. Tatul Sarafian and Ashkhen Mentese crested the bluff and reined in their mounts. Spread below them was the meager camp of the Sivas refugees. The river ran beside the camp in a cut forty feet below it, defiantly noisy, its swift, deep waters the only thing in abundance in the dying district. With the coming of night, small diamonds of firelight sparked from the idle onion fields spread at their feet.

Across the river's watery divide stood the defiant walls of the Monastery of Mesrop.

As the two riders drew near the camp, they encountered a hideous scene. Three wasted children played listlessly at a pebble game while two of their playmates lay dead at the edge of the circle. Too weak to eat, they had died with roots pulled from the soil clutched in their tiny hands. Dirt clung to their mouths and sightless eyes. The skin of the roots was barely broken where they had weakly attempted to chew some nourishment from a scant harvest.

An old crone sat nearby, pawing at the ground in dazed frustration. Tatul leapt from his horse and pressed a fist-sized chunk of flat bread between her rigid fingers. As if from thin air there suddenly appeared five more women, as crazed and naked as the first, who stalked the crone with the bread. She scrabbled away, grunting unintelligibly, shielding the prize from the rest of the scavengers.

Tatul threw bread at their bloodied backs like crumbs after pigeons. He chased them, but they were oblivious to anything but their own insanity. Ashkhen rode sadly after his friend, pulling the reins of the riderless horse, tears streaming down his cheeks. The People of the Book, these his sisters, had lost their last shred of humanity.

"God help us, Ashkhen. God help us!" Tatul whispered. "When I think how on Christmas Eve my family used to congratulate one another that we were Armenians, the first Christian nation on earth, and now there are more of us in the ground than walk upon it!"

He watched the crazed women dart away into the darkness and remembered. It was early Christmas morning long ago, the village dark and still, when from down the street came the singing voices. "He is manifested today! *Shnorhahvor dzenoont!* Christ is born; He is manifested today. Rise up, you sleepy ones, for God has come down into the world!"

A knock sounded at the door. Father in his nightgown opened the latch and there stood the choir, grinning and peering inside. The Sarafians crowded around, blinking and rubbing the slumber from their eyes. The choir sang "Praise be to God the Father, praise Him, O fortunate Christians. Rise up and come to holy church, for now is the hour of worship!"

Father closed the door. Excitedly, grandparents, aunts, cousins, siblings started talking all at once.

"We have God's Word!"

"God's Truth guides us!"

"Christ has come . . ."

" . . . and shall come again!"

"We are redeemed from sin!"

"You are Armenian and I am pleased to know you!"

"Haji, get off your brother. Christ be blessed!"

And then they dressed and poured out into the street, which became lighted by the lanterns and candles they carried as they flowed past the Muslim homes in which the unbelievers slept and moved toward the Armenian Apostolic Church. The snow crunched beneath a thousand feet that at last mashed it to water on the steps of the church. From within God's palace the lights and music and incense of almost two thousand years spilled from every window and door. Just before little Tatul crossed the threshold, he always looked up to catch a faceful of snowflakes, and it seemed to him then that he was so small, just a tiny beetle slipping through a crack at the base of a frighteningly tall mountain.

The Mass that began in the dark ended in the light. The road home stretched impossibly long, for at its end awaited a feast of lamb, stuffed grape leaves, rice pilaf hand-ground from Sarafian-grown wheat, pastry, fresh fruit, and small steaming cups of Turkish coffee.

Happy memories of better times. Would they ever come again?

"*Shnorhahvor dzenoont!*" Tatul Sarafian called sadly into the famished night. "Congratulate me, I am an Armenian!"

"Shh, brother, quiet. Someone approaches!" Ashkhen put a hand on Tatul's shoulder and peered anxiously into the dark. A horse snorted, and a bulky Turk materialized from the gloom.

"If the hungry fools could but wait, there will be boiled meat and broth shortly." Rifle cocked, the camp guard spoke with a smoker's rasp and the volume of one who spent considerable time among the deaf. "No sooner had we skinned the mule than a dozen of the dirty pig-eaters fell on the hide and tore it to pieces, devouring it without a trace. Only by the aid of Allah did we beat them off the meat. I'll tell you one thing, I'll not complain again about the food as long as I can identify it and say which part of the animal it came from. I'll inform the captain you are here." The camp guard rode off in a whirlwind of haste.

Another commotion ahead spurred the Fedayeen on. Several of the caravan's soldiers were supervising the digging of a grave by a tall woman, her dignity pulled about her in a thin wrap that had once been dark green but was now dirty and faded. Stretched along the ground beside her was the corpse of an equally tall woman, also in a faded green wrap, her hair white as washed cotton. She resembled the living woman as might a weathered statue.

"Mother," she announced to the new arrivals without emotion, her voice empty with resignation. She scraped at a slowly deepening depression in the earth with one end of a flat stick. "If you intend to rape me, tell me now so that I may make the pit large enough for two." The soldiers rolled their eyes and one made an obscene comment. Weary of talk, they told her to work faster.

Tatul fought his anger. Perhaps if he'd been on the road with these people for two months, himself starved, neglected, daily worn down by gradually worsening hopelessness, perhaps then he would think little of such shocking statements. But to hear them raw like this, uttered publicly by this poor woman who had been reduced to laying her mother to rest before a leering crowd of bored rapists, was difficult to bear.

Was his own mother lying on the ground somewhere, forgotten, stripped, violated?

Tatul dismounted, stepped forward, and gently took the stick from the unbowed daughter. Without a single noticeable change in her manner, she closely studied every move of the young man digging her mother's grave in the hard, unyielding ground. The Turk soldiers watched dumb-faced until the smell of boiled mule grew too tantalizing to ignore, and they wandered off in search of something hot and flavorful.

When the depression was at last deep enough to accept the woman, Tatul and Ashkhen respectfully placed the body—so light!—in the ground and covered her over. They listened to the daughter's rambling prayer and added their mumbled amens.

They stood with her, not wanting to leave her alone, not knowing when she would leave. A soft breeze, carried in from the river, blew at the newly turned earth and exposed the long, elegant fingers of one lifeless hand. They covered them up again and carried stones to anchor the earth, at least long enough for the caravan to move on. Tatul drew the sign of the cross on top of the mound with his finger. The daughter watched him without expression.

After a long silence, she said, "She salted me. Took me as a baby, washed me in water, salted me good, and wrapped me in cloths. My mother salted me. My mother is dead."

Tatul nodded, fighting a lump in his throat. He and his siblings had been salted by their mother, the brothers Mentese by theirs. Armenians followed the custom of the ancient Jews and washed their babies in a salt solution for medicinal purification.

Horses approached. Out of the gloom, ahead of their arrival, came Ozal's sarcasm. "Do not harm us, men of Murat Prison. We come in peace!"

Six glowering horsemen reined in, snatched from a hot meal by the two unwelcome guests. A mocking Ozal put it into words. "Again the king of criminals terrorizes the innocent? Throwing dirt on an unarmed woman's mother? You are indeed a monster, Bolu Bergema!" The captain's countenance darkened and he dropped the pretense. "What do you mean by riding in here and treating these miserable beasts with deference? You interfere with official military business. They are enemies of the state and as such are to be treated as illegal aliens under orders of extradition. Under articles of war, they are in lawful transport to lawfully constituted detainment camps, and it is for those authorities to sort them out at the conclusion of hostilities. They have brought this fate upon themselves and are not to be accorded favors—"

"*Favors?* What of simple regard for humanity? These have done nothing except to have been born into a society that freely—and eagerly—bestowed upon them the title of citizens, qualified for all the rights and protections citizens enjoy," said Sarafian with a steely calm.

"They provoked the government by acts of sedition!" shouted Ozal.

"Their only crime is the occupation of the Turkish heartland from the Caucasian frontier to the Mediterranean coast. It is a homeland that after six hundred years you—we—are no longer willing to share with them."

"They are a party of plotters who straddle the Turkish-Russian border in both geography and loyalty. They are infidels, less than human!"

"They are peasant mothers and children in search of safe haven. Their husbands and fathers have already been exterminated for their 'crimes.' Why won't you give these the asylum that it is within your power to grant?"

"Traitorous acts must not go unpunished! Today's innocents are tomorrow's insurgents. Again, you sound a great deal more like a political sympathizer than a jailed felon. Just what are you, Bolu Bergema, and where is your allegiance?" It was an accusation delivered with all the subtlety of an exploding bomb.

Tatul Sarafian looked up at the man on the horse and quietly replied, "Whatever else I am, I am a man who hates waste. To drive these people into the ground, loot their belongings, defile their humanity, and spill their blood is a terrible waste. If a person wrongs me, I will be the first to make that person regret the action. But if a peaceable person is simply in the wrong *place* in history through no fault but that of being born, then I wish to defend—no, I am *duty bound* to defend. As one who is himself misunderstood and who stands wrongfully accused, it is my duty to protect others so accused."

Ozal's lips curled in an ugly smirk. "A strangler with honor. Such a contradiction!"

Sarafian ignored the remark. "I request, my Captain, that I and my companion be allowed to carry broth to the weak. Your men might help."

Ozal's seismic anger was felt by his horse. It whirled in a tight circle, snorted, and stamped its front feet. "My men have the important task of standing watch against predators from without"—he looked pointedly across the river to the walls of the monastery—"and rebellion from within." The cold stare he gave Tatul could have been interpreted by a child. "These innocents of yours sent raiding parties into Bismil. They stole food and farm tools to sell farther along the route. It seems that their Christian principles do not sustain prolonged hardship.

"If they cannot come to the dispensary for food, then they are too weak to continue, and to feed them would be a waste. The strong may be fed, the weak allowed to die. I prefer that to letting them prey on the good citizens of Hekim Khan under cover of darkness!"

As if they could rise to change positions, let alone threaten a town. Tatul saw Ashkhen tighten a fist and encircled his wrist with a strong, rough hand. He shook his head, and Ashkhen reluctantly nodded. They were of no use to anyone dead.

"You wish to strike me, Mentese?"

"No, my Captain, he is angry at the times," Sarafian answered, "and angry that the Third Pillar of Islam is now so twisted as to exclude these suffering ones because they are Christian."

The last thing Ozal wanted was to debate religion in front of these men. He wanted most to drag these convicts behind his horse at a full gallop and see what leaked out. But he needed more facts. Though he and his men had their strong suspicions, the soldiers were a volatile mix of boys straight off the farm, career military, and pardoned convicts full of admiration for the audacious Bergema and his display of raw courage in the cockpit. It would be dangerous to force them into a choice.

Again, Ozal berated himself for risking the wager in the first place. He did not need some scrappy boy in their midst rising to mythical proportions. He needed the bloody business to end, his record free of insurrection, and his reposting after the war to a secluded lagoon on the south coast.

Tatul read the captain's predicament in Ozal's face. He needed to carefully exploit the affections so quickly won in yesterday's cockfight. "*Sakat*, the duty to give alms, is one of the most important commands in all Islam," he rushed on, making his appeal to each of the men in turn. "Muhammed the Magnanimous ordained it and meant it as the only tax on Muslims. Why? To provide for the poor, the needy, the wayfarer, the freeing of slaves, and the aid of those in debt. It is a mercy tax, yet how much mercy have these poor ones known since the order to vacate came down on them like a sentence of death?" One or two nodded begrudgingly, faces troubled. Most cast a furtive glance at the captain.

Suddenly Tatul brightened, flashed an enormous smile, and threw his arms wide. "Ah, but my newest brothers, you have itchy, running sores from squirming in this hole of an outpost for so long." He whirled counterclockwise, feet dancing a mesmerizing blur. "My name is magic in Stamboul. Bolu the Unquenchable opens doors to the richest bathhouses, hotels, and parlors of pleasure ever known! I have the words to give you that will open those golden doors as smoothly as if they were hinged in goose grease. Perhaps your commander might release you a few at a time to go salvage your humanity and return as new men!"

They lifted knowing eyebrows and murmured in ribald enthusiasm loud enough for the captain to hear.

Ozal had heard enough. "A pretty speech, Bolu, but you tread dangerously close to insubordination with your talk of refugee mistreatment. My men have a job to do. Bad things happen in times of war. It's not clean and orderly, and there's never enough for all. Torture is too good for traitors.

"Nonetheless, you and your companion may fill a bucket with soup and make the rounds if you've the stomach for it, but I'll not spare another man for nurse duty. When the slop is gone, report to my tent without delay."

He tightened the reins and was set to give spur when Sarafian grabbed the bridle. "Oh, Captain, one thing more, I beg you!"

"What now?"

"Spare one man to return to Hekim Khan to seek clothing for the women who are without. Let them not perish from nakedness. We two will take his place."

Ozal debated whether to shoot Bergema and be done with it. The man was a blister on his rump. But maybe he could use that to his advantage. The war was a disaster for Turkey. Defeat was likely. Ozal bet his manhood there would be an international tribunal over the displacement of the Armenians. He might find favor with just one or two acts of compassion. He'd guess Bergema could be very persuasive before the judgment seat. And if he did have connections in Constantinople outside conventional circles . . .

Ozal motioned to one of his men. "You! Go to town and return with covering for these scarecrows. However, collect the necessary garments only from the females of Armenia, for I know they would want to be the ones to help their own."

And are the ones who have but the clothes on their backs to give, thought Tatul bitterly. He sincerely hoped Ozal would not have the satisfaction of their refusing to help.

Adrine would not let that happen.

The man departed for Hekim Khan, and Tatul and Ashkhen began to haul pots of the gamey-smelling bouillon from cluster to cluster of the haggard outcasts. At least they would get some liquid and nourishment into their wasted bodies. Turk farmers and villagers sold the refugees drinking water from the Euphrates for what last bits of gold a few of them had left for barter. Many had nothing of value and would have died of thirst that night had it not been for the soup. The guards kept a wary eye and made certain no one slipped to the river for a free drink. For their vigilance, they received a share of the gold.

For three hours the two Fedayeen ladled and rationed the pungent mix to the dazed assembly. Some were too tired or sickened to acknowledge the meal; others smiled weakly or wept silently. One woman fed her wasted child like a mother bird, cooling the hot liquid in her own mouth before dribbling it between the cracked and peeling lips of her feeble little boy. When Tatul spilled some of the precious broth on his hand, a toothless grandmother without shoes suckled his fingers dry.

A man with a limp arm refused his portion, the hatred in his eyes more powerful than the ache in his belly. Another, scalp bloody with sores, greedily gulped down a portion followed by a long and noisy belch. The unexpected sound so surprised him that he laughed merrily, and Tatul with him.

But for the most part, it was a long and dreary business, and when a shout arose at the coming of a woeful wagon of thin, ragged clothing, the ladles scraped the bottom of the buckets for the last time.

Tatul and Ashkhen distributed the garments as best they

could, but most of the deranged drones were still only half clad. *Bless you, sisters of Hekim Khan,* Tatul thought. *You did not close your hand to the need of others, though you must now yourselves be close to naked. May you be warmed by your act of kindness and gowned by your unselfishness. If I but could, I would clothe you all in royal raiment. One day, God willing, I shall!*

Instantly, he scoffed at the empty promise. Tatul the Dreamer was back again. He of the seaside villas, dashing husband of a raven-eyed beauty, father of many polite and placid children—idiot without equal. Tatul the Practical knew all too well what God willed. God willed to place beloved Armenia into the fiery furnace and leave her there to writhe and pop and scream while the world yawned and gave another turn on its axis.

It was with fierce resolve that Tatul Sarafian entered the firelight of a more reflective and quite drunken Captain Ozal. The captain reclined with the exaggerated importance of a caged sultan in the doorway of a stained brown canvas tent. Scattered about him on the ground were his guards, wary as they could be, given the amount of gin and fermented rice mash that had arrived with the clothing wagon. They were vigilant without remembering why. And why, for that matter, were their guns loaded? Were they really in danger from a caravan of starved and half-mad infidels?

"You wished to see me, Captain?" Tatul bowed.

At the back of the tent, Ashkhen Mentese slid to his belly and carefully slit the cloth along the bottom seam. When the cut was half again as wide as a man, he slipped inside with the agility of a cobra. Orange firelight lit the front wall of the shelter with volcanic intensity, the lower half of Ozal's legs clearly visible in the gap at the front of the tent. Swift hands felt bedding and spare clothing, within seconds locating the exquisite dagger that was a gift from Bolu. The dagger vanished up Ashkhen's sleeve, and Ashkhen disappeared from the tent as if evaporated.

Tatul waited while Ozal assembled the fragments of his clouded brain. The black waters of the Euphrates rushed away below them as if eager to leave before the worst happened. On the opposite bank, the walls of the monastery glowed in silver moonshine, and bright chips of flame illuminated the ancient courtyard of the apostolic priests.

Ozal peered at the ex-convict framed against the stars. Was there much more to Bolu Bergema than talk? He looked determined, but was he more than a skeleton hung with a few pounds of flesh?

"It is time for the pleasantries to end," Ozal spoke carefully. "Something must be done about you."

Tatul stiffened. He felt Ashkhen press against his back in the shadows, felt the cool smoothness of the hand-tooled stiletto pass between them. No matter how much drink jumbled their faculties, Ozal's men would sober fast enough at the first sign of trouble.

"What, sir, do you mean?"

"I mean that you must earn your way, and the Armenian women are a drain on the treasury. We've had our little fun, and you and your companions have had sufficient hours to cuddle your harem.

"It is well past time to return to matters of war. The cockfight was a brief diversion, nothing more. The wager was a novelty among men too long without the refinements of the fairer sex. We must now return to our senses, and you, sir, must earn your keep like every other man in the government's employ." Ozal lifted a ladle of water, moistened two fingers of his right hand and pressed them against his eyes. "At first light, I go to the railway stop at Malatya for resupplies. Raisins, grain, dried mutton. My men grow slow from lack of food. You will march your harem to the deserts. Upon my return, I will find no trace of them. If I were you, I would take them all on a tour of the breathtaking ravine that has rendered so many Armenians quite speechless." Ozal clearly expected his grin to be matched by one of Bergema's.

Tatul betrayed no emotion. "Yes, my Captain. And in gratitude for taking us into your company and sharing so willingly the spoils of Hekim Khan, I present you with this extraordinary blade, identical twin to the one presented to you at the cockpit."

He stopped dead in his tracks. The hair rose on the back of his neck. From across the river came the deep, cavernous tones of chanting:

"Mystery ... Holy Mystery ... divined by the Twelve ... they

who walked with God . . . Jesus Christ . . . He is Grace. . . ."

Ozal and his men staggered to their feet, grabbing for their rifles. Across the waters, bright with moonlight, ghostly sentinels of men stood dark as rocks along the edge of the far bank. Bearded faces of flickering light and shadow floated in circlets of candle glow. The incantations carried on the stillness, tongues from another world declaring glory to God in the Highest.

"Silence, you stupid fools!" Ozal bawled into the night. "I swear I will burn you and your compound to the ground and feed your insignificant ashes to the cattle!"

"Mystery . . . Holy Mystery . . . that saves . . . renews . . . and unites all things in Christ . . ."

"Who do you call upon?!" Ozal shouted. "Who hears you?" He ran along the bank, stabbing the air with his fists, twenty men at his heels. He kicked at a pile of moaning rags lying in the dirt and dragged up a weak stick of an Armenian woman and thrust her forward. "Here, look now upon the people of Jesus. See how well they are. See how generous is their God!"

"We believe in one God, the Father, the Almighty . . ."

At the words of gold from the Nicene Creed, the living dead rose from the cold earth and staggered and crawled to the riverbank. Slowly at first, then more quickly they shuffled and stumbled forward, each word of the age-old confession a sacred tonic to ravaged and wasted flesh and bones. The refugee apparitions, even the most demented, stood or lay facing the holy glow, their lips moving to the affirmation of faith.

" . . . and in one Lord, Jesus Christ, the Son of God . . . was made man . . . suffered and was crucified . . . and rose again . . . and is to come . . . to judge the living and the dead. . . ."

Ozal stopped and listened to the unified whispers and chants in the surrounding darkness. His revulsion toward the monks was more than hatred—it was fear. Mesrop was a safe haven for the Christian oppressed. Where was the safe haven for Ozal? The mosque was a place of echoes, and one was thought weak if he could not find answers in the *Shahidah*, the Muslim profession of faith: "There is no God but Allah and Muhammed is his prophet." It was cradle song, dirge, password, war cry, and hallelujah. No one questioned that it was not enough.

But the monks at Mesrop were the keepers of an ancient Christian faith of miracles and resurrection, of a God so big, yet so personally near. If it was all speculation and magic, why would otherwise healthy men with all the human appetites dress in black, build a fortress in the desert, and pore over ancient manuscripts and pray ancient prayers that were full of thanksgiving and questions? While all the world and its woes spun around them, they lived in the vortex untouched, immovable, unshakable. They loved their Christ and were nourished by Him. Ozal felt so distant from Allah, who had no redeemer son and was in all ways unapproachable. But to feel otherwise was considered empty sentimentality. Allah did not save. He was not grace. He was duty. He was five daily prayers, alms for the poor, a month of fasting, and a pilgrimage to Mecca.

The captain of the Twelfth Army Corps felt trapped. What did these monks of Jesus know? What peace had they found that Neelam Ozal, locked in Allah, had no hope of finding?

He could have crossed the river long ago, killed the lot of them, and leveled their monastery. What would that have accomplished? For every one killed, two would take his place. Besides, they welcomed death, and he would not give them the pleasure of anything they welcomed.

Swift as death an image of his mother sprang to mind. She crossed herself, muttered an unintelligible prayer, and told her crying son to stop or the Holy Spirit would suck his breath away while he slept and he would never awaken.

Ozal yanked a rifle from the hands of the nearest soldier and fired wildly into the night. "Silence!" he screamed into the dark. "Do not pretend to be so holy and set apart! You are Armenians who feed off the garbage heaps of men's souls! You should be exterminated inside the rat hole you have dug for yourselves in the desert!" One by one, the circlets of light on the opposite bank went out.

The chant grew louder in darkness and with it the chorus across the river.

"... also in the Holy Spirit ... the perfect ... who preached in the apostles and dwelt in the saints ..."

Ozal and his men fired volley after volley into the darkness to protect themselves from priests they could not see. The holy men concluded the Creed and began again.

Ozal threw a hand into the air. His men lowered their rifles. Without a moment's hesitation, the captain again grabbed the weak Armenian woman and thrust her forward. He raised the rifle's muzzle and shot her through the back. Silent, light as thistledown, she flew over the bank and fell thirty feet to the water. The splash was no more than that of a small dog.

As if signaled by an unseen conductor, the chanting ceased.

"To Ozal the Conqueror!" shouted Tatul, glass raised. "You have our allegiance!" He sucked the fermented mash, then downed it in one stinging swirl. Anything to keep the madman from sending the entire caravan over the cliff.

"To our captain, keeper of the order, leader unmatched!" Tatul and Ashkhen ran from Turk to Turk, forcing cups of the potent beverage into each hand, enticing them back to the firelight. Another toast, and another, and they soon forgot the pile of bare humanity that cowered by the river's edge. Ozal stood for a long time just watching, then entered their midst with a wicked tale of his younger days as a foot soldier when he and his companions entered Armenian homes and ravaged larders and daughters with equal fervor.

———

Just before first light, a much clouded Ozal sent ten men to Constantinople with clear instructions from Bolu Bergema to enter the tea shop of Suleyman Talu and ask for Gopi, seller of white melons. To her, they were to say, "Bolu has sent us for what is ours. We shall be at the baths."

They were to immediately go to the nearest baths, discard their smelly uniforms to be burned, drink down a warm beverage, and sink into steamy marbled luxury. Twenty minutes later, weak from steam and dizzy with drink, weapons far from them, they would sink beneath the waters, helped to the afterlife by pleasant, and quite strong, Fedayeen bath attendants.

Hopefully, upon more sober reflection later in the day, Neelam Ozal might even send another band of men to bring back the first. They would, of course, only catch up to them beyond the grave.

Such was the beauty of Fedayeen justice.

———————

Tatul and Ashkhen dropped farther and farther back from the waning night's revelry until they were once again in deep shadow. "My brother," Tatul said, voice low but urgent, "now, this night in all haste, take your brother Misak and a wagon to the railway stop at Malatya. Secure as much food as you are able and bring it back here on the wings of God before Ozal gets there. When you return, seek the priests of the Golden Casket. They will know where we and the sisters of Armenia have gone."

Ashkhen hesitated. "How can you make your escape without us?"

Tatul embraced him, then shoved him toward his horse. "Ozal goes for resupply. We will have to deal with those he leaves behind as best we can. Now go, and may the Creator of heaven and earth part the waters for you."

"The God of all things visible and invisible keep you hidden," Ashkhen replied.

"I will kiss your return."

"Or curse your demise."

The Fedayeen blessing complete, Ashkhen Mentese left his friend at a soft, noiseless trot.

Tatul hated to see him go. He desperately searched for the rest of the plan. Perhaps the earth would open and a subterranean passage would lead them all the way to the far mountains and into the arms of the Black Wolf.

But the arms he yearned for most were those of Adrine Tevian. Without them, he would hold no one ever again. How amazing that despite all she had seen, God still dwelt in her. How surprised he was that despite all he had seen, he was still drawn to that same God.

With trembling hand he reached to an inside pouch for the snippet of hair that he had prized all these long months since dear Veron was ripped from him.

But now it was the hair of one long laid to rest in the bosom of Abraham. So many had followed her in death. Veron would understand if he now chose to live.

He breathed the scent of her one last time and released the silken treasure on the night breeze. It whirled and danced higher and higher until it was lost among the twinkling stars.

Perhaps the cold place inside him would glow warm again.

Much needed to be done before any hope of that. The Turk captain was evil personified, stripping people of dignity and life without the thinnest twinge of regret. Tatul looked to the firelight flickering against the tents, heard an outburst of lusty laughter, and recited the ancient Catholic curse against the Turk butchers. " 'As for those who say there was a time when the Son was not, or there was a time when the Holy Spirit was not, or that they came into being out of nothing, or who say that the Son of God or the Holy Spirit are of a different substance, and that they are changeable or alterable, such the apostolic holy Church does declare anathema.' "

He might have followed the curse with bloody action, but for Adrine. She deserved more than an assassin's revenge.

———————

Long after the sounds of voices and feet and the tortured turning of dry wagon wheels had faded; long after the barely human caravan had withdrawn south to a camp along the river bluff just north of Hekim Khan; long after the watery makings of mule stew had disappeared into famine-distended bellies, and the night chill had settled into road-battered bones; for very long after, a lone figure knelt huddled before a smoldering pile of ashes, calcified bones stiff with cold, breath coming in short irregular puffs, old artist hands clutching a corner fragment of the painting of the fortress at Mount Ararat.

A quarter hour past midnight on the moonlit road to Sivas, unable any longer to hear the crying of grandchildren, the lone figure drew one last shuddering breath, toppled over on his side, and was forever still.

CHAPTER 19

Frank Davidson sighed in frustration. Though Alexander Bell and Tom Watson had just made the first transcontinental telephone call, it still took him most of a month to make contact with Ambassador Morgenthau in Constantinople and get a reply.

The saber rattling was as loud as ever. Germany must cease interference with U.S. shipping or such acts of hostility would be met with forceful retaliation ... et cetera ... and so forth ... ad nauseam. More empty threats. American neutrality, however you sliced it, was in vogue to stay.

Davidson smiled, though, whenever he got that sour. Crotchety people did not last long in the consular corps. But he really did wonder at times if he could abide one more soup supper with Neman Beyit, the provincial governor. All communiqués from the American officials he had bombarded with letters seemed to say the same thing: "Hold your position. Mollify the local leadership. Protect U.S. interests in Eastern Anatolia." Mollification grew increasingly difficult to stomach.

The U.S. consulate at Harput was full—twenty men in the attic, forty women and children in the courtyard, another forty scattered throughout the upper rooms. Most had American ties and relatives willing to sponsor them, but in the current climate, they were as much at risk as an Armenian peasant who'd never heard of America.

He could claim diplomatic immunity, march them out to safety under his protection, and surrender the American-run schools again in trade. But the pasha had just refused American offers of outside aid for the Armenians, and Davidson

202

doubted Governor Beyit would want to invite the wrath of his superiors by acts of mercy. Davidson had $200,000 of Armenian gold and currency in the safe. What was the moral thing to do? He had promised those who had left their savings with him that he would see to it that the valuables were transported to the United States and every effort made to locate their rightful owners. He was certain preservation of property fell among his neutral duties, and he kept careful records. But when was the greater good served by using a portion of the valuables as ransom? He believed that time was near.

The mood in Harput worsened by the hour. The Turks issued another impossible decree. All remaining Armenian households were to surrender any weapons. If the frequent random searches turned up no weapons, the family was accused of civil disobedience, of hiding illegal arms, and charged as rebels. Armenians, therefore, paid exorbitant prices for black market guns, sold to them by the Turks. These they placed in plain sight so the raiders would have something to confiscate. However, those who thought they'd beat the system soon learned that this sword had a second carefully honed edge. To have guns meant that you were clearly plotting to overthrow the government and were part of an insurrectionist scheme.

At dawn, Hovhannes Simonian, professor of art at Euphrates College, was tortured to death when a cache of guns was supposedly uncovered in a tiny cellar beneath his desk in the art classroom. Though the bloody and battered man swore that all the cellar contained were onions and potatoes, he was murdered with a heavy oak cane before truth could be sorted from hearsay.

Davidson remembered Simonian as the most genteel of bridge players. He had spent a small salary, and an even smaller allowance from relatives in Austria, buying exemption from military service for his frightened Armenian male students. At forty gold coins apiece, he had ransomed three students before his death.

Orphans as young as three wandered into town from passing refugee caravans. They shrieked and wailed in a daze, ignored by the Turks, for they were infidels, and ignored by the Armenians because they were another mouth to feed. Seldom now did a live Armenian male come through Harput who was over eleven years of age.

Davidson fought despair by staying busy. He smuggled families out at night and entertained or diverted Turk officials with tea and cakes both day and night. He gained considerable ground when the American Red Cross offered one hundred beds to convalescing Turk soldiers at the hospital in Mamouret-el-Aziz. There was even talk of an award from the Turkish Red Crescent Society for his efforts.

The moon shone silver over the ornate Persian bedspread beneath which Frank Davidson fitfully slept. His dreams were populated by runaway Armenians who kept arriving until there was standing room only in the yard and rooms of the consulate. Hundreds, thousands more beat on the gates, screaming for sanctuary as hordes of sword-wielding Muslims swooped down upon them for the kill.

A rough, meaty hand gripped his shoulder and shook. Davidson fought to remain in the dream in which he carried a family of eight on his back, running with all his strength for the Russian border but with every step sinking deeper into a great sucking pit of quicksand. "No, God, no. Let me go. . . ."

"Mr. Davidson! Mr. Davidson, please, you must come! It is most urgent. Mr. Davidson!"

The U.S. consul struggled to the surface and opened his eyes to find Gomidas the boxer swinging his employer's legs over the side of the bed. "Brothers in need," he said, thick body blocking the silver moon. "We must go at once!"

A wagon stood hitched and ready at the gate. They threw two dozen war-damaged Turk army uniforms into the back. Davidson blessed God that he'd offered to have the U.S. consulate staff repair the garments for the overtaxed medical workers. And because they hadn't managed the repairs yet, the dried grime and blood would be all the more convincing, whether the wounds and tears matched the men in them or not. The uniforms came from the hospital at Mamouret-el-Aziz, and to the hospital they would return.

Davidson was thankful as well that the consulate guests that night, a lesser police constable and his bronchitis-inflicted wife, had left early after a coughing fit that left her practically incapacitated. Frank definitely needed more sleep between acts.

They rode hard to a cave east of town. A hundred yards from the cavern, three men with aimed rifles stepped into the road, faces wrapped in masks of muslin.

"Armenian rebels," said Gomidas in a hoarse whisper. "They have many wounded."

The Armenian and the American jumped down from the wagon and were led behind an outcrop of rocks to men lying on the ground, bloodied and moaning.

One of the masked guards spoke through the muslin wrap, his deep voice muffled. "They are Armenian brothers of Harput. They hid in the cave for a week and had nearly made good their escape to the north dressed as women. Unfortunately, they blundered into a contingent of Turk soldiers who quickly discovered their true identity and began to beat them mercilessly. By the kindness of God, we were camped nearby and heard the commotion. We crept without a sound to the scene, took pity, and started firing. The Turks fled, but the Armenians are a mass of cuts, cracked ribs, and broken noses."

"Dress the injured in the military uniforms we brought and help them into the wagon," Davidson answered. "If God has not tired of us, we just might smuggle them out of the region at Turk expense."

Back at the wagon, fifteen battered passengers, wincing at the hard, cramped quarters, listened somberly to Davidson's instructions. "You are wounded Turk soldiers, ambushed near Mus. Do not talk among yourselves. Some of you won't have to put on much of an act, but if need be, feign delirium and unconsciousness. Speak only if you absolutely can't avoid it, using only the most basic responses, and only in Turkish. If one of you forgets and answers in Armenian, God have mercy on your souls!"

Every jolt and rut en route earned a fresh shower of painful protest from the passengers, but the whip-thrashed and snorting horses soon thundered into the hospital yard, where mass confusion spilled from every passageway and cot.

The Red Crescent nurses at Mamouret-el-Aziz were overrun with casualties, some from hundreds of miles distant and

many with gaping wounds and gangrenous limbs that required swift and full attention. The new arrivals were made to
lie on the floor and wait. But to pay a debt to the generous
American, the harried nurses asked no questions and quickly
and efficiently bound the wounds of the brave men of Mus in
between more serious cases.

"Allah bless you, Afyon," Davidson called to the charge
nurse, who was sharp as a carpet tack and had to wonder at
the odd wound patterns of the men's bodies compared to
their damaged clothing. But, dear heart that she was, she said
nothing. Not even when the application of an arm splint was
met with a short burst of Armenian cursing. She simply
stuffed a piece of torn sleeve in the man's mouth and continued as if nothing was amiss.

"God find you room in Paradise," she responded with a
weary smile. "Now do us a favor and get off the floor, all of
you. We need the space!"

Before daylight, all the wounded Armenians were treated,
bandaged, and helped aboard a Turk army transport train that
was headed for the battle against Russia. Some of them had
identification in their pockets signed by Frank Davidson and
embossed with the official seal of the United States of America.

As the train pulled away from the siding, Davidson prayed.
If the Fedayeen network held, mountain rebels ahead would
be awaiting the arrival of the train and snatch the fifteen citizens of Harput away at the army staging area a few miles shy
of the battlefront along the Russian border. A couple of canyons and paid Kurd mercenaries later, and the bogus soldiers
could fall gratefully into the open arms of Uncle Christian.

At dawn's light, Davidson was on his way to Malatya to
negotiate food at the railway stop. He had the feeling that a
great many supplies intended for Harput markets were actually commandeered by the Turk military and sent to the battle
zone. It seemed that these days everyone—even citizens of
Turkish descent—had to fight for each morsel received, especially when there were extra mouths to feed and outfit.

He felt justified in going. There was little official work left
to do at the consulate, and this was one way to keep an eye
on Turk dealings in the outlying district. Not that his pres-

ence prevented much ill, but at least they'd know he was watching.

He rode into the caravans of deportees from Erzurum and Erzinjan encamped near Harput. It was like riding through hell itself. Ragged, filthy ranks of widows and children moaned eerily in confusion and hunger. One child crawled on her belly toward a patch of faded grass which she had not the strength to pull. She lowered her mouth and chewed the blades with rotted teeth.

"Please, kind sir, I beg of you to take my child."

"My little ones, Mr. American, with a little food and water will serve you well. In the name of God, save them!"

Mothers held their children out to him, eyes pleading, faces contorted in agony. Limp, lifeless babies hung from fleshless arms and milkless breasts. Infants squealed weakly. Dirt-and-mucous-caked children, once healthy, took halting steps toward him like hundred-year-old dwarves. Their sunken eyes and bulbous heads looked unearthly.

Three shrieking children sat in the dirt around the body of their departed mother. They would have to beg or die.

An aged woman, face scarred somewhere in her long flight from sanity, beckoned to Davidson. "You need a coat, fine sir? I sell you this good coat of my husband's for very little." She did not need to say what had become of her husband. "I know the history of this coat. It will last someone a lifetime. It did my husband." When Davidson started to turn away, she grabbed up a set of blue-and-silver earrings. "My daughter has no further use for these. Perhaps you have someone you love with the pretty ears like my daughter had. Or this belt, woven by my mother, hand stitched by her mother, in the family fifty years, good as the day the cow gave her hide for it. A watch? You need a watch?"

It was heartbreaking. Whole generations for sale and almost everyone barefoot. Davidson swallowed hard. A man should be able to die with his shoes on and a watch in his pocket.

He'd heard that Turk military gendarmes accompanying the caravans often scared the refugees into thinking an attack by marauding Kurds was imminent. They were told to lay down their valuables, that the Turks would safeguard the goods and return them later. They rarely kept their word and systematically plundered those they were supposed to escort to safety, or allowed Kurd raiding parties to have their way with the Armenians.

Thankfully, word of the mass killings was at last reaching the United States and Europe. Reports had recently arrived in Harput that Near East Relief was raising funds for medicine and food. The many missionaries who had refused to abandon Turkey at the outbreak of war were the ideal means of administering the relief efforts. The American Board of Commissioners for Foreign Missions had outstations and missionaries throughout the country, along with scores of Protestant churches, schools, and colleges. World opinion would weaken the pasha, open the gates to relief.

It was health, welfare, and moral recovery on a large scale that might, however, take months or years. For now, the Turks would exact maximum retribution from their Armenian citizens, punish them for having controlled the nation's imports, much of its exports, and eighty percent of commerce in the Ottoman Empire. Punish them for having a lower infant mortality and for establishing a historic homeland, an immense tract of land comprising one-third of the entire country. And punish them for being infidels.

Davidson's nose recoiled at the incredible stench of sick, unwashed bodies. Dysentery and typhus were epidemic, killing half the population of outlying villages within ten days. Some Turk and Kurd villages suffered an identical fate. Few doctors, scant medical supplies, wells poisoned by the dead bodies of refugees trying to slake their thirst—Turkey had effectively slit its own throat with no plan to stop the bleeding should someone decide it was worth saving.

Word had come that Van had fallen. It was one of the few places the compliant Armenians had made a stand, and a brave one it was. They courageously faced the Turk army, which was in retreat from a losing battle with the trained Russian enemy. The Russians were coming to free Van, but the Turks marched through eighty Armenian villages first, shooting in cold blood every adult male. In three days, tens of thousands of Armenians lay murdered.

It was then the Turks had turned their rifles, machine

guns, and field artillery on the Armenian citizens of Van. Fifteen hundred Armenian men with three hundred rifles fought five thousand Turk soldiers and their weapons of war. A large part of the town went up in flames.

For a month, Armenian men, women, and children resisted their attackers until the Russian army arrived and took over the task. The Turks fled the area to massacre the Armenians in surrounding villages. A communiqué from U.S. Ambassador Henry Morgenthau listed the devastation: fifty-five thousand Armenian dead collected by Russian soldiers and cremated.

The empty wagon bounced over stones and ruts, leaving its firm, even track in the dust of ten thousand shuffling feet. They passed rows of the dead spread faceup, facedown, among the trees where they had been off-loaded from the death carts. No attempt had been made to cover the bodies or grant them respect. Tears flowed freely down the cheeks of the big boxer at Davidson's side. "I ... I want to eat the snows of Ararat before I die," he wept. "I want to take my people with me, to bathe them in the snow and heal their scars, restore their flesh, wash the terrible memories from their minds. My homeland! My poor, slaughtered homeland!"

Davidson took the reins from Kerkorkian and slipped an arm around the big man's shoulders. He ached for his Catharine's comforting embrace and the sound of her reassuring voice. A letter had arrived from her this week—nearly three months old!—and already it was tearing from being unfolded and refolded scores of times.

As always, she tried her best to keep it light, to take his mind off circumstances of separation and war and to not burden him with troubles at home. He'd told her he preferred to hear the little details of normalcy that accompanied daily life in New York. He pulled out the letter to read once again.

Albany, New York
January 27, 1916
My Dear Frank,

How mad with worry I am half the time. Your letters have grown very sporadic, and it is clear that they have been opened (by Turk or Yank?). It galls me to think of some perfect stranger pawing over your private declarations of love. Still, every word is precious to me, and I sometimes awake to find your letters have spent the night beneath the covers next to me.

Well, darling, I took your advice and came north to Cousin Florence's for the remainder of the winter. The cold is biting, and I have spent more time skating on my bustle than on my skates. My goal before spring thaw is to remain standing for a city block, then glide back on my bustle if need be!

How easily I can see you laughing at my ungainly efforts on ice. I'm smiling, too, as it does seem to have been some tonic for my ailments. The pale pink in my cheeks is deepening to rose. I think next I shall try hockey, although they frown upon it for women. We should, after all, be in the kitchen stirring hot toddies for our men. Perhaps you regret my lack of kitchen sense. Forgive me, darling, and know that if you were here, I would drown you in toddies!

Ran into an insufferable suffragette today—Jane Adams, chairman of the newly formed Woman's Peace Party. She thinks a speedy end to the war will come through a conference of neutral nations like ours, and an eventual end of all war through the creation of an international police force. Hmmmm. As long as all police are men, I don't think that's likely to happen, do you? (Of course, I want the war to end so you can come home!)

Oh, Frank, I am so torn over a woman's right to equality. Just when I'm ready to elect a woman president for the country, somebody will say, 'The hand that rocks the cradle rules the world!' Then I burst into tears because I can't give you a son, and the only cradle I'll ever rock is someone else's.

Enough melancholy. I know how difficult things must be for you. Though you hold back so much, I read between the lines. A few short paragraphs are beginning to appear in the papers about the atrocities. Don't give up trying to get the attention of others. Though German hijinks get the most play, you've got to keep pressing for equitable treatment of the Armenians and for the Turks to be held accountable for their misdeeds.

I love you, sweet Franky, and am so very proud of your achievements. President Wilson will reward your loyalty.

I just know he will! I'll write again once I return home. Until then, place this page against your cheek. It is saturated with my kisses!

> With Sweet Affection
> and Most Tender Love,
> Cath

P.S. I've found that blue cardigan sweater you thought you'd lost. It was in a pile of forgotten mending that I can't seem to ever get around to. You'll think me silly, but I wear the sweater sometimes, just to feel something of you around me. I'll not stretch it out, never fear, but I'd rather see it on you. Come soon, Franky. I'm not much good without you. C.

He folded the letter and returned it to his pocket. How thankful he was that he could hear her voice in every word. For all else that could be heard in the impoverished land of his existence was the blowing of the wind and the creaking of the wagon on the deadly road to Malatya.

CHAPTER 20

Sasun Heyd, the stationmaster at Malatya on the Berlin-to-Baghdad Railway, was not in harmony with the earth, nor with anything above or below it. Nothing written in the Qur'an or prayed in his five daily prayers to Allah or uttered by his three wives—especially that uttered by his three wives—would be half sufficient to atone for the cursed pashas and the five cars of food staples they'd caused to sit immovable outside the station, blocking the one main transport line across the entire Turkish Empire.

He paced the plugged track. "Berserk the Brilliant couldn't have done it better!" he seethed.

Heyd was beginning to sweat. He hated to sweat. He wore crisply laundered shirts and a clean pair of pants each day and mopped his brow, his underarms, and the backs of his knees at the first sign of perspiration. He kept three wives—despite their incessant nattering—to launder his clothing.

Heyd's blood had run cold when the train pulled in with its five cars guarded by soldiers with hollow stares stationed on its top and sides. Chests crisscrossed with ammunition, they disembarked, shouldered their weapons, and disappeared into the countryside to exterminate Armenians. There was no other reason for them to be here. The Russians were much farther north.

Sasun Heyd wiped his neck and narrowly missed a stream of brown spittle fired from a bored old Turk slouched on the coupling between two of the food cars. A dozen local militiamen—crippled, aged, or otherwise unfit for military service—were charged with guarding the contents.

But who was looking after the pitiful refugees who flooded in just after the food cars arrived and stretched their hands

212

toward him in desperate pleading? The attending gendarmes, smeared in the grime and blood of grim days on the march, shouted that a camp be made, and then, without even sitting for a moment's shade on the station platform, headed into town to quench unspeakable thirsts. Now Armenian refugees were encamped all over the rail yard, as far as the eye could see, in their little clusters of rags and filth.

For two days the drawn, starving masses stayed where they had been ordered to stay, though no one was there to enforce the orders. Despite the horrors they had seen, the Armenians were afraid to mutiny, to leave behind the familiar torments of a forced march for the unknown terrors to come.

Heyd the stationmaster felt sorrow for the refugees. He could not look at them, for they reminded him of the incredible failure of leadership that Turkey suffered. To shout against the pashas for poor civic management was a national sport; to look squarely into the face of their depravity was to kill all hope. He gave the deportees a wide berth—until today.

"If you move another step, I will dash your brains in with a stone!"

The threat came from just ahead of Heyd, where a tall scarecrow of a refugee in a brown coat and a shorter man in a gray vest with an enormous scowl stood over a cowering elder. Every time the old man tried to rise from his knees, he was knocked back by the fists of his two antagonists.

"Let me go!" he cried, shielding his swollen eyes and lips from the rain of fists. Blood trickled from his mouth. "I must go forward, I tell you, I must!"

"Here, stop that!" Sasun yelled, but not before the tall man hit the old one across the cheek with a flat rock. The elder, barely covered by a ragged white shirt, baggy trousers, and one-and-a-half shoes, moaned and fell on his side.

Heyd shoved his way into the circle and knelt by the beaten man. "This is government property. You cannot commit your crimes on government property. What has this man done?" This close, the old man's stink was overpowering, and Sasun cursed getting involved.

The shorter of the other two replied with an indignant sneer, as if reporting a petty thief to the magistrate. "He was moving to the front of the caravan and would not maintain his position near the rear. Those of us who are stronger and can better keep up have earned the front positions!"

The elder gasped and for all his injuries pulled himself up. He wet a thick tongue and rasped into the ear of the stationmaster. "I must not fall behind. They target stragglers. My feet are injured and I am too slow." Sasun cast a painful glance at the old man's feet poking out of shoes worn through by endless miles of walking. What he saw were barely recognizable as feet, so pulverized and covered in oozing sores that they leaked blood and gray-green infection. The nails were long and cracked and yellow with fungus.

"If he is not fit to travel, then he should be left at the roadside to be met by God's mercy," said the tall man, thick black eyebrows meeting in the middle.

"*You* are God's mercy!" shouted Sasun with a vehemence that shocked the tidy stationmaster himself. "If you are unable to save this man's life as well as your own, then have the courage to see that he does not die alone!"

The two Armenians looked at the neatly dressed Turk cradling the injured refugee. They backed away. "You who have caused our anguish now wish to tell us how to treat our own?" said the tall one incredulously. "Will you come to our fires and calm our children with amusing stories? Will you save our women from rape when the gendarmes return tonight fortified with wine and rest? Will you accompany us even so far as the next village to bear witness to our survival with your own eyes? Will you help us bury our dead? Will you?"

The reckless, accusing questions went unanswered. Heart pounding, Sasun pulled the old man up and half carried, half dragged him to the door of the station house. He kicked open the door he'd left ajar, hoisted the old man inside, and kicked the door closed. Immediately he regretted his actions.

Door shut, the old man reeking and bleeding on the carefully swept floor, Sasun could barely breathe and wondered if he was having a heart attack. Worse, he was sweating like the greased wrestlers at the cultural festival in Smyrna.

Not only had he given aid to a prisoner of the state, he had singled out one individual for special treatment. Was he to stick cotton in this man's wounds and put him back where he'd found him? Would the Armenians on the other side of that door, in order to curry favor, tell the gendarmes that the stationmaster of Malatya harbored a fugitive infidel?

He gave the old man a sip of water, then reached in the lower drawer for the medicine kit. He felt in the kit for a vial of ointment, selected a clean swab of cotton, and knelt over the visitor's crippled feet.

———

Ashkhen and Misak Mentese rolled their wagon alongside the station platform and hopped from the heat of the trail into the cool of the covered railway loading area. They rubbed and worked the kinks of the bumpy ride from their aching muscles and let their eyes scan the waiting railcars surrounded by a disheartening multitude of Armenian refugees. With each passing day, their numbers swelled, and it seemed that the whole earth was required to move or die. The now familiar stench of the sick and dead hung heavy in the air. It was uncannily still, the gathering vacuum of an electric storm robbing lungs and land of moisture until it could hurl the liquid plunder down again with sound and fury.

The station door opened and shut, and a wiry man in sweat-stained white practically flew to greet the newcomers. There was a pungent odor about him of trees and pastry and salve.

And sickness. Death. Those two were stronger in the stationmaster's presence.

"I am Sasun Heyd, railway master at Malatya. How may I serve you on this day of omens?"

"Omens?" questioned Ashkhen in Turkish, suspiciously eyeing Heyd who was suspiciously eyeing them both.

"Just look at the sky, friends. Measure the air. Something is about to happen."

The Menteses looked at each other, perplexed at this strangest of all greetings. Ashkhen felt a shiver ripple across his scalp and looked behind him to see if a cloud of pursuit was on the horizon. "We seek resupplies for the Twelfth Army Corps stationed at Hekim Khan under the command of Captain Neelam Ozal."

Heyd glanced narrowly at the single wagon, the two men, the sky, and back to the two men. Their lack of uniforms was not strange, given the shortages of war, but the lean, feral gaze in their eyes made him clammy. "Your papers of requisition?" He looked at them steadily and waited.

Ashkhen studied the glowering sky. "That is a sky heavy with omen," he said. He turned to Misak. "I think, my brother, that this is the final resting place for the bag of gold coins."

The stationmaster's suspicion grew. "Gold? What are you talking about? You asked for resupplies, and I asked for your official papers of requisition. If you do not have papers, then Allah be praised, we have come to the conclusion of our business."

Sasun nodded curtly and was about to turn on his heel when Ashkhen said, "We have something better than papers. We have gold coins. You have need of gold." It was not a question but a statement of fact.

Sasun blustered. "You are talking to a duly appointed servant of the Turkish government. Rare as it is these days, gold does not carry the power of a signature or a stamp of state. Have you neither of these, then we have little to discuss. Besides, that regiment of yours should number at least one hundred eighty souls. The two of you and one little wagon are hardly a convincing emissary from good Captain Ozal. The plains are full of pretenders today, and I do not grant the pasha's food to pretenders."

"Does this look like pretense?" With a flourish, Ashkhen removed a small dark velvet bag from inside his tunic and spread his palm with several coins of tawny gold.

Sasun's eyes leapt, but he quickly folded his arms and resumed a stern bureaucratic air. "Ah, I see. What was once a bribe in theory is now a bribe in fact. There are severe penalties for attempting to corrupt a government official. Even in these times of moral scarcity and temporal lack, not everyone has chosen the low road. No papers, no resupplies."

Misak, who so far had not spoken a word, stepped forward. "Excuse my brother's brashness," he said, "but it was not until you mentioned the portent of this day that the offer was made. It is very obvious that you need this gold. That removes it from any hint of scandal and places it squarely in the category of providence." He smiled the most pleasant smile Sasun had seen since his first child by wife number two had recited the Five Pillars of Islam without stammering.

"Why do you say I need this gold?" Sasun asked.

"Why, most esteemed government official, four truths are quite obvious. One, the rails on either end of the five cars occupying your station are caked in dust, an indication that no new freight has traveled over them in days and that you have probably missed a payday or two in all the confusion. Why should your loyalty go unrewarded? Two, it would appear that you are all but deserted by whatever other national government officers ought to be present if the powers in Constantinople truly care about this shipment. Therefore, at this moment you are the pasha's only mouthpiece for the railway station at Malatya, and the power to act is yours alone. Three, food does not keep in heated railway cars indefinitely. How would it look if you allowed the goods to spoil? Four, local militia are not empowered to do the work of federal officials; therefore, these who guard the train would be in violation should they attempt to unload the supplies aboard that train."

"And your conclusion?" Heyd found it increasingly difficult to take his eyes off the gold coins on Ashkhen's palm.

"That we, being part of the national Twelfth Army Corps at Hekim Khan, offer all assistance to the only appointed federal power at Malatya in unloading and distributing the food in the name of the pasha, all of the pashas. And that you receive this gold in partial payment for loyal service in difficult times. And your conclusion, Stationmaster?"

Sasun thought of cool sea breezes, azure blue waters, and natter-free living. "I have business to attend to in my office should you need me. Otherwise, enjoy your brief stay in Malatya!"

Ashkhen replaced the coins in their velvet bag and passed it to the stationmaster with a slight bow.

Quickly, as if at any moment demons of destruction might fly from the sinister clouds, the Menteses ran from pocket to pocket of refugees, conscripting in rapid Armenian the most lucid and able-bodied among them, whatever their age or sex. At first, despite their famine, the leery Armenians argued and were reluctant to invite the wrath of their absent overseers. But the Menteses cajoled and convinced until, quiet as fleshless specters, the small army of the chosen swarmed into and over the waiting food cars.

A generous portion was afforded each militiaman as promissory payment against wages. With nothing left to guard, they took their food and went home.

With antlike efficiency, the deportees in one half hour stripped the railcars of every crumb, every leaf, every morsel of grain. Six tons of food vanished among them like corn in a crowded barnyard.

They filled the Mentese wagon level with the sideboards. Extra sacks of flour cushioned the wagon seat with the ingredients of the staff of life. The load was covered in canvas and satisfied the close inspection of Misak and Ashkhen. Too full, the wagon would draw attention. The one hundred Armenian sisters would just have to practice frugality.

The wagon loaded and secured, the Menteses looked out over the encampment. The same dreary pockets of wasted humanity. The same appearance of hopelessness and death. No sign that anything had changed.

Misak's sharp eyes found the one difference. Away off the end of the station platform, a little lice-infested girl with rickety legs played with two moist peach pits, her scabby lips wet with juice. Her dull, crusted hair was pulled back with a strip of bright red flour sacking.

The splash of life was only visible a few brief seconds before the girl's mother wrapped her head once again in a dusty, unwashed scarf the color of earth. A puff of wind chose that moment to rain more grit on the miserable camp. It coated the girl's mouth a muddy brown.

Without the dab of color, Misak soon lost sight of the little girl in the mass of milling refugees, and it was a loss he found most difficult to bear. But at least now there was something in her belly that would keep her alive a few more days. Time enough for another miracle.

———

A lone horseman caught Ozal's company close to noon on the outskirts of Malatya.

Other than an early morning pair of rough farmers in a creaking wagon on the way back to their turnips and leeks, hauling a load of flour for their families, the sixty military men on horseback and a train of six supply carriages had met no other travelers on the deserted road. In an abrupt exchange of greetings, during which the farmers pulled off into a field to allow the Twelfth Army provisioners to pass, Ozal learned that plenty of flour had been left behind in Malatya.

But now, at the sound of thundering hooves approaching from the rear, the captain called the supply train to a sudden halt. He turned to face the approaching messenger who came madly on, cloak flying horizontally behind, reins whipping wildly, racing steed slick with foam.

Face set in a grim half-smile, Ozal waited for his lieutenant.

The horse, barely under control and coated in dirt and saliva, plowed to a wheezing stop in front of the officer.

"Bergema is an impostor!" gasped the lieutenant. "Murat Prison still stands. No one knows of a strangler or even a petty thief by that name. But the townspeople have recently had a brush with four Armenian anarchists on horseback, so have villages all along a corridor out of the north." He paused for a mighty gulp of air. "They are Fedayeen, good Captain, as certain as the sun. And that's not all. The traitorous Bergema is rumored to be the infamous Fox—straight from the bosom of Kevork Chavoush, the Black Wolf!"

The troops broke out in angry curses and an excited babble of disbelief.

"Silence!" commanded Ozal, who ground his teeth and looked sharply at the messenger drenched in sweat. "To warrant those illegitimate sons of Satan coming so great a distance at so monumental a risk, they had to have been summoned." His eyes glittered and narrowed. "It does not take a palace scholar to guess the identity of the one who screamed for the Fedayeen dogs. The two of them have played in the river together, and she is named the *bash kadin* of his harem. All the while, he eats my meat and drinks my wine. He calls me captain to my face and swine to my rear. And now he plots to steal my property out from under me. I should have trusted my instincts!"

Ozal, the heat of rage visibly rising in the veins of his neck and forehead, slashed at the air with an imaginary riding crop. Mocked by its absence, he tore a rifle from the grip of the closest soldier, whirled about in the saddle, took aim at the horrified messenger, and shot the wasted, straining horse out from under him.

"There is no time for delay," he said, voice low, yet audible to his shocked and silent men. "This will be our food for now. Quarter it and load it on. Turn the caravan around and make all haste for Hekim Khan. Set some village women to work cooking stew while we hunt the Fox. It won't be much of a hunt. He can't have gone far with all that baggage, and by the looks of this weather, he'll wish he were in hell. It will be a bloody day, but by its close the vultures will thank us!"

———

The abandoned buildings of Old Hekim Khan just to the northeast of the newer quarter took to the torch as if soaked in gasoline. The six kegs of gunpowder from the garrison created an aerial display so bright that witnesses swore the flash of the blasts reflected off the billowing storm clouds overhead.

Scores of the remaining Twelfth Army contingent, having just escorted the refugee caravan past town and onto the road to the internment camps, had no sooner turned around than the near distance blazed yellow-orange with flame.

They converged on the run with a stream of the last of the Turk soldiers pouring from the center of town, some on horses, most on foot, still pulling on a second boot or hastily cramming shirttails inside trousers. Several were weaponless but fully prepared to choke the life out of Armenian renegades with their bare hands. Not a few looked bewildered. Who could have predicted an insurrectionist attack this far out on the plains?

Out of sight, below the bluff at the river's edge, Tatul Sarafian and Azniz Mentese washed black powder from their hands. They waited for the ringing in their ears to subside before returning south at a lope.

———

The repeated blasts shook the walls of the old hotel with a frightening force.

"Sisters of Armenia, we bow in prayer." Slowly they sank to their knees—Fark, in his green fez and billowy attire, and the one hundred thirty women and children, crammed shoulder to shoulder before him.

"In the name of Christ Jesus the Conqueror by whose stripes we are healed and by whose blood we are saved; in the name of all the glorious apostles, saints, and martyrs of the Holy Faith who did gladly succumb to all manner of destruction by stone or sword; in that Name that is above all names, we humbly beseech you, God the Almighty, to take us away now across the river to your fortress walls at Mesrop. Grant us safe crossing and sanctuary. Grant us a happy and holy reception. And though we walk through the valley of the shadow of death, keep us from the enemies of the faith—"

"And allow us to see the blessed wood, the Cross of Noah made from the Ark of salvation!" cried Adrine Tevian, almost more excited than fearful. The room filled with murmured assent.

"Into your hands, O good Lord, we commend our spirits. It is in the name and for the sake of Jesus the Only Begotten that we pray. Amen," Fark finished.

The room echoed with fervent amens. Then the women, wrapped in what meager clothing remained from the rags they'd surrendered for the refugee caravan, some carrying children in their arms or clasped close to them, filed out into the glowering daylight. Isabel Petrosian smiled at Adrine and made the sign of the cross. Leaning against her, lips trembling and faint with fear, Hannah Mereshian paused to grasp Adrine's hands.

"Go with God, good Hannah," Adrine said. "Your feet are clean, dear sister. You are Christ's and He is Prince of Heaven!"

Adelina Yanikian, her wide-eyed boy in a cloth sling about her neck, pressed gently against Hannah's back until she moved through the doorway.

"Forward, sisters, forward!" urged Adrine, who stood by the door, smiled, and caressed the cheek of each one who passed. Some were still engaged in fervent prayer. "Remember Lot's wife and do not turn back!" she instructed.

They stepped out into the hostile streets. The heavens opened and the rains descended. The wind howled and moaned among the houses and shops of Hekim Khan, but no one emerged, no one stopped them, no one helped. They were alone.

When the hotel had emptied, Adrine said a special prayer for Tatul, Azniz, Misak, and Ashkhen. She followed the others along the street's five shops to the opening between Zarene the carpet weaver's and a boarded-up bakery. From there, it was twenty paces to the edge of the embankment, then down a long slippery path that angled fifty paces across the face of the slope and out across a narrow gravel beach to the water's edge. It should not take them all more than a quarter hour to assemble at the ferry landing and the rafts that would take them across the Kuru River.

Adrine stopped, sensing someone at her back. "Yes, who is it?" she demanded, not turning to look.

Sosi Emre, the Turk washerwoman, stepped up beside Adrine, little Kenan in her arms and both soggy with rain. "We have come to say good-bye." The poor woman's face quivered with sorrow, and Kenan's sniffles were loud in the empty room.

Adrine smiled sadly, took her friend's hand and gripped it hard. "But we are the two Marys," she said and reached out to smooth the lines of anguish in the woman's face. "Easter won't be the same without you. Come with us, Sosi. I am so afraid they will harm you."

Sosi looked down and swallowed hard. "How would we be received among your people? How would Kenan be treated by the other children?"

"As one of us!" said Adrine with a vehemence that surprised them both. "You have treated us righteously, and your reward is in heaven. I haven't the right to ask you to leave your home, but if you stay, my heart tells me we shall both regret it."

Sosi gazed at the resoluteness in Adrine's expression, then she whispered in her son's ear. His sad eyes brightened, and he whispered something in return. Sosi smiled. "Kenan says that if Ardem can come, we should follow." At the mention of its name, a younger image of Giaour the cat stuck its head out of Kenan's shirt, then withdrew back inside the instant a raindrop pelted its black-and-white nose.

Adrine laughed. "Yes, yes! After all, it's an Armenian cat with an Armenian name. I'll get Giaour so they'll have each other for company!"

Hand in hand, the three humans and one cat ran through the rain to find Giaour and catch the others headed for the river.

They were all refugees now.

CHAPTER 21

Frank Davidson brought the wagon to a stop at the Malatya train station just as the stationmaster cinched the last rope tight on the canvas covering his own wagon. Sasun Heyd was calmer now, and that allowed the cedar, cloves, and anise to do their job. He turned to the two men and smiled without the slightest hint of odorous offense.

"Frank, my friend! Gomidas, what a delight! But so sad your faces. Not trouble at the consulate, I hope?" Heyd was feeling good, and he fairly bounced on the balls of his feet. Early on he'd guessed Davidson's extracurricular activities, but he couldn't help liking the man and the generous way he rewarded Heyd for ordering whatever supplies he needed—and for keeping his mouth shut. It was a mutually beneficial arrangement, and the stationmaster would far rather deal with a liberal-handed American than a rabid Turk national any day of the week.

"It is a trail of death from here to Harput," Davidson replied heavily. "We have seen things no man should be required to see. How fare you and your accomplished wives, Sasun?"

Heyd's smile faltered. He did not want to talk about the natterers he was about to leave behind. Not that their welfare concerned him. They had their sewing machines and could talk any man out of a means of support. "They are adequate. Thank you for asking. The Older has gout, the Middle a goiter, but the Younger is just afflicted with the fast tongue." He grinned, thinking it not at all strange to call his wives by their chronology rather than by their names.

Davidson did not smile, and Gomidas said not a word. Davidson shook his head at the sight of countless more Armenians being marched and starved to death. But the big boxer looked through and beyond the idle railcars and the milling refugees as if fixed upon some far horizon of thought.

"We don't wish to take up a great deal of your time, Sasun," said Davidson. "We received word that a shipment of staples has arrived, and we need to restock the consulate kitchen."

The stationmaster studied his nails nervously. "You certainly must be entertaining a large number of Turk officials these days," he said, casting a hesitant glance at the covering on his wagon. "I'm surprised Washington allows the expense, but then that's none of my affair. Regardless, it is a moot question. There is no food in these railcars, and I have errands to run. You'll excuse me?" Was that sweat rising in his armpits?

"Was there *ever* food in these railcars, and if so, where has it gone?" Davidson demanded.

Heyd's neck beaded perspiration, and he lost his smile. "While I don't think I care for the tone in your voice, Consul Davidson, let me say that of course in the history of these railcars, they have undoubtedly carried foodstuffs upon occasion."

"Oh, for the love of heaven, that's not what I'm asking, and you know it!" Davidson exploded. "Where has the food gone that I was told recently arrived in those cars? And let me add that I would be reluctant but willing to make this a matter of diplomatic importance faster than you can snap your fingers!"

That did not fit at all well with Sasun Heyd's immediate plans, so he promptly replaced his smile and forced his mind off the salty secretions now gathering behind his knees. "Come, let us be reasonable, Mr. Davidson. You request normal answers in abnormal times. There was food in those cars, of course, but now they are empty. Logically, you want to know where it has gone. Logic has no place in the current political climate. And if I may, let me say that if I stand here much longer, I will have to answer to a power even more formidable than you. Most of the former food was destined for the Twelfth Army regiment stationed at Hekim Khan, and those supply wagons should arrive anytime soon. I do not wish to be in the way when they do. As Allah is my witness, I am sincerely hoping that they came and took the former food in the night without my knowledge, or I will be just another rat exterminator at the Smyrna docks!" His weak smile was meant to solicit Davidson's sympathy, but all it earned was dark reproach.

"The *former* food? You talk in circles! That is no explanation at all. I will speak to your superiors. Now, if you will excuse me, I will go to meet these army supply wagons or go all the way to Hekim Khan if I have to. But I will have my explanation, and it will make sense!" Davidson returned to his seat in the wagon and angrily seized the reins. "Who commands the garrison at Hekim Khan?"

Sasun sighed. "Captain Neelam Ozal, friend."

Frank Davidson snapped the reins, and the horse reluctantly turned the wagon in a tight circle toward Hekim Khan. On his way past the stationmaster, Davidson shouted, "Ozal, you say? Don't believe I've heard mention of that name."

"Neelam Ozal," Heyd repeated, the name's sour taste upon his tongue. Sasun felt a twinge of regret for his friend from Harput. Whatever contact Davidson made with the notorious Captain Ozal, he would never ever forget the name.

But Sasun Heyd would try his best to forget it. And Malatya. And his job at the suffocating little stop on the Berlin-to-Baghdad Railway.

After the two men from Harput were but a distant speck, Sasun climbed up into the wagon and urged his horse northwest toward Gurin. From there, the balmy bays of Smyrna were half a country due west. He'd first considered going south to Tarsus and booking passage on a steamer, but south was not a good direction for anyone in these troubled times.

Besides, he had a passenger, and the longer the old man was kept from sight, the better their chances of escape. He turned and lifted the canvas and saw that the bruised Armenian slept the sleep of the drugged. Opium was almost good as gold in these troubled times. It helped people forget.

He passed the outstretched arms of an Armenian mother and daughter begging by the roadside and wondered why he had chosen to rescue an old one over a child. Was it because it required less of a long-term investment?

He shoved the disturbing question from his mind. It was something one of his wives would ask, or all three in chorus.

Sasun Heyd preferred to think of it as needing a grandfather.

The stationmaster urged his horse to a fast walk and wondered where in Gurin a man could obtain a fresh shirt.

Misak and Ashkhen Mentese waited below the far side of the bridge at Sisus. Thunder rumbled, and the air was charged with a crackling intensity. The sky was inky as sin.

The fuse at their feet ran twenty paces uphill to three powder kegs strategically placed beneath the main struts of the roadbed suspended over the tributary of the River Euphrates.

This was the fabled land of Assyrian Queen Semiramis, of Hittite mining settlements, and the headquarters for the Roman *Legio XII Fulminata*. According to a favorite Armenian legend, in response to the prayers of the Christian soldiers in the famed legion, lightning struck the Roman opponents and the battle was won.

The Menteses said a devout prayer that upon this day lightning would strike a second time.

Thunder crashed directly above them and it poured rain. Visibility worsened until they wondered if they would be able to spot the enemy when he arrived. Rivulets of mud cascaded down the embankment and turned the footing treacherous.

With a cry of frustration, Misak clawed his way uphill toward the kegs. Ashkhen caught a retreating foot and dragged his brother back through the mud to their hiding place in a clump of bushes. He grabbed him in a squirming headlock.

"You have maggots for brains!" Ashkhen hissed in Misak's ear.

"The fuse is soaked and useless!" Misak spit back.

"Of course it is, but we wait and pray for the rain to slacken. Under the bridge, all is dry. We wait and when we know beyond doubt they come, we light the dry length as close to the bridge as we dare. Your way, we blow ourselves to pieces, and then what good are we to the Fox?"

Misak quieted in his brother's arms. Ashkhen kissed the younger Mentese's cheek and smacked the top of the boy's head with an open hand. "Hotblood!" he chastised.

"Brute!" Misak shot back, but with a slight grin. They both had to dig in their heels to remain on the slippery hillside.

———

Hand in hand the Armenian sisters snaked a path from the bluff down the steep slope of the east riverbank to the little-used ferry landing. With a ferocious crack and rolling concussion, the thunder cannonaded above their heads. The shock of it flattened them against the embankment like trampled grass, soaked and shivering.

"Rise, up, get up!" Adrine urged them each time, shouting to be heard above the fury. She smiled and laughed and made a game of it, trying desperately to calm their fears and quiet the squalling children. Privately, she questioned the sanity of the flight to freedom. Maybe if they stayed, by some miracle they would be allowed to continue to serve their Turk masters until the war was done and the survivors could be sorted out. If the soldiers caught them escaping, for certain they would be butchered on the spot.

Then she remembered Ozal's hands on her shoulders, his foul riding crop beneath her chin, the ravine of the dead, filling with each passing caravan. If they did not at least attempt to escape, Ozal would desecrate the bodies of these women she had come to love. "Get up, sisters, come! It is not far!"

Through the driving rain, she could just make out the cracked and weathered assembly of rusted pulleys that held the wire cables swooping low over the roaring Kuru River. The cables extended to a twin assembly of pulleys on the opposite bank, which was obscured in mist. The motorized winch that in former days pulled the conveyance directly across the river and back had long since quit running. Ground creatures now built nests in the ancient gears.

Secured by ropes to the base of the near pulley assembly were two ferries, no more than large rafts, crudely assembled of wooden planks and crossbeams lashed to squares of inflated goat bladders. Ozal had not permitted the use of the poorly maintained craft in months. In theory, each ferry could take twelve passengers on a calm day, or twenty-four between them each crossing.

They were one hundred thirty-three souls, with Tatul and Azniz aboard to steer each trip. Seven crossings would do it.

Adrine peered through the rain at the rising water and bit

her lip. Rain hissed on the water, the rapids swelling to a boil. The tilted wooden cable tower looked as if it would topple into the torrent at any moment. She couldn't recall when it had been built—it was one of her first memories as a child. Its cracked and splintered construction, barely visible through the slanting rain, looked frail and ancient.

She felt faint, stepped out of line, and lay down in the streaming grasses to rest. The women had to remain calm. Panic was their worst enemy now. She shook with the cold and the sight of the flooded river. *Father, Son, and Holy Spirit, take us across.*

The rain battered her back, and the cold of it quickly penetrated thin flesh and into her bones. The rain beat against her head. She felt as if she would never be warm again.

"Adrine!" someone called to her.

Tatul?

"Adrine," chided Sosi Emre again, pulling her friend to her feet. Kenan, wet and shaking, looked miserable. "Come, Adrine, we must keep moving."

———

Tatul waited at the ferry landing, the multicolored sash of the Fedayeen now proudly, defiantly, bound at his waist. Misgiving gnawed his stomach, and a hard knot of apprehension pressed against his heart. The pitiful procession of mothers and daughters, little children crying for dry clothes and a warm fire, made its way toward him like lambs to slaughter. Little lambs that had placed their trust in the Fox. Perhaps little *dead* lambs.

The storm howled in angry, sodden blasts that whipped the rain-swollen river into a maelstrom of clashing waves. Tatul looked at Azniz, who struggled to hold one raft against the shore by a rope line, and smiled encouragement. Azniz returned a brave nod.

Tatul held the shore line of the second raft wrapped around one wrist and stretched his other hand toward a mother and child urged forward by Fark the eunuch. "Come, mother," Tatul called, blowing the rain from his mouth. "Take my hand—quickly now!"

Once aboard, Fark helped the woman and child find a

place on the slick wooden decking and showed them how to grip the ropes that held the platform to the flotation bladders. One by one, the frightened, resolute women took their places aboard the sloshing craft and tried their best to quiet the terrified children.

"Keep their heads down!" Fark shouted. "Don't let them look at the water!"

Tatul strained to see Adrine through the streaming rain. He thought he saw her, and then it was as if the earth swallowed her up. He could not remember so fierce a storm. It was either heaven's cover or hell unleashed, he didn't know which. Whatever it was, it would rapidly extinguish the explosion site, and Ozal's soldiers would discover the suspicious absence of Bergema and the Menteses. Enraged, they would soon descend like a swarm of rabid bats.

Lightning lit the riverside in a blinding flash, and Tatul looked up. "Help us!" he screamed at the sky. "Take us across!"

A woman midway in the procession mistook his agitation and thought he had spotted movement behind them at the top of the bank. "We are discovered! Oh, God, they're coming to kill us!"

Confusion erupted. Some women shoved others aside and fell in their mad rush down the bank.

The alarm spread. "Why are we being punished?" another wailed. "God take us!"

"The children! The children! Throw them in the river!"

Tatul thrust the rope into the hands of one of the sturdier sisters waiting to board the raft and dove for the legs of another racing for the water's edge with her bundled child. They fell in the weeds, and Tatul tore the girl from her mother's arms. He scrambled out of reach, sat on his heels, back bowed, and sheltered the terrified child against his chest. Man and girl presented a slender shield between the raging waters and the panicked women.

"Drown her!" shrieked the wild-eyed woman who lunged for her daughter but slipped and fell again in the thickening muck. Other mothers hesitated but tensed, fully prepared to cheat capture and hurl their children into the river.

"No!" Tatul shouted at the soaked, mud-smeared women.

"If you kill your children, you hand victory to the enemy. This little one is the future of Armenia, the seed of a new homeland. Ozal's soldiers are distracted by the explosion, and you saw Ozal leave town with your own eyes. He has not returned. Have courage; have faith!" He said it, even though he felt little possessed of either attribute.

Adrine, matted and disheveled in her spare covering, materialized from the downpour and took the girl in her arms. She spied the scarf of many colors at his waist. Heart pounding, she looked at Tatul with wonder and love. She turned, shoulder against his arm, and faced the sisters now clumped at the river's edge.

He felt her tremble.

"Women of Ararat, Mothers of the Homeland, do not forget your heritage." Adrine was their magnet, their proud voice. They listened. "Saints Thaddeus and Bartholomew carried the Light to our ancestors in A.D. 43. We are the Armenian *Apostolic* Church. We are bold in God, temples of God's Spirit. Rise up, take hold of Christ, and stay fixed on the Cross of Noah, there"—she pointed behind her—"just across that river. God took him through the flood, and He will do the same for us. Believe, sisters, believe! And if still you doubt, see the sign of the Fedayeen tied at this man's waist. This is no thief, no convict. This, good women of God, is our brother! When your heart fails you, think of the scarf and how brave Bolu Bergema ransomed us all from the hand of death!"

Now it was his turn to look at her in wonder. Silent, worried faces set determinedly, other women, including Sosi Emre, stepped away from the distraught mothers. Backs to the river, they formed a chain of resistance and looked steadily into the eyes of suffering. The despairing ones, so thin they looked ghostly transparent in the lightning's glare, would not be comforted and wailed in sorrow. They gripped their children to their chests or beneath their arms, with knuckles white as death.

The second raft took most of the remaining passengers and Tatul as the steersman. He looked longingly at Adrine, the faithful Fark by her side, and prepared to cast off.

He stretched out an arm toward her. "Come, brave heart, room for one more."

Adrine hesitated, wiped the water from her eyes, and thrust Sosi and her boy forward. "Here are your passengers," she said stoutly. But Sosi shook her head. "If you stay, we stay," said the Turk washerwoman.

Another woman, face a fearful mix of hope and terror, quickly stepped forward, a one-year-old in her arms. Adrine waded through the shallows with her and helped mother and child aboard.

Fark shouted to Tatul. "It looks, my courageous Fox, as if your lady will serve you well after all."

Adrine heard and her heart soared with the truth. The Fox was neither apparition nor fable. He lived, and he'd called her "brave heart"!

Their eyes met. The camp cook and the legendary Fedayee knew in that instant it would not be their last rescue. God would use them again to safeguard lives and protect the innocent.

Without a word between them, they dreaded the coming separation. The swelling Kuru might as well have been the great sea, so deep was the divide. In a rush of mutual understanding, they realized each had become the other's anchor. Adrine smiled wanly and made the sign of the cross over her heart.

Tatul returned the sign with a sad smile. He called to her. "One day we shall explore what we feel, when we are dry and the River Kuru is no longer with us."

She nodded and prayed that God would give them the chance. "You are Fedayee," she said. "We must succeed!"

He wanted to run back and kiss her but gathered in the rope instead. He felt in his shirt and tossed her Ozal's riding crop. Loathsome as it was for both Adrine and Tatul, it represented the captain's strength over them. When it was kept from him, he seemed less formidable. She frowned at it but held it tightly.

How Tatul hated to leave that bedraggled little band so defenseless. Too bad being Fedayee wasn't some divine power after all. If she but knew how little the Fox really had to offer.

With Azniz manning the tiller of the lead raft, Tatul the tiller of the second, they pushed off through the shallows and made for the mainstream, the umbilical cords of rope playing out behind them. The unrelenting rain pounded against the little rafts with cold hard fists, and the power of the river pulled them in.

————

Three hours away at Sisus Bridge, Ashkhen shook Misak awake. "They come."

The brother looked where Ashkhen pointed, and gradually, like shimmering wraiths, men and mounts took solid form in the far mists. They moved at a trot, the slower pace dictated by the intensifying storm.

Slowly, deliberately, careful to stay hidden behind rock and bush, the Menteses made their way back to the bridge. Now they could hear clipped bits of conversation, the splash of hooves, and the snort of horses.

Worry raked at Ashkhen's thoughts. The rain had not softened, but only worsened. Ozal came much too soon, and where were the supply wagons? Had he prepared his own surprise? But if his leaving town was a ruse and he meant to catch the Fedayeen in a snare, why had he traveled so far from Hekim Khan?

The answers would have to wait. The Menteses needed to stop Ozal here to give the Fox time to ferry the women across at Hekim Khan. It was a detour of many miles to the next bridge crossing and would stall Ozal by half a day or more. By then, and by God's miraculous intervention, all of the women would be safe inside the monastery.

The slick hillside gushed streamlets of water and provided no secure foothold. Every step forward crumbled beneath them, and they slid farther down the slope, dangerously close to exposure. The river below was visibly rising from the flash runoff.

Ashkhen and Misak fought their way upslope. The elder motioned to the younger to observe. Misak stopped. Ashkhen took one step up. Another. By stepping into clumps of vegetation securely held by the roots, and not directly on the muddy earth, they at last began to make progress.

"Stop!"

The Menteses froze. Ozal's order sounded above the fury. Horses and riders halted.

Seconds passed like hours, and every fiber of the brothers' beings shouted for release. Ashkhen, certain they were discovered, could feel Ozal's eyes peeling the skin from his back. He hoped the wagon was well enough hidden with brush. Misak's leg started to cramp, and a cry of pain was upon his lips when his brother forced a stick between his teeth. He bit down hard and fought to stay upright.

————

"I don't like it." Ozal stood in his stirrups and scanned the bridge ahead. Carefully he examined the roadbed above and below, the uprights and rails of the creaky old crossing. "No, I don't like it," he said again, low as if talking to himself.

He dismounted, handed the reins to his lieutenant, walked to the side of the road, and slid partway down the embankment. Crouched, hands on thighs, he peered intently through the watery gloom. He looked down, blinked the water from his eyes, then up again to a place beneath the far end of the bridge.

They were clearly distinguishable this time. Three gunpowder kegs, military issue, snugged up under the main support struts, ready to blow the bridge into the sky.

Ozal motioned for silence, then pointed. Two more officers dismounted and slid downhill to better vantage points. Their eyes fixed on the kegs, and they nodded their understanding. Again motioning for silence, Ozal returned to his horse and led it on foot to the near end of the bridge, his men right behind him. They paused. Ozal remounted. They remounted. Ozal raised his arm slowly. When it dropped, they would charge across the bridge.

Lightning lit the structure in stark light. It wasn't much of a bridge, but it was all the bridge they needed.

————

Ozal knew.

There wasn't time to ignite the fuse. Headstrong Misak was sure to balk.

"Brother," Ashkhen whispered, "give me your hand."

Misak, gasping from the hot pain in his calf, reached out, fully expecting his brother to pull him up the steep slope.

Instead, Ashkhen grabbed his brother's wrist and gave a mighty shove. Misak Mentese flew backward and fell twenty feet into the Euphrates.

"God help you!" Ashkhen cried, then turned and bounded from plant to plant up the eroding hillside, a dagger clenched in his teeth, eyes riveted on the kegs of explosives.

"Charge!" bellowed Captain Ozal and the horses sprang forward.

Ashkhen reached the nearest keg and plunged his dagger deep in its side. A blue-black stream of powder gushed out and was soon joined by two identical streams from the other kegs.

Overhead, the clatter of hooves and the shouts of assassins rained down upon the Armenian from Ardahan.

His feet slipped out from under him, and Ashkhen Mentese stabbed at the earth. The dagger caught and held. Alternately stabbing and crawling, he pulled himself back to the kegs, all the way praying a blessing on his people, his country, and his soul.

Neelam Ozal, his officers, and ten of his enlisted men cleared the bridge. "Ride hard!" he shouted.

Ashken leaned over the bleeding kegs and struck iron to flint.

The thunderous blast blew the Fedayee apart and tore the end from the bridge. Eight soldiers and horses were caught in the direct blast. The sixteen riders behind them yanked back on their reins before sliding forward and down. With a mighty wrench and rush of wind, the remaining bridge structure buckled and pitched into the surging river. One man leapt from his horse to the bridge rail and rode it down until it tore from the roadbed moorings and swung free, dangling him high above the raging deluge.

Below, horses and riders thrashed for their lives, swept downstream by the twisting torrent closing over them, repeatedly rammed against the bridge superstructure just ahead of them. Lightning tore the sky, and for one terrible instant, illuminated a logjam of struggling flesh, both beastly and human. Then the swirl of pleading, squalling life was gone, swallowed by the river that had become a boiling sea.

The lone survivor swinging from the bridge rail lunged for the main structural support still anchored to the embankment, missed, and fell screaming into the flood.

Thunder cracked and rolled. The ground shook. The fragile soil collapsed. Mountains of mud, rocks, and trees tumbled into the waters as if covering over the grave.

Captain Ozal rode on toward Hekim Khan and did not come back for his regiment. "Ride, you fools, ride!" he screamed at the men who remained. No matter the loss, the Fox must not be allowed to escape. They whipped their horses into a flying lather.

"Faster!" the captain roared, "or they shall make good their escape!"

Lightning flashed, rains hammered the earth, the waters rose, and the men of the Twelfth Army Corps rode faster.

CHAPTER 22

As soon as they nosed into the strong, rain-swollen current, the rafts swung downstream. Each was tethered by ropes to the system of pulleys connected to the wooden assembly sunk in the riverbank. Once they had off-loaded their passengers on the other side, the steersmen would shout at Fark to retrieve them, and hand over hand, the others would drag the rafts back for another load.

The river here was ten horses across, nose-to-tail, compared to normally four horses. The rising gray waters gushed from the throat of the leftward bend above the town and raced past the ferry landing as if desperate to escape the stifling pull of Hekim Khan. The shallows behind them where Adrine had freed the little boy in the reed boat were shallows no more.

Tatul and Azniz worked the rudders and attempted to angle the rafts neither so little as to be swept away downstream nor so sharply as to capsize. Each haul rope was attached to a ring in the center of a chain the width of the raft so that it could be reeled back to the landing at Hekim Khan. The sagging cable stretched wooden tower to wooden tower was their only orientation in the soupy gray onslaught.

The current wrenched them downstream to the chilling roar and hiss of river and rain. Tatul's muscles knotted and fought the giant pull. His brain screamed prayers that no one would lose her grip.

One woman near the center of his raft lifted a defiant fist and shook it at heaven. "Why?" she raged. "We are Christians and still you turn a deaf ear. Why have you not avenged our dead husbands and sons? Why?"

One or two others added their mumbled accusations, but

most braced against the cold and the river waves that alternately drenched them and drained off their bent backs. Tatul did not contradict the accusers. Resentment kept a body warm, and he wasn't at all sure what he could say in defense of God.

"We have but ourselves to blame!" came a thin, reedy rejoinder from somewhere at the far edge of the raft. "Most of us lived as atheists going through religious motions. What are we to expect but God's punishment?"

The others cast curses at her and told her to be still.

"Who let this Turk on board?" one mocked. Another derisively demanded to know, "Who granted you sainthood?"

But the one they reviled was not easily silenced. "I do not pardon the Turks, but as a people we put too much stock in our wealth and possessions, in our precious achievements. We should have been on our knees praying for our souls and the souls of the Turks!"

This was met with angry shouts. "How would you pray for a Turk who split open the womb of your pregnant sister just to see if he rightly guessed the sex of the child within?" More shouts. A shove. "If you want to spend time with your precious Turks in hell, then over you go!" Arms reached to force the unwelcome passenger overboard, and she half fell, one leg in the water, one on the raft.

"Stop!" yelled Tatul, trying desperately to steady the raft and quell the riot. "You behave as animals!"

A child shrieked. From out of the gloom came the rush of the far bank. With a mighty jolt, the raft collided with the shore, and a bloodcurdling cry tore from the woman struggling to keep her place on the raft. The leg trailing in the water was pinned between the raft and the shore.

Tatul leaned hard on the rudder. The craft swung away from the bank, then grounded to rest in the mud and gravel, under a sheltering overhang of rock and scraggly shrubs on the low-lying west bank. A gaping gash in the injured woman's knee showed bone and trailed blood to the landing, coloring the shallows crimson. Azniz had already grounded his raft farther downstream, and those passengers hastened along the bank to hold fast Tatul's raft. The women and children splashed and floundered ashore in their haste to be off the river.

Quickly someone tore away a length of threadbare garment, fashioned a tourniquet, and bound the injured woman's leg above the wound. Another sacrificed a sleeve of her dress for a bandage. A third tipped a carefully hoarded bottle of liquid between the woman's moaning lips. The nurse's pained eyes met Tatul's angry ones. "She said too much," she murmured, biting her lip and looking away.

The thunder and lightning subsided and moved on, but the rains poured incessantly.

From back across the river came singing. " 'Christ, my Christ, my heavenly shield . . .' " Brave Adrine held choir practice.

"Ready, Azniz, my brother?" Tatul called to his friend. The pale Mentese, whose crossing had been no less taxing, nodded. "Wait here," Sarafian ordered the women. "Huddle together for warmth. When everyone's across, we'll make for the monastery."

"If first we do not die of exposure," a mother complained, her child's teeth chattering like dice in a cup.

The singing from across the river died, and Tatul shouted, "Fark! Adrine Tevian! Pull!"

Again. A third time.

Within seconds, each steersman felt a tug. Thin hands pushed the ferries off the slippery bank. Ever so gradually, the rafts edged back into the river for the return journey.

A dozen women at a time hauled back on the slick ropes until their arms threatened to snap. Colorful Fark, a barking streak of perpetual motion, organized a fresh dozen to stand alongside the others and one by one take the line from shaking, weakened hands.

"That's a good harem," he joked. "I see that soft silks, milk baths, and bejeweled navels have not spoiled you!"

The banter took anxious minds off their peril. "Swallow your scurvy tongue, old fig!" they chided in return.

Fark worriedly examined the two badly frayed haul ropes being ground away by the corroded pulleys. If they snapped now, the rafts and their steersmen would plunge downstream, unstoppable, to be lost in the crushing deluge below. Yet they dare not go back to town to search for a newer replacement. Besides, there wasn't time. Fark prayed what rope they had would hold, then recited the Nicene Creed.

Adrine helped choose the line crews, subtly including one of the more distraught women in with the stronger, thereby scattering the most volatile and suicide prone. It was good that they labored and kept their minds off the top of the bank eighty feet above. As the passage of time was swallowed by gray rain, gray river, and ever grayer skies, Adrine found herself glancing more often at the ragged line of bush and rock that defined the top of the bank where the women had come over the crest from the road in front of the hotel and made their way down the well-worn trail. She prayed for a legion of angels to blind the soldiers, or for the sun to fail and inky blackness to fall. Whenever she stared too hard, fatigue and a muddled mind convinced her of guns where there were no guns, of wicked eyes without bodies, and bodies without eyes.

They worked without ceasing, forth and back and forth again, each time made more difficult by the steadily rising waters. Four trips, five, and a sixth. Children cried. Women moaned, their hands cramped and bloody from the coarse rope, and yelled their petitions for divine mercy. The winds howled back and hurled knives of cold through thin, soaked clothing and lank frames.

And mercy came down. No lives lost. No guns. No Ozal.

"It is a storm from Mother Ararat!" shouted Fark jubilantly, sniffing the air with exaggerated zest. "Smell the snow, sisters. It has the scent of pitch and gopher wood in it. Again God's ship sets sail upon the flood! Again the children of Adam and Eve are spared! What soldiers? What death squads? For us the Red Sea holds no threat!"

On the sixth return trip, even Tatul Sarafian breathed easier. "One more, God above. One last crossing, and then maybe you and I should talk again."

The landing at Hekim Khan was a pulverized slough of mud. The last remaining—Fark, Sosi, Adrine, and ten of the hardiest Armenian sisters—gathered in the rope, hand by torn hand, weary minds unthinking, bodies on the verge of collapse. Tatul, alone on his raft, was three raft lengths from landing, the lone Azniz and his raft close behind that.

Without warning, the haul rope connecting Tatul to land parted like rotted wood. Fark, Adrine, and the five women behind them jerked back and fell in a heap. The racing current, as if glad to finally claim one of the rickety craft, whipped it downstream, slowly turning like a hat in a whirlpool. Tatul heard Adrine's faint scream from shore, turned, and threw himself against the tiller to avoid a massive rock outcrop leaning away from the bank.

The raft yawed right and the rudder snapped in two. Tatul fell into the rear wake, grabbed for the line securing the goat bladders, and held on.

The force of the impact drove the raft vertically up the face of the rock outcrop. The raft held suspended for a moment like a newly sawn tree, then, pushed by the power of the river, it started to fall back on Tatul. Instinctively, he dove beneath the surface.

The raft smacked the water and broke in two. Flotation bladders squirted loose in the churning confusion. Lungs near bursting, Tatul grabbed wildly for one of the black air bags and missed. The surge pounded him against the unyielding outcrop of stone.

His mind stalled. Horrible black curtains of night wrapped a part of his brain in thick layers of darkness. He struggled to stay conscious. *Bladder. Got to get one. Mine . . . the goat's?*

On the third try his arm snagged a ropey nest of bladders that lifted him to the surface. He exploded from the water and gulped glorious sweet air and dazedly wondered where he was. Hands and arms beneath his shoulders and legs pulled him from the river and turned him on his side to cough and retch the water from sodden lungs. Images swam before his eyes, and voices babbled unintelligibly around him. Adrine's hands on his head and neck. An angel's? Wet, tangled hair in his face. Warm drops of something on his cheeks.

He regained his faculties between the grunting forms of Azniz and Fark, the former in possession of the Fox's arms, the latter a firm hold on the Fox's legs. They stumbled with their half-drowned load back along the riverbank toward the one remaining raft. The slick footing was so unsure that, even in his rattled state, Tatul assessed his chances of being pitched again into the river were quite good. He squirmed in their grip, and they set him down.

"Thank you, brothers, thank you! Your services are no longer required." It was then he saw the stricken face of Adrine Tevian. Mirrored in the dear woman's eyes was the reality of just how close he'd come to dying and an affection he couldn't bear to name.

"Forgive me, Adrine. I fear I have concerned you needlessly." He took her hand, but she pulled back in pain. Gently, he opened her fingers and exposed the raw, oozing wounds of the rope. Before he thought, he bent and touched warm lips to the injuries.

Startled that he would be so bold in the presence of others, Adrine gasped. Tatul, flustered, looked to Fark for guidance. But with sudden speed, the little gnome bolted for the ferry landing. Tatul looked at the ground, a place of similar interest for Adrine's gaze. "I . . . I unthinkingly did the first thing my mother did before dressing my wounds as a child. Of course, you're no child . . . I mean, you're someone's child, certainly, but no small child in need of . . . of . . ." His voice trailed lamely away, and Adrine turned from him so that he could not see her smile.

"We must haste," snapped Tatul irritably. "We invite the devil's own dirt standing here. Fark will bind those hands on the other side. Quickly, I say!"

Adrine ran ahead. The feel of his strong neck muscles, the contours of his noble face, made her fingers tingle and anesthetized the stinging pain in her palms. *Thank you, God, for restoring him to . . . to me.*

They were too many for the remaining raft, but no other choice presented itself and they crowded aboard. No sooner had they launched into the grab of the river than they saw, too late, that the water had risen mightily, and now a mob of deadly projectiles had joined the racing tumult—a wagon tongue, parts of buildings, tree limbs, and whole trees, their snarled, glistening roots flying downriver dark as a witch's mane.

The wind howled in torment between the banks. The heavy, slanting rain bent the passengers over, feet and hands frantically digging for a secure hold in ropes and planking.

Two or three hung half out over the water, so little room was available.

Tatul and Azniz wrestled the tiller, but the swollen current ferociously refused to yield. Helpless as a toy boat, the cumbersome craft yanked into the mainstream, twisted, and rushed downstream stern-first.

"Pray!" shouted Adrine above the howl.

"By the wounds of Jesus," Fark's high voice implored, "still the waves!"

The raft began to swing about-face toward the far bank, but the shore came on too fast. They swept past the normal landing site, over a huge swell in the rapids, and down into a caldron of branches, farm implements, and a drowned cow caught in the thick arms of a tree, its trunk imbedded in the shore.

The downstream edge of the raft was sucked under the bole of the tree with a sickening crunch and held. The back edge reared to the sky. The passengers fell into the snarl of flotsam and grabbed for a hold among the branches and debris.

Adrine felt Fark pushing her from behind, and she stumbled forward against the awful flow of the current that threatened to tear her from the tree. Again and again her feet broke through the slick tangle. Each time she clawed back, gaining shore a little at a time. She tried not to see into the frozen stare of the lifeless cow snared belly-up in the hag tree's grip. Even in death, the look of dumb trust remained.

She followed the trunk of the tree to the top of the bank and to the ruined, gaping hole where once the tree had stood anchored in soil. She fell to her knees in the grass, hands clasped, uttering gratitude in short, breathless gasps.

Fark pulled her to her feet and pushed her ahead. "Pray on your feet," he said kindly. "We shall soon die of the cold. Keep moving, sisters, that's the way. Keep moving." She caught the gnarled hand of an old woman and the small, slender hand of a young girl. They stumbled forward together.

The wind died, but impossibly, the rain fell still harder and turned the earth to mush. Adrine's feet no longer existed, all feeling lost in the numbing cold. They had literally fled with nothing but the clothes on their backs and not a thread fit to be buried in.

And then the Fox was there and lifted the little girl into his arms. "Catch hold of my sash!" he shouted to Adrine. "Your friend, too!"

His strength and stride carried Adrine and the old woman swiftly forward as if they grasped the wings of Mercury. They pulled and half carried one another up and along the bank in their haste to find the rest of the sisters and then seek the monastery and refuge.

They lurched along the shore until at last they reached the landing where all the other sisters and children had been left.

A sea of mud. Footprints upon footprints. A child's carved figure of a wooden pony poking from a puddle.

But no child. No sisters. No life.

They stared uncomprehending for a moment, then Tatul explored the perimeter for signs of a trail. "Here!" he called. "They must have hastened to the monastery. This way!"

"*Halt!* Do not move, or by Muhammed, the Seal of the Prophets, you Fedayeen dogs will be shot for treason!"

The command, shouted from across the river, was as paralyzing as snake venom.

"Stay," rasped Tatul to the others. Slowly, he pivoted to face the source of the command and looked up.

Shock stabbed his loins with daggers of bitter disappointment. Above them, for fifty paces along its grassy crest, the high opposite riverbank bristled with grim-faced Turk soldiers, weapons trained down on the shivering escapees. But, thank heaven, still no Ozal. These were the thirty-five remnant troops of Hekim Khan under subordinate leadership, angry and disoriented by the diversionary blast from the town's old quarter. Could they be stalled? "We have not come so far to be stopped now," he shouted back. "We have a right to protection and a future."

With a resounding crack, a rifle muzzle flashed orange. The bullet tore a corner of fringe from the sash about Tatul's waist and left a searing hot trail across the surface of one thigh. Adrine screamed in pain.

From the corner of an eye, Sarafian saw her go down. Then, as if someone pulled a lever releasing a false floor beneath, the entire slope upon which the soldiers stood sheared from the riverbank with a roar and fell into the River Kuru.

The mud slide, triggered by the rifleshot, crashed down in a grinding churn of men, weapons, trees, and earth. An ocean of water separated them, filled them, and bore them under the waves. Their cries of terror were quickly swallowed as the mighty flood closed over them and swept them away to a watery death.

Tatul rushed to the still form so pale against the mud. Adrine lay facedown, blood seeping from a bullet wound in the right hip, a frightening look of eternal peace about her. In shock, Tatul lifted her from the mire and pressed her fragile body to his chest, less weight than a new, wet calf.

For a moment, stunned and weeping, Tatul and his little company stared unbelieving at the massive gash in the land where seconds before a small army had stood. They waited for more troops to appear at the new brink of the far bank. All that came were swiftly dying winds and softening rains.

He did not feel the burning in his side. He pressed an ear to Adrine's chest. The seconds were eons in which no one moved but watched the dark, sorrowful eyes of the Fox.

Those eyes squeezed shut at last, and with that a sob tore from the Fedayee's throat. "She lives!" he cried. "Thank God Almighty, my brave one lives!"

But how thin the rhythm of her heart and how cold the skin. They must not delay. "Come," Tatul commanded. "Haste to the monastery. Move!"

They turned. And stopped.

Before them stood another wall of men.

Black hoods. Black cassocks.

Not one made a sound.

The silent monks of Mesrop.

CHAPTER 23

The water swirled about his neck and forced itself down his throat. His nose and mouth fell below the surge, and when he panicked, he gulped more water, then fought to stretch his neck and face out of the river. He vomited, choked, then clamped his mouth against another wave of water rushing to fill his belly to death.

Misak Mentese was caught in the crook of a splintery snag stretched across a narrowing of the river channel, one foot wedged tightly in an underwater vise of twisted branches. The water had risen from his chest to past his chin in the half hour he'd been trapped there. "God, my God!" he gasped. "Hold not my sins against me. . . ."

The awful roar and suck of the floodwaters faded in the numbing cold. Misak's limbs slowed. His chin gently slipped beneath the waves. He choked and jerked awake, with barely enough strength to stretch clear of the river for one more breath. Too soon he felt himself sinking back, no feeling in his knees, no way to support his weight for another push up.

"*Yavroos! Yavroos!* Dear one, come!" It was his mother calling him in for *gatnabour*, the rice pudding that always made him smile. He was late gathering the peas and now it was so dark. He thought she should be angry, but her voice was sweet with love.

Marooned in death, Mother's little *yavroos* opened his arms to her embrace.

———

"Did you hear something?" asked U.S. Consul Frank Davidson, a half hour out of Malatya. He'd heard a sound different than the thunder, more the distant crash of shattering glass.

"No, but I felt it," said Gomidas Kerkorian, the stable keeper. "An explosion somewhere ahead."

For another fifteen minutes they rode in uneasy silence, then welcomed the return of the previous discussion, tiresome as it was.

"Martin Luther said he would rather be ruled by a competent Turk than an incompetent Christian," Davidson asserted, then clucked at the horse and felt for the twentieth time if his collar had one more button to keep the wind and rain out. It did not.

"That presumes one can find a competent Turk," snorted Kerkorian. They had argued the politics of the Ottoman Empire for the past fifteen kilometers, hunkered beneath heavy oilskins. More profitable to search among goose eggs for a golden one than to debate Ottoman affairs. And about as productive.

"Confound this weather!" grumbled Davidson, geehawing the poor mud-caked nag out of sheer ornery frustration. "I have never seen the likes of this storm anywhere in the world! Eastern Anatolia is supposed to blister you in summer and make ice of you in winter. No one said anything about it hemorrhaging rain in the spring!"

They sought shelter in the lee of a bluff and attempted to build a fire, but the rains switched direction, and it became the lesser of miseries to keep the wagon moving.

"Smell that?" Kerkorian asked eventually. "Gunpowder."

They rounded a wide bend to the right on the approach to the bridge at Sisus. The river tore past on their left with incredible speed—one great roiling artery of water rushing to the heart of the sea, scouring every stick and loose rock ahead of it like a brawny fist thrust down a coat sleeve in haste.

It had apparently taken the bridge with it. The road ended thirty feet above the water. What twisted remains yet clung to the embankment were rapidly being undermined by a river out of control.

"This is a bad business," Davidson said, shaking his head at the devastation.

"Look, there!" cried Gomidas, pointing to a clot of brush

on the opposite bank. Caught in its tangle was the upper body of a lifeless Turk soldier.

Davidson jumped to the ground. "It must be the military from Hekim Khan. The way the bridge structure's shredded, this is our explosion. There's one of their wagons."

High on the far bank, looking forlornly down as if half convinced to follow the dead, was the Menteses' sodden horse still attached to its wagon.

"Quickly!" Davidson ran downstream at a trot, Gomidas at his heels. "Any survivors won't last long in this."

They searched the racing waters for signs of life. The footing was treacherous, and more than once it took a swift grab to keep from falling into the wild river. When they reached the narrows and the monstrous tangle of debris that all but dammed it, they were ill-prepared for the chaos of men and horses caught in a graveyard of fallen trees and twisted wreckage poking above the churning maelstrom. Two dead soldiers chased one other in a foaming whirlpool, caught in a perpetual *danse macabre*.

"Nothing to be done for these poor infidels!" Gomidas shouted above the gale and the hungry storm waters. "We should turn back now before the roads become impassable."

Davidson stared hard at one tree that stretched the width of the maelstrom, stuck fast in the shattered remains of the bridge and whatever else had floated down from farm and settlement. "We can make it across that tree if we go now. Most of the water's passing under that mess, but it's rapidly building up and will soon spill over. Leave the wagon—we'll appropriate the one on the other side—but bring the chest from the consulate and the foodstuffs. We've got to hurry."

Kerkorian looked at the bodies and hesitated. "I don't expect you to come," Davidson said kindly. "But I've got a bad feeling about this one. Something terrible happened here, and the answers may lie in Hekim Khan."

The stable keeper stared once more at the carnage. "The executioner is ever changing," he said grimly and turned to give his employer a look of deep sadness. "I will not abandon you, my friend. Lead on."

They ran back as swiftly as possible over the mud-slickened terrain and relieved their wagon of a canvas bag of dried fruit and jerked meat and a small padlocked brown leather chest with metal clasps. Gomidas slapped the cover of the box. "Are you convinced this is worth the risk?" he asked Davidson.

"That," replied the American consul determinedly, "contains life and death for many."

Without another word, the muscled Armenian shouldered the chest. Davidson slung the canvas bag onto his back, unhitched the horse, and slapped its rump. The two rushed back to the ghastly tangle. Already the water had risen another inch. They removed their sodden slickers and prayed for divine traction on the slippery crossing.

Carefully they crept out onto the pileup, trying to keep their eyes off the racing waters beneath and on the snarl of dark branches and splintered wood that caught at their clothes like the devil's own fingers. They made it onto the thick trunk of the tree. Each time a new piece of debris rammed their precarious barge and sent a shudder through the whole fragile assembly, they held their breath and prayed.

Gradually, they progressed along the trunk to midstream, gasping and chattering with shock from the combination of icy rain and chilling river. Just five more minutes and they could kiss the good earth again.

Davidson waited for the gentle pugilist ahead of him to continue on, but there was no movement. "What is it?"

"It climbs up here!" Kerkorian yelled back. "I need two hands free. Straddle the tree trunk, and I'll ease the chest down to you."

Davidson hugged the trunk with his legs and wedged the bag of food securely in a notch formed by two broken limbs. He leaned sideways around a thick, vertical bough. "Careful!" he called. "Let her down easy!"

Slowly Gomidas sank onto the tree and lowered the chest by a single handle. Davidson stretched to take it from him but couldn't quite reach it. "No good. Can you come down a bit more?"

His left leg twisted under him, Gomidas attempted to straighten it out. Off balance, he struggled to keep a grip on the tree and in so doing, loosened his grip on the handle. The chest shifted with a rattle and slipped out of his fingers.

Davidson made a swipe for the box, but it tumbled end over end out of reach.

"A stupid mule I am!" yelled Gomidas, trying to twist about to see. "Is it there or is it gone?"

"Watch yourself!" Davidson yelled back, tempted to agree with the stable keeper's personal assessment.

Davidson peered down and smiled to see a corner of the chest sticking out of a matted cradle of shore grass and weeds. "I see it!"

There was something else.

A man's head.

Davidson groaned.

The head moved.

At first he thought it was the action of the waves jostling a corpse about, but then there was a sputter of air and a feeble, unintelligible cry.

"What did you say?" asked an anxious Gomidas.

"Not me," Davidson said, looking about for secure footing. "We've a man here, and he appears to be alive. There's room to stand, but be careful. Don't step on him or the lock box. Hurry! His face just went below water. He must be caught—"

While Frank Davidson cupped the man's chin and kept his head above water, Kerkorian cautiously slid into the water and felt for the man's feet. One was free, but the other was caught fast.

"I can't hold him much longer!" Desperately, Davidson watched the stranded man's face go slack. Was he dead or just unconscious? Suddenly, there was no resistance to the man's body, and again he slid below the surface. Davidson, his muscles cramping in the iron cold, fought to hold on to the tree and support the man's dead weight. "God in heaven, hurry!" urged the consul through leaden lips.

Gomidas had to release his hold on the tree if there was any hope of saving the enemy of his people.

"What, man, what?" Davidson searched Kerkorian's face and saw the resentment there. "Why do you hesitate? Save this man now, and trust God to sort the sheep from the goats!"

With a wrenching sob of regret, Gomidas Kerkorian dove under and wrapped strong hands around the trapped leg.

Imagining it was the neck of Interior Minister Talaat Pasha, he gave one mighty yank. The knot of branches snapped and the foot floated free.

"Praise God! All right, now, get back up on the tree. I'll hoist him up high as I can, then you grab under the arms and haul him up."

They grunted and strained, warmed now by the mutual act of saving a life. They got him onto the tree and slapped him until he roused and coughed water from sodden lungs. When he was spent from retching, he muttered on deliriously, barely above a whisper. Davidson leaned close to decipher the words.

Impatiently, chilled to the core, Kerkorian waited to hear what the infidel had to say. Davidson wasn't talking. "What does he whine?" Gomidas asked mockingly. "That he is cold and wishes to lie by the fire with old women?"

"I don't understand it," Davidson said noncommittally. "Perhaps you can make out what he's saying."

Throwing up his hands in exasperation, Gomidas bent an ear to the mumbler's mouth. "*Ya-yavroos*," he heard and his eyes grew large. "*Yavroos! Yavroos!*"

Gomidas looked at Davidson, who was grinning like a court jester.

"Despite yourself, you have saved an Armenian," laughed the American. "Of course, if you'd rather put him back . . ."

Gomidas gave his employer a look of disgust. "I wouldn't be so smug if I were you. He may speak Armenian, but why was he here with these infidels? And he's blinder than a wall. He called you *yavroos*, his little dear one." Kerkorian managed a grin, and both men laughed before cautiously removing the survivor from the far end of the river jam and carrying him over to the abandoned wagon.

They removed his wet clothing, placed him in old horse blankets and empty grain sacks among the flour sacks in the back of the commandeered wagon, then retrieved the leather chest and the food bag.

Consul Davidson, dry sacking around his shoulders, lifted the canvas cover and checked their passenger once more. His violent shivering rocked the wagon. "I'll join him," Davidson said. "Two bodies stay warmer than one."

"You drive," Gomidas answered, handing over the reins.

Before disappearing beneath the canvas, he leaned on one elbow and smiled. "On my bones is more meat with which to heat. Besides, this is a brother Armenian. So few of them are spared, I wish to be near him and give him of the life you have given me."

His throat tight, Davidson cinched the canvas down. Kerkorian's voice came once more from the wagon bed. "And you can believe that before the wagon reaches Hekim Khan, I will have this man's story!"

Davidson smiled, slapped the canvas, and urged the bewildered horse forward against the slanting rain.

They went nearly three miles before the giant plug of debris clogging the tributary to the River Euphrates broke under the strain and spilled its mighty wall of water and entombed dead like entrails onto the divided plains of eastern Anatolia.

CHAPTER 24

From across the courtyard, Adrine's deep hacking cough threatened to either send Tatul's pulse racing or stop it altogether.

At least the earth breathed easier. The sun mounted the horizon in a crush of rose and pink, streaked with peach and lemon. The rains were over, and the sun thirstily began its work of blotting the earth, reclaiming the waters so wantonly spilled. It was the morning peace of a child, all innocence and soft repose.

Yet the monks did not sleep. In shifts they kept the watch, uttering prayers, rifles ready, hearts clear. Eighty of them were assigned to Mesrop, Monastery of the Golden Casket. Forty remained at the monastery, and the rest were dispatched to the far corners of Anatolia to minister and die for the faith. They believed fervently in the ancient "Truce of God," which forbade wars on holy days and during Lent. They defended to the death the "Peace of God," which declared immunity from attack to peasants, the clergy, and to sacred places. For three centuries, the monastery walls had stood inviolate through kings and sultans and barbarians alike.

It was a city of refuge, a sanctuary, and many of the older priests and brothers could recall times when a life was spared inside the healing walls of Mesrop. Not a few believed it was because the monastery was home of the Golden Casket, the true resting place of Noah's Ark, in the Inner Room inside the Inner Hall of the Inner Courtyard. Within the ornate gold cabinet, beyond the two gold doors festooned with cherubim and seraphim, reposed a red cross of petrified wood measuring thirty-one centimeters tall, twenty-four centimeters wide, and three centimeters thick. Bishop Benedict alone held the power to hold, view, or display the sacred icon fashioned from the very wood that saved humankind from total annihilation. He alone vowed obedience under the Rule of St. Benedict and was therefore the true descendant of St. Anthony of the desert.

Only one other Cross of the Ark existed, at Echmiadzen, the monastery at the feet of Mother Ararat. Both had been obtained by St. Jacob of Nisibis who, one legend claimed, stood at the bottom of Ararat while a human chain of worthy Armenian males passed the sacred piece of wine red wood hand to hand down from the Ark at fifteen thousand feet to Jacob on the plain. He took the ancient material and fashioned it into two priceless crosses, an act that earned him canonization. Thus was the Living Faith preserved in two crosses of red wood, burning brightly in the pagan darkness of eastern Turkey.

Beyond the Casket, beyond the walls, yet near them, peasant women came to meet the sun and to work the fields in their baggy pantaloons, long-sleeved blouses, and veils. Dressed in purple, black, orange, and burgundy, the Turks liked to till and plant and cultivate within sight of Mesrop. For centuries before they were born, it had stood. Someday their daughters' daughters' daughters would gaze upon the same walls and till, plant, and cultivate the same soil. The Christian monks doctored the Muslim children and purchased food from their neighbors. What made them so evil that they and their people should be starved and shot? Those who fought the wars could go kill themselves somewhere else. Here, in the shadow of Mesrop, peace reigned.

The Armenian women and children of Hekim Khan lay under the sun in the outer courtyard of Mesrop, sun-warm on the outside, God-warm on the inside. Sleep, unmolested by soldier or tempest, was abundantly free. The wild, stormy crossing of the Kuru still raged inside them, boiling to the surface in nightmarish cries by day and night. But immediately upon their coughing, bedraggled entrance into Mesrop, they found a plenitude of kindly monks who moved among them with a compassionate intensity.

"Oh, Great Deliverer, you have brought your daughters and their innocent babies through the sea to dry land, and for this we exalt you, the All-High and Almighty," prayed Bishop

Benedict, surrounded by scores of shivering, weary refugees.

"Praise be to the Great Deliverer," muttered the survivors faintly, more moan than speech.

"O Maker of Fire and Flood, accept our gratitude for simple pleasures and use them to restore and revive each sister and child gathered here."

"Praise be to the Maker of Fire and Flood."

The amens were fervent and brief. Soaked clothing was quickly replaced with thick robes of rough fiber and soft tunics, plainly woven but warm and dry. Hot water for bathing appeared in great hearth-heated kettles carried on wooden poles by pairs of monks and emptied into copper tubs. Soothing ointment for multiple sores and abrasions was brought in little clay pots. They were safe here. Food was plain but plentiful. It was the first time the younger children had seen honey, and the golden treasure magically transformed mealy tubers into sweet treats.

For once the Armenian sisters thought they might live to see a new homeland. For now, it was enough to lie curled beneath the blankets and garments of the kindly, silent monks, there among the trees, among the tombstones and sarcophagi of dead saints.

"Bite on this," said Hannah Mereshian, handing a clean, tightly twisted rag to the woman whose leg had been pinned between the raft and the shore. Silently, fearful eyes wide with pain never leaving Hannah's face, the woman lay back in the arms of Adelina Yanikian and placed the rag in her mouth. Nearby, Adelina's little son nestled against a tired young girl whose rope-burned palms received a soothing balm from a crooked brown pot painted with tiny purple flowers circling its rim.

Remembering the Easter feel of kindly hands bathing her old, hard feet, Hannah tenderly applied salve to the ragged leg wound that flared red and raw from knee to midshin. Tears streamed from the injured woman's eyes, but she never uttered a sound, nor ceased to bite the twisted rag.

Nearby, Isabel Petrosian fought back other tears while wiping the runny noses of two boys fussing in their mothers' arms. She felt their chests and heads and tried to hide the frown at the fever burning there. Her own chest was tight with missing Ahbet, her brave young suitor who had stroked her head when she was ill.

"Nothing worse than a sick bride!" Ahbet's mother had huffed, no girl good enough for her fine son.

"Nothing better than to nurse one back to health!" his gentle reply had come, the feel of cool lips against her clammy brow.

Isabel grinned at the boys and tickled their ribs. They squirmed and rewarded her with irritated smiles.

A chill passed among the sick and injured. Had they survived the river only to die between the walls of Mesrop? Was Ozal here, too, slithering closer each moment, about to release the poison of his fangs?

Sarafian did not rest, pacing the courtyard restlessly. He had not stopped the bullet that struck his beloved Adrine, though his body had slowed it considerably. The priests were able to remove it from near the surface, but feared she might have been too long emaciated to fight back against the infection of the wound and the cold that settled in her lungs.

And more. The fox, cunning and sly, outwitted his rivals by doubling behind the hounds that hunted him. Tatul the Fox did not even know on this fine morning where the hounds were. Should he leave sleeping dogs lie or entice the hounds out onto thin ice, then leap clear at the last moment while the heavier hounds fell through?

What was Ozal up to? When would he strike? He had not appeared among the ill-fated men who died in the riverbank cave-in. How many men did he have left? Had Misak and Ashkhen been able to elude him?

When Adrine had finally come to, she had first asked if he was all right, then for some water. It shocked him how utterly taken he was with her and yet how utterly incapable he was of sparing her further distress.

He found her on a soft, warm cot in the center of the sunny courtyard. She rested at the feet of a speaker monk who was reading to her from some ancient monastic text. " 'I am as intimately united to Him as the marriage bond. My spirit is His Spirit; my heart having long ago ceased to beat now beats with the divine heartbeat. I am one with the One and am hidden, nowhere, and am no one just as He is lost, forgotten, unknown by the world He made and sustains. I am a hidden outcome of His redemption, an exiled channel of His mercy, a messenger of His boundless love. . . . ' "

Brother Victory's soothing baritone was interrupted by another fit of hoarse, metallic coughing. Adrine doubled up, knees to chest, and in her sallowness, seemed visibly to shrink inside the large brown robe like a nut in a shell. She was alive, and for now, that was miracle enough. Sosi Emre approached with a small clay cup of tea, murky with the friars' special blend of medicinal herbs. Tatul took it from her and knelt by Adrine's cot.

He placed the back of his hand tenderly against her cheek, and the warm brown eyes blinked open. He felt a faint pressure against his hand and caught his breath. But a new wave of coughing seized her, and it was more than a minute before it subsided and she straightened again, small and brittle.

Tatul supported Adrine's head and held the tea to her lips. She sipped a little, a little more, then waved the cup away. "The sun," she said weakly. "Grandmother would be out in such a sun."

Brother Victory slipped quietly away. Giaour the cat took his place, all licks and nibblings in a vigorous attempt to correct the storm damage to her fur coat.

Adrine noted the silence and turned to see Tatul's troubled face. It was the face of a good man, a merchant, a statesman, a king. She could see that face on a theater poster, in a painting on a wall of the most opulent hotel in Berlin. The books at the mission school spoke of a life so much larger than anything she had yet lived, and here was a face to match that life.

"Thank you," she whispered.

Tatul preferred her faint smile to that of the sun, but her physical lightness frightened him, as did the stabs of pain that contorted her features every time she coughed. The wound would not heal unless she remained still. "Why do you thank me?" he asked.

She carefully sipped two deep breaths before answering. "You and Fark and Azniz removed us from the lake of fire. Without you, I have no doubt we would be piled dead in the ravine. It was the greatest bravery to come into a town where you knew no one and were so outnumbered. I am glad you are no Bolu Bergema!"

He laughed with too much bitterness.

Her face clouded over. "Why do you laugh at that? Why?"

He was upsetting her, which made it more difficult for her to draw breath. He was silent for a time and, without being aware of it, smoothed her brow until she calmed and the times of coughing grew further apart. He thought she had gone to sleep when she said, "Tell me your secrets, Tatul Sarafian. Does it bother you that I prefer your real name to your assumed one?"

He shook his head and wondered how much to say. It was still early, but a whisper of activity gradually filled the court- yard of the industrious priests. Morning prayers had long ago been said and breakfast eaten by those not fasting. Now there were manuscripts to be studied, Scriptures to be meditated upon, musical instruments to be played, gardens to be worked, chickens and goats to be tended. And always time was taken for blessed worship seven times between dawn and dark.

A huge collection of artifacts was part of the monastery treasure—valuable carpets, metal and wooden icons, a library of more than two thousand priceless ancient manuscripts and books. At times like these, Tatul yearned to be a priest on an internal quest for humility, purity, sanctity. But he was not that. He was a mountain rebel disguised as a cowherd. He was a sinner and the brother of assassins, heart dark with hate. He was not worthy to make the Ararat pilgrimage. If Ozal walked through that gate, Tatul Sarafian would happily gouge his eyes out and make him crawl on all fours the rest of his days.

Tatul winced. He had forced Adrine Tevian to crawl on all fours. Is that the best ruse the Fox could devise, to harm this one he cared so deeply about?

Her gentle hand brushed his. "Forgive me," he said. "I was just thinking how very unlike a fox I really am. That is the name I was given by Kevork Chavoush, the Black Wolf, but to date, I have not behaved much like a fox."

He needed to scout the surrounding river land. Perhaps torch the dense brush to flush Ozal into the open. The most dangerous madman was a hidden one.

The warm eyes watching him hardened. "Oh? Does a fox lose his scent by running through a flock of sheep or herd of cattle? Is that not what you did when you entered Ozal's do- main as an escaped prisoner? Do you not hunt with your nose, appear and disappear at will, sleep with the roots in the hole of a sandy bank? Does . . ." She choked then, and another long coughing fit ensued.

"Perhaps I should leave you. You must rest if you are to heal. You were so wet and cold." Tatul made to leave. He could feel Ozal close-by. The young Fedayee had to get beyond the monastery walls. To hunt.

Or be hunted.

"Don't go," she said in a weary rasp. She took his hand, turned it palm up, inspected it, and kissed the thick, callused skin. He looked at her, amazed at her boldness. She held up her hands, the rope burns salved and wrapped in cloths. "You started the healing process with a kiss. Now, please sir, tell me a story."

He laughed at her little-girl flirtations despite the pain and pulled the blankets more tightly to her chin. "Of whom shall I speak? Of old King Tiridates III who proposed to our ancient mother Hripsime? When she rejected his offer of marriage and refused to forsake the Christian faith, he promptly killed the thirty-three virgins who supported her and bore witness to Christ by their faithfulness."

She nodded. "That's a good start. Now tell me about you, your family, the town of your birth. Leave nothing out, or I shall call on the secretary of the Fedayeen to verify the facts." He laughed with her and held her close when the coughing returned. And stole those moments when she was distracted to scan the women, the monks, the courtyard, the walls.

They learned more of each other but talked not of what to do about the growing love between them.

And while he told his stories and scanned the interior of Mesrop, the Fox sniffed the air and paid heed to the hairs at the back of his neck. He knew the women needed rest and time to heal, but he knew also that the only way to live again was to greatly increase the distance between them and the rabid hounds of Hekim Khan.

———

Fark tried to get him to rest during the night watch, but Tatul could not sleep while frail Adrine lay feverish. The priests boiled and applied every medicament and poultice they

knew to concoct, but it was as if she'd waited weeks and
months for a safe place to lay aside the stiff resolve that had
carried her so long.

The sisters came in twos and threes to lay hands on Adrine
and to pray with fervency for her restoration. Tatul watched
them, watched the monks join in, read Scriptures, and apply
the warm oil of healing. But a great block in his own heart
kept him at a distance, fearful she might not recover and he
would be made to live without her.

He approached the aging friar Victory to ask the question
that kindled acrimony in his heart. "Why, brother? Though I
am found wanting in the wake of your great kindness, tell me
why that kindness did not cross the river before now and minister the mercies of God to those enslaved by Ozal, or intercept
the southern death caravans on their slow descent into hell?
Why have you shut yourselves up with your prayers and your
food in this pretty little garden while our homeland is strangled and mothers and fathers led in chains to the slaughter?
Answer me!"

At first it seemed that Victory was in some kind of medi-
tative trance and would not answer, but then, slowly, as if returning from a far place, he spoke. "Are you so sure we have
not gone out? We do so as the angels, taking on the appearance of farmer, plowman, or highway inspector to slip bread
into a grandmother's shawl, to give Christian burial to a dead
son, to steal away an entire family and bring them here to be
healed and smuggled north. We cannot save them all, but by
God's providential hand, we do as we're able, but not that
which would bring down the unholy wrath upon our refuge.
We act when the discernment of centuries says to act."

Victory, head shaven, one old cheek drawn slack with a
stroke, looked deep into the Fox. "I sense that your question
is one you have asked many times of yourself and the work of
the Fedayeen. You strike selectively and only a privileged few
are the glad recipients of your cunning. Is it random, Tatul
Sarafian, or a choice made in the heavenlies? When you rode
here in response to a cry for help, how many starving Armenians did you pass on the way? The caravan of refugees just
removed to the south—were they sacrificed in favor of the one
you love and her sisters? Oh, do not look so ashamed, as if

love is a meddler. For love between you to flower in the midst of demons is evidence of the divine, and in that we glory. It will be that which heals her.

"The questions you ask are sure to drive a man crazy, and you may ill afford to lose your sanity with so many looking to you for salvation. Save whom you've been called to save, and know that the rest fly to the bosom of the crucified Christ, the scars of their horrors forever erased from their memories."

Tatul knelt and pressed his lips to the old monk's hand. It was rough as hide and smelled of earth. And when the sanctified hand reached out and took his, it was with the grip of an archangel.

———

Another morning and bath day, nearly twenty-four hours since the crossing. A few of the women and children were sick with a variety of ailments, but most felt quite improved after two good meals, clean bedding, and lots of bed rest. Once they'd taken their fill of sun, the women and children were moved to the interior cloister cells to sleep and rest on the hard plank beds under the watchful eyes of guard monks. The remainder of the brothers took up temporary residence in the courtyard.

Several large kettles of water were kept boiling constantly to moisten the air of Mesrop and to provide the endless brews the brothers applied to the outsides and insides of their patients.

The rest of the steamy water went into the baths. Much splashing and laughter ensued in the copper tubs; so much can hope be contained in a small portion of soap and a good bit of swirling about in the warm therapy of heated waters. Brother Correction kept insisting on ten droppersful in each bath of a vile blue potion he said would draw the poison from the system, but few saw any sense in drawing the poison out while squirting the venom in. Bishop Benedict put an end to the screams when he pronounced Brother Correction's liquid "anathema and an unfit instrument of Christian charity." The good brother's feelings were repaired when Sosi Emre made him a buttery pastry of soured goat's milk and dried apricots. With a smack of appreciative lips, he was still licking stubby fingers long after the last crumb disappeared.

The lighthearted banter was medicine to Adrine. She even

sat up a few minutes and teased Brother Correction herself. "Let us send your liquid to the Russian front. Two drops in each Turk stewpot and the war will be won inside a week!"

At midday prayers the entire company gathered inside the prayer hall with the brothers of Mesrop to seek God. Six of the silent monks remained on guard on the walls, suspicious of every bird that called.

"O merciful Master of soil and sky, we the humblest of thy children come on bended knee to thank our Father's kind heart and to ask our Father's giving spirit to meet the basic needs of another day. Kohren Vartanian's little girl has stomach cramps. If it be disease, we beg thy divine intervention; if it be the beginning of womanhood, we celebrate thy perfect plan. Grant us normalcy, good Father, so that we do not jump at every natural thing and call that which is good sin, or that which is sin good. . . ."

The Fox listened to the prayers of Bishop Benedict as if they were his mother's lullabies and heard the music in them. They were earthy and plain and direct, not at all the elaborate, flowery petitions he remembered from his childhood church, but more the conversation of a son with a concerned and giving father. They poured over the women of Hekim Khan like mild ointment over a burning rash. The ill ringed the walls, reclining on soft wool mats arranged by the monks.

"Adrine Tevian . . ."

Tatul felt a swelling of the knot in his heart.

". . . continues to wrestle against the flames of infirmity, intrepid, defiant, better but still in need. We ask thee, loving Father, to pick up the fight for her, shield her from permanent harm, breathe into her nostrils the winds of heaven and grant her gentle repose in the crook of the Shepherd's strong arm.

"Ada Janjikian's left eye grows dim, Father . . ."

And so it went, each spoken request met with a murmur of renewed faith from the sisters who knelt, heads bowed, some weeping, a few clucking reassurances to fussing children, others still as stone in private struggle with a God they once thought they knew, who had in war become so unfamiliar, demanding, and distant. It did not escape Sarafian's notice that the latter sisters received an extra measure of patient attention from the priests.

"Elizabeth Sarian, Father, has such pain in her feet. . . ."

CHAPTER 25

It was two hours past midnight, when even the foxes occupy their dens.

A shaft of silver moonshine illuminated the rough stones of the absent monk's narrow cell, patches of light falling upon a high study desk and stool, a tall four-legged stand with porcelain washbasin, and a wooden wall brace bearing one spare, hooded brown cloak. Directly below it sat a small wooden clothes chest. The chest stood at the foot of a hard bed of planking that was chained to the wall and spread with an unmonklike cushion of blankets. In the center of those blankets, fever broken and breath steady, lay Adrine Tevian.

Beside her, on the floor, burned a small candle in a brass holder.

The spartan room opened doorless onto a long hall of cells—with three and four women and children to a cell—which, thirty paces along, turned at a right angle and continued past individual cells for another ten paces. Fark slept in the cell adjoining Adrine's tiny one-monk compartment.

The lone sentinels at the four corners of the monastery walls drew their cloaks tighter about them in the night chill. A half-dozen monks walked in silent supplication among the sleeping guests, praying in dead-of-night discipline for that other half of the world bathed in daylight.

Adrine dreamed. She was alone on a raft, searching a quiet stretch of the river for Tatul, who swam alongside like a laughing fish, then dove deep out of sight, teasing her. Why didn't he come up for air? She leaned out as far as she dared and searched the black depths until her eyes hurt.

How long she stared at the monk in the doorway to her

cell, face hidden deep inside the humble hood, was impossible to tell in the feeble light. But in that half world between sleep and wakefulness, she saw the figure enter partway, hesitate, start at an approaching swell of prayers from down the hall, then evaporate.

Time stopped and Adrine floated downriver, splashing the cavorting Tatul just beyond reach.

The cloaked figure stood at a distance, as if waiting on shore for the raft to run aground. At one point, it started forward, waded into the shallows, hands raised, fingers groping the air, and it frightened her. She whimpered aloud, and it vanished at the sound. Then the current caught the raft and swung it around the end of a rock.

A little sand beach hove into sight, and she leaned forward to grab the branches of the water birch and pull herself to shore, Tatul pushing the raft from behind. She leaned out over the still shadows and saw the reflection of a hooded robe.

Adrine awoke with a start and saw that she was kneeling and straining far forward over the end of the bed, peering at the cloaked figure. She wondered which of the vigilant monks was he.

"Hello," she called.

He did not respond but stood there tall, hands clasped inside the sleeves of the cloak. She smiled and relaxed. The silent brothers seemed the most at ease in their wordless worlds.

From the size of him, she guessed, "Brother Ransom?"

He acknowledged her astute powers with a slight bow.

"Praise God from whom all things issue," she called in blessing.

Brother Ransom bowed again and she lay back, thinking he would leave her cell now that she was accounted for.

Suddenly, with a rabid snarl he was on her, a suffocating weight, encircling her throat with a length of rope. Pain stabbed her side. She screamed and clawed back, tearing away the hood of secrecy.

The contorted face of Captain Ozal panted over her, raining flecks of spittle and sweat into her mouth and eyes. "You wretched little harlot, thinking you can entice me with wet lips and dancing eyes, and then escape with that lying scum of a traitor. You will give me what I came for, and then I will end your miserable life!"

He pressed insistently against her. The rope tightened and bright streaks of light exploded across her brain. Adrine fought to breathe; fists pounded the bed; fingers clawed the blankets, and still no air.

Gunfire sounded from the courtyard, then shouts of alarm. Stumbling commotion in the next cell. A light in the hall. The flash of a blade above her.

Instinctively, Adrine reared up, heard cartilage grind against bone, and felt the splash of something warm against her cheek. Ozal slapped her with such force she almost lost consciousness. *O my Lord, spare me this death.*

"You'll only get one chance to use it. Choose well."

Tatul's words, almost audible, welled up from her memory. With the last ounce of strength she possessed, she reached inside the folds of her garment and withdrew Ozal's own riding crop. As if seized by an angel, her arm reared back and whipped the crop a slashing blow across her attacker's eyes. A ferocious roar filled the room, and back swung her arm for another smashing blow across Ozal's face.

The rope slackened. Adrine fell to the floor, vision swirling, gasping for breath. Somewhere ahead of her a blur of red and green filled the room, and two bodies became one in deadly combat. With a splintering crash, the chains anchoring the bed broke, and the monster of Hekim Khan and the brave little eunuch fell to the floor. The sickening sound of blade meeting flesh—two, three, four times. Urgent shouts of "Here, here! Down here!" Many feet pounding to the rescue even as two feet fled the room.

The tiny cell filled with bright light and a babble of anxious men. One voice distinguished itself from the rest. "Dear Adrine, my sweet, you are wounded! I only left for a half hour to think. Tell me, where are you injured, where?"

Her sore, knotted throat could produce no speech, and he thought the worst. Strong, gentle hands stroked her. Loving arms engulfed her.

"Good Fark is badly hurt!" someone shouted. "Bayoneted. Turk military issue!"

"Ozal!" she choked out and collapsed against Tatul's

chest. From inside him she heard an anguished cry torn from the center of his being. The name of the dreaded Ozal passed from mouth to mouth down the hall and into the courtyard like a ricocheting bullet.

He fought to think, to command. At length he said calmly, "Take her back to the courtyard and give her wound a fresh dressing."

Someone—a brother monk—took her from him.

Tatul Sarafian lifted Fark the Faithful, grand eunuch of Abdulhamid, in his arms. The Fedayee took two steps and stumbled to his knees in grief. He felt the feeble pulse of his friend and heard the labored breath. He buried his face in the thin jacket and wept.

Suddenly he straightened, hugged Fark to his breast, and marched up the stairs to the ramparts. Brushing past the startled monks who scanned the night for invading demons, he stepped onto the south wall. The Fox raised the old man in outstretched arms.

"Cowards!" he shrieked at the night. "Murderers of mothers and infants! You may rob our dignity and destroy our bodies, but you will never quench our spirits! Long before your misbegotten ancestors trampled our homeland, Ararat stood. Tonight she remains, not one stone shorter than when Christ the Creator commanded her to rise from the plain of Anatolia or when Father Noah stepped from the Ark onto her dry shoulders. And long, long after the beetles have feasted on your flesh, she will live and her snows will cleanse the homeland of every dark sin and trace of spoilage left by your passing! In the name of all that is holy, Armenia shall live again!"

A volley of rifle fire cracked the night. Screams erupted in the courtyard. The monks scrambled to pull Tatul and Fark down behind the protective wall.

"They have come to finish us!" The women shouted their hysteria.

"We are to be slaughtered inside the walls of our own church!"

"God is the enemy!"

The sharp slap of flesh on flesh met the final blasphemy. Sister confronted sister. "Foolish mule! Do not turn against

God, or we are all surely doomed. Who do you think has kept us alive this long?"

More streaks of orange flame split the darkness beyond. The crack of each bullet was felt deep within the bones of all who sought the shelter of Mesrop.

Tatul took Fark to the healing priests and laid him at their feet. With a stormy look at Bishop Benedict, hand gripping the dagger inside his cloak, the Fox turned to run from Mesrop far into the night.

"No, Fedayee." Benedict blocked his path. "If you take revenge on one, many will die."

Tatul made to step around the tall, bearded cleric but found his way again blocked by the determined priest.

"Move aside, Bishop," said the Fox, danger in his tone. "It would not do for us to come to blows."

Eyes of an ancient intensity pierced Sarafian to the core. "Were he here, the Black Wolf would tell you to await the dawn. Madmen reject reason. If you go out there, two madmen will be loose, and the results shall be dreadful to all."

"Madness just walked into the sleeping chambers, strangled one, and attempted to slice another to death. Fark may die. You cannot ask me to sit and wait until day as if postponing a trip to the bakery! How can you propose to know the mind of Chavoush?"

The answer came in the silence that passed between them, the sparks of wisdom bright as shooting stars that flashed in the old priestly gaze. Benedict confirmed it. "Long ago, I rode with his father, the Great Wolf, and watched him bite the umbilical cord and slap the bare bottom of a husky, bellowing male child and declare the boy to be Black Wolf, champion of his people."

Tatul felt a tremor of Fedayeen recognition rattle his backbone. "You are—"

"Dark Falcon, my Fox," said the priest. For a long time they embraced, each breathing deep the pungent odors of a thousand cooking fires and the musky high-mountain wilderness.

Suddenly a cruel voice sounded from behind Sarafian. "How touching. Two infidels enjoying their last good-byes."

Tatul whirled, dagger raised.

Neelam Ozal, nose crooked and caked with blood, an ugly raw red X torn across his features, greeted him with a pistol barrel aimed at the Fedayee's right eye. "I think maybe it's time we again discussed the future of your eyesight, don't you?" the captain snarled.

Four Turk soldiers, rifles at the ready, disarmed Tatul and roughly searched the priest for weapons, finding none. Screams of fear turned the air desperate. From where he stood, Tatul could see other priests being herded by torchlight into the courtyard, their hands raised.

Beyond them, in the darkness along the base of the far wall, someone else, maybe two, darted past keeping low to the ground.

Who were they? If Ozal's men, why hide now that the trap was sprung? Sarafian searched wildly about for Adrine.

"The harlot?" spit Ozal. His eyes locked with the Fedayee's. "She lives, although I must say she's not nearly as feisty as when she served me. Can't you take better care of your concubine?" He laughed coldly at the hatred in Tatul's look. "Love thine enemies, Bolu the Impostor. Do good to those who do wrong to you. Bless those who revile you and say all manner of evil against you falsely. Of course, in your case, just what is false?"

The captain's enjoyment was enormous. He circled Tatul, watching the captive's every twitch. "I don't mean to be critical," he taunted, "but your battlements were easily penetrated. Can you really expect slaves of religion to give a proper defense? It was simple enough to slip inside and wrap my fingers around the scrawny little neck of your harem slave, but the stroke of genius was remaining within the walls when you assumed we were immediately run off by your pathetic little army."

Ozal warmed to his tale of military genius and practically crowed, "How easy it was to hide among the shadows, away from the scene of alarm, and to enter the courtyard from a completely different and unexpected direction. And then to mingle among the frightened women, face shielded by the cowl, a comforting hand here, a calming influence there, a reassuring pat on a crying child's head. So easy. And then to fire shots into the night, beyond the walls, so that your attention was ever focused outward—it was too easy. I think maybe your desire has overpowered your reason!"

Tatul's eyes blazed, and the brash, impetuous youth he had trained so hard to subdue burst from him. "And what of the ease, shrewd Captain, with which you were beaten back by a weak and wounded maid? It appears that she altered your appearance quite dramatically and for the better!"

Ozal's battered face turned thick and deep red with loathing. With great difficulty, he fought back the rage. "Bring her!" he ordered.

Two of the riflemen went to Adrine's mat by the fire and yanked her to her feet. She stumbled, cried out, and was half walked, half dragged back to Ozal. With a triumphant laugh, he searched her for the riding crop, hands groping over her body until they closed on the whip.

"Strip her!" he roared, with quick side glances of gratification at Tatul Sarafian sweating and straining against his captors. The sadistic whip flicked playfully beneath the Armenian's chin.

Suddenly two forms appeared as if from nowhere, one arising directly behind Ozal.

A small circle of hardened steel pressed deep into the soft flesh at the base of Ozal's skull.

No one had to tell him not to move.

Frank Davidson rasped hotly into the captain's ear. "Tell your good Turk regiment to lay down their arms, or I am going to make paste of your brains!"

"Put down your rifles!" Ozal choked out. "On the ground. Now! Don't hesitate, you fools. Lay them down!"

Across the compound, eight others forfeited their weapons and were quickly taken into the custody of the Church.

The screaming and sobbing among the women instantly subsided. Tatul rushed to take Adrine into his arms but was shocked when suddenly Misak Mentese appeared and embraced him before he had hardly moved. Azniz pounded his brother Misak on the back in happy greeting. A strapping Armenian with bulging biceps stood nearby the stocky, broad-shouldered American stranger whose gun spoke so convincingly. The American released Ozal into the grip of the burly Brother Integrity, who made the prisoner lie facedown on a stone bench while Brother Correction tied his hands.

Misak made the introductions, told of his harrowing adventures and timely rescue by Davidson and Gomidas. Ashkhen's puzzling actions at the River Sisus disturbed them all, and they feared the worst. "He must have died in the bridge blast," Misak concluded sadly. "It is the only explanation for his disappearance." The others nodded grimly.

Davidson looked at Tatul. "I have heard your name spoken by my guests at the consulate. With a good deal of awe and respect, I might add."

Tatul acknowledged the words with a nod and rapidly filled in the new arrivals on the recent harrowing events of the crossing in the flood and the shooting of Adrine Tevian.

Misak looked doubly stricken. "Adrine has the courage of three Fedayeen. I am sorry she has suffered, my brother."

Tatul nodded appreciatively. "And I am sorry for Ashkhen, our brother."

Misak looked at the ground.

"It's impossible to tell how many Turks escaped the explosion at the bridge," Davidson began. "Tracks in the road didn't last long in that rain."

Davidson smoothed the close-cropped hair that fit his scalp so neatly and pointed at several partly sodden sacks of flour, onions, and bread his party had brought in with them. "Rain-kissed provisions," he said wryly, "lightly seasoned with river water, road dirt, and wagon grit. Soup that practically makes itself!"

Tatul smiled despite everything. He hadn't spent much time with Americans. They could be refreshingly inane.

"Misak told us all you have endured," Davidson said. "Rest assured that though we did a cursory search, we saw no sign of surviving Turk military along the road from Malatya or anywhere in Hekim Khan. The townspeople were less than forthcoming, but they seem just as glad to be out from under Captain Ozal and his occupation force."

Recognizing Sarafian's position with the people, he nodded respectfully to the serious young man. "Mr. Sarafian, you have a plan?"

Tatul Sarafian did not know whether to laugh or cry. He should be home in Erzurum milking cows. Instead, hundreds

of eyes watched, hundreds of ears strained for a plan that
would lead, if not to freedom, to a haven without rape and
death. He sighed and attempted a slender smile. "I have behaved, Mr. Davidson, like the fox in Aesop's fable, jumping
again and again for the lowest clusters of some very fine
grapes. Grapes of a restored homeland where I might govern
myself and laugh with my wife, father my children, grow the
biggest herd of milk cows that ever chewed the cud in the
shadow of Ararat . . ." He paused, searching Bishop Benedict's
gray-bearded visage for the rest of the dream, ". . . and worship
God with all my heart, mind, and strength." A chorus of murmured amens greeted the words. Tatul looked at the wistful
faces of the women, eyes tightly shut to preserve a like vision
that all of them harbored to some degree.

He continued. "But my legs are tired from leaping, and I
must at last say with the earnest fox, 'Those grapes are sour.
Though I could reach them, I would not eat them.' We have
been a docile, peasant people too long. We will never be safe
from the barbarian so long as we content ourselves with pas-
tures green and peas of plenty. Those of us with the means
must stop the Turk by force. We have to go back to the homes
of Armenia and force the squatter Muslims out. It will take
time. It will cost lives. But like the Jews, we have too long been
the outcasts. It is long past time for us to be heard!"

Ozal, facedown on the stone bench, laughed derisively. "I'll
tell you who's not been heard from in some time, you lying
fox! Where do you suppose the rest of my men are and what
might they be doing while you hide behind monks and
women? You've not yet accounted for all of us—"

"Do not speak!" ordered the Fox and motioned for a man
to return the muzzle of a rifle to the captain's neck. The children were beginning to quiet and their mothers with them.
Tatul would not tolerate another wave of anxiety generated by
the crazed Turk.

"If he speaks again, break his teeth with your gun barrel,"
Sarafian said. "Come," he said to the others, "let us go where
we do not have to breathe his air."

At a safe distance from Ozal's ears, the Fox spoke again.
"For now, we must secure these women and children. Father
Benedict and the brothers of Mesrop have offered to shelter

the sisters and assist them on their way to freedom in the north. My brothers and I will make our way north to the Caucasus Mountains and rejoin the Fedayeen. Our work will be to avenge the illegal treatment of Turkish citizens and to smuggle Armenians into Russia."

Davidson nodded.

The American consul grasped Sarafian's hand. "I commend you for the foolish yet brave flight across the river. You must command the very angels!"

Tatul pulled away. "I command nothing, Mr. Davidson. I cannot control my own heart—least of all can I order the angels!"

Adrine's rasping cough carried on the night breeze. Sarafian's head jerked toward the sound, the torment of a helpless lover straining from every pore.

"Is she better?" Davidson asked.

"Some. Have you any medicines?" Tatul's voice cracked.

"No, nothing so good as a monk's recipe."

The cough ended in a groan that brought Tatul and the American to her side. Pale Adrine lay on the cot, the great black robes of Bishop Benedict hovering over her like the raven of death. His hand moved over her head and breast in a circular motion. Her neck was laid bare to the gentle sponging of Brother Victory. Terrified of losing her, Tatul grabbed the dark priest's wrist and yanked back. The hand contained a large jeweled cross of ancient wood, the grain deeply stained blood red.

Their eyes locked, the cross reflected in the holy man's compassionate gaze. Some of the women nearby saw the ancient relic and prostrated themselves on the ground. "It is the irresistible power of God himself," the old priestly lips said. "The power that cleanses, the power that heals, the power that saves!"

And then he pressed the symbol of Supreme Sacrifice against Tatul's forehead before placing it against Adrine's. "Man has done what man can do," the bishop said. "Now watch God work."

He rose, placed the cross inside its golden casket, and raised the sacred box once to the starlit sky. Brother Benedict placed the wet cloth in Tatul's hand, smiled in lopsided reassurance, and returned to the holy repository where the Cross of the Ark was kept.

It was as if time slowed and all else retreated. Tatul knelt, bent until his head touched her arm, and prayed with all his being.

"Grant me her heart to possess, and she mine," he prayed.

He felt her hand light across the back of his neck and heard a tired voice. "It is true . . . the rumors all true. The Cross of Noah . . . here . . . like Grandmother said!"

He remained with her, guarding her from the terrors within and those beyond the walls of Mesrop.

Later that night after Adrine had settled into a long, exhausted sleep, Tatul Sarafian stared hard into the inky darkness, Neelam Ozal's question gnawing at him. Where were the remaining Turk soldiers of Hekim Khan?

Or was what bothered him more the sneering accusation that the Fedayeen's Fox used monks and women for his shield?

Misak stood strong beside Tatul. "You need rest," the Mentese brother told him. "Ozal is bluffing. Let it go until light. If there are any more of them, they'll not strike again so soon—not without their commander."

Tatul frowned at the spots of green and gold light swimming before his eyes. He was tired and beginning to see movement where there was none. He'd slept little since the river crossing, and it had taken a toll. But one troubling thought would not let go.

"I'm more concerned that they haven't struck. We are prisoners here until they do. And I don't know about you, brother, but I became a Fedayee to fight. If I'd wanted to join a monastery, I would have taken the vows. No, the only way to get out of here and on with the struggle is to lure the rest of the rats into the open. The longer we wait, the longer they have to regroup and gain reinforcements."

"But we can't find them in the dark," protested Misak.

"No, we can't," Tatul murmured, giving Misak a friendly pat on the cheek. "To find rats in the dark, you must send another rat."

Save for a few distant voices, the night grew quiet again, exhaustion heavy on fragile bodies and anxious hearts. Stars without end powdered the heavens.

———

Neelam Ozal counted the stars. He waited and watched on the stone bench in the center of the courtyard, willing himself to be snatched back into the night beyond the walls. This pathetic collection of women, children, priests, and rebels was no match for the sons of the Ottoman Empire. Maybe the Young Turks had botched the war, but they knew how to eradicate Christian parasites. No meddlers from within or without could prevent the washing of the land. Turkey was for Turks and damnation to those who thought otherwise.

He had pretended to sleep, but now the captain raised his head from the bench on which he reclined and was surprised to see that the two guards stationed nearby were no longer in sight. They had left him unwatched and unbound. Idiots! *They have so little to do with intelligence. Small wonder they're so easily duped.* He looked about, saw that no one was near, and sat up.

Perhaps the guards went to relieve themselves and lost their way, he thought with growing contempt. He stood and cautiously made his way past library and prayer rooms to a door in the north wall. He heard distant laughter and saw a knot of men congregated around a fire, no doubt joking and celebrating at the Turks' expense. He'd gamble his rank of captain that that's where he'd find the guards.

Ozal paused, backed up to the iron ring of the door and searched the moonlit courtyard for signs of discovery, listening for cries of alarm.

None came. The attention of the monks who patrolled the perimeter of the wall was at the other end of the monastery. They stupidly believed any invasion would come only from the south. With one last congratulatory smile, Neelam Ozal turned the iron ring, slipped through the stone doorway, and melted into the night.

———

By dawn's first light, Tatul knew that Fark, though weak,

would live. Tatul bowed his head in silent thanks and marveled at the old eunuch's endurance. He had survived too much to die by surprise.

The body of Brother Fullness, from whom Ozal had taken life and cloak, was placed in the personal sarcophagus belonging to Bishop Benedict. Though heavy of heart, Tatul watched the last rites and knew here was fit repose for the ambushed monk.

"Brother Fullness lies now in your bosom, Son of Heaven." Bishop Benedict intoned the words of burial. "Gather him to your divine heart, care for him in the great aloneness, and may he awaken by the crystal sea. In the name of Father, Son, and Spirit, so shall it be."

The tomb was sealed and the dread of an old familiar evil gripped the living like the talons of the predator.

Tatul watched a greatly improved Adrine take rice pudding and tea, grateful for her resilience. But there was little talk among the refugees.

The brothers Mentese watched Tatul and waited for a sign. It was not long in coming.

The Fox looked to the north, to Ararat, nostrils sifting the air for scent, ears alert to every sound beyond the courtyard. Eyes narrow, jaw set in grim resolve, he slid a hand inside his shirt and fingered the lock of dark hair next to his skin. He had taken it from her just before dawn while she slept in the crook of his arm, fatigued from the night's ordeal. He breathed the air she breathed, held the wisp of her hair to his cheek, and the whole crazy plan was born. It was mad, insane, and worthy of a fox. Would she go along? Would the American?

It was time to lure the hounds out onto the ice.

The Fox turned. Azniz placed a fist over his heart. Misak did the same.

Tatul Sarafian returned the salute.

The Fedayeen were ready to ride.

CHAPTER 26

The sun rose high in the sky five hours after Brother Fullness had been laid to rest. The road north and east to the Turk towns of Arapkir and Kemaliye and the Turk Mountains of Munzur was rough and rutted. The storm had worked its worst, and erosion had scoured away great chunks of the roadbed. In some places, entire sections were washed out or lay under deep pools of standing water. There was much wading and backtracking through the fields, and progress was slow.

The one hundred Armenian sisters of Hekim Khan sloshed through ankle-deep mud and clung together in ragged chains of six and eight to safely negotiate the ruined road. Prayers were said for the sun to suck the land of excess water, but where it would put it, no one knew.

The women had come through much together. Now they clung with hard, curled fingers to their few belongings, slung over a shoulder or bound to a thin waist by strips of faded cloth. Each wore a head wrap of serviceable fabric supplied by the kindly monks. Those at the rear of the procession wore long, loose cloaks, again courtesy of the brothers. A few had even foregone sleep to sew fresh cloth into dresses or billowy blouses and pantaloons for the journey, the first new garments most of them had seen in months.

It was small consolation in a land demented by war. Mothers hugged hope to their withered breasts, for there was little else. No cries for food. No begging to stop for shade. No children.

Ahead, in the sodden fields on both sides of the broken track, veiled Turk women hunched over the earth like half people searching for their remainder. They scrabbled in the wet soil with bare hands or makeshift spades. They looked for winter tubers to tide them over the spring, but dreamed of figs and olives and sun-bright oranges.

————

Neelam Ozal, and the last eight soldiers of the garrison at Hekim Khan, rose from the reeds along the banks of the Kuru astride the sturdy mounts that had swum the river two nights before.

Slowly, deliberately, they walked their horses onto the road and stopped. Ozal scanned once more the backs of the Armenian women leaving Mesrop, lowered the glasses, and popped a small handful of pine nuts into his mouth. He chewed thoughtfully, then turned the glasses back on the solid, unmoving walls of the monastery. No movement outside the gates either, nor sign of anyone inside. All was prayerful, peaceful calm.

Too peaceful.

Ozal spit husks, studied the mane of his mount, and sniffed the air. He felt the sting of the ugly red welts and knew he would bear their scar forever. He should have choked the life from that infuriating harlot while he'd had her in his grip. He would have if her traitorous eunuch hadn't suddenly appeared. To think that a servant of the last great sultan was now a Fedayee collaborator made Ozal's stomach boil. That's what came of trusting infidel scum. When he became pasha, Captain Ozal would entrust a few surviving Armenians with one important task only—licking his boots clean, morning and evening.

His Armenian mother should have shined his Turk father's boots and told him that the fact he was an invalid did not matter in her eyes. She should have admired him for his brain and his commitment to her and done all within her power to make him feel still part of the human race. Instead, she told him that he was no longer fit for this earth. She threw her wedding commitment in his face and left him for dead.

Armenians could not be trusted.

He scanned the backs of the Armenian women again, looking for one in particular. There she was, at the head of the file, a rugged staff in one hand like some heroic female Moses leading the way to the Promised Land. Where did she draw her accursed strength? Rest, good food in sufficient quantity, whatever mystery potions the priests had given her, and some inner quality that made her a fighter. She would say it was God. But Ozal knew better. He'd seen it before. It was the Armenian refusal to get out of the way and die.

Ozal watched another woman walk at Adrine Tevian's side and help her over the difficult places. It was probably that conniving bride of Hekim Khan who had tried to lie her friends out of trouble. What an unprotected imbecile she was, one who no longer merited even the scant cover of Fedayeen scum! The women had been forced to leave the monastery so that Bolu the Impostor could concentrate on more pressing matters—like saving his own skin. In fact, the little night raid had probably sped up the process.

Neelam Ozal would wager his lungs that the boy was even now negotiating some deal with the greedy priests, a deal that would fatten the pockets of the Wolf himself. Nothing like a nice war to shore up a shaky power base. Once Ozal finished with the women and wired for reinforcements from Adiyaman, the Fox would lead him to the Wolf, and there would be boot licking on a grand scale.

Make no mistake. Some Armenians would survive the purge. They were like reptiles that lie dormant in the mud until revived by spring rains. Now these wretched vermin were on the move again, going north, thinking they could escape their sentence of death.

But not if he could prevent it! The Armenians had brought down plague and disaster upon the land. They had slaughtered Ozal's men at Sisus. Another died last night, and eight more were taken captive on the botched attempt to cripple the Fox by killing his woman. And where were the rest of the garrison he'd left to go secure supplies at Malatya? Armenian assassins had slain them all and apparently eaten them! Not a trace left.

Ozal fought the anger and thought of their surprise when the dawn revealed the captain's escape. That must have been what drove the Fox into hiding this morning and convinced him to cut his losses and send the women out. It was a line of thinking that made Ozal very happy.

Still, his greater job was to cleanse the region. He must keep an even mind and think it through if he was to outfox the Fox. "Why have they abandoned the children?" he pondered aloud.

His lieutenant waited to see if the captain would answer his own question.

"They have been sold for bread," Ozal concluded with a disgusted smile. "It is the new economy. The scabby priests will in turn resell them to the farmers for cheap labor. They will be used until they drop. Then their carcasses will be worked into the soil as fertilizer!" He laughed dryly, a sound mimicked by his men. The lieutenant nodded in witless admiration for his commander's ability to read the otherwise inexplicable actions of the infidels.

Ozal relaxed. "The Fox has found its den." He spoke low, grinding another batch of pine nuts between molars. "Christ's monks and rebel butchers seem to have much in common! They like their creature comforts. Come, let us pay the women one last visit. As in the divine sayings of Muhammed, 'I was a hidden treasure and desired to be known; therefore I created the creation in order that I might be known.'"

He felt the tender, oozing welts on his face and stiffened. He had vowed never to have an Armenian woman, but with her he would have his revenge. "I, Neelam Ozal, desire to be known to one woman in particular. You, my good men, may have the rest!" They muttered their enthusiasm, having been too long without women.

The river made a crooked bend to the left and blocked them from view at the monastery. Quietly, carefully, Ozal's men made their way along the water's edge, staying well below the top of the bank. Where the river bent back to the right and the road continued straight, the Turk horsemen emerged from the river and fell in a good distance behind the women.

It was two or three minutes before someone raised the alarm. "Dear God in heaven, it is him! We are doomed!"

Fearful cries rippled through the columns of women. They tried to hurry faster, but feet weighed down by caked mud did not respond.

Ozal, who enjoyed the panic, kept the horses at a fast walk and loudly observed, "Look at them stumble and scurry! You'd think they'd ride horses, but it appears they much prefer being close to the mud from which they crawled. Foolish things. They were never meant to walk upright!" He laughed with bitter sarcasm and was joined by a chorus of eight.

"Courage, sisters!" a strong voice called, and Ozal jerked in the saddle as if stuck in the eye with a burning brand. Adrine Tevian led them once again. She would regret this day. He would begin with her face. . . .

A clear, sweet voice rose over the panicked tumult. " 'Christ, my Christ, my heavenly shield; thy Word, thy Word, thy Truth I shall wield!' "

A few took up the words, and the hymn began to swell as the women quickened the pace past the bent Turk women rooting out the earth's shabby yield without so much as a glance at the passing parade.

"Allah is most great! Allah is most great!" roared Ozal, his men quickly joining the attempt to drown out the thin, reedy efforts of the terrified women. "I testify there is no god except Allah! I testify that Muhammed is the messenger of God—"

" 'Behold, believe, our crucified King! Revived, alive, His hosannas ring!' "

"God is most great! God is most great! There is no god except God!" Ozal's men continued their chant.

"Do you know what amazes me, Lieutenant?" Ozal bellowed.

"No, most excellent Captain, what amazes you?" the lieutenant shouted.

"That these fools are not listed among the Seven Wonders of the Ancient World! They should come right after the Pyramids of Giza and the Colossus of Rhodes. We could call them the Sirens of Holy Harlotry who sing so desperately on their way to the gallows! Look at those in the rear, how slow and clumsy and fat-hipped they are, even though they starve! They walk like apes in those stupid cloaks, undoubtedly the holy garments of the Fat Fathers of Mesrop. Such fools!"

The Turk remnant of the Twelfth Army Corps gripped the reins of their sturdy mounts and switched to a trot, eager to finish off the troublesome women. They passed the fields where the veiled Turk women labored so hard. They did not see one woman straighten and signal the others.

Ahead of the soldiers, now just thirty lengths in front, the women came to an abrupt halt. With a sudden crystal clarity, Captain Ozal understood. A roaring filled his head from within. The ice cracked and the hounds fell through.

DELIVER US FROM EVIL

Cloaks, veils, and head covers fell away to reveal not robed women directly in front of him, but monks with rifles primed and aimed. Ozal wheeled his horse about, only to face a second phalanx of "farmers," also male, also armed, most with heads shorn in the style of the cloistered brothers of Christ. Wildly, Ozal quickly counted eighteen Christian men—and eighteen rifles.

In their midst stood the Fox and by his side Frank Davidson, American Consul at Harput. Davidson, face drawn, looked at Tatul Sarafian, then back at the cornered Ozal. He spat on the road and strode forward.

As though fueled by images of the thousands of hacked and bloated Armenians he'd seen, Davidson reached up and grabbed the Turk commander's uniform and wrenched him from the saddle. He shoved him to his knees in front of Sarafian. Neelam Ozal sank in the mud, small but defiant.

The other Turks were relieved of their weapons, unceremoniously hauled from their mounts, and thrust to the ground behind their leader. While they cringed in fear from those they'd persecuted, Ozal's mouth twisted with all the remorse of a cornered weasel. He tore open the top of the military tunic and turned his face aside to expose a sweat-stained neck and a throbbing jugular that betrayed his inner turmoil. "To the victor the spoils!" he shouted. "Do it now, in front of your concubines so they can see what a brave butcher you are!"

The cords stood bulging out on Tatul's neck as a flush of anger crossed his face. Sliding a dagger from his waistband, he stood over the monster who had wreaked so much suffering and yanked his head back by the hair. He bent and peered straight into the captain's bulging eyes. "Do not blink," he said. "I want to know the exact moment that life leaves your stinking shell!" His grip tightened on the knife. Ozal swallowed.

"No, my brother, no!" Adrine pressed forward through the crowd to stand at Tatul's side. She saw the involuntary thankfulness speed across Ozal's straining face, then looked away from the jagged welts that she had put there. "Life is God's to give and take," she said.

Nor could she make a life with a man who routinely killed for political gain or even for national retribution, however justified. Her heart thundered with the loudest prayer of her life.

Stay his hand, my Lord, stay his hand!

An eerie hush fell over the assembly. Adrine felt the hair rise on her arms. All about her the sisters said nothing but bent and took up stones and sticks. Faces young and old looked in judgment at the men on their knees in the mud.

"Kill the filthy rapists!" a woman shrieked, striking a young Turk in the side with her rock.

"Make them crawl for mercy, then show them none!" howled another, brandishing the thick cudgel of a tree root.

"Murdering mongrels!" yelled a third.

Some small stones and bits of wood rained down on the soldiers but quickly subsided. If possible, the men on the ground cowering before refugees looked more pitiful than the women ever had.

Adrine held up a hand. "Hymns and revenge should not pour from the same spout. Don't let them poison your well, sisters. Put down your weapons. Think of your children," she said as calmly as she could manage. "They will have their mothers back now. They are the fruit from which the new Armenia will spring. Tend the fruit, sisters. Tend the fruit."

Never before had such a fight waged within the Fox. Who on earth would judge him ill for ending so ruthless and immoral a maggot as Neelam Ozal? Armenians who survived the forced marches and the death camps would hail him a hero. The Wolf would accord him a hero's return, and he would be legend among the legendary Fedayeen. As a man of honor and the son of Serop Sarafian, himself a man of great honor, Tatul would be less than honorable to pardon this festering boil of a man.

But of all the passions that beat against him now, the strongest, the purest, the most undeniable, was a deep longing for Adrine. It was preposterous that he should have fallen in love now, here, under impossible conditions. But her strength, her goodness, her fire held infinite allure. And more, she, in the midst of hell, held out the hope of God. Why was that so important to him?

"A fox does not kill the hounds, only outthinks them," came her soft reassurances. She was weeping. "You have done that, Tatul, that and more. Find in your heart a more fitting punishment than slaughter. Seek a justice with which you can live."

He felt the tension drain from his arm and the hand that

held the knife. With a look at the anxious eyes of his fellow Fedayeen, Tatul released Ozal's scalp and shoved him over backward. "Your life has been spared," he said, "though I cannot begin to know why. Misak, I give this pathetic man into your care. If he gives you one ripple of trouble, drag him behind a horse until he wears as thin as the sisters of Hekim Khan."

Tatul went to her, hands at his side, yearning for her embrace, but not here before base men. "Come, Adrine Tevian, stand with me by the river's edge while I think of a sentence. I would then ask that you accompany me while it is carried out. You ... you steady me."

She smiled at him and felt a weakness at the late turn of events. Grandmother's little goose had come to love when at her lowest, when all was but lost. And yet it was a love as impossible as the circumstances from which it sprang. He was a wild pony with no rider, a wanted seditionist who slept on the ground and lived in mountain caves.

But then, what did she have to offer? One cat and a leather riding crop were about the extent of her dowry. And the ability to cook, should there ever again be anything decent to cook. She grinned unexpectedly. Apparently she had one thing more to offer: a dormant sense of humor.

At the water, she watched him tear a clod of grass out by the roots and throw it. Spinning soil, the clod smacked the surface and floated south.

"For all my talk, maybe that is the way we shall all go—forced south to burn in the desert. Who cares about Armenia, Adrine? Who beyond our suffering borders cares whether we live or die?"

Adrine sat on the grass and flipped pebbles. She tried to get each to enter the water in the exact spot as its predecessor. She liked the musical plop they made. It was such a normal sound.

"I have met a great number of people who care," she said. "The German and American missionaries care. Frank Davidson cares. The world cares, Tatul, but the news comes to them slowly. If we lose faith now and answer vengeance with vengeance, we are the sorry ones. What will we have learned? Kill those who disagree with us? Live to ourselves and let no one else in? Bitter lessons indeed for our children." She looked away, embarrassed. "Our children" sounded so forward. She hadn't meant hers and his.

Had she?

"Our children will have no homeland to call their own," Tatul replied evenly. The way he said "our children" gave her hope.

"They will if we fight for one. Do you honestly think the proud Armenian people who have claimed the cross for centuries can be broken in one short fight? No! We are survivors and have been since Noah danced in victory on the heights of Ararat!"

He was silent for a very long time. "Adrine?" he asked at last.

"Yes?" It came out small and quiet, afraid of what she wasn't sure.

"My father is alive. I must believe that. He was too brave, too kind, too needed to die."

She said nothing. A man's dreams were his food.

"Adrine?"

"Yes?"

"I like your courage and ... and that you still believe. Maybe, if you rode with me, I might believe again."

Ride with him? It was her greatest wish!

He had ridden the wind to save her.

He the Fox.

She his lady.

Adrine looked around. He was standing near, looking down at her, forlorn and confused. It was not possible for the rushing of the river to cover the pounding of her heart.

"Will you kiss me, Adrine? It ... it's been so long." He grinned shyly, lopsided, as if fearful of joy.

She stood to her feet by the river and their lips met, ragged refugee and hunted rebel. Her imagination flew to long ago daydreams and the train station in Berlin. A mysterious dark man in a beautifully tailored suit. A red flower in his right lapel.

Silly little goose.

CHAPTER 27

The wagon turned from the main road leading to the Syrian internment camps, south out of Hekim Khan. The wheels jumped and spit rocks from under the tightly packed load of Turk prisoners. The wagon tilted downward into the ravine where the rains seemed not to have altered a thing.

The prisoners, hands tied behind their backs, heard the vultures before they caught sight of the first one soaring along behind the wagon in silent black witness. The soldiers twisted and hiked their torsos about to catch a better view of the approaching pit and the feathered grave tenders who flew low and glutted over the feasting grounds.

Ozal's defiance began to slip. Sweat beaded on his skin, and his left cheek spasmed uncontrollably.

The powerful stench of human decay rolled up to meet the wagon. "Mercy, Allah the Most Compassionate!" shouted the captives. "Allah forbid that we should perish! Allah All-Wise, All-Holy, All-Just, keep us from hell!"

They could not call God the Father. To the Muslim, human beings were not children of God. To imply kinship was to trivialize God the Untouchable. They pled with him nonetheless. "Allah is One, the Eternal God. He will not forget us as we have forgotten him!"

Tatul, Adrine, and Frank Davidson sat atop the wagon seat and pressed scarves soaked in lemon water to their noses. Gomidas stood in back, grimly holding to the sides of the lurching wagon. Azniz and Misak trotted along behind. The boxer and the Mentese brothers kept their guns on the prisoners.

Deeper they descended into the canyon, the stink thickening with each turn of the wheels. Ozal's lieutenant began to retch and finally vomited on the Turk next to him. Icy fear gripped them all.

The wagon slowed, coming to a stop five paces from the brink of the mass grave. The prisoners were ordered down from the wagon bed to stand shaking and sweating as far from Captain Ozal as they could manage. It didn't take the minister of defense to see who was to blame for their troubles. Ozal, the self-assured, had ruined their lives.

"Do something!" one of them screamed in the captain's face. "This was your command, so command!"

Ozal used his shoulder to knock the man almost over the edge. The accuser sprawled on his face, then scrambled back from the rim, mewling like a half-crazed child.

"What's the use!?" another prisoner blubbered. "We did not pray enough. We did not feed the poor. We made our own path to hell. Let us accept the Day of Reckoning."

Face grim, sick in his soul, Tatul Sarafian faced the captain and his men to pronounce sentence. "Because I am compelled by a higher power"—he looked to Adrine Tevian at his side— "I condemn you to the very pit to which you have consigned the innocent, *but* not with the same malice. You have hope of survival, something of which your victims had none. Hands to remain tied, you shall be lowered by ropes into the pit before you and left to find your own way out. If you work together, it is possible for all of you to untie one another and help each other scale the canyon walls. If you quarrel or abandon one another to your separate fates, you will die or be driven mad. May God have mercy on your souls."

Tatul knew there was only the slimmest of chances that the wild-eyed men before him would form a survival team and reason their way out. It would mean freeing one another's hands, splicing the ropes together to make an escape line, finding footholds, scouting a reasonable route, and selflessly pulling one another hand over hand up the sheer cliff face— all the while held to earth by the putrefying flesh of their unarmed victims.

Maybe, if they could somehow remove Ozal from the equation . . .

"One more mercy I will extend you. Any who wish may be

blindfolded prior to descent. And before the sentence is carried out, Adrine Tevian has requested a moment of prayer."

"That harlot will not pray for me!" Ozal complained. "I should have taken her when I had the chance."

Tensing, Tatul nodded to Gomidas, who quickly gagged the captain with one of the blindfolds and showed him the knuckles of his hammy fist. The captain settled into sullen silence.

"O God, have mercy on the souls of these men," Adrine began, then faltered. "Help me find forgiveness for them in my heart." The tears spilled. "Give me the courage to outlive their wickedness and the terrible wrongs they have done to my people. Help me, Father. . . ."

She turned and started up the road leading from the Valley of Death.

She did not look back.

CHAPTER 28

"It daily grows more dangerous to move in the open. I shall take you to the Russian border myself," Davidson said the next morning.

Adrine, Tatul, and the two Menteses, all disguised in women's clothing, nodded their gratitude.

"Well, it only makes sense. I know those who run the underground escape stations and where they are located. They'll feed us and give us the latest information on the safest routes. We'll take old Chester here in case of emergencies." He affectionately patted the brown chest beneath the wagon seat. "I think the owners would like to know that some of their worldly earnings went toward the safe passage of the Fox and his lady!"

Adrine blushed. There were a great many miles left before they had any real hope of lasting happiness. But she secretly liked the sound of "his lady."

Brothers Victory and Confidence loaded the last few supplies into the wagon bed, including six rifles and plentiful ammunition. Big Brother Integrity gave them each an awkward hug.

The immediate plan was simple. Gomidas would make haste on horseback for the consulate in Harput to check on matters there. He would explain the consul's absence as another extended circuit of American mission outposts. Thank God the Muslims were loathe to storm the American consulate for fear of bringing the United States into the war.

Fark would stay behind and ready the women for the final phase of their arduous escape. Davidson, Tatul, Adrine, and the Menteses Azniz and Misak would travel to Binbasar at the

Russian border and the Monastery of St. Timothy.

From there, Adrine and Tatul would ride into Russia, sealed inside burial caskets. Once Tatul and Adrine were safely away back to the Wolf, the Menteses would return to Mesrop with Davidson to oversee the exodus. Safety, they knew, was in the Caucasus Mountains that straddled the oft-disputed borderlands between Russia and Turkey. Stretching nine hundred kilometers between the Black and Caspian Seas, it was the towering stronghold of the Fedayeen. It sliced through ancient Armenia with a formidable bastion of rock, snow, and timber, an impenetrable maze of canyons and deadly cliffs. Those who held the heights held the border.

The good monks of St. Timothy's would accept the seal of Bishop Benedict. They were carpenter priests and suppliers of coffins to the war effort. Many were the refugees who had found safety among the coffins. Here they stopped and were fed; their sores and injuries treated; their sins confessed and prayed for. The men of St. Timothy's had planted the rumor that diphtheria and typhoid fever were occupational hazards of handling the war dead. Most often they and their monastery were given a wide berth by the living enemy.

Tatul smiled thinly. Odd, he thought. Odd that doomed Armenians should find new life among the casualties of war.

The women refugees would travel by wagon, dressed as monks of the order of silent brothers should they encounter Turk interrogators en route. The vocal brothers would remind the Turks that the wagons were on divine business. The good brothers of St. Timothy's had requested additional hands for making caskets, and the brothers of Mesrop were only too happy to send in reinforcements.

Surely it was a small deception, permissible in times of war. The bishop vowed to personally take the matter before the Mercy Seat.

Money from Davidson's leather chest would buy specially marked coffins to ferry the sisters of Hekim Khan over the border amidst the confusion of battle casualties. It had been successfully done with smaller groups of escapees, and plans were laid to divide the women and their children into smaller, safer cadres of eight or ten for the journey north.

Prayers were begun immediately for the audacious undertaking.

Adrine took both sides in her heart's debate whether or not she should remain with the sisters and help them make their escape, but in the end she reluctantly left them in the good hands of Fark and the humble heroes of Mesrop.

It was Fark who made it clear when he said, "You have the two rarest qualities for which Armenia is so desperate: faith and will. Go with the Fox, fight the good fight, and stop the bleeding. Though he must resign his neutral position to do so, good Consul Davidson will take your struggle to the world media and press for a war crimes trial. You will be sorely needed to restore order and find justice once the Allies have Turkey in a vise. Leave the harem smuggling—and freeing—to me!"

Dozens of kindly wrinkles grinned in unison. Adrine playfully knocked the little green felt hat away and affectionately kissed the top of the little man's head.

It was past time to part. Davidson embraced Gomidas, his loyal stable keeper and companion. It would be a month or more before they saw each other again, yet no words passed between them.

Tatul wrapped little Fark in a hug worthy of the Wolf and lifted him off the ground, careful of his healing wounds. "Take tea and caution, my little man." Sarafian spoke the blessing gruffly. "Perhaps one day we shall find ourselves another harem to free."

Fark wiped his eyes. "One more compliant and with a great deal more meat on its bones, I pray," he said. "Set me down this instant or these cuts of mine will open all over again!"

Adrine completed tearful embraces with Bishop Benedict, the kindly monks—even the silent ones were weeping—the sisters and their babies, but still she did not see the one face she could not leave without bidding farewell.

"I won't be long," she said to Tatul. "I promise."

She found Sosi and little Kenan in the far corner of the Prayer Hall. She stood there a long time in silence, watching the devoted mother stroke the hair of her son. Finally she caught Kenan's sad eyes, smiled, and took Giaour from behind her back. "She doesn't care for long wagon rides," Adrine said, voice cracking. "Will you take good care of her just as you have her kitten?"

Kenan's eyes opened wide, and he looked at his mother for approval. Sosi Emre said nothing but nodded, and the boy gathered the newest addition to the growing family into his arms.

"What is it, Sosi? What troubles you?" Adrine placed the palm of one hand softly against her friend's cheek.

Sosi looked up, her expression bittersweet with joy, separation, and apprehension. "You have given me something beyond words—a peace here." She patted her left breast. "I, a follower of Islam, taught to hold Christians in contempt, found acceptance with you and a new freedom. But now I am losing you, and it weighed on me, so I came here to this prayer room and asked Jesus the Savior to accept me just as you did. Now I know that even though you must go, I am no longer an outsider to the kingdom of Jesus, but am forever inside the sanctuary of God the Father." Tears tumbled into her lap. "He is the first true father I've ever had. Mine beat me and told me that he could not feed another female mouth. I . . . I had to survive as best I could. Kenan's father, an Arab I think, left me at a caravansary, then rode off with his camels to another tent farther on. Don't hate me, Adrine, but I can never be so good as you." She sobbed against her friend, and now it was Kenan's turn to stroke his mother.

"Shush, shush," comforted Adrine. "Such talk! You are a daughter of Christ, and your sins are drowned in the sea. I know this, Sosi, for I have been forgiven many of my own. You shall ever be the woman who gave Easter back to me and fed the multitude with goat's milk and bits of cucumber. And now you are the mother of my cat!"

Sosi looked up in surprise, half crying, half laughing. The bright, wet face of Adrine was doing the same.

"You be strong for the sisters, Sosi. You're one of them now," said Adrine.

"I will sing the Christ songs," Sosi promised. "I will give them Easter all year-round!"

When they had kissed each other and said their good-byes, Adrine ran from the room.

———

The miles melted behind, the highways and Armenian villages eerily emptied of humanity save for three wretched caravans of refugees bowed and limping southward. It was heartbreaking to ride through their sea of outstretched arms, unable to assist, forced to meet their mournful begging with helpless silence. Each knot of Turk drovers they passed looked wilder than the last, feverishly eyeing the wagon of veiled women with suspicion and hunger. When stopped, Davidson explained that he was on official American consulate business, bringing medical nurse replacements for the remote Red Crescent hospital at Kars on the Russian front. He would tap a foot against the leather chest beneath the seat—also eyed hungrily—and say, "Save many lives!" The drovers assumed it was vaccine.

For safety's sake, they bypassed Erzurum, Tatul's birthplace. It was all he could do to refrain from bolting home, but the acrid smell of smoldering ashes, the sight of dwellings and businesses smashed and destroyed, the vision of his murdered beloved and the tearful faces of his family sobered him. There was no home to go home to.

Word had come that his parents were sighted in Urfa, then further news that just his mother and two children had reached an internment camp at Deir-el-Zor. His rebel contacts looked and inquired and bribed where necessary, but never did they find a trace of the Sarafian family. Then the reports had stopped altogether. At times, he was crazy with worry and wondering; at others, he left them with God and prayed for their souls. Hundreds of thousands were missing, and there was little hope of discovering their fate. To dwell on the loss was to pile wound upon wound.

Adrine had heard nothing at all. Long ago she had given her family over to the Father.

At Karakurt, someone dashed from the gathering shadows and tossed a tiny, bleating infant into the wagon and vanished. Adrine clutched the wasted babe to her breast, rocking it gently, murmuring soft words of comfort all the while. At Selim the baby died—exhaled a last shallow breath and never took another—and was laid to rest in the hollow between two rocks.

They were numb from asking what it all meant. Would they ever know?

The Menteses slept. Adrine did not speak for the longest time, jostling like a rag doll against Tatul at every stone and depression in the road. What did he intend? No woman had penetrated the Fedayeen stronghold. It was a man's world, one step removed from animal existence. Would he really take her to meet the Wolf, or would he send her to live with the Russians? She felt the restless tension hardening his muscles, heard the little sighs of exasperation as though his racing mind and heart warred over a thought they were sifting.

"Tatul—"

"—Adrine!"

"Yes?"

"I . . . I have been thinking. I have something important that I must do."

Her heart sank quicker than the winter sun. He was not made for political solutions. He was Fedayee first, last, always. He would shed Turk blood until Armenia was vindicated or he was beheaded by the executioner. Until the world grew wise to the slaughter and the western forces prevailed against the Ottomans, the Armenians would continue to die in remote desolation, and the brave Fedayeen could do no more about it than a nest of angry hornets. The exodus of a hundred wasted women, no matter how miraculous, in no way signified the saving of a homeland.

The hounds would have her dear Fox, not she.

"You have shown me what I must do," he said, his enthusiasm growing.

She bit her cheek. Her talk of a more clever fox had served only to convince him his cause was righteous after all.

"I must go and finish what I have purposed to do. I must make my pilgrimage!"

Adrine Tevian. Good little goose. Always the peacemaker. Yet justice for him comes most swiftly at the end of a dagger. How could I hope to change that? Now he will venture up into the snowy reaches of Ararat, and I will lose him. What, no blessed hymns come to mind just now? Have you no right to happiness? Have you eggplant for brains?

"You are so quiet. Be happy for me. Be happy for ... for us. Because of you I have done the righteous thing and spared my enemies. And that means I am worthy at last to worship the God of The Landing Place. But Bishop Benedict taught me that we don't have to climb mountains to raise an altar to the Lord. God has come among us. We are His altars. My reasonable and most pleasing sacrifice is to fight for a self-governing Armenia. Will you fight with me, Adrine, here, by my side?"

He removed the incongruous head covering and veil that covered his smile, turned her face to his, and kissed her forehead. A far light burned in the dark and dangerous eyes. "Justice!" he said, hissing the two syllables for all the strength of their meaning. "I will rise close to where God dwells in the heavens and ask Him to seal our cause in His. I will find a way to pray for the infidels and make an offering of my pride and the hatred that galls me with fire. Then you and I will rise, and together we will seek justice for the dead and a new homeland for the living."

Unable to prevent it, Adrine's heart soared against all odds and met his in the air. "How, my Fox, how will this be?"

His flashing eyes streamed tears. "How? You ask me how? I know not how, only that we must." Excitedly, he reached inside his waistband, extracted a tiny scrap of worn paper, and reverently unfolded it. " 'And on the seventeenth day of the seventh month, the ark came to rest on the mountains of Ararat,' " he read, voice quavering, " 'and on the first day of the tenth month the tops of the mountains became visible.'

"Adrine, my love, we have come through the terrible flood of the past few days. Now we will come through the flood that has overtaken our homeland. Like Noah and his family, in the depths of my soul I can see the tops of the mountains once again! War is for a season. We will fight beside the Wolf and force the Young Turk madmen to face their crimes and receive their just punishment. We will hide their plans, disrupt their rail shipments, 'borrow' their officers, and always leave the mark of our passing—a tuft of shiny red fox hairs protruding from the barrels of their guns or from the sleeping ears of the first in command!

"Together, we will help restore the pride of the Armenian people in themselves as People of the Book, People of a More Excellent Way! It is dangerous work, but you will have the protection of the Fedayeen, I promise you that, and there is no greater protection on earth than to be safe in the lair of the Wolf!"

She looked at him with intense longing, then tossed her head proudly. "It is not protection I seek, my fine Fedayee, but to stay the fist of vengeance and raise the hand of justice!"

Theirs was fanciful, giddy talk, and Adrine wanted more. Her suddenly explosive imagination saw his ridiculous women's garb fall away to reveal a magnificent gray wool suit of western cut, a—what did the French call it?—a *chapeau* of finest felt, expertly blocked by European hatters, a watch of burnished gold, and a finely manicured hand holding out a tight Parisian nosegay just for her. In her extravagance, she fancied in the other hand an exquisite cane of translucent tortoiseshell, tipped at the small end by gold, capped at the large end by a bevy of jewels. A boutonniere of wine red roses completed the ensemble. She laughed in delight at the vision of a dapper Fox and blessed the days she'd spent in stifling schoolrooms listening to the missionary teacher drone on. Oh, she would enjoy this ride! And she hadn't yet hauled out the well-worn future of herself, independent businesswoman taking tea and cakes in her private rail compartment en route to Berlin....

Suddenly, his look turned dark and piercing. The intensity of his gaze made her flush. "The Sarafian family would welcome you to the center of the house," he said in blessing. "Father Serop would bid you come to place your feet beneath the communal blanket and dip your hand in the communal dish."

With a stab of regret, she thought of old six-toed Uncle Saras under that blanket. Family. Shared laughter. Small, common dreams of good marriages, many grandchildren, a second Christmas goose.

All shattered. The blanket torn. The family broken, scattered, missing. Armenia was bleating weakly like a bear-mauled lamb.

She felt his finger beneath her chin, his rough thumb wipe

a tear from her thin cheek. Tatul's eyes sparked with a determined light, and she looked far into them for the hope of Armenia. He was carved from the very rocks they rattled past, and it was then she knew without doubt that Armenia would again form from the soil and streams of the forgiving earth. By God's good grace, by the holy martyred blood of St. Andrew the First Called, and by the redeeming shed blood of Christ the Righteous, Armenia would rise again!

Azniz and Misak Mentese, napping together like two big hairy sisters, snorted and turned, brushing at imaginary flies. Adrine rested her head against Tatul's shoulder, and for the weary woman, it was enough.

They continued north through the tortured land, and for once it did not intrude.

EPILOGUE

Several days later in the foothills of the disputed Caucasus borderlands, a siren wailed a dirge for the Turk dead, and the death wagon came to a halt in the murky dusk. A large-caliber Russian artillery barrage, bright as a meteor shower, lit the barren, remote canyons beyond. Small-arms fire popped and echoed down the craggy battlefield, drowning the cries of the wounded. The dead lay crooked and twisted in dark clumps like birds shot from the sky.

Two holy men in heavy black vestments and tall black hats of the orthodox Order of St. Timothy looked up, placed their palms together, and nodded once to the three people on horseback, all dressed once again as men and silhouetted against the rocks.

The priests stepped down from the wagon, untied the ropes securing the load, and waited.

The three horsemen dismounted and two bent to the ground. They straightened, a six-foot rectangular wooden box between them. The third man helped first the front man hoist the box to his shoulder with a grunt, then ran to help the rear man do likewise.

With slow, careful steps, the two bearers lowered their burden down the jagged ravine, the third helping to steady the load whichever way it shifted.

"The devils of Christ have slain another?" The utterance came unexpectedly out of the darkness.

Startled by the sudden unknown voice, the men stumbled and nearly lost their hold on the box.

A filthy, sweating Turk fighter materialized from the gloom and lit a cigarette. He was thinly dressed for the conditions and as foul of mood as he was of body.

A priest recovered first. "Your opposition suffers worse," he replied with stony reserve. "For every Turk we collect, there are two Armenian dead. Can't someone remember the face of peace?"

The Turk ignored the priest's sarcasm and rejoined with some of his own. "It is good that Allah makes our bullets go twice as far. Two Christ-lovers at every shot is good use of government issue! It will teach them to fight with Russian scum against us."

Uneasy silence met the remark. The coffin bearers waited, but the Turk did not leave. He smoked. He watched.

They eyed his rifle. Old and battered, like much of the Turk armament, but able to open a man's insides to inspection. They outnumbered him, to be sure, but he had the markings of rank. Four more would come looking for him if he was too long overdue. The coffin bearers wouldn't invite unwanted attention unless things turned ugly.

The priest cleared his throat. The coffin bearers adjusted the load and moved on. They stepped on to the wagon track, crossed in front of the soldier, and slid the box on top of other identical boxes piled in the wagon bed.

The third bearer remained in the shadows, hastening back up the draw to a second coffin.

"Another?" asked the Turk, a harder edge to the question. "Tell me, priest, did the Virgin who suckled the infant Christ know what a murderous people she birthed?"

The friar who had not yet spoken reached inside his vestments.

The soldier stiffened and snapped his rifle level. "Easy, priest!"

Slowly the hand withdrew and with it a circle of flat bread. The arm extended the food to the Turk.

Hungrily, the man snatched the bread from the priest's grasp and immediately tore a piece and sniffed it cautiously. "I see what you intend," he sneered. He pinched the fire from the end of his cigarette and slipped the remaining tobacco behind one ear. He stuffed a bite of bread into his mouth. "Feed the enemy, placate the Muslims, earn your reward in heaven will you? Well, I tell you, you may be able to fool these hirelings of yours. What are they, anyway? Scurvy Kurd vultures who help you dispose of the dead? Inbred Turk peasants with all the brains of a weevil? But I am not fooled. Allah does not smile down on those who deal treachery to his people. Do not waste any more time getting these good Turks buried. Nor shall you have any dead Armenians in this load, or I swear by Paradise that I shall cut you down like the diseased dogs you are!"

He walked to the priest who had given him the bread and spit the contents of his mouth into the holy man's face. "You handle the dead, Christ-man, and so we let you live. Do not forget that." The friar of St. Timothy's did not move except to blink back the man's wrath, bits of moist bread clinging to his beard. The Turk threw the remaining bread into the dirt and ground it under the heel of a boot.

The two coffin bearers scrambled quickly up the hillside and bent to the remaining box. They hoisted it to their shoulders and hastily began the descent, the third man hanging back, face averted.

Still the Turk did not leave. He studied their every move. The men passed by, the sweat rolling down their faces, and felt the drill of his suspicious gaze. He glanced uphill to the one in the darkness.

The men rounded the wagon and wrestled the last coffin into place atop the load. It was then they discovered they had been holding their breath and gratefully expelled it almost in unison. They turned to jump down from the grisly cargo.

The priests hastened to retie the ropes that held the dead in place.

"Wait!"

Everyone froze. For one brief, unreal moment, the bright burst of bombs and the banging of rifle fire melted into one. It was a moment in time that trapped them all.

"I want to inspect that last box," the Turk said. "Remove the lid."

The men in the wagon dared not look at each other. Their eyes met the priests'. The message that passed between them was but a blink.

A thunderous explosion two hundred yards downslope from them shattered the night. Everyone dove for cover, but in the confusion, a coffin, dislodged from the pile when the men in the wagon jumped for safety, fell heavily to the ground and split open.

The Turk soldier stared into the blank eyes and bloodied uniform of a fellow infantryman, a red crescent stitched into the lapel of a grimy shirt.

"You stupid fools!" the Turk rifleman shouted, jumping to his feet and reshouldering his weapon. There was fear in his voice. "Get these heroes of the Ottoman Empire away from the front lines and buried immediately. If you allow any disease to escape from these corpses, I'll have you all shot!"

With that, he ran pell-mell into the night toward the distant lights of battle.

With a renewed urgency, the men recrated the dead man, placed the coffin back in the wagon bed, and helped the brothers of St. Timothy's secure the ties.

Then the three men from the hillside lit matches and looked at the end of the uppermost coffins for the two with tiny crosses etched in the wood. On these they placed their hands and said a prayer for divine safety.

Inside the coffins, Adrine and Tatul added their fervent amens.

When the three casket bearers slapped the wood in farewell, an answering knock sounded from within each of the branded coffins. The men smiled at the priests, made the sign of the cross, and received it in return. With a snap of the reins, the wagon moved off north toward a range of hulking shapes in the distant night.

The Caucasus Mountains.

Somewhere between the wagon and a hidden Fedayee cave high above the carnage, the Black Wolf and his men roamed at will, throwing fear into the enemy. Toward him, encased inside a coffin in a cargo of coffins, came the Fox. But it was no corpse's heart that beat so loud and strong inside that particular box. It was the beat of the living, of the free. It was the rhythm of a profound love for the courageous woman inside the box that knocked against his in the jostling death wagon, the dear woman who had said yes to the crossing of the borderland from tyranny to self-determination, from death to life.

The three bearers returned to their horses, mounted, and formed a solemn circle. They leaned to the center, right arms extended palms down. Horses moving, they linked thumbs and little fingers, prayed the Lord's Prayer, and broke with a soft shout of solidarity.

Their keen eyes followed the wagon down a narrow draw, across a small stream, and up a muddy track where the cargo of the living and the dead disappeared into the trees. A quarter hour into the forest, the living would emerge from their tombs of wood to fresh mounts and a meal of jerked mutton and water.

From there to the Wolf was a long day's journey into the mountains of Noah.

The three watching horsemen—one American and two Armenian brothers—waited and prayed. Another rocket blast lit the sky before they turned south toward Hekim Khan and rode abreast into the unknown.

AFTERWORD

"Who, after all, speaks today of the annihilation of the Armenians?"

Adolph Hitler
August 22, 1939

Hitler's chilling words were spoken to his military commanders on the eve of the invasion of Poland, just twenty years after the slaughter of Armenia. With true admiration for the Ottoman solution, the German leader drew inspiration from the ease with which a "problem" people had been all but eradicated in the first genocide of the twentieth century.

Hitler, of course, went on to match, if not exceed, the Turks in depravity. His was a single-minded quest to dispose of the Jews with a ghastly efficiency even more calculated than that experienced by the Armenians. It was the world's indifference to the Armenians that got him started. Not until six million Jews later was he finally stopped.

The Armenian holocaust of World War I remains one of the most distressing chapters in human history. To this day, despite volumes of eyewitness accounts to the contrary, historical revisionists, like those who deny the Jewish holocaust, attempt to minimize the Armenian death toll or shift the blame. The truth of the matter is that of Turkey's two million Armenians, one-half to three-fourths were annihilated between 1915 and 1923. The Turkish government's strategy of systematic deportation and execution of its lawful Armenian citizens effectively erased one-third to one-half of all Armenians from the face of the earth.

The Armenians are an industrious, creative, resilient people. Nearly three hundred thousand escaped over the Russian border. Many fled to the United States, where today lives one of the largest concentrations of people of Armenian descent. Finally, on September 23, 1991, after decades of communist rule, the Republic of Armenia declared its independence from the Soviet Union, and a revised Armenian homeland was born. But it is one cut off from the vast lands of Eastern Anatolia where *Deliver Us From Evil* takes place. Those lands, the very heart of ancient Armenia, remain a part of modern Turkey.

But it is by no means the end of the story. Though most of the holocaust survivors have died, succeeding generations keep their memory alive. The Martyrs' Monument in the Armenian capital of Yerevan is an imposing granite memorial that shelters an eternal flame in honor of those who suffered so horrible a fate at the hands of their neighbors.

Why did so many die? Why was so little done by the rest of the world to stop the killing? Why did God allow the Armenians to suffer such ghastly persecution? If America had entered the war sooner, might Turkey have refrained from so great a slaughter of its own citizens? It is right to ask these questions, but not all can be answered. The region of Eastern Anatolia, where much of the genocide took place, was then an extremely remote and little-known part of the world. Once word did begin to leak out, however, mission societies and relief agencies from Europe and the United States took multiplied tons of food and medicines to the aid of the Armenian refugees and established orphanages, where concerted effort was made to reunite families with their displaced, abandoned, or abducted children.

Neutral American observers were stationed all across Turkey during that time. A steady stream of their cables flowed to the U.S. State Department, and the message was the same: "The Young Turks are engaged in the murder of a nation."

Two million Armenians, descendants of the first country on earth to embrace Christianity as the state religion, were known by the name "The People of the Book." The Bible was their sacred text, their rule of life, and for sixteen of their twenty-five centuries of history, they had kept the faith through conquerors and conquests.

More than that, Armenian historians traced their lineage

back to Hayk, a great-great grandson of Noah the Patriarch, and claimed eastern Anatolia at the foot of Mount Ararat their geographical homeland. For all of recorded history they maintained a devotion to the one true God, and when they were told of Jesus Christ by Saint Gregory the Illuminator, they joyfully bent the knee before the Son of God.

Consequently, they aided and abetted the Crusaders in their attempts to convert Muslims by force, and the bad blood that resulted returned to haunt the Armenians when the Ottoman Empire seized control of the land by the sixteenth century. Though religious persecution was strong, Armenian merchants were a vital part of the economy and begrudgingly tolerated for their adroit business practices. But on its last gasp by the end of the nineteenth century and in search of a scapegoat, the Ottoman Empire, led by despot Sultan Abdul Hamid II, went on a rampage among the six provinces of Armenia. The news emerged only through the heroic efforts of German and American missionaries, who estimated the death toll at nearly two hundred thousand Armenian men, women, and children. That slaughter set the stage for the even more devastating events of World War I.

Western Europe reacted with revulsion once the full extent of the Armenian genocide came to light, and harsh terms were meted out to Turkey by the Allies in the postwar settlement. A war crimes trial was initiated by the Turks themselves, but few were punished. Occasional assassination attempts by Armenian zealots against Turkey's government officials continue to this day, in retribution for the unconfessed sins of the past. Some are successful.

All of the central characters and incidents in this novel are fiction. The colorful Fedayeen were Armenian freedom fighters, with many individual legends among them, including Kevork Chavoush, the Black Wolf.

Frank Davidson, American Consul at Harput, is closely based on the life of Leslie Davis, a brave and compassionate U.S. consular officer, who was every bit as caring and heroic as his fictional counterpart. He served several mission stations and knew the good husbands, wives, and children who treated the sick and labored for a meager harvest of souls in a very isolated region. He knew their joys and defeats, took them medicines for their illnesses, and enjoyed their pies and friendship. From three days to two weeks away by horseback, they constituted his "circuit." Though he never knew what each visit would hold, he enjoyed their companionship and counted them among his closest friends. The detailed Davis journals formed an extremely valuable part of my research. He risked his life to champion the cause of the Armenians in his district. Freedom lovers everywhere are in his debt.

The kind monks at Mesrop and St. Timothy's are a composite of the many religious orders over the centuries who have set themselves apart to the glory of God. Keepers of an ancient faith, they have the gratitude of all who received sanctuary, physical sustenance, and a saving knowledge of Christ at their praying hands.

Finally, who can know the mind of God? As Job and others learned, the Creator is above and beyond His creation, and who is man to question Him? I do believe that many of those Armenians who died before their time went on to a glorious reward. Still, the Armenian holocaust drained much of the life from the ancient Armenian faith. Every earthquake that strikes Turkey today is considered by some of the remaining survivors and their descendants to be a direct punishment from God for the Ottoman crimes of World War I.

For other Armenians, however, there is a renewed optimism and a resurgence of the joyous personal walk of faith typified by Adrine Tevian. They again embrace their beliefs with Christian fervor and look forward to the day in heaven when every knee shall bow before the throne of God, all tears shall be wiped away, and war and all its horrors shall be no more.

The story of the Armenian holocaust, as terrible as it is, provides a haunting reminder that left unchecked, wickedness corrupts and destroys. Rulers and nations must be held accountable for the treatment of their citizens, and those of us who know the fruits of freedom have an obligation to call them to account.

God bless those who do.